The Barnstorming Mustanger

Shona, something for you to read when the weather is too bad to go flying.

Love C.

Ted Barber

*Best Regards
Ted Barber*

BARBER INDUSTRIES, INC.
Orovada, Nevada

I would like to thank my wife, Margaret, son Curtis, and daughter-in-law, Fern, also Ruth Tipton, for their valuable assistance in putting this story together, without whose help this book could not have been written.

All Rights Reserved
Manufactured in the United States
Published by Barber Industries, Inc.
Post Office Box 5
Orovada, NV 89425

ISBN 0-9617858-0-2

CONTENTS

THE PILOT'S CREED

When the earth retreats beneath my rising plane, I feel the challenge of those who first ventured into the heavens, those who risked so much to carry on through the lean years toward man's conquest of the air and those who, today, with me, are striving to uphold and advance the glory of aviation. I am conscious of a responsibility akin to that of a sea captain. I must be the master of my ship, of myself, and of every emergency. I must back my ability with keen judgment, accuracy, and unfaltering confidence. My fearlessness must be tempered with caution and wisdom. I must know my airplane in order that I may recognize its limitations and appreciate its possibilities. I must have for my plane even greater regard than a seaman has for his ship. As my sea is far greater, my ship far faster, so must I, the pilot, be more sure.

Author Unknown

FOREWORD

Early in life Ted Barber had a strong determination to fly but had no clearly marked road to follow. He began his flying career in the 1920's, and by trying to make a living with his airplane through the Great Depression, he had a real struggle for existence. Among other ventures, he used his flying skills in an effort to support his family by capturing wild horses in our western states.

Pilots of that period who did not have a certain degree of venturesome spirit, even recklessness at times, in their makeup never learned what they could do with their aircraft when the going got tough. During his years of flying open-cockpit, OX5-powered biplanes, he experienced his share of power failures and crash landings.

Ted knows first-hand the sound of a landing gear collapsing and the wheels tearing their way up through the fabric and spruce of the bottom wings, the sound of wood propellers splintering and flying in all directions, and the sounds associated with a power pole tearing off both left wings.

He knows the feeling of desperation when jumping out of his doomed airplane just before it plunges over the top of a high mountain, followed by the feeling of despair at being alone and injured on top of an 8,000-foot mountain, and he knows the smell of death from crashes where other pilots were not as fortunate.

He also knows the good feeling when a sudden power failure

caused a forced landing, and his plane stopped undamaged two-thirds of the way across a 450-foot field. This time it had been necessary to bend over the top of a small pine tree with the bottom wing to get down onto the field. The tailskid mark was only six feet from an irrigation ditch inside the field.

This is Ted's story in his own words, as a pioneer aviator. It is a true unembellished account of flying as it was in earlier days, by a man who is still here to tell it. His flying adventures have become legendary in Nevada and central and southern Oregon. Pilots of today will find much food for thought in his reflections.

Many noble themes have been woven into the stories of early-day aviation. In those days the air was an alien element into which pilots ventured at their peril—and many did not survive. The complete story of aviation can never be told. It can only be seen through the eyes of the person who is telling it. This is the story of one man's experience.

Ruth Tipton, Nevada Historian
Winnemucca, Nevada

PREFACE

I have a desire to put on paper what I have learned about flying. Not just the one-two-three of which way to push or pull the controls, but also some of the experiences I have had while doing it.

I would like for this to be as if you and I were sitting across the table from each other, with our favorite drinks before us—probably coffee, stronger if you prefer—and we are visiting and talking about things that have gone before in our lives. All our words are not words of great wisdom and are not necessarily in chronological order.

In the beginning it was more of a stunt just to get an airplane off the ground, and venturesome people paid high prices for short rides in flying machines. This generated income that financed what we now know as the aviation industry.

If anyone had a clear blueprint of the course aviation was to follow, it was not very obvious because it went off in a lot of different directions before it became a recognizable industry and settled down to the course that seems so obvious to us now.

There was a lot of barking up wrong trees in the early days of aviation, and even much of this after I came along. Individually, the early pioneers traveled unbeaten paths, roads beset with temptations, opportunities and dangers that no other traveler met.

In the early days of flying there were oodles of theories and even superstitions that have been proven false now. There was a belief that a pilot should fly with his left hand because of the sensitive "feel" that was supposed to have been required to be developed in the left arm muscles to fly an airplane.

It was believed this sensitive "feel" could be developed in the left arm better than in the right arm because the left arm is closer to the heart; and also because we do so much heavy work with our right arm, such as chopping wood and cranking Model T Fords. This heavy work would tend to destroy the supersensitive "feel" that is required to fly an airplane. The throttle was on the right side of the Standard J-1 airplane for this reason. It seems that something only a little less than a spiritual connection was required to fly an airplane.

There were many theories and beliefs that caused heated discussions with almost anyone you met in the aviation business about almost anything relating to an airplane. There were more questions than answers: should it be a biplane, monoplane or triplane? Should it have the propeller in front or behind? Should it have wheels or floats? Should it have a stick or a wheel control? What wing curve is best? There was no end of things to argue about, and many people had strong opinions, but few facts.

Many of today's pilots would shrink up and disappear if they were subjected to the hardships the pilots of 50 and 60 years ago endured. When I think of the pilots who get such a great thrill out of flying their antique biplanes, I wonder how much they would have enjoyed all the "other" aspects of flying the OX5-powered biplanes in the 1920's and 1930's—where they would have been flying them for "real," and having their meals coordinated with the money they could have generated with them, not just for romantic sentiment.

Airplanes and airways have become so sophisticated and over-regulated by bureaucratic laws that we yearn for the "good old days" when the skies were not so crowded and the OX5-powered biplanes were "king of the skies."

This yearning for the "good old days" and the romantic OX5-powered biplanes takes on a twist that results in a sleek little biplane that has "super" features such as super power, super aerodynamic features, and you have a biplane that is super for aerobatics at airshows, but it is a complete stranger to the barnstorming biplanes of earlier days.

It was only the infusion of large quantities of money our government paid out through the military and Post Office Department that got our military and airmail planes operating and modernized. It was the unlimited money World War II put at the disposal of the aviation industry that brought modern engineering to aircraft design, as we see it today. The pilots of the OX5 barnstorming days had none of this. With the tools they had at hand they did what they could with them. Our modern airplanes today have more dependable engines, the aircraft structures have better engineering, are stronger and lighter and have better aerodynamic features. Pilots of today often fly many years and thousands of hours without having a power failure.

During my barnstorming days wing flaps had not been invented, and trim tabs had not been developed. The Waco 9 I was flying did not even have an adjustable stabilizer. When I had a full gas tank, I had to hold a constant light back pressure on the stick to hold the nose up; and when I had a heavy load in the front cockpit, I had to hold a constant forward pressure to keep the nose down. On rare occasions when I had exactly the right weight in the gas tank and in the front cockpit, the plane was properly balanced.

In my fishing-pole glider days, 1925, the airplanes barnstorming our country were mostly Jennys and Standards. The big names in aviation were the real early pioneers, or World War I pilots, or in some cases civilian pilots who had managed to get military training. Lindbergh was one of these, followed by civilian pilots such as myself. Most of them (including me) had little to offer except an intense desire to fly.

As I look back over the years of my experience with aviation, I realize I have had the privilege of living through the most exciting period of human history and have witnessed many, and have participated in some, of the developments that have brought us to where we are today.

Those of us who made a living with an airplane, or at least tried to, during that period, had a real struggle for existence. With our unsophisticated aircraft and limited experience and knowledge, we were always searching for ways to make our airplanes useful to society.

Much of the pioneering had already been done as I emerged on the scene. I was only 10 years old when World War I ended, so it was in the 1920's when I was learning to spread my wings.

I was not one of the early barnstormers; I was probably the last barnstormer. I hung on, trying to make a living with my airplane after other pilots saw the handwriting on the wall and went to more sensible ways to earn a living.

I could have made more money over the years if I had gotten a job doing almost anything else, but it would not have been as rewarding. Just the fact that I have had the privilege of participating in the most exciting venture in the history of our society is very satisfying to me. The fact that I have never made the "big time" disturbs me not at all. The spice of life is in the journey, not in the destination, and I have had an interesting journey.In my early years I heard only one drummer to march to. This drumbeat was coming from the sky, but it was far off and difficult to tell if it originated above the heavy overcast that was present much of the time, or if it originated behind some faraway hills.

I started out as a small boy in a struggle for personal achievement in a complex world, trying to reach goals that seemed, and perhaps were, beyond my reach. But eventually I did reach some of these goals and succeeded in living a life along the general lines of my boyhood interests. But I found the world as complex after I grew up as I found it as a small boy.

After 70-odd years I figured a good way to get things into focus would be to try to get it all on paper. Fortunately, over the years, without the slightest talent or qualifications for writing, I had kept a large amount of rough handwritten notes covering many of my experiences and thoughts. Eventually I decided to get serious enough about writing to try to put my thoughts on paper, with the help of my accumulated notes.

Some time back I even studied writing, hoping it would help me put my story in an orderly fashion. One of the things I learned was a little confusing. I learned that in order to write a successful story, facts are not essential, but it is very important to have a crisis, climax and conclusion, in that order. Facts have always been a very important part of my life. I haven't always had them, but in my profession life itself depends on facts. It was in the interest of self preservation that I was constantly searching for them. As for crises, climaxes and conclusions, I have had more crises than climaxes and conclusions.

x

1

EARLY FAMILY LIFE

This story actually begins before I entered this world. Back in Missouri my father's first wife died of hydrophobia. She got this by washing their dog's bedding after the dog had died. They had one son, my half brother Ed, who died in 1919 from an injury he received in the Navy in World War I; I was 11 years old when Ed died. After my father's first wife died, he married Ina Grawl, the girl who was to become my mother. He worked on a section crew, repairing railroad tracks, and I still have the large pocket watch he had to buy to meet the railroad standards in order to hold that job. He bought the best watch in the store in 1895, an Elgin for $15.

My family lived in Missouri and Kansas, then moved west and settled in the small company-store type of sawmill town of Wendling in western Oregon, where my father worked in the sawmill.

Wendling was the end of the line for the railroad as well as for the dirt road to the outside world. It was in big timber country 22 miles northeast of Eugene, in the Willamette Valley 150 miles south of Portland. At its high point the population was about 500. We left Wendling in 1923, and some years later the sawmill closed and the town ceased to exist. Today road maps show Wendling as a ghost town.

When my parents moved west they had, in addition to Ed, three sons and a daughter—Clayton, Thad, Elta and Vance, in that order. My mother's mother and father moved west with them. My brother Cordis and I were born in the west. I was the last. Cordis was two years older than me.

When I entered this world in the spring of 1908, the western frontiers had only recently been settled. This was just a few

1

years after the wagon trains had brought the earlier settlers west. The golden spike that established rail transportation across the United States had been driven into place only 39 years earlier, May 10, 1869. Horse-drawn stagecoaches and horse-drawn freight wagons were common throughout the land.

Since my arrival, presidents have risen and fallen. Important and unimportant people have come and gone. Members of my

Down on the farm. Left to right—brothers Vance, Cordis and Teddy. Mother made all the clothes visible, except the shoes, with her foot-powered sewing machine.

own family have been born, educated, graduated, hired, fired, married, divorced, and some have died. Yet, the sun rises, crosses the sky and sets each day, not even noticing.

I was oblivious to all such goings on as I embarked on this one-way journey through life. My little world was wrapped securely around me, and I was concerned only with the small parts of it that touched me.

My father built a small unpainted house on the outskirts of Wendling, where Cordis and I were born. My grandparents Grawl built a larger house, also unpainted, near the center of town.

When I was two years old, in 1910, my father bought some land about a mile down the road toward Eugene, cleared the land and built a new house there, also unpainted. He continued to work at the sawmill as he developed the farm.

In 1910 a forest fire got out of control and burned all the houses in Wendling, including the house I was born in, and Grawl's house. All the men were busy saving the sawmill, which they did save, so they still had their jobs, but they lost their homes and most of their belongings. Our house on the farm was out of the path of the fire and did not burn.

I don't remember a lot of details of my first few years. One early thing I do remember is when we went to Eugene on the train in 1912 to a big celebration of some kind—it was probably a Fourth-of-July celebration—in the city park. I was four years old, the park was crowded with people, there was music, and someone always had to hold me up to the water fountain to get a drink, and someone always had to go with me to find the restrooms, which were outdoor toilets with no plumbing.

Everyone was all excited because Teddy Roosevelt was there and he made a long-winded speech. He had just recently been President of the United States. Also, he was famous for having run up a hill called San Juan.

These things didn't excite my young imagination as much as the fact that I was seeing and hearing the man who wrote the big book we had at home that told all about his experiences hunting wild animals in Africa. All this made a big impression on me; in fact, I was named after Teddy Roosevelt. It was only recently I learned the teddy bear is also named after him. All small children have a teddy bear some time or other in their lives. I did. A child can talk over all his problems and dreams

3

and things with a teddy bear. They are good listeners and they don't go around blabbing everything they know, and sometimes they even tell you things.

One of the pleasures people my present age have is the privilege of looking back over the years and seeing things from a distance that dim closer distractions of the time and gives us an opportunity to have a different perspective than was possible in the days we lived these experiences.

Most happenings of my early childhood are completely erased from my memory, but there are a few things that stand out. I remember my early childhood as being a very pleasant period in my life. We lived in the country, on a farm, in a valley. There were mountains all around, in big timber country, with lots of smaller trees and bushes, with no open country.

My father and four brothers, Clayton, Thad, Vance and Cordis, were all hunters, and sometimes trappers, seeking a wide variety of wild game. Birds as large as ducks and geese, and other wild game from small to as large as deer, bear and timber wolves. I was very young during part of this period.

I grew up in such an environment where it seemed natural to kill things.

When I was far too young to shoot a real gun, such as a .22, I had an air rifle that shot BB's. One day, there was a small brown brush bird, probably a wren, under a bush in our front yard. I shot it and killed it. I had never killed anything before.

Seeing that pretty little bird as a dead bird suddenly bothered me, and I felt I had done something very wrong to have killed it. I was too young then, and am too old now, to remember what my beliefs in God might have been at that time, but I do remember that a lot of communications passed between God and me regarding that little bird, and it bothered me for a long time. In fact, I still think about it at times and wonder why we destroy things like that which are doing us no harm.

As I became older, my parents thought my brothers were getting to be old enough to have a. 22 rifle to hunt with, so they purchased a single shot .22 rifle for them to use. The whole family was out in the yard taking practice shots at a snag, some distance away, using .22 short cartridges. When the bullet hit the snag, we could hear it hit.

I was really too young to shoot a .22, but I kept coaxing to shoot it and finally they decided to let me try. Cordis told me I would have to shoot at something closer than the snag because I was too young to pull the trigger hard enough to shoot that far. Anyway, I got to shoot the .22, and it was finally decided I could shoot at the snag. I probably missed it.

In those days the angels and the devils were given credit for almost everything that happened. In this way the people avoided responsibility for their actions, much as they do today. However, even in those days almost every kid above the fourth grade knew the father of the family was Santa Claus; but there was still some mystery about the Paul Bunyan type of person who built the mountains and the plains and rivers and oceans and things of that nature. Even the grownups hadn't figured out exactly who the angels and God were. In fact they, we, haven't quite got that figured out yet.

There were two other small towns, Marcola and Mabel, within four miles of Wendling: Marcola, west on the road to Eugene; Mabel, north over a high timbered ridge. To go to Mabel, we first had to go to Marcola, but sometimes we walked to Mabel, and that was shorter, just over the hills north. We probably never ventured out any farther than these two other small towns before the Buick entered our lives, except on special occasions when we went to Eugene, 22 miles away, by train. On the train there was a toilet we flushed by pulling on a string that hung down from a water tank on the wall. That was a new experience for us.

There was a moving picture theater in Marcola, three miles down the creek from Wendling. On special occasions we went, sometimes walked, to Marcola to see the moving picture shows.

From about five to ten years of age I heard a lot of talk about World War I in Europe, that was being fought to end all wars and to make the world safe for democracy.

My oldest brother, Clayton, joined the army. My brother Thad, a couple of years younger, was disappointed that they wouldn't accept him because his eyes didn't meet their standards.

Clayton wanted to be a fighter pilot, and he did get into that branch of the service; he was stationed at Kelly Field in Texas, where the army trained pilots. But he became a cook. He had his first ride in an airplane when he bought a ride with a barnstormer at Eugene after the war was over.

When he saw he was not going to get to be a fighter pilot, he transferred to the observation balloon department. But even then, when his outfit was shipped "over there," he was in an army hospital in Texas almost dead with the flu, so he didn't even get in on that part of the fighting. He sent me a picture of a Newport fighter airplane from Kelly Field. I still have it.

Any place 20 miles or more from home was a strange outside world in my early years. My father liked to go around places like the country store or the train depot and visit with people he did not know, also with people he did know; but I believe especially with people he did not know, and they talked about things in which they had a common interest. Then when he came home, he would tell us about these visits and things that were happening in the outside world. I have tried things of this nature but I do not get the same results he did.

Only a generation before me the oldsters remembered some of the highlights of their lives. These memories dealt with such things as the joys and hardships associated with working with horses, saddles and wagons, and all the things you could do and the places you could go with such mobile equipment, and the adventure and romance connected with this activity.

When I was very young, my mother and father took a vacation trip in the western part of Oregon, in big timber country, and were gone from home a week or two. They took the family team and wagon, and all of us kids stayed home, the older taking care of the younger.

At their farthest point they could have been all of 30 and maybe even 40 miles from home, much farther than I had ever been or ever would be from home for a long, long time. They must have really had the time of their lives. When they came back, they talked a great deal about many of the far away places they had been, and their experiences on the trip.

When I was seven years old, I had a serious experience with pneumonia and was carried to the railroad, about a mile away, on a stretcher. The train made a special stop to pick me up, and I was taken to a Eugene hospital, over 20 miles away, where they operated on my left lung. The doctors gave up hope for my recovery and my parents had decided which coffin they would put my body in. Somehow I fooled them and within three months I was able to be taken home, where my mother kept a close watch over me for a long time.

I remember enjoying my early years in school at Wendling, and I especially liked two of my teachers there, Neva Downing and Arnold Collier. However, school work never came easy for me, and I was never at the head of my class in anything.

My health remained a serious problem for quite a few years. The doctors advised my parents to get me out of western Oregon into a drier climate. Because of this I spent three winters with Uncle Cal and Aunt Bluebell in north-central Oregon between then and when we left Wendling in 1923. My first winter with them was for the school years of 1918-1919, at the very small one-store, one-room schoolhouse town of Olex where Uncle Cal operated an automobile repair shop. I was 10 years old and still weak from my earlier sickness, and very lonely, being away from home, family and friends, for the first time. The house we lived in that winter still stands.

I spent my school vacation in 1919 back home, down on the farm near Wendling. Then for the school year 1919-1920 I was back with Uncle Cal and Aunt Bluebell. They had sold the garage and leased a 2,000-acre wheat ranch north of Olex. I was less lonesome there because there were more things on the wheat ranch that interested me—farm machinery, goose hunting, etc. I was in the fifth grade and walked three and one-half miles to Olex to school and back each day. Also, I was the janitor at the schoolhouse, so I had to be the first one there to get a fire going in the wood-burning stove before the others arrived.

The goose hunting was in the fall, after harvest. We dug holes large enough for one man and a bottle of whiskey, or a few bottles of home brew. Then we covered the fresh dirt from the holes with straw that was already in the field. We put out some cardboard decoys that were shaped and painted to look like geese. Sometimes we staked out live geese that had been crippled.

I bought a secondhand single-shot 12-gauge shotgun. I was a little small for shooting it but I wanted to hunt with the men. The first time I shot it, it knocked me flat on the ground, but I did learn to shoot it okay.

The sheriff from Yakima, Washington, arrived each fall for hunting. He always brought several one-gallon crock jugs full of "applejack" that he had made in his still that had a silver coil. He was mighty proud of his still with a silver coil and it sure made good "applejack." The first time I took a swig out of one of his jugs it hit me almost as hard as the first time I fired my shotgun.

Bluebell had all the geese she wanted to cook, and there were nearly always geese hanging on the screened in front porch during hunting season. I sold geese for $1 each to hunters who didn't get any. I wanted to sell enough geese so I could buy a bicycle, but I never sold that many.

One day some city-type hunters with fancy guns and other equipment, as well as the usual refreshments, came out and went hunting. I saw a nice big flock of geese fly over them, and they did a lot of shooting, but none of the geese fell. I kept watching the geese, and after they passed the hunters one of them fell. I walked over and picked it up. When the hunters came in that evening they didn't have a goose. So I sold them the goose they had shot for $1. They were happy to get it. I thought that was a pretty slick stunt to pull on them.

I used to dream about taming a whole flock of geese and harnessing them to a small basket and have them fly me up in the air, but that project never "got off the ground."

At the end of this school year I went back to my family, but not to the farm. My father had sold the farm and had moved to

After a day of goose hunting on the wheat ranch. I was 12 years old and am holding my 12-gauge shotgun.

a small unpainted house on the south side of Wendling, and he was busy building two more rooms on it so it would be large enough for our family. Grandmother Grawl was living with us now, since my grandfather had died while walking home from his work at the sawmill while I was at the wheat ranch. I had made some real progress at improving my health during the two winters with Uncle Cal and Aunt Bluebell.

At Wendling I delivered papers for about two months. With the money I earned I bought an old wreck of a bicycle and fixed it up. Also, I purchased part of the lumber I needed to build a small workshop. There was a small creek nearby, and I was going to run a circle saw and an emery wheel with water power from this creek. I was 12 years old.

I built a wooden flume to carry the water over my four-foot water wheel, but couldn't get enough power out of it to operate the emery wheel or the circle saw.

My third winter with Uncle Cal and Aunt Bluebell started in the fall of 1922. They lived on the same ranch, but in the other large white house that was one mile farther north. So I had four and one-half miles to walk to school that year.

One of the hired hands, Ned Norton, built me a steam engine that really worked. It didn't do anything, but after building a good hot fire under the five-gallon boiler and getting steam pressure up, the wheels went around.

I had my 15th birthday the following spring before school was out, and after school was out I stayed on as a hired hand and really enjoyed that period.

There was no electricity on the wheat ranch. The windmill in the barnyard pumped water into a large high tank. This cold water was piped into the kitchen. There was no hot water in the kitchen, except in the hot water reservoir on the right side of the cook stove, that we filled with a bucket.

Two of the hired hands had this crazy idea of getting out of bed in the morning and, before getting dressed, to walk about 75 yards out to the building that was under this water tank, and take a very cold shower; and they got me to doing it also. Some mornings we walked barefooted on several inches of crusted snow to get there. Then we put our clothes on before walking back to the bunkhouse. If you think a cold shower under these conditions, before breakfast, doesn't wake you up, you are not paying attention. I don't believe I missed one morning doing that all the rest of the time I was there, and I have never been healthier than I was at that time.

Uncle Cal would be considered a master mechanic for his time and era. When the neighbors were still farming with mules, Cal was using Holt Caterpillars. He did his own maintenance and overhaul work on everything there. I got in on this part of the work also, as a helper, which included pouring new main and connecting rod bearings, and even pouring new bearings in the main gear housings of the transmissions. I pumped the air for the forge for the blacksmith. At first it was a large bellows type blower. Then they installed a rotary type that blew air by turning a crank. On some of the blacksmith jobs I would swing the sledge hammer while the blacksmith held the hot iron on the anvil. This shop work held my interest as much as anything I did on the wheat ranch.

By no stretch of the imagination could Uncle Cal be considered an outlaw, or in any way a bad citizen. He was well liked and respected among his neighbors. If he ever had any enemies, I never knew about it. This period was during the prohibition days. Cal made his own home brew and he bought his drinking liquor from his friends who made it.

One local man Cal had known for many years, Jim Owens, lived off the main road, up in a deep canyon. He had a partner, Charley Wilson, who had drifted into the area, and together they operated a whiskey still and did a pretty good job of supplying the moonshine for that area.

Charley had been caught and arrested several times but they couldn't keep him in jail. He broke out of every jail they put him in. These men were good friends of Cal's and I was well acquainted with both of them. One time after Charley had broken out of the jail at Condon, about 20 miles away, he came to the wheat ranch on foot and Cal loaned him a saddle horse to help him escape.

One day Cal and Bluebell and I had gone to Arlington in the Model T Ford. We stayed in town to go to a movie, and it was almost midnight when we started home. Cal was getting low on liquor, so we drove up to Owens' place to replenish his stock. They parked the Model T Ford by the front gate and walked to the house. They said they wouldn't be gone long so I sat in the car. There were no lights in the house when we parked. After they knocked at the door some windows lit up and they went inside. I waited for them to come back.

10

Suddenly someone came walking out of the dark and up to the Model T right beside me, holding a hogleg-type six-shooter that looked like it was about a foot long, and it was pointed right at me. In a voice that sounded like he meant business, Charley asked, "What the hell do you want here?"

It didn't take me long to tell him what I wanted. Then of course he recognized me, and I recognized him and everything was okay and he went into the house. Apparently when we drove up, Charley had been over a ridge to wherever their still was.

After I left the wheat ranch, I heard the law caught Charley again. This time they recognized him as the man who had murdered his wife and children in Oklahoma. They held him until a lawman from Oklahoma arrived to take him back. On the way to Oklahoma he was handcuffed to the lawman and had an Oregon boot on one of his legs. An Oregon boot is a heavy iron ball chained to a prisoner's leg.

They were sleeping in an upper berth on the train. Charley took his watch apart, got some tools out of it, and picked the lock on the handcuffs. Then he climbed down out of the upper berth and left. In doing this he stepped on a woman's hand in the lower berth. She woke up, and then she woke up the lawman, and they started looking for Charley.

They found him on top of one of the cars, trying to pick the lock to get the Oregon boot off his leg. If he had succeeded in getting it off, he would have jumped off the train. I never heard any more about Charley, but I still remember him and his big six-shooter.

I had a wide variety of jobs on the wheat ranch. I drove machinery, drove mules, hauled wheat to Arlington with the Model T Ford truck that had hard rubber tires. I also made trips to Arlington behind a long string of mules, pulling wagons loaded with wheat. On the mules and wagon hauling I was just a passenger. I was too young to handle that kind of a job, my job was to help load and unload the wheat, 100-pound sacks, which in itself was a pretty big job for a 15-year-old boy. Sometimes the mule skinner would let me handle the lines out on the open road. One time he let me make the 90-degree left turn through our gate when we got back to the ranch with empty wagons. It took some doing to get that long string of mules and wagons through that gate, and I felt real proud of myself when I did that.

I did a lot of growing up during my three periods with Uncle Cal and Aunt Bluebell—especially during the two periods on the wheat ranch. When my work ended that fall, I bought a secondhand Harley Davidson motorcycle for $50 and headed for Bend, about a 150-mile trip over dirt roads, quite an adventure for me.

The main reason for the move to Bend was to get me permanently into the drier climate east of the Cascade Mountains. Because of my health problems I had spent nine years getting through the first six grades of school, and still had the seventh and eighth grades of school ahead of me. Even during this period my health did not permit me to take part in the physical exercise class at school, although in general my health gave me very few problems when I took care of myself.

But I am getting ahead of my story—

Down on the farm at Wendling some of our neighbors were buying automobiles, Model T Fords mostly. My father decided to buy one, but he wanted something a little better than a Model T, so he bought a Buick, complete with a top and removable side curtains. That Buick was a big thing in our lives. It greatly increased our horizons, but in those days cars were not well engineered or well built. The Buick gave so much mechanical trouble that we eventually owned a Dort and a Star, which were not much better, if any.

For the remainder of my father's and mother's lives, they never did own a really good automobile; there were a lot of lemons in those days. Now we pay too much for automobiles, but at least we are getting something that will give us dependable transportation.

In my "growing up years," even with automobiles that had not reached a very high degree of perfection mechanically, we were reaching out farther and seeing more, and seeing it more often, than in the horse and wagon days. As time progressed, family cars became a little better, and the roads and tires were a little better, so family trips on weekends and holidays up to 50 or 100 miles were not uncommon.

After World War I war surplus OX5-powered Jenny airplanes were available to the public, brand new, for $500. My father talked about buying one but to my regret he never did. It was probably one of the best decisions he ever made. Anyway, I decided flying would be the life for me. I was too naive and innocent in the ways of the world to know I couldn't do it, but I did.

At 12, after we had moved to Wendling and I had built my workshop, I made keys for neighbors who had lost theirs, and I made broomholders and sold them, but mostly I just experimented with things I was interested in.

One day in 1920 at Wendling I was sitting at our kitchen table alone, way back in a corner. I heard a motor. My mother was out in the yard and she called me and said there was an airplane flying over. There were chairs in my way so I climbed right over the top of the table to get out to see it. The airplane was from Eugene, 22 miles away, and was the first airplane I had ever seen. I didn't know it then but it was an OX5-powered Curtiss Jenny.

Leaflets were dropped saying Stetson hats were to be dropped over Eugene for those who could catch them, as an advertising stunt, at a big celebration that was coming up, probably the Fourth of July.

In those days a great deal of my thinking about airplanes could be described as daydreaming. It would not have meant much to me at this young age if I would have realized I would be 19 years old before the first transcontinental air passenger would be flown across the United States; on July 5, 1927, he landed in Reno.

Ever since I had a little model airplane at age five down on the farm, the motivating force behind me was my desire to fly. There were times I had other interests. For instance in 1922, at Wendling, a friend built a radio, a one-tube regenerative set that used earphones for receiving; it did not have a loudspeaker. This was the only radio in Wendling at that time.

The boy who built it used to broadcast with it. He and his friends played music and sang and just had a good time, not knowing if it was really broadcasting until they started receiving letters from listeners, some of them from as far away as the state of Washington. Then they stopped because they had no license to broadcast and they were afraid they might get into trouble with the law.

I bought the radio from him for $50 when he decided to build a larger radio that would have a loudspeaker, but I never tried to do any broadcasting with it.

At the time I bought this radio, there was one other radio in Wendling. The union at the sawmill paid $500 for it, and it had a loudspeaker. It was a large set that consisted of several units that filled a table about the size of a kitchen table, and the batteries were on the floor under the table.

For some time my interest in radios was pretty strong, probably because I could get my hands on a radio, and there was no way I could get my hands on an airplane at that time. But my interest in radios could not overpower my interest in airplanes.

At an early age I developed a strong desire to fly. Not having the slightest idea of the obstacles that lay between me and reaching that goal. Something else I did not understand in my early years was that the human spirit does not recognize barriers that might stop lesser things.

THE DREAMS LIFE IS MADE OF

I saw some airplanes sailing
    Sailing through the sky
They looked like silver dragons
    Way up there so high.

Past the horizon they did sail
    See them you could no more
Then hurrying toward the house
    I heard another roar.

It was a tri-motored monoplane
    And looked so huge to me
I thought if I were up there too
    Above the world I would be.

If I were an airplane pilot
    I'd sail right up to Mars
After seeing all the planets
    I'd look at all the stars.

After seeing all these things
    I'd sail right back to earth
And tell all the people down below
    What a trip like that is worth.

2

IN THE BEGINNING

There were no airplanes when my father was born in 1870. His father had ideas and ambitions about building a machine that would fly. He said someday he was going to build one, but he never got around to doing it. There were more immediate things that had to be done for survival, such as putting shoes on the mule and plowing the south 40. My father also had flying ambitions which he never accomplished.

I was born four-and-a-half years after the Wright Brothers made their first flight, and three years before our government bought its first airplane. So as I was growing up, man-carrying flying machines actually existed, but just barely. I was several months old when the first cross-country flight was made, 10 miles out and 10 miles back. The world's altitude record was about 300 feet, and the top speed was about 40 miles per hour. A public opinion poll would have shown people almost completely ignorant of the fact that an airplane had ever flown.

At age five, I received a small model airplane as a premium for selling jewelry. This little airplane flew very well and contributed to my interest in flying. I spent a lot of time trying to figure out how to build an airplane big enough to ride in. I was six when World War I started and no doubt heard a lot of talk about airplanes of the war. No doubt this made a deep impression on my flying ambitions.

When I was in the fourth grade, we were having a spelling match. I was usually at the bottom of the class in spelling and was at the foot of the line for our team. The score was tied with but one more word to spell. It was my turn, and the teacher said, "Teddy, spell 'aeroplane.'" I spelled it correctly and became the hero of the hour. The teacher later told me he knew I could spell "aeroplane," that's why he gave it to me.

15

Designing, building and flying kites occupied much of my time. One spring morning before time to go to school, I was flying my six-foot bow kite and had out 1,000 feet of string with the kite high over Wendling. Realizing I would be late for school, I tied the string to a small tree and let the kite fly as I went to school. To my surprise it was still in the air at noon, and to my greater surprise it was still in the air when school was out that evening. This kite flight raised quite a lot of comment and interest around town.

Before leaving Wendling in 1923, I had read all the books on aviation in the Eugene library, and at Bend I read all the books there on aviation and all they could order from the state library in Salem. Even so this was not very many books.

When living on the wheat farm, the folks there talked about ''jack-o'-lanterns.'' These were balls of fire that drifted slowly across a field a few feet above the ground. It seems almost everyone there had seen them, but no one knew what they were. One night an equipment operator was plowing on the night shift, and he saw one of these jack-o'-lanterns moving slowly across the field he was plowing. He thought it was his boss out there checking up on him; he got mad and quit his job the next day. I finally saw one of these balls of fire about one foot in diameter, a couple of hundred yards away, not over 10 feet above the ground moving slowly. Other members of the family and crew saw it also. Today these would probably be called U.F.O.'s.

OAKLEY G. KELLY

One day when I was out in the field burning weeds, an airplane suddenly came flying low, coming right at me, barely higher than the fences, flying very fast due to the velocity of the tailwind. It was a DeHaviland DH4 with a 12-cylinder, 400-horsepower Liberty engine. It came very close to me, and I could see the pilot plainly. This was the closest I had ever been to an airplane in actual flight.

The Portland newspaper the next day had an article about the flight. Oakley G. Kelly, commander of the army air base at Pearson Field, Vancouver, Washington, had set a speed record from Pearson Field to Pendleton, Oregon. Kelly and John A. Macready had made the first nonstop flight across the United

States a few weeks earlier. Thus the flight I witnessed was aviation history in the making.

Later Kelly, flying a DeHaviland and accompanied by six Jennys, landed on the Arlington, Oregon, airport 14 miles north of us. Three of these Jennys were taking off in formation. Kelly's DeHaviland was sitting on the field with its engine running, waiting to take off after the Jennys were in the air. As the Jennys were taking off, one of them locked wings with the DeHaviland, badly wrecking both planes. No one was hurt.

Kelly said the pilot of the wrecked Jenny had been nicknamed "The German Ace" because he had wrecked more of our airplanes than the Germans did.

We drove up from the ranch to see the wrecked airplanes. The Army had hired two men with 12-hour shifts to guard them. The night guard was a 19-year-old boy I knew who agreed to trade his guard job for my ranch job for the duration of the airplane cleanup and repair.

The Jenny was dismantled and the salvageable parts were loaded on a truck and hauled back to Pearson Field. Two new wings and other necessary parts were brought to repair the DeHaviland. Pop Bacon, the head mechanic at Pearson Field, and a helper arrived to do the repair work on the planes. The badly damaged parts, mostly wings, were put in a pile to be burned at the end of the salvage operation. When the repairs were completed and the DeHaviland was ready to fly, Kelly arrived to fly it back to Vancouver. I tried to convince him he should let me take the damaged wings home to the ranch to build a glider, but I lost that battle, and the wings were burned.

TEX RANKIN AND VERN BOOKWALTER

At a later date (1924) I became acquainted with Tex Rankin when he was barnstorming through central Oregon with his Curtiss Oreole. In 1925 both he and Vern Bookwalter flew into central Oregon. Tex was flying a Curtiss C-6 Standard and Vern was flying a Hisso Standard. Sometime after their barnstorming period Vern married Pop Bacon's daughter.

Tex and Vern were both early pioneers in aviation. Tex operated flying schools in the Northwest in the 1920's and 1930's, and he won the World's Championship for aerobatic flying. During World War II he operated a large flying school at Tulare, California, training pilots for the military.

Vern became an early day airmail pilot. He was one of the first pilots on the West Coast airmail runs. One day on an airmail run in bad weather, flying an open cockpit J-4 Travelair biplane, his destination was Medford, Oregon. But when he arrived where he thought Medford should have been, he couldn't find it because the whole area was socked in solid. When his gas ran out, he stepped over the side and came down in his parachute.

Vern was the only pilot I ever knew whose pilot license was signed by Orville Wright.

The last time I saw Vern, about 1930, he was working on an amphibian on Pearson Field, Vancouver, Washington. (This was the field where I had made my first solo flight in an OX5 Waco 10 in 1929.) As I walked across the field, I came to this amphibian and one man was working on it. All I could see of him was his feet sticking out. It was Vern Bookwalter, and he "took five" while we visited a few minutes. He was getting his amphibian ready to fly to Alaska. He must have liked what he saw up there, since he spent the rest of his life flying in Alaska and died a natural death there several years ago.

During one of their barnstorming tours through central Oregon in 1925, Vern and Tex were flying from the same field where later that same year I flew my fishing pole glider. And they were passing the time with conversation as they, and I, waited for someone to come out to the field who would spend a few dollars for rides in their airplanes. As I listened to two real pioneers in aviation discussing ideas and problems that they faced, and as I think back over more than 60 years, it is interesting to try to put the pieces together and see what the picture is. Actually it comes out blurred.

Vern said to Tex, "There will always be a demand for good flight instructors." Well, at the time that sounded great, but how about the time near the end of World War II when war contracts were suddenly shut off. The machine shop where I was working was laying off workers because of losing their war contracts.

We lived in Burbank, California, and our local airport, Whiteman Field, wanted to hire a flight instructor. I had had years of experience, so I talked to them about the job. Andy Devine, of movie fame, was there. He was part owner of the field. I was told pilots with war experience would have preference. I could not compete with that. I was only a flight instructor during World War II and had no combat experience, so I could not qualify under those rules. I pursued the subject no further, moved to Nevada and became a farmer and a wild horse mustanger.

While on the wheat ranch in 1922 and 1923, I was corresponding with a flying school in Lincoln, Nebraska, with the idea that I might be able to go back there and work in their airplane factory and earn enough money to buy flying lessons. They built the Lincoln Standard J-1 airplane there, and I thought they would probably have work for me. However, during this period I was only 14 and 15 years old and such a venture was not in the cards for me. I learned later that if I could have gone to Lincoln when I wanted to I would have been there while Lindbergh was learning to fly there.

MY FIRST FLIGHT

During the fall of 1924, when I lived in Bend, Oregon, I heard someone say an airplane would be coming sometime that week to take pictures for the lumber companies. It was indeed a novelty for an airplane to come to Bend; we had lived there for over a year and hadn't seen one. I watched and listened without success until Saturday morning. While I was sitting on top of the woodshed searching the skies, I heard the dim sound of an airplane motor. Finally it appeared, made a circle over town, then headed southeast as though it didn't have the slightest intention of landing.

I heard it was going to land about five miles out of town, so I decided to walk out to see it. After stuffing my pockets full of apples and getting directions, I started down the road. After about seven miles, including a shortcut through the sagebrush, I saw the plane with the following printed on the side: "CURTISS OREOLE 150 H.P. 115 M.P.H. THIS PILOT HAS CARRIED OVER 5,000 PASSENGERS." My spirits soared high. This was the first airplane I had seen in central Oregon.

Only one man was at the plane when I arrived, and he was working on the oil pump. I kept him so busy answering questions that he almost forgot how to put it back together. He lacked one tap having enough to finish the job, and as I was searching my pockets for a tap, I found the apples I had put there before starting out. I thought I might get a free ride if I gave the apples to him. He told me his name was Tex Rankin, and he accepted the apples with a smile since he hadn't had anything to eat that day.

Although I already knew the control movements, I asked Tex how they worked, figuring he would tell me what all the instruments were for. He told me to get in and see if I could figure it out for myself. I got in the pilot's seat and imagined I was just starting out for a flight over the trenches encountering several German Fokkers and sending them down in flames. Finally I made a perfect three-point landing without a scratch. I thought to myself, "Maybe I can really fly someday."

Tex was having trouble under the left wing where he was patching a hole in the fabric. I got down there and helped him until his driver, Glen Hoover, and his helper, Woody, arrived with some lunch and drinking water. They asked me to eat with them, but I was so interested in the airplane I had lost my appetite. (They probably would have rather had me eat with them so I couldn't ask so many questions.) One thing that seemed strange to me was that they always referred to the airplane as a ship. I had never thought of an airplane as being a ship.

I got about 200 feet in front of the ship to see if the wings were trued up okay and discovered the left wing had more angle of attack than the right wing. Tex explained that the wash of the propeller had a tendency to push the left wing down so it had to have more lift than the right wing.

Although he had come here to take pictures, he said he would take up passengers Sunday if the weather was all right. I asked him how much he would charge, and he said he wasn't sure because he didn't know how many passengers he could take at one time. The ship was built for two besides the pilot, but that field was small, and the elevation was 3,600 feet, which made the air light. The field was sandy, so he didn't know whether he could get enough speed to raise over the trees with two passengers in the ship.

If he could take two passengers at a time, the price would be $5, but if he could only take one passenger at a time, the price would be $7.50.

"Would you like to go up?" he asked.

"Can you give me enough work to earn a ride, or maybe I can sell tickets for you?"

"You be out here in the morning, and I will take you up for nothing. I want to see how much of a load I can get off the field with."

"I'll be here," I told him, "and if you think it will be necessary, I will stay here all night and watch the ship for you. If the wind comes up, it might wreck the machine unless someone is at the controls to keep it from turning turtle or leaving the ground. I'm sure I could handle the controls all right."

"No, that will be OK," Tex said. We have some sacks here to fill with sand and tie to the wings and tail. We will set the ship's tail into the prevailing winds, and if the wind does blow very hard, it will have a tendency to push the ship down instead of raising it up. Then the sand bags will keep it from turning over if the wind strikes it from the side."

I helped fill the sacks and put the canvas over the engine and cockpits.

Tex said he wouldn't be out there until about 9 o'clock in the morning, and he didn't like to leave the ship unguarded as somebody might take something from it. I promised him I would be out there by six o'clock.

Early the next morning, my father took me to the field in our car at 5:30 a.m. The canvas was still on the ship so there was really nothing much to see until Tex got out there.

He finally came at 10 o'clock. He said he would have been there earlier, but it wouldn't be a good day to fly anyway. We went to the nearest farmhouse, which was about half a mile away, to get some water for the radiator. After filling the radiator, cleaning the sparkplugs, oiling the motor, and otherwise getting it in shape to go, Woody got in the rear cockpit, and Tex handled the propeller. The motor started on the first pull after choking it a few times.

After the engine was warmed up, Tex got in and gave her the gas, and like an over-anxious goose, the ship started swiftly forward across the field. It raised gracefully from the ground, soaring over the sagebrush and jack pines. After making three circles over the field, he made what appeared to be a swift dive and landed. That was the most beautiful flight I had ever seen.

Tex taxied up close to where we were standing and motioned for us to come over there. With the engine still running, he indicated that Glen Hoover and I should get in the front cockpit. He told us to not raise our heads high enough for the wind to hit them until we were well in the air because it would slow the

21

machine down. There was a windshield so we could look out a little anyway.

The engine roared like a steady thunderstorm, then we were moving swiftly over the ground. It seemed as though the ship was never going to rise, but finally it leaped into the air, then the wheels thumped the ground and seemed to drag heavily with the power still on. The fence loomed up in front of us and some scattered jack pines were just beyond the fence. I remembered I had noticed an irrigation ditch on this side of the fence large enough to wreck us if we hit it.

Suddenly the ship leaped into the air like an eagle, this time to stay. It swung to the right, then to the left, to miss two jack pines we weren't high enough to get over. The noise was almost deafening.

As soon as we were off the ground and clear of the trees, I poked my head out and took in all the scenery. A steady blast of cool crisp wind fanned my face, and the ship rode the invisible air currents like a boat rides the waves on the ocean. As the ship changed air currents, we would fall and rise again as if by some magic hand. The earth was gradually dropping away from us. I looked down, what seemed thousands of feet, and there was a small silver line stretching for miles. It must be the irrigation ditch. The green alfalfa fields, the miniature houses, and the numerous crossroads all seemed more beautiful than ever before as they passed slowly beneath us.

The town was below us, and I could hardly recognize anything until we had made a couple of circles and looked things over from different angles. The river was very small, and the footbridge looked more like a 2x4 crossing the river than a bridge. We hit several air currents that caused the ship to rise and fall suddenly.

One thing that seemed to impress me was the fact that there was no sensation of movement or speed as I had expected there would be. The wings were stiff and motionless and as innocent looking as a board. I could see only a dim blur the diameter of the propeller, that had no sign of movement whatever, and I could see objects right through this blur almost as clearly as if it wasn't there.

After flying for 10 or 15 minutes, we headed back for the field. With the motor idling, we were gradually losing altitude, and as we neared the field, we were about 100 feet high. Tex pulled the throttle back and nosed her down.

There was no windsock on the field. Tex just supposed the wind was still blowing the same as it had been when we took off. It had changed, and we were coming in with a tailwind, which was not a nice thing to do with the fast-landing Curtiss Oreole. However, after a thrilling maneuver which Tex later explained was a sideslip, we touched the ground with a smooth thud on all three points. We had been traveling at a high rate of speed due to the tailwind and nearly hit the fence before we came to a stop.

In the process of taxiing back to the place where we took off, I really got a sensation of speed and motion. The sand the propeller kicked up was more like a blizzard on the Sahara Desert than a flying field.

At this time Glen Hoover and his brother Bob had just started hauling passengers between Bend and Portland with their new Packard car Glen used to transport Tex and Woody to and from the field. They called their passenger service the Bend Portland Bus Line. This service prospered and grew into what is now Trailways Bus Lines. Bob Hoover was president of Trailways Bus Lines for many years, until he retired. The president of Trailways Bus Lines still lives in Bend.

FISHING-POLE GLIDER

Shortly after we moved to Bend, I became acquainted with 10-year-old Cloyde Artmen, and we built model airplanes and model gliders together. One of the boys in our area told me he knew where there was a wrecked airplane about five miles out of town, so we walked out to see it. Most of it had been hauled away, but the damaged wings were still there. I figured it was either a Jenny or a Standard J-1 airplane. There was something sacred about anything that was part of an airplane, and it shouldn't be wasted.

I figured I could build a full-sized glider with these wings and managed to get them hauled to our place and started working to build a glider. Cloyde and I worked together on this project, but before we had made much progress, his family moved to the state of Washington. I continued with another boy, Jack, as my partner.

As work progressed, I decided the glider would be too heavy and changed to a design made with cane fishing poles that could be purchased at our local hardware store for 25 cents

23

each. This glider had three wings, one above the other. When the triplane glider was finished, a few very short trial flights convinced me it was not properly balanced and that it did not have good lift. The cloth had not been treated with anything to make it airtight.

I sawed off the top wing and made the other two wings longer, then painted the cloth with calcimine from the hardware store to make it airtight. Calcimine is not waterproof, so when it rained, the wings soaked up water like a dishrag and I couldn't fly again until the wings dried out.

The biplane glider balanced much better than the three-wing design and it had satisfactory lift. The wing span was 27 feet, 4-foot cord, 4½-foot gap, and 18-inch stagger. The glider had no ribs in the wings. I purchased the cheapest possible unbleached muslin at a local store at seven cents per square yard and had one thickness of the cloth between the front and rear

The fishing poles I used to build my 1925 gliders. Also seen in the picture is the back end of my Model T Ford, for which I had paid $5.

fishing poles. The cloth was hand-sewn around the poles. In flight, the air pressure would push up on the cloth between the poles and form the wing curve. Where the compression struts and the interplane struts connected to the fishing pole spars, I notched them a little, used glue, and wrapped them securely with ordinary store string. Also, where the extensions were spliced on the two wings, I overlapped the fishing poles about 12 inches and wrapped them with string and glue.

The fuselage, horizontal stabilizer, and rudder were all made with ½x¾-inch pine molding, put together with gusset plates. I made these gusset plates from tin cut from tomato cans with tin snips and installed them with brads. No glue was used on the gusset plates. This is where Jack and I parted company. He was not completely sold on using fishing poles to build the wings. He said if we used anything smaller than two-by-fours to hold the tail on, he wouldn't have anything to do with it. (Years later Jack died on the death march of Corregidor. He had

My first 1925 fishing-pole glider was this triplane, with a biplane horizontal stabilizer, seen on the right side of the picture. This glider did not fly well, so I sawed off the top wing and increased the span of the lower wings and used a monoplane horizontal stabilizer. That glider flew very well.

become a radio operator on a submarine and was captured by the Japanese.)

All the wire bracing on the wings was piano wire and turn-buckles. The tail was braced to the wings with four stovepipe wires on each side. The handholds for picking the glider up were two spruce I-beams from the rear spars of the damaged airplane wings. I installed these in the center of the bottom wing with string and glue.

When flying the glider, I wore no harness of any kind and had no place to stand or sit. My only security while airborne was a good solid grip on these two I-beams.

In order to launch the glider, I tied on a tow rope with a bow knot. To release the rope, I could pull the loose end of the knot. However, if I let loose of one of my handholds to pull this rope, I would fall out of the glider; so I was not able to release the tow line on the first few flights until I made other arrangements.

After changing the glider from a three-winger to a two-winger and treating the cloth with calcimine to make it air-tight, I could run into a light wind, jump up, and become airborne for a very short distance. Now I was ready to make a flight behind a tow car. I had my father's four-cylinder Star car. There were three other boys there, none of whom knew how to drive. I gave the oldest boy a quick driving lesson.

I told him to slowly increase his speed until I was three or four feet off the ground, then gradually slow down until I landed, then stop. I wanted to get the feel of how the glider balanced and handled before getting very high.

Finally everything was ready. The driver was behind the wheel; one boy was standing on the running board looking back at the glider so he could tell the driver when to slow down after I became airborne. There was no wind.

As the car started moving, I ran to keep up with it. The speed kept increasing. The glider was trying to lift me but the tail was too high. We were going so fast I would not be able to run any faster, but he continued increasing the speed.

I decided I was holding the I-beams too far forward, so with great effort I slipped my hands back about six inches. That was too much! The nose of the glider came up, and we headed for the sky like a homesick angel.

When the boys in the tow car saw me about 75 feet in the air and still climbing steeply, they were afraid to slow down and just kept going. I reached the end of my 150-foot tow line and was looking almost straight down into the tow car and wondering, "What do I do now?"

If I had let loose of the I-beams to move my hands forward, I would have fallen out of the glider. I leaned forward as far as I could, but that was not far enough to get the nose down. I finally succeeded in getting my knees on the forward fishing pole, put my head between the two front interplane struts, and braced my shoulders against these struts. With this accomplished, the nose came down and the glider began to lose altitude about the time the tow car had come near the end of the field.

It would be the understatement of all time to say that was a great thrill being that high. It was a lot more than I had bargained for. I felt better as I got closer to the ground. The tow line was completely slack so I was on my own. The next problem was to decide when to start moving my weight back to lose some speed for the landing.

As the ground got closer, I started moving my weight back. The right wing dropped at a steep angle, and the glider slipped steeply into the ground to the right. The right wing hit the ground and was smashed. Then my feet hit but not very hard, and I was able to hold up the rest of the craft to keep it from being further damaged. I spent two weeks rebuilding the glider.

In reviewing the flight, it was obvious I had leveled off too

Fishing-pole glider, Bend, Oregon, 1925. I was 17 years old. This glider lifted me off the ground at 15 miles per hour behind a tow car.

high and stalled, which caused the right wing to drop. After repairing the damaged glider, I had a better idea where to take hold of the I-beams for proper balance, and my driver became better at handling the car. As we both gained experience, I succeeded in making quite a few short flights without gaining too much altitude. Then I began making longer flights and getting more altitude. I never again flew as high with that glider as on that first flight.

Being towed behind the car, the glider lifted me off the ground at 15 miles per hour with no wind. This was excellent lift considering the ground elevation was 3,600 feet above sea level. The farmer's field was three-quarters of a mile long, but it was narrow. The driver had instructions to slow down at a certain place to leave slack in the rope so I could nose down and experiment with different gliding speeds and practice flaring out for the landing.

The climb was a cinch. As long as the tow rope was pulling, I had unlimited power, so no matter how steep the glider climbed there was no danger of stalling. Controlling the gliding speed after the tow line became slack, staying within the limited side boundaries of the field, and learning to flare out properly for the landing were all challenges for me.

The glider seemed to be plenty strong and light enough to handle. By shifting my weight forward and backward, I had good control up and down. Shifting my weight to one side or the other did not give me very good control for keeping the wings level or for rolling into and out of turns. I figured the lateral control could be improved by installing ailerons near the wing tips. Eventually I made two rope half loops from the front fishing pole to the rear pole, and after becoming airborne, I could put my feet in these rope loops and stand in them. Then I could let loose of the spruce I-beams without the danger of falling out of the glider.

After a little practice, I was getting pretty good at being able to control the angle of climb while being towed and controlling the angle of glide coming down. I also learned about where and when to flare out from the glide to make a good running landing. Lateral control still needed to be improved.

On one flight, after I had installed the rope loops to stand in after takeoff, I was just under 100 feet above the ground with both feet in these rope loops when apparently an unexpected air current dropped my left wing. I shifted my weight to the right as far as possible but the left wing stayed down, causing the glider to turn to the left. The car that was towing me was soon near my right wing tip. This was pulling the glider to the right, causing the left bank to get even steeper. Within seconds, I would completely lose control if this situation continued. I let loose of the right I-beam, pulled the slip knot, and released the tow line.

After releasing the tow line, I was able to get the wings level, but now was headed north instead of east. At least that emergency was behind me and the glider was under control again; but as the ground got nearer, another situation was developing. There was a barbed-wire fence in front of me; and I did not have enough altitude to get over it and was too high to land before reaching it.

There was a large irrigation ditch, with no water in it, on my side of the fence. I did not like the idea of getting tangled up in a barbed-wire fence, so I moved my weight forward and dropped into the far side of the ditch and came to an abrupt stop about two feet from the fence. I was badly shaken, and the glider suffered considerable damage. It was never rebuilt. I

When I built this fishing pole glider in 1925, I was a member of the American Society for the Promotion of Aviation. That is the reason for the A.S.P.A. on the rudder.

had done considerable flying with this glider, and it had been damaged only on its first and last flights. It had given me a real taste of flying, and I knew I would never be satisfied without doing more.

NATIONAL AIR RACES–1927

I seemed to be at some sort of crossroads in my life, and was having a problem trying to decide which road to take. After experiencing a real taste of flying, I was more convinced than ever there was no other course in life for me except to fly.

It came to my attention that the Aeronautics Branch of the Department of Commerce was issuing a transport pilot license to pilots who had 200 hours in the air. I wrote a letter to this department asking them if I could qualify for a transport pilot license if I flew my glider 200 hours behind a tow car. They said, "No."

I considered my fishing-pole glider very successful, up to a point. However, it was damaged again and stored in a farmer's barn, and it needed more than repairing. It also needed some ailerons for better lateral control.

I came to the conclusion that designing and building my own airplane was my best bet for getting some flying experience. I began drawing plans to build a larger machine, using larger fishing poles, with wheels for a landing gear, and using a motorcycle engine for power. I still have some of those plans.

Two years later, I visited the National Air Races in Spokane, Washington, along with 25,000 other people. There were more Jennys and Standards there than any other types of planes, but there were also other more modern airplanes.

After the show ended each afternoon, the field was opened for commercial flying. Some flew passengers, and a lot of people were buying rides. When it got dark, there were still passengers waiting for rides, and several pilots continued flying passengers after dark. This was an army field, and the officer in charge did not like the idea of planes flying passengers after dark. He gave orders to turn out the lights, even though there were still planes in the air loaded with passengers. They kept circling, waiting for someone to turn on the lights so they could see to land. It was a contest to see if some plane would run out of gas before the lights were turned back on.

An OX5 Jenny was forced to land because his gas was too

low; however, his engine was still running as he came in for a landing. It was too dark for the pilot to judge his altitude, and he hit the ground in a full sideslip. The landing gear collapsed, the bottom wings were destroyed, the fuselage was broken just back of the rear cockpit, and the propeller was broken. The two passengers and the pilot were not injured. The lights went back on so the other pilots could see to land, but that ended the night flying.

Nick Mamer, the fixed-base operator at the Spokane airport, owned the Jenny that crashed there in the dark. He was later a captain for Northwest Airlines and lost his life on a Lockheed Electra when the tail section broke off in stormy weather.

One airplane at the air races boasted brass bushings with graphite in the brass so the wheels didn't have to be removed to grease them. Another plane had wheel brakes. This was a big help in steering while taxiing, as well as enabling a quicker stop after landing. Eddie Stinson was there with his new cabin biplane, the one with the wheel brakes. Eddie Stinson was a famous pilot, airplane designer and manufacturer during that period. He finally lost his life in an airplane crash. There was an all-metal Hamilton mid-wing cabin monoplane with a Wright J-5 engine that carried six people. I helped two mechanics grind the valves on one of the cylinders on this plane one night, and it won the efficiency contest the next day.

The unlimited speed race was run with two biplanes, the Army's and the Navy's. These two planes were so fast they would not fly them cross-country but shipped them to the air races in railroad boxcars, and assembled them right there on the field; they were disassembled and shipped out after the races. I do not remember which plane won the race but remember its speed was 225 miles per hour. (Just 10 years later Northwest Airlines was operating an airline through Spokane with Lockheed Electras. Their cruising speed was 225 miles per hour.)

Three Boeing pursuit planes flew in formation right in front of the grandstand about 10 feet off the ground and pulled up into a beautiful loop. They were biplanes with Wasp radial nine-cylinder engines. They did not have retractable landing gears. One of these planes pulled out of his loop too late, and when it hit the ground, the landing gear collapsed. The right wheel broke the right lower wing; both spars were broken and the wing was pushed up over a foot at the break; the metal propeller dug into the ground and was badly twisted out of shape.

Then the plane bounced back into the air and flew very low right over the grandstand, directly over my head. One of the wheels rolled over and hit a 12-year-old boy who was standing in front of the grandstand, and he was taken away in an ambulance. The plane went out of sight behind the grandstand. In a short while it appeared in front of the spectators without any part of its landing gear. The engine was making odd noises. The plane landed nose high, and after the tail touched the ground, the belly dropped to the ground. The plane slid forward on its belly. Then the engine dug into the ground, raising a large cloud of dust. The tail raised real high, then settled back down. As the ambulance went screaming out toward it, it came to a stop right side up. The ambulance crew pulled the pilot out of the plane, but he wasn't even hurt. The boy who was hit by the wheel was not seriously hurt, either.

3

TEX RANKIN'S FLYING SCHOOL

After seeing the National Air Races at Spokane, I decided the proper course for me was to learn to fly at a regular flying school instead of continuing with my home-built ideas. In the spring of 1928 I made the 200-mile trip to Portland on my motorcycle and signed up with Tex Rankin's flying school, then went back to Bend to continue working in the box factory (wood boxes) at $37\frac{1}{2}$ cents per hour to save the money needed to start my flying lessons. To speed up my learning, I took Rankin's home study course back to Bend and studied it.

Rankin's Flying School was located on the north bank of the Willamette River by Swan Island. Sand was being dredged from the bottom of the river at that time to build up Swan Island to make it into Portland's airport. Tri-motored Bach airplanes were operating from Rankin's field on regular airline service up and down the West Coast. This was the fastest airline in the United States, with a cruising speed of 150 miles per hour. Those Bach airplanes had a 450-horsepower Wasp engine on the nose and two 165-horsepower Comet engines under the wings.

At an airshow in Eugene, before going to Portland to start my flight training, I bought 20 minutes of dual instructions in an OX5 Jenny for $5. The pilot wanted $10, but $5 was all I had and he wanted that pretty badly also. I was to learn more about this sort of thing later. This was my first flight training, and today I am proud of the fact that I had 20 minutes of flight instructions in the now famous OX5 Jenny of World War I.

Late in 1928 I left for Portland to start actual flight training. I took everything Rankin offered; a shop course on engines, a shop course on airframes, and classroom studies on theory of flight, meteorology, navigation, engines and airframes. For experience I helped service airplanes at the flying field.

With my background in designing, building and flying model airplanes and gliders, my fishing-pole glider experience, and having studied many books on aviation, I figured learning to fly would be easy. This was not the case. Learning to fly was very difficult, and there were others who seemed to learn it faster and better than I did; nevertheless, in due time, I completed the 50-hour flying course successfully.

Tex Rankin and his two brothers, Dick and Dud, Art Walters, and Morris King, had been my flight instructors. One thing I and several of the other students enjoyed was that when we flew with Dud Rankin he had a favorite fishing place on the Willamette River where we solo students would land, after Dud had "checked us out." Then we would practice solo landings in a farmer's field that just happened to be right nearby, while Dud fished. When I finished my flight training, I had a total of 55 hours of flight experience, including both dual instruction and solo flying, and an Oregon State pilot's license.

FLYING CLUB

Before I finished my flight training, I had found an OX5 Waco 9 at Corvallis for sale at $1,600; so I hopped a freight train back to Bend and spent a few days organizing a flying club. Sixteen members put in $100 each, which gave us the cash we needed to buy the Waco. I now had created a flying job for myself and had 16 eager flying students as a starter. Even if I would have known about the world-shaking stock market crash that would happen within the next 90 days, I would not have let it worry me.

When I shook hands with Dick Rankin and said goodbye, he said, "It's a big sky out there Ted. Don't tempt it."

As I was climbing out of Rankin's field heading into my future, Dick remarked to those near him, "Well there goes Ted Barber. If he is still alive next spring, he will be a damn good pilot."

That day, August 15, 1929, as I pointed the nose of the Waco 9 up into the Columbia River Gorge on my way to Bend, I had a full gas tank and two passengers and suitcases crowded into the front cockpit. This was my first payload as a commercial pilot, and I had a great feeling of accomplishment and great expectations for the future.

However, it didn't take me long to realize my learning days were not over. I had started this business with the firm conviction that if there was anything I did not know about flying, it surely could not be very important. But as time progressed, I discovered there was a great deal about flying I did not know.

Flying was a game of adventure in which we were not only dealing with the things we understood but, in so many cases, with forces and elements we did not understand. Even today flying is something that is never completely learned. No one person will ever know all there is to know about flying.

It is more understandable today than it was back in those days, that not only the early barnstorming pilots, but also our government, didn't understand how best to handle the various situations encountered, considering the fact that bureaucracy entered into it. Human and civil rights as associated with aviation were words that had not been recognized yet.

In those days, carburetor ice was not understood. The hazards of high-speed flight were unknown. Rudder and aileron control coordination and quick-stall-recovery were not properly understood.

Many planes of those days were improperly balanced, giving them dangerous spinning characteristics. In many cases, each pilot used his individual understanding and techniques for many of his maneuvers.

After this first flight to Bend, I enjoyed a long honeymoon period with flying. This seemed like being on a continuous paid vacation. On my student flights I was learning more from them than they were from me, and on the passenger flights I thought it was really something for people to pay me to take them for a ride in an airplane. I enjoyed it more than they did, and furthermore, I got to fly the airplane.

There were only 32 airplanes in the whole state of Oregon as I established myself as the first fixed-base operator and barnstormer in the central part of Oregon. About 28 of those were located on the west side of the Cascade Mountains. I was on the east side. So mid-air collisions were not a big problem on my side of the mountains. I was operating the only commercial flying business in central Oregon, with the only airplane in over a 50,000-square-mile area.

My first flying in Bend was to start 16 anxious students out on their flight training. On the first day of flight training, after each flight, the other students would crowd around the one who had just finished his flight and ask questions. "How did it go?," etc.

One remark when asked how it went was, "Well, Ted interfered with the controls a few times." Another's comment was, "Old Ted looked like Jesus Christ up there in that front cockpit." The rest of the students' impressions of their first flying lesson fell somewhere between these too extremes. Only now could I begin to sympathize with some of the problems my flight instructors had while trying desperately to teach me to fly.

Our airport at Bend, Knott Field, was 3,600 feet above sea level. There was a lot of difference between flying a 90-horsepower OX5 airplane at sea level and flying it in the central Oregon area where field elevations range from 3,000 to 6,000 feet above sea level.

Up to the time I started flying at Bend, I had seen only two OX5-powered airplanes land there, a Waco 9 and an American Eagle. The American Eagle crashed while trying to take off, and it was hauled away on a truck. All the other airplanes I had seen land at Bend had 150 horsepower or more, so I was trying something that had not been done before.

One day a student and I flew to Sisters, 20 miles northwest of Bend, to sell airplane rides. Sisters did not have a good landing field so I landed on a 600-foot oval shaped racetrack near town, and discovered that by using some rough ground I had another 200 feet at the west end to help get the takeoff roll started. This gave me 800 feet to become airborne, then about 200 feet of sagebrush before coming to a fence. Then there was about one-fourth mile to get over some tall pine trees; there was a gap in one place that looked wide enough to fly through. In the center of this gap was a small tree about half as tall as the larger ones. I was not sure about getting over the tall trees, but felt sure I could get over the small tree.

After landing and looking the situation over, I flew over town solo to drop out some leaflets advertising airplane rides for $2.50. Several people came out to the "airport." Two men who weighed at least 200 pounds each decided to buy an airplane ride. I was not very enthusiastic about the prospects of getting this heavy load off that short field and over those trees; however, I was in no position to turn down $5, so I loaded these fellows in the plane and used the full 200 feet of rough ground to get the takeoff roll started.

I succeeded in getting the airplane into the air and in clearing the fence but was unable to get any extra speed or lift. There was just enough lift to keep the airplane in the air. I headed for the gap in the trees, and the closer I got to those trees the more doubtful it looked about even getting over the small tree. There appeared to be a little more gap to the left of the small tree than to the right, so I lined up with this gap. By now I felt sure there was not enough gap for the plane to get through, but I had no choice.

At the point of expected impact I closed my eyes, and strangely enough, nothing happened. I opened my eyes, and the trees were behind us. We proceeded nonchalantly on our way, and I was able to get above the next trees we came to. This flight concluded satisfactorily. More people came out who were not as heavy, and there was now less gas in the tank so there were no more problems.

At a later time, I was flying at Sisters one day each week to teach a small class of students. One of my students had made a small windsock and put it up on a pole. One day a pilot from Seattle flying an OX5 American Eagle was flying over that area. While lost and low on gas, he saw the windsock and landed. He found out where he was, got some gas, and crashed on his takeoff. (He broke about 10 feet out of the top of two trees.) He took the engine back to Seattle, left the rest of the plane, and reported me to the federal aeronautics inspector at Portland for having a windsock at a field he said was not safe to fly from. The inspector told him there was no law against anyone putting up a windsock anywhere and that when he got his pilot license it was supposed to mean he could tell an airport when he saw one.

Finally we pilots of the high country got to feeling a little superior to the pilots of the low country. A takeoff was not just a simple case of opening the throttle, then pulling the stick back to get off the ground. There was a little more to it than that, and sometimes learning exactly what this was separated the men from the boys. In our advertising we said, "Learn to fly at Bend, and you can fly anywhere."

In those days, the words "general aviation" had not been invented. OX5's and Hisso's were the most commonly used engines. Cabin planes were not widely accepted for teaching students to fly. You had to be out in the open so the wind would hit you in the face in order to learn to fly properly. Otherwise, how could you ever learn to avoid skidding and slipping in turns?

In 1929, airplanes were not widely accepted by our society. Even after World War I, where airplanes, dirigibles, and balloons were all used extensively, our military leaders failed to recognize the possibilities of the flying machine. I planned to help change this attitude by proving an airplane could be useful.

NIGHT FLIGHT

Shortly after establishing the flying business at Bend, I had a charter flight to Portland. Two men had some business there, then wanted to fly back to Bend, a two-and-one-half hour flight each way.

We got off to an early start, and because the Cascade Mountains were covered with clouds, we went north to the Columbia River at the Dalles, then west down the Columbia River Gorge to Portland.

This was in the prohibition days, but I noticed before we took off from Bend that my passengers had smuggled a bottle of the forbidden spirits on board. They sampled its contents rather sparingly on the flight to Portland.

We landed at Portland's Swan Island Airport. I had the plane gassed and waited impatiently throughout the day for my passengers because I wanted to get back to Bend before dark. The Waco had no lights, and I didn't even have a flashlight or any matches. When they finally arrived back at the airport, the sun was already down. There was no way we could get home before dark.

The weather was clear except for the clouds that still covered the mountains. I phoned Bend and asked my brother, Cordis, if he could get three or four cars to drive out to Knott Field and turn their lights on the field when I flew over town so I could see to land. Then we took off in the fading light and headed for Bend.

As the darkness overcame the daylight, ground objects became indistinct and blurred. The steady bluish flames from my two exhaust pipes cast their glow on the sides of the fuselage. The faithful Waco grew in stature as earthly objects dimmed, and someone turned the stars on, one at a time at first, then whole clusters as darkness completely won its contest with daylight and the whole sky became brightly lighted with stars as night took over completely.

The magnificence of the sky filled with shining jewels lost its charm only when I looked at the total darkness below. Except for occasional car lights on roads, and the lights of widely spaced towns on our path, everything below was black and featureless. The engine wouldn't dare quit now, or would it? Flying, like religion, some of it at least, was done on faith.

By now, my two passengers had become highly inebriated as they passed their bottle of fortification back and forth until it was finally empty. Then they tossed it overboard, and it disappeared into the darkness below.

As darkness won its complete victory, the Columbia River Gorge was now far behind us. We were flying south, and I knew the country below well enough to identify the lights of each town that showed up ahead and slowly passed behind us.

It had been a long day, and the steady drone of the engine was contributing to my drowsiness; I was having to exert considerable effort to stay awake at the controls. As we approached the northern edge of the lights of Bend, my engine suddenly stopped. I was sleepy no more.

It was too dark to see even a dim outline of any open area. I knew the ground within my gliding range consisted of rolling hills, rocks and trees, plus the Deschutes river. There was a large dam at the north edge of Bend; I could see the reflection of two lights from the water of this dam. I figured landing in the water would be better than in the hills, trees and rocks I could not see.

As I was losing altitude and getting lined up to approach the water for a dunking and a cold swim to shore, I put my left hand on the throttle and discovered it was closed. This surprised me. I pushed the throttle open and had full power again. One of the passengers had just accidentally bumped the throttle in the front cockpit and closed it.

We continued flying toward Knott Field which was seven

miles southeast of Bend. Now I was hoping Cordis had been able to get three or four cars to drive out to the airport so I would have enough light to see to land. This was my first night flying experience and would be my first night landing. As I approached the area where I knew the airport was, I was not prepared for what happened next. Suddenly all of Knott Field lit up like daylight. There had to be a hundred cars down there with their lights on. We were being welcomed home as if we were just completing the first nonstop flight around the world. The next day, the local newspaper made a front-page story out of the first night flight into central Oregon.

I kept pretty busy on student instruction, passenger flights, and charter flights, and was the only one in the area capable of doing the daily maintenance work and occasional repair jobs that were normal to operating a flying business. The plane had not been exactly in top condition when we bought it. The fabric was pretty bad; there were some broken ribs in the lower wings, and eventually the engine needed overhauling.

When winter was coming on, we rented a building in town and completely rebuilt the plane, clear down to stripping all the old paint off the steel tubing of the fuselage. With a home-built rib jig, we made new ribs to replace the damaged ones. We majored the engine, poured new main and connecting rod bearings, and hand-scraped them. Some of the students offered their help, and this work went very well. By the spring of 1930, we had a Waco 9 that was in the best of condition.

The planes of that period did not have a steerable tailwheel. They just had an iron skid on the tail, and they did not have wheel brakes. When we were operating out of fields 600 or 800 feet long, it was necessary on the landings to get them on the ground before very much of the field went by. "Neither the runway behind you, or the altitude above you has any value to you," according to "Ye Book of Rules For Flying Fools."

MID-AIR REPAIRS

One day Cordis and I were out on a barnstorming tour headed for the small town of Shaniko. One sparkplug wire came off, so the engine was missing. We still had power enough to get to Shaniko, find a field, land, and repair the wire. But I figured if we flew over town with our engine hitting on only seven cylinders, the people might be reluctant to buy rides in our airplane, so I decided to try to put the wire back on the sparkplug while we were flying.

Cordis was flying the plane from the rear cockpit, and I was riding in the front. I got out on the right lower wing walk and moved cautiously forward. The OX5 engine had single ignition, with the cylinder heads extending out of the cowlings. There were steel tube wing struts for me to hold onto, but I could not reach the sparkplug wire very well while I was standing on the wing. When working on the engine while on the ground, it was common practice for me to stand on top of the wheel to reach the engine. So I reached out with my right foot and stepped on top of the right wheel. Because we were in the air, there was nothing to prevent the wheel from turning, and as soon as my weight was on the wheel, it started turning. I got the thrill of my life. Even straight down it was a long way to the ground.

I had a good hold on the wing strut with one hand and did not fall. By keeping both feet on the wing walk, I finally succeeded in getting the wire back on the sparkplug. When we flew over Shaniko, our engine was running smoothly on all eight cylinders.

Eventually we were getting caught up on our flight training, and passenger flights were slowing down. Our problem was that we were getting deeper into the depression, and fewer people had money to spend for flying.

We had changed our name from the Bend Flying Club to Bend Flying Service, Incorporated, of which I was president. We were incorporated for $10,000, which was ample for what we were doing. We considered incorporating for more money and selling stock through some stockbrokers from Chicago, with whom we had held several meetings. If we had done this, we planned to buy two or three tri-motored Fords, for $50,000 each, and start an airline through central Oregon.

Also, we considered sending the airplane and me to a project in southern Nevada where the federal government was going to start building a large new dam in the Las Vegas area, called Boulder Dam, later renamed Hoover Dam. We could have been the first flying service at this project.

I liked the airline idea and I liked the Boulder Dam idea. I would have liked anything that would have kept us in business.

However, our board of directors couldn't decide on either of these projects. The decision that was finally made was to sell the Waco 9 to me on terms I could afford, and I started out on my own.

There was still a big sky out there and I still had an area of over 50,000 square miles to call my own, but it was becoming harder and harder to find enough business to continue operating. Becoming an aerial gypsy and barnstorming from town to

Ted Barber, Knott Field, Bend, Oregon, 1929. OX5 Waco 9 with a Travelair landing gear.

town seemed to generate more income than staying in one place.

In a way, barnstorming was comparable to an eagle flying the countryside looking for fresh meat for his next meal. That is what I was doing. Any place I found suitable refreshments was my home for that day, or until the refreshments ran out.

THE WINDOW IN THE SKY

The deepest blessing God can give
    Is not that man shall always live
But that the time allotted here
    Be spent where he is always near.

And where can man more closely be
    Than in the sky where he can see
The glory of the earth below
    And space up where he can not go.

Soaring far above the ground,
    Sometimes flying fast as sound,
He knows that only moments lie
    From sudden death and men who fly.

When the day that he must go
    Dawns bright as freshly fallen snow,
Full of faith the pilot flies
    Through a window in the skies.

Probing spaces yet unknown
    Places he has never flown
Leaving all earthbound things
    He rises on eternal wings.

For him who found that God was near
    And greeted death without a fear,
Think not that he's forever gone
    But through a window he has flown.

4

DENIO RODEO–PARACHUTE JUMP

Business was so slow around Bend that I spent more time barnstorming from one small town to another than I spent at Bend. It was becoming harder and harder to find enough business to continue operating.

Early one summer morning, I flew into the town of Dayville on the John Day River and landed in a small farm field in a hilly area. Some people came out from town after I had dropped leaflets advertising airplane rides, and I started flying passengers.

Ideal air conditions were an absolute necessity in order to use this field, and there was no better field available in any direction that would have been close enough to use. I was in the air with a man and his wife when an unacceptable wind came up from the wrong direction. I made several trial runs on this field from different angles and finally decided to try a landing. Before I got stopped, I went through a barbed-wire fence. The propeller and landing gear had been lined up between two fence posts, which did considerable damage to the fabric and ribs on the lower wings, especially from the rear spars to the trailing edge of the wings.

The Waco 9 had ailerons only on the top wings, and it was pretty sluggish on aileron control. I figure that while I had to rebuild the bottom wings anyway, this would be a good time to put ailerons on the lower wings. With this in mind, I flew to Burns, where I would be able to get the material needed to do this.

I purchased some pine lumber and some unbleached muslin and proceeded to build ailerons. I bought some cupboard door hinges to mount them, and from a wrecked American Eagle I found two pieces of light steel tubing to connect the lower ailerons to the upper ailerons so they would both work together. Cupboard door hinges were also used on each end of these steel tubes. With this conversion, I had better aileron control with four ailerons.

Sometime after installing ailerons on the lower wings, I was barnstorming in southern Oregon south of Burns. I landed in a hayfield called the HL Meadow, below Frank Henry's place at the base of the Steens Mountains. In a few days, Frank was putting on a two-day Fourth-of-July celebration at Denio, Oregon, on the Oregon-Nevada border. A good passenger hauling business could be expected there.

An old man lived in a cabin a few miles west of Frank's place, out in the middle of Catlow valley. Frank wanted to make arrangements with him to stay at the ranch to take care of his livestock while the rest of us went to Denio for the celebration. I flew Frank out to this fellow's cabin so they could discuss the situation. The old man could be described as a hermit, living in a cabin right out in the middle of the large flat valley. As we flew over his cabin, we could see him out in his yard, within a hundred feet or so of his cabin. We landed in the wild hay that was everywhere and taxied right up to his cabin.

He was picking hay, and I mean he was really picking it. It is, perhaps, hard to believe, but he was actually picking it by hand. He would stoop over and pick a handful of hay with his right hand, then hold the picked hay in his left arm while he picked more hay. When he got an armload, he would walk over to the haystack which was near his house, deposit the hay, then walk out and pick another armload of hay. He said the sheep men bring their sheep down in the valley to winter, and he expected to have 20 or 25 tons of hay picked and in the stack ready to sell.

Frank suggested that he would be glad to loan him horses and a mower and a rake so he could put up more hay. He refused this because he was too far out in the country, and when something broke down, as it always does, there would be too much delay and expense in getting it repaired. Then Frank offered to loan him a scythe so he could get more hay in by hand. He also refused a scythe which would get dull and cause him trouble.

As the day of the big celebration approached, my thoughts were on all the money I would make at this two-day Fourth of July Rodeo. I set the Waco down on the cleared landing strip in the sagebrush as the sun started peeking over the low hills to the east. The high mountains were west and much closer. It had been a short flight from Frank Henry's ranch to Denio, and I was eager to not miss a beat on the events of the next two days.

My landing strip was within 100 yards of the rodeo grounds. The hotel, about 100 yards northeast of the corrals, was just a large ranch house. There were two bars about a quarter of a mile above (west) of the corrals and hotel. Also there was a bar in the hotel. Not bad accommodations considering this was in the days of prohibition when it was against the law to have, sell, or consume alcoholic beverages.

Even at this early hour there were people moving about, and there I was, Johnny-on-the-Spot, ready to fly passengers during the big event. My altimeter showed a field elevation of 4,500 feet above sea level, but that wasn't asking too much of an OX5 Waco 9 was it? Or was it?

Within a short while after landing, I was in the air with two passengers, and gradually more arrived. Bill, my helper, kept tickets sold ahead and had a five-gallon can of gas ready for me to put in as I needed it. Everything was going along fine until later in the day, as the air became warmer and warmer and started losing some of its integrity.

I had always been told a downdraft over level ground would not put an airplane into the ground. A downdraft is a body of air moving down; and over level ground when this body of air reaches the ground, it must flatten out. Therefore, you would not be in a downdraft after you get closer to the ground.

As I was taking off with a man and a girl as passengers, I encountered a downdraft that did not seem to know anything about these rules. I made a normal takeoff and climbed normally to about 50 feet of altitude. I had passed the boundary of my landing strip and was flying over sagebrush when the plane started to sink rapidly. The situation looked serious, and I laid the plane over in a right bank, hoping to find better air a little to the right. I never did get a chance to find out. The downdraft never did let up, and it put me right on down into the ground.

There was no time to get the wings level before it struck the ground, but I did get the stick all the way back before it hit. The first thing that hit the ground was the right lower wing tip. Full left aileron was on when it hit, so the right aileron was down and took the worst beating. The cupboard door hinges on my homemade aileron broke, and eyewitnesses said the aileron flew end-over-end about 30 feet into the air. The right wing tip hitting first threw the plane sideways. Then the wheels hit the ground, and this put the left wing into the ground with more force than the right wing had hit. By the time this had happened, I had moved the stick to the left to protect the left lower aileron so it was not damaged. The plane stopped within about 300 feet without further damage except that the fabric on both lower wings was badly torn and the left rear wing spar was broken at the wing strut fitting.

After the plane had quit bouncing itself around in the sagebrush and had come to a complete stop and all the noises had died down, I was still aware of some confusion. My water-cooled engine was boiling over. The radiator was under the top wing in front of my passengers. Boiling water was spewing out of the radiator onto the underside of the top wing and running back on the wing and falling onto the passengers in the front cockpit. They were screaming for someone to get them out of there;they must have thought they were being boiled in oil. As soon as I saw what the situation was, I got out, unfastened their safety belt, and got them out. The water was still coming back on them, and it was still hot, though by the time it reached them it was not hot enough to really do them any permanent damage. They were more scared than hurt.

With the condition the plane was in now, it was not possible to make a parachute jump that day as we had advertised. The crowd was very disappointed when they learned the parachute jump had been postponed.

One of my ex-students, Cy Ralston, was the pilot who had flown at the celebration there the year before. He had also advertised a parachute jump but he did not put one on either. His jumper was an experienced jumper, but when it came time to make the jump, he decided that for a 4,000-foot elevation and a hot day, and because he had only a 24-foot Russel Lobe parachute he had borrowed from me, it was not safe to make the jump. However, they did go up and drop the parachute with a 100-pound sandbag, and everyone agreed that if a man had hit the ground as hard as that sandbag did, he would have died.

This still left the crowd dissatisfied. At a time like this the crowd would rather have seen a man killed than have a parachute jump postponed. The Russel Lobe parachute was not a good parachute. Several jumpers had been killed or injured while jumping with it, and the manufacturer became involved in lawsuits and went out of business.

You can see how the crowd felt when they learned there would not be a parachute jump that first day of the celebration. I told them that if certain hasty repairs could be made to my plane, I would still make the jump that was scheduled for the next day.

Bill and I made a quick trip back over the mountains in a borrowed pickup to Frank's place and borrowed a spare bedsheet for patching. All good barnstormers carried dope and thinner, so I now had the materials to patch the wings. We worked on the plane until it was too dark to see what we were doing, then spent the rest of the night at the dance. As soon as daylight started to break, we left the dance and went back to work on the plane.

Shortly after the sun had come up, everyone had left the dance and were in various attitudes of retirement. Just Bill and I were laboring in a stupor on the crippled airplane. We looked up from our work at the sound of an old Model T Ford that came chugging down a dirt road near us. There was no top on the car, and there were two very drunk Indians in the front seat. The back seat was empty.

The Indian village, which was temporarily set up by the Indians who came to the celebration, consisted of about a dozen tepees that were about a quarter of a mile below the corrals and hotel. There were two bars about a fourth of a mile above and west of the corrals and hotel. These two Indians were on their way from the bars to their tepees. As they were about 100 yards from us, the right front door flew open as the Model T bumped crazily along the road, and the Indian who was sitting on the right went rolling out into the sagebrush. As he rolled to a stop, he lay motionless, never moving a muscle that we could see. The one driving didn't even miss him as he continued driving toward the tepees.

Bill and I were tired and about half punch-drunk from lack of sleep. We were becoming intoxicated from breathing the fumes from the nitrate dope and thinner we were using to patch the holes in the fabric. So we kept right on with our work.

About an hour later, the rickety old Model T came chugging back up the road from the Indian village. This time there were three Indians in it who did not seem to be as much under the influence of moonshine as the other two had been. They were obviously looking for something, as they were driving slowly and watching both sides of the road. When they came to their pal, who still lay motionless out in the sagebrush, they stopped and loaded him in the car and returned to their tepees.

About 10 a.m., Bill and I drove up to the bars in search of drinking water and food. The town was like a scene from a western novel. On every porch there were unconscious men sprawled out, some half drooping from chairs at various points along the board sidewalk. There were two white men and one Indian lying out in the middle of the street. We had a quick breakfast and went back to the plane. We were still racing against time to get the plane ready for the parachute jump. The right lower aileron was not damaged; the wood screws that were used to mount the hinges had just pulled out. We replaced them, and the day wore on slowly.

The rodeo got started about noon. There was a light breeze blowing, and it was very hot. My parachute was a 32-foot Thompson Brothers balloon pack. It was made especially for exhibition jumping. When it was packed, it looked more like a sack of potatoes than a parachute. The large bulky bag containing the parachute was tied solidly to the walk on the left lower wing. The jumper wore a harness and rode in the open front cockpit. The jumper's harness was not attached to the parachute until the jumping altitude was reached, usually around 2,000 feet. Then the jumper climbed carefully out to where the parachute was, stooped over, and snapped four large harness snaps from the parachute to his harness. Up to this point great care was taken to not slip or fall, for to do so would be to come down without the parachute.

When the jump was made, the pilot, maintaining a low airspeed, would apply full left rudder to get the plane's tail out of the way of the top of the parachute as it came out of the bag. As the jumper fell, his weight would pull the parachute out of the bag; the bag always remained solidly attached to the airplane. After the parachute opened, the 32 shroud lines from the

Something whizzed past my face. I reached my arms around under my head and picked the knife out of the air. It had fallen out of one of my leg pockets.

parachute came down to a large aluminum ring, about 14 inches in diameter. This aluminum ring was above the jumper's head but close enough to be reached. From this ring a rope came down to each side of the jumper's harness. These two ropes were attached to the harness by four large snaps near the jumper's hips.

At long last the plane was as ready as we could get it. The left rear wing spar was still badly broken, but everything else was in fair condition, so I decided to make the jump. I would not carry passengers because of the broken spar. It was then I discovered I had forgotten to bring the parachute harness the jumper had to wear. At the hotel there was a sort of blacksmith shop. We found an old leather harness that had been worn out and discarded, and we found some copper rivets and iron rings.

We hastily put together a makeshift harness. Some of the fellows did not think our homemade harness was strong enough, but it looked satisfactory to me. We announced our intentions and took to the air about 3:30 p.m. The rodeo came to a halt so everyone could watch this breathtaking event. Even after we were in the air, because of their previous disappointments, many of the spectators would have bet odds we would find some reason for not jumping.

Bill was at the controls and I was in the front cockpit with the parachute harness on. Normally we would have climbed to 2,000 feet in about 10 minutes, but the air was very light that day, and the broken spar in the left wing caused some loss of lift. By the time we had been in the air 15 minutes, we had gained only 500 feet, and at 30 minutes we had gained only 800 feet. It looked as if we would not be able to get any higher, so I signalled Bill to get into position for the jump.

He tried to talk me out of it because I had never before made a jump from less than 2,000 feet. With the air as light as it was, I was sure to make a hard landing, but my reputation was at stake, and I would never be able to face that crowd if I landed without making the jump.

I wore a white coverall-type flying suit that had large pockets in the legs both above and below the knees. In one of these pockets was a large folding hunting knife borrowed at the last minute from one of the spectators. It was good to have a knife with me when I jumped, so if one or two shroud lines became tangled and prevented the parachute from opening properly, I could reach up and cut the lines that were causing the trouble and still get the parachute open. The fellow who loaned me the knife had asked me to be sure and not lose his precious knife.

About one mile before reaching the jumping position, I started out of the front cockpit to get my harness snapped onto the parachute. I got into position and untied and removed the one-fourth inch rope that held the mouth of the parachute bag closed. As we reached the jumping position, my mind was not at ease, but I was convinced that was the only way down for me.

As I look back on this, it is understandable why there have been so many mishaps at airshows. It is easy to get yourself into a situation where you are forced to do certain things against your better judgment because you know the crowd expects it of you.

As we reached the jumping position, I gave Bill the signal to cut the throttle and get the tail of the plane out of the path of the top of the parachute as it came out of the bag. Then I dropped backwards off the trailing edge of the wing.

The parachute came out of the bag, caught the wind, and opened in fine shape. I was still attached to the parachute, so my homemade harness had passed its test.

If I had jumped from 2,000 feet, I would have gone through my regular procedure of pulling the shroud lines on one side of the parachute until the chute would partially collapse for about a 500-foot drop. Then I would revolve over and over, forward then backward, being suspended from my hips. After doing this, I would hook my toes into the aluminum ring above my head, and with my head hanging down, wave my arms at the crowd.

Because of my limited altitude, I dispensed with the first two showoff maneuvers. I just turned upside down and hung by my toes from the aluminum ring. As I started to wave my arms at the crowd, I felt something whiz past my face. I immediately thought of the borrowed knife in one of my leg pockets, and I reached my arms around under my head and grabbed the knife out of the air without ever having seen it.

By the time I had released the aluminum ring with my toes and turned right side up and put the knife back in my pocket, I realized I was approaching the ground at a terrific speed. I had installed a landing cord on this parachute. This consisted of a 1/4-inch clothesline rope fastened at the top center aperture of the parachute; the other end of the line was tied down where I could reach it easily. When about to land, I would reach up as far as I could and pull down on this cord. This would pull the top of the parachute down, which would spread the sides some and slow down the descent for the landing.

This descent was dangerously fast. I gave the cord a long pull but was still falling too fast. I held the cord with one hand while I reached up with the other hand and pulled it again. I was getting a little panicky as I reached up and gave it the third pull as I contacted the ground.

It is probably a good thing I did not start pulling this cord any sooner, or I may have turned the parachute wrong side out. It gives you a very helpless feeling when you can see you are falling too fast and there is nothing you can do to slow down the rate of fall. I was not a professionally trained parachute jumper; all I knew about it was learned from talking to other jumpers and from experience. My theory was to not land stiff and not land limp but to land with just a certain tension in the muscles that would absorb part of the jolt, then to roll, maintaining some muscle tension so as to get as many parts as possible on the ground. In this manner, no one part of the body took all the jolt. This was in the days before the word skydiving had been invented.

I contacted the ground drifting backwards. Right after hitting the ground, I became a human ball rolling out through the sagebrush. It was fortunate this was an area with no rocks. When I came to a stop, the light breeze carried my parachute to one side, and it settled onto the brush beside me. I got to my feet and started feeling and moving various parts of my anatomy to learn if everything still functioned. Nothing was out of order except my clothes were torn some.

I had landed about 200 yards from the crowd, and as I got to my feet, everyone arrived there at once. Bill was bringing the plane in for a landing. I had never seen such a wild crowd. When they discovered I was still alive and not even hurt, they picked me up and carried me into the saloon at the hotel on their shoulders. They set me on the bar, and everyone was buying drinks for the crowd. They insisted I drink a bottle of beer. I offered some resistance, but inasmuch as I would not be flying passengers anyway, I gave in to avoid bloodshed. I realized the commercial value I was to the owner of the bar, so I sat there and enjoyed the company of the group as first one man then another bought drinks for everyone at the bar. There were enough people there who knew I didn't drink, so I got by with one bottle of beer, but Bill did not stop at one bottle.

Someone passed the hat among the crowd, and they collected over $30 for me, which came in handy considering I did not make much other money there. I had expected to take in about $300 for the two days.

With the celebration over, there was the problem of getting my plane 300 miles back home and rebuilding the wing with the broken spar. It would have been quite costly to have it dismantled and hauled home on a truck so I decided to fly it home.

I departed in the early morning for smoother air and held the airspeed down to a minimum to avoid unnecessary strain on the damaged wing. The altitude was held over 4,000 feet above the ground for smoother air.

As I reached Bend after that long, monotonous flight at such low speed, I was getting impatient to get on the ground, so I closed the throttle and allowed the gliding speed to increase considerably while losing altitude. Suddenly this increased airspeed caused the tip of my broken wing to begin a violent flutter. This could have torn something loose if it had continued. I rapidly brought the nose up and held a slow glide the rest of the way in.

After dismantling the wings, stripping the fabric off the damaged wing and removing the bolts, fittings, ribs, etc., I gently lifted the broken spar out in two pieces. There was not even a splinter holding the two pieces together.

Knott Field, Bend, Oregon, 1929. One of my students in front of my home and office.

54

5

VIRGINIA'S JUMP

This Waco 9 was my only possession and a very fragile one at that. On every flight I was gambling with all my earthly possessions. Like a gambler playing blackjack. On every take-off it was like having a cash bet on the table, but the odds seemed more or less in my favor on these bets. Even at that, sometimes I envied those with simpler jobs like maybe sweeping the streets, or punching a time clock almost anywhere.

We had only a safety belt between us and the ground. I thought about this when we were upside down in an open cockpit biplane, no shoulder straps and no parachute. Once in this position I felt, and saw, my dollar watch slip out of my shirt pocket and head for the ground, several thousand feet below, but my hands were too involved with the controls to make a grab for it. Sometimes we found ourselves in situations where the best we were capable of doing just wasn't quite good enough. Then there were those happier easier moments that took the sting out of the sadder ones.

Through all of my OX5 flying days, and including the period when I was corralling horses in Nevada in 1933, the federal aeronautics inspectors considered me an outlaw, or at least a fly in their ointment, because I was not licensed under the federal aviation laws. But I was not violating any laws; I was operating under the Oregon State laws.

For one thing the federal laws required a jumper to have an extra parachute when they jumped, so they would have an extra chance if the first parachute failed to open, but the state laws did not require this extra parachute. I used only one parachute when I jumped, although I had an extra one, the 24-foot

Russel Lobe parachute, that would have made me legal under the federal laws.

We purchased this parachute new in the spring of 1930, for $250. But I had learned it was not safe to jump with it. Several jumpers had been killed or injured using the Russel Lobe parachutes, and the manufacturers were being sued and went out of business. I had never jumped with it, although I had worn it several times while test flying rebuilt airplanes, and while doing stunts at airshows.

Tex Rankin's brother, Dud, had a Russel Lobe parachute he wore while doing stunts. After he heard some bad things about it he dropped it with a sand-bag and it never opened. He didn't wear it any more.

I had the feeling the federal inspectors were not really concerned over anyone's safety as much as they were over getting everyone to just live up to their rules, and many of their rules didn't make much sense. Besides, I was trying to make a living with my airplane, and living under their rules would have complicated that.

One day a girl, Virginia Smead, was to make a parachute jump from my plane, with my regular balloon pack parachute that was tied to the lower wing, next to the fuselage.

The mouth of the parachute bag was tied shut with a light string; the jumper's weight would break the string and allow the parachute to come out of the bag. The bag stayed on the airplane.

We climbed to 2,000 feet above the field. Virginia climbed out of the front cockpit and snapped the four harness snaps to the parachute, and when I was in the right position, I gave her the signal to jump.

When I looked over the side, expecting to see the parachute opening, I saw the parachute was still in the bag and Virginia was nowhere to be seen. Finally I located her, dangling at the end of the ropes, down under the wing. She weighed less than 120 pounds, and her weight had not broken the string that held the mouth of the parachute bag closed.

There was no way she could reach the wing to climb back in, and no way I could reach her.

If I landed on the airport with her dragging below the plane, she was sure to be injured. I considered landing in the water in Mirror Pond, right in the center of Bend, in shallow water. I figured she would not be injured in a water landing, and I would be able to help her get unfastened from the parachute and get her out of the water. Also I could drop a note to the ground and have help from the ground and an ambulance standing by. Such were some of the choices we had in the OX5 flying days.

However, there was another possible way out of this predicament. If I could break the string that was keeping the parachute in the bag, she could still finish her jump.

I could not reach the parachute bag while sitting in the seat, but by standing up in the rear cockpit I could just barely reach the mouth of the bag with my right hand while still keeping my left hand on top of the control stick.

I managed to get two fingers inside the bag where the string was, but I was not able to pull hard enough to break the string, and I really tried. Apparently the bag had been tied shut with a string that was stronger than it should have been. On all the jumps we made with this parachute after this experience, we used a one-quarter-inch rope instead of a string, and the jumper had instructions to remove the rope just before jumping.

With my left hand I shoved forward on the control stick and put the plane in a steep dive for about 500 feet. Then as I pulled out of the dive real fast, I pulled hard on the mouth of the bag and the string broke. The added centrifugal force of pulling out of the dive, along with me pulling at the mouth of the bag with my two fingers, did the job.

The parachute came out of the bag and opened in fine shape, so the jump was completed with no further problems.

However, this is not the end of the story. I discovered I had ruptured myself in that go around, and I had an operation to repair my hernia.

Now, you might think our scientists have accomplished a lot in recent years developing our modern electronic communications systems. But we had almost the equivalent of this back in 1930. It was called the grapevine, and through this system word of this experience traveled at approximately the speed of light.

While I was in the hospital, a federal aeronautics inspector came to Bend and inspected my airplane. He had no jurisdiction over me because I was operating under the Oregon State laws. He avoided talking to me and I did not know he was in town. He went back to Portland and told the state inspector I was flying an unsafe airplane. He said it had a broken spar in the wings.

The state inspector came to Bend and talked to me in the hospital before he went out to the airport to inspect my airplane. I told him I did not know of any broken spars in my wings and that if there was "anything" unsafe about my airplane I wanted to fix it before doing any more flying. When he went out to the airport and inspected the plane, he could not find any broken spars.

He went back to Portland and told the federal inspector he could not find a broken spar in my airplane. Then both inspectors came to Bend and gave my airplane a close inspection and discovered there were two broken spars. Both rear spars in the bottom wings were broken where the interplane struts attach to the spars.

When we bought this Waco, it had spent all its time in the wet area of western Oregon, about three years. Rain water had apparently run down the rear struts, onto the rear spars and had caused dry-rot.

The result was that the top half of these spars had dry-rot at this place, and a hard push down, or negative load, caused the upper half of them to break. I still figure the federal inspector probably supplied the push-down that broke them, but even so, I do not hold this against him, as I have never had any desire to fly an unairworthy airplane. What I resent is his underhanded manner of handling the situation. Aviation inspectors should be helpful in such situations, not antagonistic. There has never been a time when any hard feelings ever existed between state inspectors and myself.

This development caused a lot of excitement in official circles and three members of the State Board of Aeronautics came to Bend and held a sort of Kangaroo court. I was the defendant.

I was out of the hospital and was able to get around, but my doctor had told me not to do any work, or flying, for at least 30 days.

We met in a hotel room where the members of the State Board of Aeronautics were staying. There were no lawyers present. We just openly discussed all aspects of my life and my flying activities. There were no heated arguments, no accusations, just a friendly discussion of events.

The outcome: The State Board of Aeronautics and the state inspector were under a lot of pressure. They could not find where I was violating any laws, but because of the pressure they were under from the federal inspector, they felt they had to do "something." So their final suggestion was that if I would willingly surrender my Oregon State pilot license to them for 30 days, it would get them off the "hook." And it would not do me any harm because my doctor had told me I couldn't fly for 30 days anyway. I agreed to this, so that is the way it was settled.

This got them off the "hook," and it brought happiness to the federal inspector by making me look guilty of something.

I didn't feel guilty of anything. In fact all present said I was not guilty of anything. Some people receive awards for accomplishing less than I had accomplished with my flying in central Oregon. It rubbed me the wrong direction to do this, but I agreed to this verdict as a favor to the state aeronautics inspector and the State Board of Aeronautics. I was developing the feeling that in the aviation world of the federal inspectors, pilots did not live under the same rules as the other people, who lived in a democracy that had a government "of, by and for the people," a government where a person is innocent until proven guilty and has the right to a trial by jury. Everyone loves a puppy, but when that puppy grows up and becomes a dog a different set of rules apply. I was no longer a puppy; I was now living under the dog rules. It seemed to me that to the federal inspectors friendly cooperation and fair play were foreign thoughts.

In the early 1930's, over 50 years ago, I thought it was ridiculous that our government had chosen aviation as the only thing it served as a dictator over. Pilots had lost all citizenship rights regarding aviation. Anything the aeronautics inspector said was law, and different inspectors said different things.

An example of this is the experience Bill Anderson had with them. He had purchased a new Hisso Eaglerock. He hired a pilot and they were barnstorming in the western states. An aeronautics inspector grounded his plane because the gas sediment bowl was glass and it might break. So Bill couldn't fly again until he discarded the glass sediment bowl and installed a metal one. Obviously this glass sediment bowl had been approved before the plane left the factory—by a federal aeronautics inspector. Bill could not buy a metal bowl, so he had a machine shop make one for him, at considerable cost.

Later he was flying in another area and a different inspector grounded his plane because he had a metal bowl he could not see through to know when it had collected some dirt and needed cleaning.

In one case a pilot in western Oregon lost his pilot license because he wrote a bad check. The inspector said he didn't want pilots flying around the country giving aviation a bad name.

In situations like these if the pilots involved had any natural rights that were guaranteed by the Constitution, or the Bill of Rights, they were simply ignored. Anyway, it would look silly and would have been an exercise in futility for a barnstorming pilot with 30 cents in his pocket to have hired a lawyer and started a long drawn-out court battle with the United States Government.

One day two Zenith airplanes had flown down from Alaska and landed on my field at Bend. The owner, Mr. A.A. Bennett, and the pilot of the other plane, Elbert Parmenter, were planning to start an airline through central Oregon from Portland to Boise, Idaho. They tied their planes to the fence near my hangar and left in a car for a few days' business contacts. While they were gone, an inspector arrived and proceeded to inspect their airplanes. He had a knife he seemed to be very proud of, and he used it to cut several holes in the fabric of the planes in order to complete his inspection. Then he left, leaving the holes in the fabric. He did not tell me anything about what his inspection revealed.

When the crew returned, they discovered the holes in the fabric of their airplanes, and they were mad enough to bite nails in two. They had to spend two days patching the holes.

Time marched on, and somehow we managed to live under these kinds of dictatorial rules that did undergo many variations and changes over the years. At first it was the Aeronautics Branch of the Department of Commerce, then it became the Civil Aeronautics Authority, CAA; now they call it the Federal Aviation Authority, FAA. They just seem to keep changing it a little from time to time, but many of their rules are still not a credit to a country that spends so much of its time telling the rest of the world how much freedom we have. I have heard people say we would have lost World War II if our military aviation had been operating under our civil aviation rules. On the other hand, it is so much better than we had before that we should be thankful for small favors.

I still figure it was ridiculous that our government had chosen aviation to be the only part of our lives they chose to operate under the equivalent of a dictatorship that we undereducated and undernourished barnstormers were living under. It was so different from what I had learned in school about our having a government "of, by and for, the people."

Only a few years later we were conditioned to hate dictators as we began fighting two prominent dictators across the ocean, Hitler and Mussolini. Of course, Japan also, across the other ocean. I don't believe Japan was called a dictatorship at that time, but they were mad at us for reasons us common folks didn't then, or even yet, fully understand. Actually they were the ones who started the fight, and I still do not know why.

A curious thing happened in fighting the two dictators east of us. The man who was probably the world's worst dictator, Joe Stalin, was also fighting them. We gave old Joe billions of dollars worth of hardware to help him fight Hitler and Mussolini. Even a wild animal can be friendly if you feed him, and that is the way it was with old Joe. But after the war we quit feeding him and he became wild again.

Before World War II started, I had talked to several people, voicing my objections to our government's dictatorship over aviation. I pointed out how ridiculous it would be if our government operated this kind of dictatorship over the automobile industry, and what a hardship it would place on the automobile industry and the customers who purchase their cars if this should ever happen.

Of course, I knew this could never happen in the automotive industry. It was too well organized before this type of dictatorship was invented, and it was strong enough to fight back. I just used this line to point out how unfair it was to the aviation industry to operate it under this form of dictatorship and that changes should be made so we could operate our aviation industry under the same rules the automotive industry operated under.

Well, time has progressed, and the rules have been changed, but the change has been in the other direction. Now that our government has learned how to operate a dictatorship and still call it a democracy, our automotive industry is now operated under approximately the same type of dictatorship the aviation business is operated under. We don't call it a dictatorship, we call it bureaucracy, but it adds up to the same thing. Government by pressure groups, government without common sense, government by people we do not know, control, or understand. So now we are entering the era of seat-belt laws and airbag laws, that, like our wild horse protection laws, are being pushed by highly vocal minorities, with common sense being ignored.

This Waco 9 didn't exactly set the world on fire, but it did give a lot of Oregon residents their first view of the world through the eyes of an eagle, and at the same time it was teaching its pilot a lot about how to fly an airplane.

One day, in the middle of the winter, I landed on a farm field at the edge of the small town of Plush, Oregon, on a few inches of packed, frozen snow, in a cattle feed lot. A few minutes after I landed, it seemed that the town's whole population arrived on foot to look at the flying machine. They said this was the first airplane that ever landed there.

The weather was clear but bitter cold. One lady looked at that 8-foot propeller and said she didn't understand why I needed such a large fan in this cold weather.

A half dozen boys climbed up on the wing walks on both sides of the fuselage and were looking in the cockpits. I was watching them and didn't say anything to them as I visited with the people in the crowd.

The father of some of these boys arrived and ordered all of them to get off the airplane. Then he climbed up on the left wing walk to get a better look inside; and he stepped off the walk and his foot went clear through the wing. He was very embarrassed. I told him that was no big deal, that I could patch the fabric when the weather warmed up a little.

6

FORCED LANDINGS

One Sunday in the early fall of 1930, I had four forced landings and another one the following morning. I was out on a barnstorming tour with my OX5 Waco 9. My helper Bill was with me. He and his partner had owned an OX5 Waco 10, and before he had wrecked it, Bill had built up about 90 hours of flying experience.

We were at Frank Henry's ranch in southern Oregon, on the east edge of Catlow Valley. The Henrys had twin girls our age. Bill and I had spent some time Saturday thinking about the dance the Henrys were putting on at the town of Andrews that night.

Andrews was on the other side, east, of the Steens Mountains, and we looked forward to spending an enjoyable night there, and also of making some money flying passengers the following day. Andrews was a very small town, but a good crowd would gather from the surrounding ranches for the dance. We figured the dance would last until daylight Sunday morning, and almost everyone would be feeling good enough by that time to want to ride in the airplane. I trusted Bill's flying ability, so we flipped a coin to see who would fly the twins over the mountains. Bill won. Neither of us had ever been to Andrews, and we had no idea where a place could be found suitable to land the airplane.

As evening approached, Bill took off with the precious cargo. I stayed behind and came over a few hours later in the car. I was a little uneasy about where Bill might find a place to land.

When we finally arrived in the car, after dark, Bill and the girls were there. They had arrived safely, but Bill told me he could not find a decent place to land closer than seven miles from the dance hall. He had landed in a small clearing just across the street from the dance hall and figured I could fly out of there solo early in the morning while the air was heavy and fly up to the other field to carry passengers. That might ruin our chances of doing much business, as we could not expect our dancing crowd to drive that far to ride in an airplane. We went through the night, however, with much dancing and merriment. There was a good turnout at the dance. There was plenty of bootleg moonshine available, and the "spirits" of the crowd held out very well. When it started breaking daylight Sunday morning, I was out warming up my trusty OX5 engine and walking over the little field, stepping off distances, trying to determine if I could fly passengers from it. I finally decided that by using some rough ground at the west end of the field, and by making about a 20-degree right turn on the takeoff run, I could get 800 feet before having to clear a barbed-wire fence.

The field was about 4,400 feet above sea level. It was sandy and soft, but the takeoff run was slightly downhill, and dropped about five feet in 800 feet, which was in my favor. A west wind would spoil everything because there were trees and buildings at the west end of the field.

As the orchestra was playing "Home Sweet Home," it was light enough for me to see to take off. I made one solo flight to achieve a complete warm-up on my engine and to check the field. Everything looked good enough, so I landed and announced that I was ready for passengers.

Bill kept tickets sold ahead, and he kept a five-gallon can of gas handy. Every two or three hops, I would shut off the engine long enough to put in the five gallons of gas. The gas load had to be kept light so there would be a better chance of getting over that fence. There was no wind, which was better than a tailwind. The air was cool and heavy. The takeoff required so much of my attention that I gave very little thought to the flying except to buzz around for about 10 minutes for two $2.50 passenger fares and get back down.

On one flight, I had a man and his wife who were willing to pay extra if I would fly them out over their gold mine, about 20 miles out in the mountains. Every takeoff was so close that I talked to the Lord a little after making it. This takeoff was as successful as the rest, but approximately a 10-mile-per-hour south wind had come up. This was a crosswind on the takeoff which did not seem to bother too much.

As I was working for altitude to fly out to the gold mine, I was about five miles from my field and had gained about 100 feet of altitude flying with a direct tailwind. The mountains were on my left and the valley was on my right; the ridges and draws were running at right angles to my line of flight. Suddenly without warning, the gas line broke and the engine stopped. I was in a maximum climb so I had no reserve airspeed. The thought that passed through my mind was to land headwind. I immediately laid the plane over in a fairly steep right bank and dropped the nose to maintain a safe gliding speed.

With my limited altitude and low airspeed, I had no sooner established the right bank, when I realized it was hopeless to complete a 180-degree turn from such low altitude. I quickly applied full left aileron and full left rudder, but my airspeed by then was so low that the controls were sluggish and the plane did not respond. I held them on anyway because there was nothing else that would help.

By this time, even though I was not yet recovered from the right bank, I had to start bringing the nose up to prevent hitting the ground. Now the wings were slowly leveling out as I brought the stick the rest of the way back to the full back position for the landing. Contact was made with the ground and sagebrush just as the wings became level. This goes down in my memory as the only landing I have ever made with all three controls in their extreme positions—full left rudder, full left aileron and full back stick.

It was a surprisingly smooth three-point landing. Providence, not I, placed it midway between two draws on a ridge with hardly any rocks. Even the sagebrush was not tall enough to tear but very few holes in the fabric of the bottom wings and fuselage.

One of the important rules every flying student learns is to never try to turn close to the ground with a dead engine, but when the chips are down, we all do it. It seems hard to know by what rights some pilots remain alive while others pay the supreme sacrifice for errors in judgment in such an emergency. Even when you are alert and trying hard to do things right, things can stack up against you to where you have to put everything you have into it just to stay alive.

A friend of mine was killed on takeoff as a result of an engine failure at about 200 feet. He was solo in good air conditions with plenty of flat sagebrush ground ahead of him where he could have landed with a dead engine with only minor damage to his plane. We can only guess that he tried to turn with a dead engine to get back to the airport to save his OX5 Waco 10.

I made a rather hasty repair on the broken gas line, and a crew of Basques volunteered to help me cut enough sagebrush so I was able to make a solo takeoff and fly back to my regular field within about two hours. The same two passengers met me there, climbed back in the airplane, and we completed the flight.

The forced landing, instead of scaring my passengers, seemed to increase their confidence. They learned the plane could be landed in hills with a dead engine without killing anyone.

Along about noon, I was still doing business and had several tickets sold in advance. On this flight, my passengers were two young ladies; we had about 500 feet of altitude, and the flight was nearly completed, when the same gas line broke again.

On a previous occasion when I had some trouble, I had spliced about 6 inches on the end of one propeller blade and apparently did not get it properly balanced. This set up a vibration that was causing the gas line to break. However, I hadn't had any trouble before. On this second forced landing, I was down over the valley where the sagebrush was taller and thicker and the rocks were larger and thicker also. The rocks were not easy to see because of the tall sagebrush.

This power failure was not even comparable to the one earlier. This time I had plenty of altitude, about 500 feet, and cruising airspeed. However, I did not know what it was because I had no airspeed indicator, but I did know it was several miles per hour above a stalling speed. So there were no problems in getting the nose down and maneuvering into my selected landing area.

Only the Lord knew exactly what would happen after I made contact with the ground. With the tall sagebrush, there was no way to see what rocks and ditches might be in front of me. In such a situation, the life-or-death decisions are made before hitting the ground, but the damage is done after impact.

As I maneuvered into the landing area, there was no sweat. In fact, it was so routine it was almost monotonous. The tension came after contact was made with the ground. Here was where it was finally decided whether I got off free, or whether the airplane was completely demolished, or maybe something between these two extremes.

It is strange, the difference between those two forced landings. On the first one, I came so close to stalling out and spinning in that I would have gladly settled for any kind of damage that could have been caused by rocks or uneven ground. On the second forced landing, there were no hazards of stalling or spinning so I was vitally concerned about what damage there would be to my airplane after it contacted the ground.

I selected a spot on the side of a ridge and made a successful landing, except that the taller sagebrush tore more holes in the fabric of my bottom wings and fuselage. I had not yet patched the holes caused by the first forced landing. This time a tire blew out on the rocks and the tailskid was broken.

There was no welding equipment in the area, so the commercial activities were ended for that day. I had taken in almost $100, so it could have been worse. In fact, it was due to get worse, but I did not realize this yet.

While I repaired the tire, another volunteer crew of Basques cleared sagebrush for me. They did it okay, but were not as enthusiastic this time, so I was reluctant to ask them to clear more than was absolutely necessary. By the time the tire was repaired, they had cleared a strip about 350 feet long directly down the ridge into a headwind which was stronger now and from the west. Storm clouds were rapidly forming over the mountains to the west. There were another 300 or 400 feet of sagebrush between the lower end of the cleared strip and a barbed-wire fence.

It was getting late in the evening. I was to fly the buckaroo boss at the P Ranch over the mountains with me. This was the largest cattle ranch in the United States at that time and was owned by the Swift Meat Packing Company. Everyone else had gone home. I had to take him or leave him stranded.

Because of the west wind, I could not make another takeoff from the field I had been using. With the broken tailskid and the approaching darkness, I did not like the idea of making a solo takeoff, then landing at the larger hay meadow to pick up my passenger, then make another takeoff. So I loaded him and his suitcase in.

I placed two small rocks in front of the wheels because there were no brakes. Now, by holding the stick all the way back, I opened the throttle wide open to build up full power, then shoved the stick full forward, violently kicked full rudder both ways, and jumped the rocks under full power. That is an old trick to utilize the full length of the runway. On a difficult take-off the runway behind you is the most useless thing in the world. Especially if it is only 350 feet long to start with. As I progressed down this 350-foot runway, things did not look very encouraging.

When I reached the end of the runway, I hauled back for maximum lift and succeeded in raising the wheels off the ground, but could not lift the wheels or the propeller out of the sagebrush. I knew that would prevent me from gaining the speed needed to lift over the fence.

Seeing what might take place in the next few seconds, I lined the propeller up between two fence posts as I had done many times before. As I approached the fence, I made one final ef-fort for maximum lift and succeeded in raising the plane enough so the front lower wing spars cleared the fence posts. But the posts cut large gashes in the lower wings from the front spars back. We hit the ground again just beyond the fence. This was forced landing number three. It was on lower ground where the sagebrush was much taller than before, but there were no rocks here.

By this time, the fabric on the bottom wings and the bottom of the fuselage was really in shreds, and some of the ribs and the trailing edge of the bottom wing were broken. Optimisti-cally, I reasoned that most of the damage was on the back half of the wings and most of the lift was on the front half of the wings. A nearby rancher brought his wagon over, and when we put the tail of the airplane on the back of his wagon, the wings cleared the sagebrush. We cut a hole in the fence where I had just come through it and towed the plane back to the top (east end) of the 350-foot strip.

It was getting dark, the wind velocity was increasing, and it was starting to rain. There was not a lot of time to sit around and make decisions. I left my passenger and his suitcase be-

68

hind, but I don't think he minded that. I succeeded in making a solo takeoff and headed for the Steens Mountains, hoping to get to the HL Meadow on the other side of the mountains before it got too dark to land. I figured Frank Henry would turn his pickup lights on the meadow if that was necessary so I could see to land.

NIGHT LANDING

I headed for the small town of Fields first, to follow the road over the mountains. It was getting pretty dark, and I would be less apt to get lost if I could follow the road. Fields lay at the base of the mountains on the east side, but I miscalculated the force of the headwinds and downdrafts up there in the mountains.

I was headed up the canyon the road was in and was still fighting unsuccessfully for altitude, hampered by the strong headwind and downdrafts and by the torn fabric on my wings. The road was in the lowest pass, but it was getting so dark I could no longer see the road. I got in the wrong canyon and was still trying in vain to get the altitude needed to get over the mountains. Progress to this point had been very slow, and I was quite concerned about my gas supply. The gas gauge was in front of the front windshield, and could not be read in the dark.

I battled the air currents until it became apparent I was not going to get over the mountains. I had no flashlight and no matches, but by holding my dollar watch up in a certain position, I could see what time it was. By estimating the amount of gas that was in the tank when I took off, I figured there were about five minutes of gas left when I finally decided to give up trying to get over those mountains.

Suddenly, I felt very tired and weary. I had not had any sleep the night before. I had put in a strenuous day with very little to eat. What lay immediately ahead made what lay behind look like child's play. I realized what a critical situation I was in. A solution had to be found fast, or this flight and possibly my whole flying career could end in disaster. I apologized to the airplane for getting it into this impossible situation, and promised to do all I could to get it down safely.

Much as I would have liked to, there was no possible way to

reverse the events that had already happened. A crash landing in those mountains in stormy weather in the dark was not my idea of a satisfactory solution to the problem.

Because of the low fuel supply, if I did not find a solution to my problem very soon, any major alternatives to a crash landing would be taken out of my hands. and I did not seem to have the vaguest idea how to avoid the almost inevitable ending of this flight.

I do not recall experiencing any period of great fear. It seems I merely suddenly recognized the hopelessness of the situation. This was not something in a storybook. This was for real. Here was the faithful OX5 Waco 9 that had carried me many hundreds of hours through the air in many adventures. Now my foolhardiness had gotten it into a situation I was not capable of getting it out of with any degree of satisfaction.

There was some comfort in the fact that I was the only person on board. There was no one else's safety to be concerned about. The odds stacked up against me strongly. As I flew through the darkness, each beat of the engine brought me closer to the last drop of gasoline that would give me a dead engine. Beyond this, I could visualize nothing but a crash. I stood a fair chance to survive, if with a dead engine in the dark, I could keep the plane under control until the point of impact. As hopeless as this situation looked, there just had to be a way out. There is very little satisfaction in figuring out how an accident could have been avoided after it happens. I needed the answers right then.

If I could maintain a safe speed in the dark; if I could resist the temptation to try to guess where the ground was and level off too high and stall or spin in; if I could maintain an inflexible iron nerve and keep a safe gliding speed until contact was made with the ground; and if I could be lucky enough to contact the ground where it was reasonably level with no rock walls, I would have a chance.

Normally this would seem like a rather simple thing to do because any pilot with my flying experience should know how to maintain a safe gliding speed. When the chips are down a pilot can develop the feeling that any instant he is about to slam into something solid, and his tendency is to slow down and to keep on slowing down trying to guess the point of impact. Then he slows down some more just before hitting. If one does this, and if he misjudges and slows down too much while still too high, the result is a stall, possibly even a tailspin. At this point there would not be enough room to recover.

Common sense, if there was any in this situation, told me the very best I could hope for was a crash landing, but I figured if I stayed right in there and did the right thing all the way through, it might be a minor crash instead of a major one.

As soon as I had realized I could not get over the mountains, my limited fuel supply had become my main concern, and my immediate goal was to try to get the airplane safely on the ground anywhere. I had decided the mountains were not the place for me and had headed for the flat country east of the mountains.

As I reached flat country, I was able to fly lower with a reasonable degree of safety. By flying just above fence-post level, I had located a dirt road that showed up as a light color compared to the darkness of the rest of the area. I figured Denio, a small town on the Oregon-Nevada border, lay somewhere on the road south of Fields. How could I be sure I was following the right road? I might be following a road going in an easterly direction. The turn of events had been so confusing I did not know for sure if Denio was north or south of me. Anyway, I followed this dirt road because it might lead me to something. Even if the road didn't lead me to something, if I crashed along it somewhere I would be better off than being many miles from a road.

This was a sparsely settled part of the country; even if you were on a road, you could still be many miles from nowhere. If you were not on a road, you had no idea where to go to find habitation.

Because of the darkness I was flying very low to keep the road in sight. This flight altitude was higher than fences but lower than telephone poles. Although I knew there were no telephone poles in that part of the country, there were other things higher than fences, such as hay derricks and windmills.

I sat there in the darkness realizing my gas was about gone. Any second the engine would stop. The stakes were the same and as real as they are for the pilot who goes down in combat. If I bit the dust that night, I would be just another renegade civilian barnstormer who had climbed too far out on a limb, and it broke off. My accident would be a mark against aviation, the thing I was trying so hard to promote. The public would be further convinced that airplanes are just dangerous playthings that are not here to stay and have no practical value except in time of war.

As I strained my eyes out into the darkness trying to see, realizing that any second the gas tank would be empty and that fan up front would stop turning, I had the feeling I was playing some kind of a poker game with the devil. It looked to me like he was holding all the aces, and the last card was about to be played. God sat across the table with a passive look on his face. He was not in the game, just looking on. I think He owned the joint. I kept a close eye on Him as I tried to figure a way out of this dilemma, hoping He would slip me some cards under the table. The cards presently in my hand did not look like winners.

I had a helpless feeling sitting there with my feet on the rudder bar and my hands on the stick and throttle. All the books I had read and all my flight training and experience did not tell me what to do with these controls under such circumstances in order to terminate this flight in a satisfactory manner.

It is a strange feeling to be sailing along smoothly and safely, knowing that any minute your plane and maybe you too will probably be a pile of wreckage. It is like sitting on a stick of dynamite with the fuse lit, not knowing what split second it might explode or if some miracle may yet come along and save the situation.

All the cards you hold in your hand say you will lose, but there is always a chance that at the last minute, if you stay right in there, you may even yet pull an ace out of the deck in time to do some good.

Something more than just what can be seen will be lost. You look over the orderly fashion of the design and structure of your plane, and you realize this plane means more to you than just dollars and cents. Even the patches and rips in the wings have come to be a part of it, and there seems to be something about the plane other than the material and visible.

The fact that I found myself in such a predicament showed poor planning, but realizing that was of no particular help. This knowledge should keep me from permitting myself to ever get into this type of situation again, that is, if I come out of this okay. I had to concentrate on what could be done to get out of this predicament in the best possible way.

I felt fully capable of handling my airplane, but in my weary and fatigued condition I did not know how good my thinking was. Up to this point, I had never wrecked an airplane other than minor damage such as going through fences. I had never collapsed a landing gear or torn any wings off or anything like that. Now the odds seemed so thoroughly stacked against me but I could get some comfort from the fact that I hadn't panicked. Although I was very tense, my hand was not shaking on the controls, and I believed I was thinking clearly.

As I continued to follow that road, it was only a light-colored line with no detail, all else was dark and featureless. If I just closed the throttle, turned off the gas and switch, and crash-landed, the outcome could be very questionable in the darkness.

My friend, Bill Fletcher, chief pilot for the Shell Oil Company, was caught one time in the dark. It was barely light enough for him to make out the dim outline of a farmer's field, and he headed for it, but he could not see the rock ledge in the center of the field. He died on the way to the hospital. If I tried this type of landing there would be small hopes of saving my airplane, and if I were seriously injured, there would be no one to help me.

I really had no idea where I was or where any town or ranch was. The road I was following seemed to be going east or southeast across that large valley, and I had confidence I was flying away from the mountains on flat ground. I discovered later the road was going south at the base of the mountains. If I had been on the right side of the road, I would have flown head on into a high ridge that came down to the road from the mountains.

It was so dark I could hardly see the torn fabric on the bottom wings flapping in the wind. The last card was about to be played in this poker game, and it looked to me like the devil was holding all the aces.

Suddenly I saw a dim outline of something dark on my right and circled to get a closer look. It looked like trees with some buildings among them, but there were no lights. Then, after another circle, I saw a light come in a window. Then other windows lit up. I decided that was the place for me as there was not enough gas to go anywhere else.

A crash landing here, regardless of the results, would be better than anywhere else away from habitation. It is surprising how much comfort you can get in a situation like that just knowing someone is down there, and if you crash, you will not be alone.

By the time I made a couple of circles, I saw someone carry a lantern from the house to another building. Then garage doors opened. A car backed out of the garage and went out through a gate and headed down a road. I didn't know what his plan was, but I was sure he had something in mind to help me. I figured he might be headed for someplace a good many miles down the road to show me a place to land. My gas was too low to go anywhere except where I was. I was expecting the engine to stop any second and could not understand what had kept it running this long.

My eyes were becoming accustomed to the darkness to a certain extent, and I had located a small field close to the house. I was trying to stay in a position to aim for it if the engine quit. The next day I learned this field was a small garden about 150 feet by 300 feet with a fence all around it and one across the center.

Under the circumstances my judgment of distance was not very accurate, and that was the only clearing I could see. I had an approach to this little field all planned in case the engine stopped. I did not realize until the next day that this approach would have put me into that field with a tailwind. There was a pretty strong wind blowing, and I knew approximately which direction it was coming from. The fact that I had planned a tailwind landing was proof that my thinking was not very clear. Inability to think clearly can shorten a man's life in the flying business.

All the while I was watching the progress of that car with great interest. Perhaps this was the Lord slipping me a card under the table. About one-half mile from the house the car turned and went through a gate and shined its lights on a hayfield. I reasoned that the Lord would not go to all that trouble to get those car lights on the hay meadow unless He intended for me to make proper use of them, so I lost no time heading over there.

Normally, I would make at least one trial pass in a strange situation like this before trying to land; but I was afraid to risk my gas, so I made one desperate bid for a landing. Those who are skilled in the art of flying will realize the difficulties that are involved in setting an airplane down, even on a power approach, at night in turbulent, stormy air with a wind blowing from an unknown direction at an unknown velocity. It was difficult to judge the limited area lit up by one set of car lights.

Those car lights shined clear across the field and showed me some willows on the far side. The lights were shining directly in my eyes, which was a rather serious handicap, but I was so thankful for those lights I hardly gave that a thought. On this approach, I held my altitude as high as possible to still make it without overshooting. I wanted to be sure to make it if my engine quit on the approach. I held the airspeed as close to a stall as could be done with still enough reserve speed to level off before contacting the ground. I succeeded in landing and coming to a stop on the portion of the ground covered by the lights. No other part of the field was visible.

No one, if he has never landed an airplane under these circumstances, can ever know the feeling that is experienced in the final stages of such a landing after things have progressed to a point where you can see "you have made it." Up to this point there is not the slightest reason for relaxing or even hardly hoping, and the tension one is under throughout a flight of this kind is completely indescribable. It was a grand feeling to get my feet on solid ground and to see my airplane setting there all in one piece with no damage except what it already had.

I never enjoyed a bed so much in my life as the one in the spare bedroom of that ranch house.

As I laid my head into the large fluffy pillow and spread out to get as much of my body as possible in contact with that soft but solidly earthbound mattress, I enjoyed a peaceful comfort I had not known existed. It had been a strenuous day, and I was very tired. The only thing I had eaten during the day was a couple of sandwiches, a piece of cake, and some soda pop while repairing the flat tire, but I was now too tired to be interested in food.

I would almost doze off and my body would be going through the rising and falling and general churning around up there over those mountains in the rough air, and I would see the shredded fabric on my lower wings riffling and fluttering in the wind. Then I would wake up enough to turn over and present another part of my body to that mattress to become reconvinced I was safely back on the ground, and the airplane was tied outside to a barbed-wire fence. I solemnly promised the Lord I would never again put Him on such a spot where He would have to go to so much trouble to get me safely back to earth.

Sunday morning, over at Frank Henry's ranch, they were pretty much concerned about me when I had not arrived there Saturday night as I had planned. They had a lot of confidence, perhaps too much confidence, in my ability to get down safely if I got into trouble. Nevertheless, Frank and Bill decided to drive over to Andrews and investigate.

When they arrived in Andrews, they met my passenger who was still looking for a ride over the mountains. Of course he told them I took off Saturday evening for Frank's place. They really began to get concerned about the situation when they learned this, and the three of them drove down to Fields where they knew I should have flown over before reaching the mountains.

At Fields, they were told the airplane had flown over there after dark, bucking strong headwinds and rain, and that the last they saw of the plane it was too low to get over the mountains. This information made the situation look even worse. So they headed back over the mountains and stopped and looked for the remains of the plane at various points, in hopes of locating it that way.

Their plan was that if they did not locate the plane by the time they reached the ranch, they were going down to the P Ranch at Frenchglen and send out all the riders they could on saddle horses to cover the mountains in a search. As they scanned the mountains from the road, they could imagine all sorts of things, and Frank told me later there were some tears shed.

I was not in the mood for rushing myself that morning. As for western hospitality, the Ralph Grove family who had helped me get safely to earth had all of that you ever heard about. It was a beautiful clear day. There was no wind, and the sun was shining with all its glory. When I walked that morning, I placed each foot solidly on the ground before lifting the next one. The good firm earth felt good under my feet.

When I put a stick down in the lowest corner of the gas tank, there was not even a little bit of moisture on it; the tank was completely dry. After putting 10 gallons of car gas in the plane, I took to the air about 10 a.m. and headed back over the route of the night before. The air was clear and smooth, and even with the damaged wings, the plane gained altitude rapidly, confirming my earlier thinking that most of the lift is on the front of the wings and most of the damage was on the back of the wings.

I crossed the summit with 9,000 feet of altitude, so I throttled back slightly and leveled off. About this time I saw Frank and Bill and my passenger of the previous day beside their pickup on the mountain road. From this altitude I did not know who it was or what they were doing up there. They saw me and headed for the ranch.

Having cleared the summit with plenty of reserve altitude, I was sailing along in smooth air. I felt as though there was not a worry in the world, when all at once, without warning, a terrific vibration and noise developed. I grabbed for the throttle and closed it, as I pulled the nose up sharply to reduce airspeed and thereby get the propeller to slow down sooner.

The engine was bouncing around dangerously. The top of the engine cowl was moving up and down several inches at a time until the propeller lost its momentum. I did not know what the trouble was, but it acted like a propeller badly out of balance, or something seriously wrong with the engine.

After the engine slowed down to its idling RPM, there was comparative smoothness, and it was idling okay. I figured the trouble was in the propeller and I had a good idea what it was. About two months earlier, the propeller had been damaged, and a few inches were broken off one of the blades; a new tip had been spliced on it. This splice was apparently weakened on the trip through the fence the day before, and it broke off, throwing the propeller out of balance. To this day that is the highest I have ever been when an engine failed.

Now there was another problem, another forced landing. My fifth in two days. I was right out over the middle of the mountains. A quick glance around showed my luck must be changing. With all this altitude, I was within gliding distance of the

HL Meadow just below Frank Henry's house, and that was the field where I was headed.

I continued a slow glide to keep the RPM down to eliminate vibration. No power could be used without the danger of having the engine torn clear out of the airplane. I kept the ignition switch on to keep the engine idling just in case I misjudged on the approach and would hit the barbed-wire fence. As a last resort, I would open the throttle to get over the fence. I seemed to be developing an allergy for barbed-wire fences.

The approach was good, so more power was not necessary. I turned the ignition off as soon as the fence was safely cleared. On the ground again, I surveyed the damage and discovered that of the two heavy stranded steel cables that brace the fuselage back of the engine, one was completely broken and the other was holding by only two weakened strands.

Anyway, the airplane was back over there where we could fix it again. This is why a pilot liked to have a helper along on a barnstorming tour. We had dope, thinner, and brushes but did not have patching cloth. We obtained another bed sheet and went to work on the fabric after we repaired the broken ribs and the trailing edge of the wing. Frank was a good blacksmith, and he helped me splice another tip on the propeller. He also had some good strong wire with his hay machinery that we used to replace the broken wires behind the engine. We were flying again in a few days.

Apparently someone at the dance took care of the news for the Burns newspaper. The next time we saw the paper, there was a short article about an airplane carrying a passenger at Andrews, and it mentioned the airplane had two forced landings during the day because of trouble with the vacuum tank. This was in the days before cars had fuel pumps. Cars had what were called vacuum tanks to get the gas from the tank to the carburetor. These tanks were almost always causing trouble. Any time an engine stopped, it was naturally assumed the trouble was caused by the vacuum tank. On my airplane the gas went to the carburetor by gravity. I did not need a vacuum tank to add to my problems.

I was 22 years old at the time of my Andrews experience. When looking back, it is apparent that confidence builds up much faster in a young pilot than either skill or judgment—especially judgment.

My friend Kenneth Pruitt wrote a beautiful poem about the Steens Mountains and the surrounding area. His poem brings out the beauty of a land where beauty is not so readily apparent, even to those who live there.

I too could see a beauty in this land, and also in the life I was living, that was not apparent to others, and it even eluded me much of the time. My intoxication was brought on by my love affair with flying. It was like a rainbow—you know it is there because you can see it, but it keeps moving and you can never seem to touch it.

Kenneth was writing about the land and the sky I knew so well, but it presented a different face to me. Actually I saw some of the beauty he saw, but some of the beauty of this area was dimmed by the hazards it presented to me, as I tried to conquer it with my, what is now called, an antique airplane. But it was the best we had then, and it seemed to be not quite good enough, nor was I, for the tasks I faced.

THE GOD BELOVED LAND

The God forsaken land they call it,
        As they gaze with pitying eye,
Nothing here but rocks and sagebrush,
        And a vast expanse of sky.
"We don't know how you take it,"
        These city folks declare,
"Or how you make a living,
        You surely must live on air."
They wonder at our twinkling eyes,
        And the smile we try to hide,
For in all this lonely windswept,
        Land they can see no cause for pride.
We could tell them of our ranges,
        Where the cattle and horses roam,
Of all the bands of bleating woollies,
        Claiming the desert as their own.
They may not see our fertile valleys,
        With their stands of hay and grain,
But nestled there among the hills,
        We have them all the same.

When there's water in our rivers,
　　The mosquitoes take their toll,
But that's when the feed grows tallest,
　　For the stock among the fold.
The streams are filled with flashing trout,
　　We've antelope, elk and deer.
We're a mile up nearer heaven,
　　Where the air is pure and clear.
This loneliness they talk about,
　　To us is God's own peace,
There's so much beauty all around,
　　That our thanks shall never cease.
Our sunsets glow with color,
　　And the pearly dawn of morn,
The pungent scent of sage drifts down
　　Upon breezes mountain borne.
We don't know much of city life,
　　Or where they find God there,
But in the sagebrush country,
　　We find him everywhere.
So to them we'll leave the cities,
　　Where the living is so grand,
And we'll stay with the hi-desert,
　　The God beloved land.

Kenneth Pruitt

7

CARBURETOR ICE

Today's pilots and writers have a tendency to romanticize flying the old open biplanes and airplanes of even earlier days. On rare occasions when modern pilots have opportunities to actually fly such antiques, the poor performance and sluggishness of control give them a more realistic idea of what it was really like in those days. A pilot had to be dedicated to flying to enjoy flying some of those planes. I would not trade the experiences I have had flying the open biplanes for anything, but that is a good period to look back on, not forward to. Much of my early flying was pure adventure, almost too much at times. I was not able to appreciate the romance as I was living through it. There was too much grease on my hands and in my hair and too many problems—mechanical, financial and social.

Today's students have to spend so much of their time trying to learn how to handle all their fancy electronic and navigation equipment they hardly have time to find out what they can do with their airplanes when the going gets tough. The going was really tough in much of the flying we did.

In the OX5 flying days, 365 hours in the air in one year was a lot of flying, considering all the time we spent on the ground servicing, overhauling, and rebuilding our engines and airplanes. Many of the big-name pilots of the really early days of flying never did have many actual hours in the air. In those days, 100 hours in the air would have made a full year of flying for a full-time pilot.

When I became a member of the Veteran Air Pilot's Association, over 40 years ago, the requirements for membership were 10 years of flying and 1,500 hours in the air. I was told that one of the big names in aviation had an honorary membership because he did not have 1,500 hours in the air. Nevertheless, there were 30-minute periods in the lives of those pilots that tempered their mettle more than 1,000 hours does for pilots today.

Flying was my life. Any obstacle to flying was my enemy. Anyone who offered me an honest way to earn a dollar with my airplane was my friend. I had all of central Oregon to myself. There were no other airplanes in over 50,000 square miles, so mid-air collisions were not one of my biggest problems.

The Curtiss OX5 engine in my Waco 9 developed 90-horsepower at 1,395 revolutions per minute. It had high-top pistons and a Miller overhead valve action, so when this engine was in top condition, it turned up 1,450 RPM on the blocks and was probably putting out about 100 horsepower.

Sometimes it was hard to keep all those horses harnessed and pulling in the same direction. The fluctuations in horsepower were what caused such things as the wheels coming up through the bottom wings, the propellers splintering and wings hanging up on power poles—all that sort of thing. The irregularities and mishaps drew the attention of the local press more than our successes did.

The OX5 engine was designed in 1914, and the last one was built in 1918. These engines were used in training planes, such as the famous Curtiss Jenny of World War 1, and could be purchased new as war surplus through the 1920's and the early 1930's for about $100. Most pilots in the United States before 1930 and well into the 1930's learned to fly behind OX5 engines.

When compared to the engineering and construction that went into our automobiles throughout the 1920's and even into the 1930's, the OX5 was really a pretty good engine. I never heard of an OX5 engine running over 200 hours between overhauls, and a valve job at 50 hours was not uncommon. The 400-horsepower Liberty engine of World War 1 needed a major overhaul every 72 hours, so 200 hours between overhauls was considered exceptionally good. Many piston engines today run over 2,000 hours between overhauls. One time I put over 3,000 hours on a Lycoming (135-horsepower) engine before I overhauled it, and jet engines do better than that.

The OX5 was a water-cooled engine that weighed 375 pounds dry, without water, oil, or radiator; the total weight of this engine was probably nearly 500 pounds. The Waco 9 weighed about 1,200 pounds empty. That is about what a fully loaded 90-horsepower airplane weighs today.

I would often load two heavy passengers in the Waco, along with 35 gallons of gas and whatever baggage there happened to be, bringing the total weight to around 2,000 pounds. Those horses were really pulling into the harness in situations like that, and so was the pilot, until the plane broke ground and the first fence was cleared.

The basic OX5 engine gave very little trouble. I never had any trouble with the connecting rods, the main bearings, crankshaft, timing gears, or camshaft. The problems were mostly with such things as the nonflexible three-eighths-inch copper tube gas line breaking, loss of water from the various water lines and hoses; in addition, the old Berling Magneto was a habitual troublemaker, and that is a serious problem on an engine that has single ignition.

The carburetor gave some trouble but not very much, except we did not understand carburetor ice in those days, and the carburetor did ice up frequently, which caused many forced landings.

There were no provisions for putting warm air in the carburetor, so carburetors got blamed for giving a lot of trouble when it was actually carburetor ice. The intake air passed through a warm water jacket, but that was after it had passed through the carburetor, so the warm-water jacket didn't do any good toward eliminating carburetor ice.

The carburetor had two main jets. I never kept count of how many forced landings I had that were caused by partial loss of power. After each one of these forced landings, I figured one of the jets had plugged up. I'd then take the carburetor off the engine and completely dismantle it, thoroughly clean it, and put it back together. There was seldom any dirt in the carburetor, but I figured maybe the dirt fell out when I wasn't looking.

Of course, what happened was the ice would be melted before I got the carburetor off, so the ice was not discovered. I was never sure what had caused the loss of power, so I would also remove the magneto and completely dismantle it and clean and inspect it, usually without finding anything wrong with it. Anyway, I learned a lot about carburetors and magnetos but never did cure the problem.

This same thing happened one time a few miles up the Columbia River when I was taking dual instructions in one of Tex Rankin's Waco 10's. My flight instructor, Art Walters, took over the controls and made a rather rough landing in a farmer's field. He shut off the engine; we examined it and drained the gas sediment bowl. After a few minutes, we cranked it up, and it ran fine. By this time, of course, the ice had melted.

Art figured the rough landing had jarred the dirt out of the carburetor jet, so we took off and were back in business again. So, even big operators like Rankin's School did not understand carburetor ice. It wasn't until several years later, when I was flying Piper Cubs, that I learned about carburetor ice and the proper use of the carburetor heat control for controlling it.

MAKESHIFT REPAIRS

It was quite common to have a water leak at the water pump packing nut. One time, right over the lava beds at the summit of the Cascade Mountains, water started coming out around the engine cowling (OX5 Waco 10) and getting on our windshield. We were headed for Eugene. There was no place within reach where a respectable crash landing could be made.

I wanted to see where the water was coming from, to see if it was just a gradual leak that would permit us to continue or if it was a broken water line that would cause us to lose all our water in a very short while and force us down. I climbed out of the front cockpit while my student flew the plane from the rear cockpit. I stood on the right lower wing walk and cautiously moved forward until I could look down into the engine area.

The water leak was coming from the water pump packing nut. We were not losing water very fast, and we stood a good chance of getting all the way to Eugene before losing enough water to cause the engine to get hot. As I was looking down into the engine area, I saw something that caused more concern than the water leak. The glass sediment bowl was bolted to the firewall. The copper tube gas line that went from there to the carburetor had one coil in the center about four inches in diameter to give it some flexibility. The central part of this gas line was rotating rapidly in about a two-inch circle, about the same speed the propeller was turning. This could cause a broken gas line at any instant, and there was nothing I could do to correct this situation until we could land.

I got back in the front cockpit and was a little nervous the rest of this flight, but we did get to Eugene without further trouble. Then I taped a small stick to this gas line to make it a little stiffer. After we became airborne again, on our way to Medford, I climbed out on the wing again to examine this gas line, just to be sure the taping job was successful. The problem was corrected.

Vibrations resulting from damaged and out-of-balance propellers caused some of these problems, but this was no fault of the basic design of the OX5 engine. The Great Depression of the early 1930's caused pilots to be too poor to be able to buy a new propeller when they really needed one, so we just patched up the damaged propeller and kept on flying.

Two different times when I broke a few inches off one propeller blade, I sawed the other blade off to make it balance and was back in business again. A couple of times when I broke too much off one blade to perform this type of repair, I fashioned a new metal tip from sheet metal and riveted and soldered it on the damaged blade. Then I added solder to the other blade to make it balance. These were wood propellers that had metal on the tips and leading edges. A new propeller cost $50 and that was a lot of money.

The time the top cylinder broke off the Zekely engine on our Curtiss Pusher, the whole cylinder got in the wood propeller. The propeller threw the cylinder up and forward, and it came down on my student's head. It knocked him out, so I had to land the airplane. This propeller did not have a metal leading edge; it had a cloth leading edge, and the leading edge of both these blades were badly chewed up from fighting with this cylinder.

The propeller was still in good condition except for the damaged leading edges, so I put sheet metal leading edges on it to cover up the damage. I flew that plane another 18 months with no problems from that propeller.

DEADSTICK LANDING

Barnstorming had its good points. I saw a lot of country I had never seen before, met many interesting people, and was acquiring varied and valuable flying experience, the hard way. However, being a flying gypsy can also become tiring. I was developing a desire to settle down in one place.

Bend had been my home since 1923 and my base of operations since starting commercial flying in 1929. But there was not enough flying business in Bend to exist without frequent barnstorming tours to bring in a little extra money. The Lakeview area, about 150 miles south of Bend, looked like it had possibilities, so I moved to Lakeview and operated the first commercial flying business in that area.

Business was good there for a few months. There was a good student business along with charter and local passenger flights. But eventually it was a repeat of the Bend area, and business dropped off to a point where I began looking around for another location.

One of my students there, Harry, told me he had some friends and relatives at a little town called Halfway, Oregon, who might be interested in learning to fly. We gassed up and loaded the plane with a few tools and things and headed for Halfway.

About half way to Halfway, our gas gauge was getting pretty low. The town beneath us was John Day, so we landed to get some gas. On the ground, we pooled our financial resources and discovered we had a total of 26 cents. We still had a little gas in the tank. Some people came up to the landing field and we sold them rides. By the time gas arrived at the field, we decided business might be pretty good right there in John Day, so we stayed there. To this day I have never been to Halfway, Oregon. We just got half way to Halfway, and I operated the first commercial flying business in John Day— students, passenger flights, charter flights, and more barnstorming and parachute jumps to fill in the gaps.

While at John Day, one Saturday evening after work, one of my students, Earl, who was the head mechanic at the local Chevrolet garage, and Les, a prospective student who owned the local bakery, wanted to fly to Baker, Oregon, to attend an Elks' Lodge meeting. I took a barrel of gas to the airport that afternoon in my pickup. Soon after arriving there, I filled the first five-gallon can and set it up on the plane. As I was getting ready to put it in, I discovered it was kerosene instead of gasoline. There was just enough gas in the plane to make a short flight over town and drop a note to Earl asking him to bring up a barrel of gas when he and Les came up. They finally arrived with the gas, and it was a long process to siphon it from the barrel to a five-gallon can and then siphon it from the can to the airplane tank.

I had never been to Baker so I did not know exactly how to get there. We did not have any maps, not even a road map. However, Earl and Les both said they knew the way. Earl had received only three or four 15-minute flying lessons. He had never received any instructions on stalls, spins, or landings, but he could fly satisfactorily on straight flying, and he needed the experience. Earl got into the back cockpit, which was the pilot's cockpit, and I crowded up in the front cockpit with Les and the dual controls.

After takeoff, I turned the controls over to Earl, and we proceeded on our way. Because of our late start, I knew we would get to Baker after dark. Earl and Les thought there was an airport there, and we figured someone would drive out to the airport and turn their car lights on the field after we flew over town. This was more or less standard practice in those days.

There was a heavily timbered mountain range northeast of Prairie City. By using wide-open throttle, we cleared it with a safe margin of about 500 feet. From there on, I had no idea of the proper route, but I settled back more comfortably in my seat as Earl started following a long valley that had a road running the length of it with a few scattered farms and ranches. Open fields on a route like this are as welcome as whipped cream on strawberry shortcake, especially when all else is heavy timber. I learned later this was Burnt River Valley.

The evening was getting well along. The sun had been down for some time. A high range of heavily timbered mountains was on our left, and a strong wind was coming from these mountains. Dark heavy clouds, indicating a storm area, seemed to be centered just north of these mountains, but the valley ahead looked good and open.

With a reasonable degree of relaxation, I was enjoying the flight. I could have been more relaxed if the darkness had not been approaching so rapidly with my not knowing for sure how far ahead our destination lay. I was still a little nervous over that hair-raising night adventure I had had the previous year down in southern Oregon.

Earl suddenly made a 90-degree turn to the left and headed straight for those mountains. I could see he was in no position to get over them, as they were higher than we were and we were flying in an area of strong downdrafts. I took the controls and applied full power but I could not get over these mountains either. I turned back and flew across the valley to an area of updrafts over the mountains that were on the south side of the valley. There were no instruments in the front cockpit so I did not know our altitude or RPM. But when we entered this updraft area, we climbed until we could look over the top of the mountains and could see the lights of a town 30 or 40 miles north of us. Les said he thought those lights were Baker.

When I figured we had about 2,000 feet above our mountain barrier, I headed north. As we entered the area of strong downdrafts, it seemed to me the engine was not turning up full RPM as we started a long fast drop in a downdraft. I pushed forward, hard, on the throttle, in order to get the last bit of power the engine would put out, and the throttle broke. The carburetor should have had a spring on it to hold the throttle open in a case of this kind, but the spring was not on the carburetor, and it vibrated back to about half throttle.

That meant a forced landing for sure, and it was too dark to see to make anything like a respectable forced landing. The throttle on this Waco was a homemade affair, with two small piano wires going through two copper tubes from the rear cockpit to a place near the carburetor. When the throttle was pushed open, the bottom wire opened the throttle, and when the throttle was pulled back, the top wire closed the throttle. The bottom wire that opened the throttle was broken.

I tried to explain that to Earl through our one-way speaking tube but could not get him to understand, and it was too dark for him to look at it and see the details of construction.

In the meantime, I had turned out over the direction of the valley to get out of the downdrafts, but we were still losing altitude. We had no parachutes, and I was the only person in the plane who was capable of handling it in such an emergency. Making a forced landing in the dark in an area I had never seen in the daylight, crowded up at the dual controls beside a passenger in the front seat, was not a desirable situation.

I figured we would all have a better chance for survival if I could get in the back cockpit where I could see out of both sides and could use the controls with unrestricted freedom. Also, there was a chance that if I were in the back cockpit, I might be able to get the throttle open by pushing on the top piano wire.

It was a desperate situation, and none of the possible solutions were very encouraging. I took a quick overall view of things and, right or wrong, decided on a plan of action. If I took no further action except to sit there, the result would be a crash landing in the dark. I figured it was better to follow any slight thread of hope rather than to do that, even though the risk might be greater.

I asked Les to put both feet on the rudder bar and his hand on the stick and just hold the controls steady so they would not move. Then I took our safety belt off and climbed out on the left wing. After I had both feet on the left wing, I asked Earl to get out on the right wing so I could get into the back cockpit. Earl didn't particularly like the idea, but he took his safety belt off and started to rise up in the cockpit just as the plane fell off into a tailspin to the right. This pinned him back down in the rear seat, and the added centrifugal force of the tailspin increased my weight so much it was difficult for me to move.

It seems that in my haste of getting out of the front cockpit, I had not given Les adequate instructions on the rudder, and in the darkness I had not noticed he had put both feet on the right side of the rudder bar. As his nervousness increased, he pushed with both feet, which applied right rudder; and my weight moving back on the wing, plus the wind resistance and the fact that no one was at the controls who knew what to do with them, all stacked up against us, and we were in a right-hand tailspin under about half throttle. This partial power made the spin even tighter than it would have been without power.

Neither Earl nor Les had any idea how to get an airplane out of a tailspin—in fact, they probably didn't even know it was in a tailspin—and I was not in reach of the controls. As we dropped off into this tailspin, the velocity of the wind increased to a shrill scream as it passed through the struts and wires. The mountains were dizzily whirling around as we plunged earthward. There was a sharp tingling the full length of my spine and I could feel the roots of every hair in my head as it seemed to me my hair was trying to stand on end, but of course my tight-fitting leather helmet held my hair in place.

Something had to be done and done fast. I weighed about 160

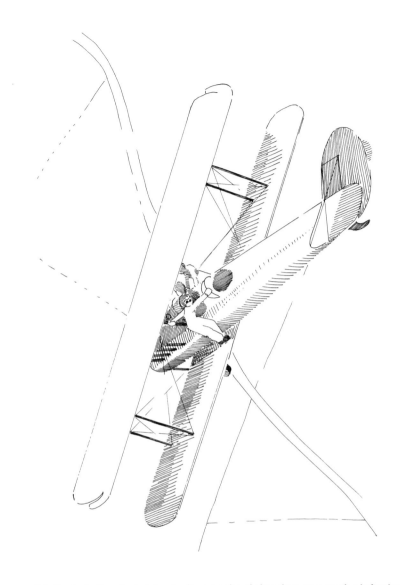

A tailspin in the dark. My student on the right wing, me on the left wing, a passenger in the front cockpit doing the wrong things with the controls, our immediate future in doubt.

pounds, but the added weight caused by the centrifugal force of the tailspin increased my weight several G's. The only possible solution was for me to get back in the front cockpit where I could get at the controls and try to get the plane out of the tailspin before we crashed. An attitude of panic here could serve no useful purpose.

Each movement was made with great difficulty as I struggled with my abnormal weight. Just moving my arm required a great amount of effort, but I finally made it back into the front cockpit and succeeded in getting the plane out of the tailspin.

Then I signaled Earl to get out on the right wing while I flew the plane so the rear cockpit would be empty the next time I got out there on the wing.

Up to this time, I had not realized what had caused the right-hand tailspin. After Earl was out on the right wing, I made the same mistake of asking Les to steady the rudder bar with his feet and the top of the stick with his hand. Then I hurriedly climbed out on the left wing again. I had no sooner gotten both feet planted on the left wing when the plane dropped off into another right-hand tailspin. This time both Earl and I were out on the wings, with only an inexperienced passenger at the controls, pressing both feet on the right side of the rudder bar.

This time the back cockpit was empty. It was farther back so I did not have as good a handhold on the wing struts, and the wing walk did not extend far enough back to give me good footing while getting in the back cockpit. This tailspin was really complicating things, but I figured I had to get into that back cockpit. So I continued with all possible haste, as I knew the ground must be getting pretty close. Any unnecessary delay could be fatal.

Finally I found myself on the back seat, and without any thought of putting my safety belt on, I reached for the controls to get the plane out of the tailspin, when I noticed my left leg was still up out of the cockpit resting against the cowling and the back windshield. The hardest part of the whole operation was to lift myself up while in this awkward position enough to get my left leg into the cockpit. It was finally accomplished, and I got the plane out of that second tailspin before contacting the ground.

I do not know how close we were to the ground or to any possible obstructions such as trees or power lines, but from what I could see through the near darkness, we were pretty close.

After recovering from that tailspin, I reached for the top throttle wire, pushed it in, and was lucky enough to get the throttle on full power again. That seemed a roundabout way to get the throttle open, but it was nice to have full power again, as it meant no forced landing in the dark. Not yet anyway.

I put my safety belt on and was circling for altitude when I noticed Earl was still hanging onto the wing struts out on the right wing. I reached out and hit him to get his attention. He would not look around at first, but he finally did look around, and I motioned for him to get in the front cockpit.

Now we were getting back to normal operations, and there seemed to be some hope for our future. With wide-open throttle, I crossed the valley to the updraft side and gained about the same altitude as before. I judged it to be about 2,000 feet higher than our mountain barrier, and headed north for the lights of Baker.

I could not read the altimeter because of the darkness, but as we reached the downdraft side, we started losing altitude again. At first, I thought we could get over the summit. This drop was very rapid, and there was nothing I could do to prevent it or slow it down. As we approached the mountains, I pushed my goggles up over my forehead and kept my head up close behind the windshield for better visibility. As we were dropping below the summit, I made a left turn and headed down a heavily timbered canyon to get back into the valley. We must have dropped about 3,000 feet before reaching the valley and getting out of the downdraft.

I flew back to the updraft side of the valley and tried this all over again with exactly the same results. This was a time-consuming operation. We were bucking a strong headwind up there. When we were headed north, our groundspeed was very low. After the third try, I saw it was hopeless and figured we probably did not have enough gas for another try. In fact, we probably did not have enough gas to get to Baker even if we were over the summit.

I do not know where the light was coming from, probably a partial moon, but by holding my dollar watch up in just the right position, I could see what time it was and figured we only had gas for five to 15 minutes (but this was a wild guess), and turned back, heading down the valley, east.

Recalling the night experience of the past year in southern Oregon, this seemed like playing the same old record over again, except this time I had the lives of two passengers on my hands. This made it all the more imperative that I do the right thing.

As I headed back toward the valley, I was getting more angry with myself for getting into such a position again after having promised the Lord I would not do it again.

A short distance down this valley, we flew over a ranch house that had lights in the windows. Circling over the house at better than 1,000 feet above it, I wanted to deliver a message to the people down there that we were in trouble and needed lights on a field to make an emergency landing. Our throttle was broken, so we were flying full power and I could not pump the throttle, so I rapidly turned the ignition switch off and on several times to try to let the people on the ground know we were in trouble.

My scheme seemed to be a success, as a car drove out of the yard and went down a dirt road. I circled and climbed above the car. A short distance from the house, the car passed through a gate into a hayfield. The car slowly made a 360-degree turn with its lights showing me two haystacks. Then it backed up to the north fence and shined its lights south, tailwind.

This meant I would have to come in facing the car lights. I did not like this but I was very thankful for those car lights. One could not expect more perfect cooperation from anyone under such circumstances. Now the rest was up to me. If I had what it took to get the plane down on the ground, those car lights were showing me I had it made.

That is easier said than done. The field was short, but there was a wind blowing, and although it was not as strong down in the valley as it was up in those mountains, it would still help me in making a slower landing and getting into a smaller field than could have been done without the wind.

In the excitement, I momentarily forgot about the broken throttle, and when the car lights settled down between those haystacks, I knew that was "it" and I closed the throttle. Then I realized what I had done. The throttle was broken and might not open again. I pushed and pulled on the top piano wire several times, with no results. The wire just bent at the carburetor end, and I got no power.

Then I reached over and turned the switch off, hoping the propeller would stop crossways so it would not get broken if we nosed over or collapsed a landing gear. I was too realistic at this stage of the game to have much hopes of being able to get down in this kind of a situation without wrecking the airplane, but I wanted to save as much of it as I could.

The propeller came to a stop almost vertically. I had a couple of thousand feet of altitude, so I dived and gained enough airspeed to rotate the propeller to a crossways position. In a way, this seemed rather insignificant considering all else that was at stake, but at the moment it seemed important. It seems that playing your cards in their proper order is as important as the kind of cards you play.

I had done this once before and gotten away with it about a year before. However, I had power on that approach to pull me up to a position where I cleared some willows, then I chopped the power, and dropped it into a hay meadow in the car lights.

This night it was different. I had two passengers with me, and the propeller was standing still. There was a strong gusty wind blowing, and I had no way of knowing how strong the wind was or if I might encounter a strong gust or a calm on the final leg of my approach. This could upset my judgment of how high or low to plan it. Jesus Christ himself could not have made an approach under such circumstances and have had any confidence in the outcome.

The only thing I could think of that gave me any comfort was that we had already survived those two tailspins up there in the dark under seemingly impossible conditions. Surely the Lord would not go to that much trouble to protect us unless He was planning on seeing us the rest of the way through.

With this thought in mind, I busied myself with the job of putting everything I had into maneuvering into position for that impossible deadstick landing. In a hundred lifetimes, a person could not have been put to a more strenuous test.

The next 60 seconds would either result in a successful landing or a crash, and it was all up to me. There was no one to lean on for help, but I did not figure it hurt any to ask the Lord for a little help in a situation like this. I had a guilty conscience with Him because of having previously promised not to ever again get into a jam where I would require so much of His attention to get me safely out of it.

The propeller was completely dead. I was approaching a field I had never seen in the daylight so I knew nothing about any possible obstructions the car lights did not show. I was landing directly into blinding car lights. The strong gusty wind could cause unpredictable air currents around unseen ground obstructions. It would have required skillful handling of an airplane to land in that field in full daylight on a power approach.

I realized it would be asking a lot to expect to get safely down on that field with so many cards stacked against me, but I could ask no less. So with grim determination I calculated the proper position and steepness for a left bank that would bring me into a suitable landing position—not too high and not too low, I hoped.

The car lights showed a fence on the far side of the field, and back of the fence was a sagebrush ridge that appeared to be about 40 feet high. I must clear that ridge, then slip, or fishtail, down into the field and come to a stop before reaching the car. I had no way of knowing what obstructions might lie out there in the darkness beyond where the car lights shown.

As we approached silently along this glide path, I experienced a feeling that leaves me at a loss to try to describe. For safety, I felt I had to aim for a position that would be just a little high as we came in over the ridge, and I succeeded in making it to perfection. Then I did a couple of violent fishtails and settled in for a smooth three-point landing near the edge of the field, rolling to a stop about three-quarters of the way across the field.

When the plane came to a stop, I could hardly believe it. I was so exhausted I just sat there in the cockpit, limp as a rag, as my passengers got out. Then I climbed slowly out and placed both feet solidly on the ground, still hardly able to believe we were safely down. Nothing ever felt so good as that nice, solid, stationary ground did to my feet. I got down on my hands and knees and spread the palms of my hands out on the ground just to feel it.

By this time the car had driven up, and the two men, the Shumway brothers, got out. All four men were standing there looking at me, so I made some remark about having dropped something and got to my feet and joined them.

Considerable conversation followed. My passengers kept remarking about how close we came to "that mountain out there." I told them I realized that, but had my goggles off and my head right up close behind the windshield, and turned down into that timbered canyon when I saw we were getting too close to those tall trees up there.

This explanation did not satisfy my passengers. They said there were no trees there, and we were so close that, if there had been a fence on it, we would have hit the fence. I could not understand that. I figured they were just overly excited because we had had a very wild ride. We all agreed we were happy to be safely on the ground.

The Shumway brothers drove Earl and Les to their meeting in Baker, and I went along with them. They were quite late. I rode back to the Shumway Ranch and spent the night there.

As we went to the plane the following morning, I saw in the daylight what Earl and Les were talking about the night before. Right out there where I made my left bank to come in on my final approach, there was a butte several hundred feet high. I do not know how I could have missed it. I had not even known it was there as I was completely engrossed in figuring the approach and glide path for that impossible deadstick landing. My passengers had seen it, and they still insisted that if there had been a fence on it, we would have hit the fence. Maybe I did have some help on that landing.

The experiences I went through that night were of a traumatic nature. They seemed to have a lasting effect on me, and I thought a lot about this in the period ahead. In fact, 54 years later, as my thoughts go back over these events, including my night flight in southern Oregon the year before, I am still mystified by it. So much of what happened seemed to be beyond my control, my ability, or even my understanding. And yet, the end results in both experiences were completely satisfactory.

In reviewing this, I cannot see where any unusual piloting skill was displayed in the southern Oregon experience. It was more just a case of extraordinary events, seemingly beyond my control, that evolved into what I see as almost a miraculously satisfactory ending.

My night experience out of John Day the following year, although different, had some similarities to the southern Oregon experience. Then, in addition to the similarities, it had an additional feature—the deadstick landing. Even to this day, I do not believe any pilot, including myself, could make that deadstick landing one time out of 100 tries. I had only one shot at it and made it. I do not believe in miracles, but also, I do not believe atheists live long in the flying business.

An important factor in both of these experiences is that I was younger then, with a more venturesome spirit than actual flying experience, or maturity. At that time I had only a few hundred hours of flying experience, compared to over 25,000 hours now.

The following is an attempt to arrive at an understanding of the elements involved in that deadstick landing.

There is a certain glide path that varies with all the changing circumstances you encounter with an airplane. There is no way of pinning this glide path down to any mathematical formula or isolating it in any way that is describable that would enable you to tell someone else exactly what it is or even to learn it precisely yourself. There are too many unknowns over which you have no control.

This Waco was manufactured in 1926; it had no wing flaps for regulating the glide path as modern planes have, and it had no wheel breaks to shorten the landing roll on the ground.

That night as I came in on my glide path, I had no way of knowing how strong the wind was down there in the bottom of the valley or exactly from which direction it was blowing, or if it might change at the last instant and upset all my calculations, even if they had been flawless.

The instant I was clear of the sagebrush ridge, I did a couple of violent fishtails and dropped in short. Most of the field was ahead of us when the plane contacted the ground in a very satisfactory three-point position.

A fishtail is a maneuver that is not taught or recommended, but there is no other maneuver that will permit you to lose altitude as quickly and land shorter over an obstruction than a fishtail. Today, most pilots know nothing about it, which is as it should be. When I learned to fly, one of my instructors, Dud Rankin, was an artist at fishtailing. I tried to get Dud to teach me the fishtail, but he would never do it. He said the only time you want to do a fishtail is after you have had at least 1,000 hours of flying experience and are flying someone else's airplane and have another job lined up. After I got to flying on my own, I kept practicing until I got pretty good at it and have never damaged an airplane yet while doing it, but I would never teach it to any of my students.

You cannot teach a thing like that. It is one maneuver you have to learn by yourself. It is like balancing a plane on the point of a pin. One little slip and you would clobber your airplane all over the field. You have to hold the controls to feel it. You do not want a student to fly that close to disaster, especially in your airplane. In anything you teach a student there has to be room for errors and corrections without undue hazards. I do not do it myself anymore. However, I would still do it if an emergency required it. In an emergency anything is legal if it will save the day. You will be surprised what you can do, if you have to.

GLIDER LANDING

The following experience illustrates how impossible it is for a pilot with a dead engine to judge accurately how to make a landing approach in an area of limited size. One day at Bend, I was flying our Eaglerock glider. We towed the glider with a car, got it up about 1,000 feet, then released it and glided around a little while, landing back on the same field we had taken off from. After releasing the towline on one particular flight, I found a pretty good updraft out from the southwest corner of the field. On the next flight I figured if I ventured out over the tall pine trees in that area, the updraft would be stronger, and I could stay up longer.

On the next flight, I gained about 1,000 feet of altitude, then released the towline and headed out "that-a-way," but the expected updraft was not there, and I lost altitude rapidly. I was embarrassed to find I was too far out and too low to get back to the airport.

There was a smaller field between me and the airport, so I maneuvered to it. This field was separated from the airport by a dirt road that had a barbed-wire fence on each side of it. Over the fence on my side of the road was a low farmer's telephone line. There was plenty of room to land the glider in this field, so I approached it with full confidence as I dropped down into the south edge of it.

About 10 feet above the ground, there was an updraft that held me in the air. At first this caused no concern because I still had plenty of room ahead to land before coming to the road, fences, and telephone wire. As I progressed across the field, the updraft continued, and finally I could see there was not enough room left for me to complete a landing on that field and get stopped before reaching the obstructions.

On this glider I was sitting out in front, out in the open, and if I went through a barbed-wire fence, it would be me who hit those wires and that is not a pleasant thought. As those ob-

98

structions got closer, I figured that if the updraft continued just a little longer, I might be able to keep the glider in the air long enough to get over the fences and telephone wire. There was not enough room to get over the fences and under the telephone wire.

As I got closer to them, I could see my only hope for a successful landing was to get over all of them. Then, just at the critical moment, the updraft petered out. Now it was a desperate situation.

As the updraft died, I dropped down low, almost touching the ground, to hold all the speed I could. As I reached the first fence and telephone wire, I pulled up for every bit of lift that was left, and the glider cleared the first fence and telephone wire with such a narrow margin that it could not have been more than a few inches.

I had not noticed until this instant that the fence posts and wires of the second fence were lying flat on the ground. I slid out onto the airport and came to a stop with my skin still intact. No damage done, except it took me some time to get my heart slowed down to its normal beat. The glider skid track was on the ground as it went over those wires. It would be hard to have a closer call than that without getting hurt.

Straight down dive in attempt to restore deaf boy's hearing.

99

8

DIVES AND TAILSPINS

I had always been told that low speeds in an airplane can get you into a lot of trouble and that high speeds represent safety. One day a young friend of mine, who was totally deaf, was brought out to the airport. I was asked to take him up and dive with him in hopes of helping his hearing. I had heard vaguely about such things being done.

With no knowledge whatever that excessive speeds in an airplane could be dangerous, I consented to cooperate in this experiment, although I did not have a great deal of confidence it would help the boy's hearing. With my deaf friend in the front cockpit, I climbed the Waco 9 to 10,000 feet above sea level, which was 6,400 feet above my airport. Without the slightest idea of what was going to happen within the next few seconds, I closed the throttle and went forward with the joystick until the nose of the airplane was headed straight down for the ground. We had no parachutes.

This airplane had hardly any longitudinal stability. Therefore no strenuous control pressures were required to hold it in this vertical dive. It was merely a case of guiding it. However, as speed was gained, and it didn't take long, the controls lost their natural feel and stiffened up from the increased airspeed so I could hardly move them.

In the first phase of this maneuver, I had an experience I never had before. In the portions of loops and split S turns and such maneuvers where the airplane is headed straight down for a short period of time, it is normal to remain solidly in the seat because of the effect of centrifugal force. However, in this straight-down dive, there was no centrifugal force.

When the dive was first entered, the airplane and I were

gaining momentum at the same rate of speed. Therefore I was still in the seat, although all gravity was lost, so I had no weight to hold me in the seat.

As the airplane gained momentum, the air resistance built up on the frontal areas of the airplane to retard its acceleration. I was in the cockpit behind the windshield and out of the airstream so there was nothing to retard my acceleration. The safety belt held me in the seat, but my head and shoulders fell forward, and I had to put my left hand on the instrument panel to hold myself back in a position where I could see what was going on, and to be able to operate the controls.

There was no airspeed indicator on the Waco, so I had no way of knowing what speed was attained in the dive. The airplane continued to gain speed until the air resistance on the plane equaled its weight. In normal level flight, my engine developed a thrust of about 400 pounds. In this dive, the thrust was the weight of the airplane, which was about 1,600 pounds, and gravity was my horsepower, which was the equivalent of about 360 horsepower. Quite naturally, I did not figure this out ahead of time. In the flying business I have figured out a lot of things "after" something unexpected happened.

I was going to hold the dive for 5,000 feet, then start pulling out at 1,400 feet above the ground. I figured if a little dive was good, a longer dive would be better. By the time we had dropped 2,000 feet, the wings, struts, wires, tail, and the entire airplane began to shake and shudder violently. It was so violent the wings and tail could have been torn off the plane instantly.

I immediately realized the seriousness of the situation. If the plane continued this shuddering and shaking dive a second too long, the wings were sure to be torn off, and if I pulled out of the dive too fast, the centrifugal force of the pull-out would tear the wings off anyway. So I was in a position where I stood to lose either way. I hauled back on the stick in an effort to get half-way between these two places where the plane would disintegrate.

It was a great relief when I had completed the recovery and the shuddering and shaking had stopped, with the airplane still in one piece. The landing wires between the wings hung loose and sagged several inches as I finished descending at a slow airspeed and landed as soon as possible. I gave the plane a good inspection and had to re-rig the wings and tail and tighten several fittings that were strained in the ordeal.

My friend's hearing was not improved, but my education was.

On a biplane, the flying wires are the wires between the wings that go from the bottom of the fuselage out to the top of the outer wing struts. These wires take the load when flying. The landing wires are the wires that go from the top of the center section struts over the fuselage, and go out to the bottom of the outer wing struts.

Along about that time, several other pilots had similar experiences. Some of them did not have so fortunate an ending. Then several articles appeared in aviation magazines warning pilots of the hazards of flying any airplane at too fast an airspeed. It was left to the individual to determine what the maximum safe airspeed was for each airplane until the Aeronautics Branch of the Department of Commerce was able to establish a set of safe airspeeds for each type and model of airplane. Today all airplanes have a red line located on their airspeed indicators. It is considered unsafe to fly any airplane past the red line.

This was not much help to me because of not having an airspeed indicator on my airplane. However, I had learned all I needed to know to avoid doing that same experiment again. At a later date when I was dismantling my plane, I found a broken wing fitting I believe was caused by that high-speed dive.

UPSIDE DOWN

After I had met up with enough experiences to take some of the wind out of my sails, I began to realize there were some things about flying I still did not understand. However, I still felt confident in my ability to just plain fly an airplane. No one could be more sure of anything than I was of the fact that at least I knew enough about flying to never get an airplane into a tailspin accidentally. That is what got most pilots into serious trouble, and I received a lot of comfort from realizing I had mastered that phase of flying.

Then one day when business was dull, I took off on a solo flight to practice forced landings, just to keep my hand in on it and see if I could pick up any new angles on the subject. This was one of the most important parts of a successful pilot's career. Success or failure, in a major way, hinged on a pilot's ability to get a plane down in an emergency without doing serious damage.

I had practiced several forced-landing approaches to small fields in the area, Then, on one of them, I had closed the throttle at about 300 feet and was in the process of making a 180-degree turn to get into my intended field. There were a few tall pines trees involved as obstructions.

With the turn about half completed, I stalled and dropped off into a tailspin. I was dangerously near the ground and normally would not have been able to recover from a tailspin from this low altitude. But quick reaction to getting the stick full forward and rapidly applying full power, so as to gain the necessary speed sooner, brought me out of this spin a few feet above the ground. I flew straight back to the airport and landed and did not practice forced landings again for quite a long time.

The instant I dropped off into that spin, I knew instinctively what had to be done if a recovery was to be made. However, I cannot find the words to describe the feeling, or the willpower, that was required to go full forward on the stick, with full power, when the nose was that close to poking itself, and me, straight into the ground.

The recovery from a tailspin, even in those old planes, was a rather simple maneuver when done a couple of thousand feet, or more, above the ground, but it was an entirely different experience to recover from a tailspin while looking the ground square in the face at such close range.

For the benefit of those who have done tailspins only in modern airplanes of today, you must understand that OX5 Waco 9's and OX5 Waco 10's stalled and spun very easily compared to modern airplanes. Hardly any backpressure was required to get the joystick all the way back. After getting it all the way back, if you merely released the stick, it would stay right back in your belly, and the spin would continue indefinitely, or until the ground was rudely contacted.

In a modern airplane, if you release the stick in a spin, it will move forward by itself, because of the inherent longitudinal stability that is built into the airplane. The airplane will automatically stop spinning and enter into a dive. It will even pull itself out of the dive if you have sufficient altitude to start with.

On the older planes, the stick would not go forward after the spin started unless it was deliberately pushed forward. Those planes would not recover from a spin unless the stick was pushed "all the way" forward. Even then you sometimes had to exercise some patience after moving the stick all the way forward before the spin would stop.

In regard to tailspins, one experience I would not care to see repeated starts out something like this—

A pilot from Alaska, Charley, flew an OX5 Waco 10 down through Oregon, barnstorming. He landed on my field at Bend and stayed two or three days. When he left, he took a young man, Bill, from Bend, with him as a helper. He told Bill he would teach him to fly in return for his help selling tickets and other help he could give.

Sometime later, they were in a farmer's field at a small town in a western state. No customers or even prospective customers were visible. This was in the Prohibition days, but they had managed to have a bottle of bootleg whiskey on hand and were generously sampling its contents.

Bill had progressed with his flight training and had made a couple of solo flights, but he had not received any instructions on tailspins. So Charley was explaining to him how to do a tailspin. Then he bet Bill $5 he couldn't go up solo, do a tailspin, recover from it, land the plane, and still be among the living. Bill accepted the bet and took to the wild blue yonder, solo, "in Charley's airplane," to prove he could do it. He did a tailspin, landed the airplane, and was still among the living.

The next time I saw Bill, he told me he was never so scared in his life as he was in that tailspin. Sometime later, Charley, like the rest of us, was not getting very rich, and he decided to sell his Waco and head back for Alaska. Bill and a young man I had taught to fly, Cy Ralston, bought the Waco and went barnstorming in the southern part of Oregon. Eventually Bill wrecked the plane, and they hauled it back to Bend on a truck. It was pretty badly damaged and they sold it for salvage.

Bill decided he wanted to get an Oregon State pilot license. He had been barnstorming without a pilot license and had about 90 hours of flying experience when he came to me for some dual instruction to prepare him for a flight test. His flying was pretty good on everything except stalls and spins.

Because of the great scare he had when he did that solo spin, he just turned white, froze up, and couldn't do anything right after he closed the throttle for his tailspin. Since I had been doing commercial flying in August, 1929, flight training had been my principal business when I was not out barnstorming, but this problem with Bill and his inability to learn to do stalls and spins had me stumped.

Many serious aircraft accidents have occurred because the pilot did not think and act correctly. I had long figured an important part of flight training is a matter of a student developing his own reflexes and training himself to have complete control of himself in tense situations. It is difficult for a student to control himself effectively if he is under a nervous strain or is just plain scared of what he is doing. Because of Bill's hair-raising experience in that first solo tailspin, he was not able to control his actions when approaching a stall or a spin.

When I started teaching him the tailspins that would be required on his flight test, I ran up against my most difficult situation as a flight instructor.

I gave him his dual in my OX5 Waco 9, using the standard one-way speaking-tube arrangement that permitted me to talk to him but he could not talk to me. This being an open cockpit biplane, I was in the front cockpit and Bill was in the rear cockpit. The windshield for the rear cockpit was between us.

After a great deal of time and effort, his stalls were fairly satisfactory, but not really good, because he still tensed up too much and seemed to be completely unconscious as to what was going on after he pulled the stick part way back. Then as we started on the tailspins, my trouble really began. I could not get him to pull his stick all the way back or to apply full rudder for the entry.

I would explain everything in detail on the ground, then we would go up, and I would demonstrate several spins in the air, carefully explaining each move as it progressed. When it came time for him to try a spin, I would talk him through it. But when it was time for him to pull the stick back, I would tell him and plead with him and coax him and yell at him and scream at him. I would turn around in my seat and motion to him, but he was just sitting there, stiff-like, and as white as a ghost.

Down on the ground, we would talk the situation over, and he could explain to me in exact detail just how to enter a spin and how to recover from a spin, but when we went back up there in the air, it was the same thing all over again.

After a great deal of instruction he did show some improvement but still was not satisfactory. The only reason I could see for his trouble was that he was still affected by the scare he received from doing that first spin solo without having had proper instructions.

All the rest of his flying was fairly satisfactory, and after a great deal of practice on spins, we both decided he wasn't getting any better, and he would either pass his test or he wouldn't pass it. We flew to Salem for his flight test.

We arrived at the Salem airport early in the morning, and Bill was to take his flight test in the afternoon. I gave him some more dual on spins, then suggested he go up solo and practice more spins before noon so he would be in better shape for the flight test.

Bill had never worn a parachute, and parachutes were required on the flight test. On this solo flight, Bill put a parachute in the rear cockpit, climbed in and strapped it on. By the time he got all the parachutes buckles fastened, he forgot to put his safety belt on.

Luckily, the inspector, Lee Eyerly, was busy in the hangar as we watched Bill climb to 3,000 feet and enter his practice spin. After three revolutions of the spin, he pushed the stick forward to recover. He held the stick forward too long, and not having his safety belt fastened, he left the seat as the plane turned upside down and started pulling negative G's. Being an open cockpit biplane, there was nothing to hold him in the airplane except that as he was leaving the plane, he succeeded in hooking his toes under the rear cowling near the rear windshield. He also got a handhold on the cowling, but he was still out of the seat and away from the controls.

As he was falling out of the seat, his knee bumped the throttle and opened it. From the ground, we could see the seat cushions as they came out of both cockpits. They strung out above the plane, as the plane was falling much faster than the seat cushions could fall. We could see Bill as he fell from the rear cockpit and hung onto the cowling with his toes and hands. We could hear the roar of the engine and the rapidly increasing whine of the wires as the speed built up in this upside-down power dive. By now he had lost about half of his altitude and was falling fast. People came running out of the office and hangars to see what was going on up there as the noise increased.

Providence, or the pull of the engine, or something, caused the plane to start around the right way and come out of the dive right side up and Bill fell back inside the rear cockpit, less than 500 feet above the ground. He managed to get back on the seat, closed the throttle, put his safety belt on, and immediately came in for a landing. He did not even try to line up on a runway; he just landed in the grass and taxied up to the hangar. As he climbed out of the plane, he was very pale and was shaking like a leaf as he asked if anyone had a cigarette.

The brace wires between the wings were floppy and loose from the strain, and I had to re-rig the wings before time for his flight test. All the seat cushions and the front control stick were lost and had to be replaced.

A flat spin is a spin in which the nose of the plane rides high on the horizon, although the plane is falling vertically. It has always been my understanding that there is no way to recover from a flat spin. However, I have talked to pilots who claim they have recovered from a flat spin. All the OX5 Wacos I have flown have spun pretty flat, but I never considered them to be fully flat spins.

This Waco 9 came as close to a flat spin as I care to get. Recovery required full forward on the stick, then a little patience, not just neutral or less that modern planes require for spin recovery. When the spin stopped, and the plane began the vertical dive that follows, it was very important to bring the stick back at this point or the plane would become inverted.

Bill did not bring the stick back when he should have, so that is exactly what happened. However, if he had had his safety belt on, the next few seconds would not have become that moment of sheer terror that he and we all experienced.

About four o'clock that afternoon, Bill went up with the inspector. They were up about an hour, and when they came down, the inspector asked Bill to go up solo and do his spins.

As he climbed for altitude, he also got a long way from the airport. None of us ever did see his spins, if any. The inspector's attention had been directed elsewhere, and when Bill came down he seemed very disappointed that no one was looking when he did his spins. The inspector did not want to send him out again, so he gave Bill his pilot license.

In spite of Bill's fear of spins, he stayed with flying. After a few years he succeeded in overcoming his fear of them, and he became a successful flight instructor on the World War II flight training programs.

This is an extreme case, but it is a true story, and it is an example of what can happen when a student is not properly instructed on the various maneuvers he must learn to perform with an airplane. Many students, under similar circumstances, would have been killed, or would have given up flying.

THE MAINTENANCE MAN

Through the history of world aviation
    Many names come to the fore
Great deeds of the past in our memory will last
    As they're joined by more and more.

When man first started his labor
    In his quest to conquer the sky
He was designer, mechanic, and pilot
    And he built a machine that would fly.

The pilot was everyone's hero
    He was brave, he was bold, he was grand
As he stood by his battered old biplane
    With his goggles and helmet in hand.

To be sure, these pilots all earned it
    To fly then you had to have guts
And they blazed their names in the hall of fame
    On wings with bailing wire struts.

But for each of our flying heroes
    There were thousands of little renown
And these were the men who worked on the planes
    But kept their feet on the ground.

We all know the name of Lindbergh
    And we've read of his flight into fame
But think, if you can, of his maintenance man.
    Can you remember his name?

And think of our war time heroes
    Gabreski, Jabara and Scott.
Can you tell me the name of their crew chief?
    A thousand to one you cannot.

Now, pilots are highly trained people
    And wings are not easily won,
But without the work of the maintenance man
    Our pilots would march with a gun.

So when you see the mighty jet aircraft
    As they mark their path through the air,
The grease-stained man with a wrench in his hand
    Is the man who put them there.

Author Unknown

Back in the OX5 barnstorming days we were our own maintenance man, our own president, vice-president, and board of
directors, also our own gas and water boy, and publicity agent.
And if we had any time left over after performing these chores,
we even flew the airplane.

As the airplane turned upside down, Bill fell out of the cockpit. He
hung on by his hands and toes as the seat cushions from both cockpits
strung out above the airplane.

9

BARNSTORMING

One day I flew a Hisso Eaglerock from Bend to John Day for the owner, and I needed a way back to Bend. I phoned my brother, Cordis, who had only 15 hours' total flying experience, and asked him to fly the Waco 9 over and pick me up. He brought a passenger with him. On the way over, he had a power failure and landed successfully on a farm field, repaired the engine, took off and continued the flight.

When we took off at John Day to fly home to Bend, I was in the front cockpit sitting beside the passenger. Cordis was in the rear cockpit doing the flying. On the takeoff run we hit a rock and blew out the left tire (26 by 4). As we lifted into the air, the tire and tube came off the wheel and stayed on the ground.

We flew on to Bend, and when we arrived there, I had to take my front control stick out so Cordis could hold full right aileron on the landing. Because of the left tire being off, he had to land on the right wheel and hold the other wheel off the ground as long as possible.

Because our passenger was in the front cockpit with me, it was not possible to move the front control stick full to the right, so I could not help him on the landing. That was a pretty big order for a student with only a few hours of flying experience, but he made a very good landing without doing any damage to the airplane.

LAKEVIEW TAKEOFF

During those OX5 barnstorming days, we seldom operated from an established airport. Many of the fields were very marginal. There were no figures we could use to determine whether or not our airplane would get out of that particular field and clear the obstructions it had to clear. To measure the length of the field, we stepped it off, taking into consideration the elevation above sea level, how soft, hard, or rough the ground was, whether it was uphill or downhill, wind direction and velocity, the temperature, load, etc. We would ask ourselves, "Is the engine putting out full power?" Maybe we had better make a solo test hop first just to check things out before putting our load in, and do we have our rabbit's foot with us today?

Today there are sets of well-established figures that give this information for each type of airplane. Charts and computers give you the minimum distance needed for a takeoff for the conditions that exist at that particular time at that particular place. That is called doing it by the book.

We operated from experience, feel, instinct, and sometimes by squeezing our rabbit's foot just right. Before we had the experience, we went out and got the experience and went on from there. If we came up with the wrong answers, we might have a repair job on our hands, or we might be looking around for another airplane, or our heirs might be looking around to see how much they could get for the salvage.

One day on the Redmond field with the Waco 9, I was flying with my students when Bill Dibble flew in from Portland and landed with his OX5 Waco 10. He had a passenger with him. After filling his gas tank, he was worried about being able to get his plane off the field, which was about 1,800 feet long and had juniper trees all around it.

Bill took a package of cigarettes out of his pocket and handed them to a bystander. He said, "Here, I don't need these." Then he got in his plane and took off. After watching his takeoff, we all agreed he did not need those cigarettes.

I have had my share of takeoffs where there was a reasonable doubt when I opened the throttle to start the takeoff roll. There were times I didn't make it, and there were times I made it by a very small margin.

One day at Lakeview, flying the Waco 9, I had a full tank of gas, two heavy passengers, and 50 pounds of twine to deliver to a sheep camp at Hart Mountain where they were shearing sheep. I was a little suspicious that some of my 90 horses were not pulling their fair share in the harness.

The field was 4,800 feet above sea level with a dirt runway

1,800 feet long, high power lines at the south end of the field, and two telephone wires at the north end of the field. The telephone wires were not as high as the power line at the south end. It was a hot day with no steady wind, but there was an occasional light breeze from the north. I had no problem deciding which way to try the takeoff because the north end had the lowest wires, and when there was a little wind, it came from the north.

I taxied to the south end of the field. There was no wind. I put two small rocks in front of the wheels, so I could get full power before starting the takeoff roll. Then I shoved full forward on the stick, followed by full rudder both directions several times to jump the rocks.

The slow agonizing takeoff roll started. After a while, the tail came up off the ground. Then after even more of the runway got behind us, it was noticeable that the wings were trying to do their job. Finally, I was able to lift the wheels off the ground, but too much of the runway was behind us. The north end of the runway and telephone wires were too close. I cut the power and got back on the ground. The runway was behind us now, and we were rolling in scattered sagebrush, tall grass and weeds. I groundlooped to the left to avoid hitting the fence that was under the telephone wires—no damage to the plane.

I taxied back to my hangar, which was about in the center of the runway, north and south. I stopped in front of the hangar wondering what to do now. I took my safety belt off and was standing up in the rear cockpit. The engine was still running. My passengers were still in the front cockpit when I noticed the windsock was full of wind from the north.

Now, if I could get in the air before that wind stopped, I would have it made. So I dropped down on my seat and started taxiing fast to the south end of the field. I did not take time to put my safety belt on or to lower my goggles from my forehead, because I figured that wind would not last long, and I had to get over those telephone wires before the wind stopped.

As soon as I reached the south end of the runway, I started the takeoff roll. We lifted into the air much sooner this time and had more runway ahead, but as we got closer to the wires, the wind seemed to be stopping. Now we were too close to have room to stop, so I continued.

As we approached the wires, I pulled back for maximum lift.

We cleared the wires by inches. Now I was in a complete power stall. Of course, I had on full power as I shoved the nose down and headed for the ground. Just before hitting the ground, I came full back on the stick, and we hit hard on all three points in a farmer's field.

With the throttle still wide open, I went forward with the stick to raise the tail. The next fence we came to, I pulled back for maximum lift and succeeded in getting over it and remaining airborne. After we were five miles from the airport, I had to sacrifice some airspeed to get over some willows.

This valley was 4,800 feet above sea level, and the sheep camp at our destination was 6,000 feet. There was a high range of mountains to get over before I could even head that direction. I had power enough to remain airborne but had to hunt for favorable air currents to climb. In this way an OX5 barnstorming pilot learns a lot about soaring. He does it with full power.

A steel tube went across the front cockpit in front of my passengers. I saw four hands with white knuckles gripping this tube as I circled in and out of canyons, hunting for updrafts to put us over those mountains. We made it.

Years later, I had an occasion to work with a brother of one of my passengers on that flight, and he knew all about it. The routine of day-to-day activities is forgotten before the moon changes, but with an experience like that, the details are remembered 50 years later.

10

There finally came a time when I decided I wanted to fly something a little better than a beat-up old Waco 9, but we were right in the middle of the Great Depression of the early 1930's. There were airplanes better than OX5 Waco 9's, but they all cost money I did not have. Eventually, I came up with an idea for getting my hands on the money to buy a better airplane.

I decided to put on one big airshow in which I would put my Waco 9 in a tailspin, set it on fire, and jump out with a parachute. After kicking the idea around for some time, the Veterans of Foreign Wars (VFW) agreed to sponsor the show. We obtained written permission from the Oregon State Board of Aeronautics and went on from there. We had tickets printed, were getting our advertising started, and began selling tickets.

Two of my students, Al and Chet Varnes, had a sister, Margaret, who worked in an office in Bend. Margaret was also selling tickets for us. At this time I had not met her, but later I did, and eventually (two weeks after our first date) we were married. We had a daughter and a son, Beverly and Curtis, and now have 10 grandchildren and six great grandchildren.

As publicity mounted on our big event there was criticism, and the State Board of Aeronautics sent me a letter withdrawing its permission. Board officials claimed the centrifugal force in the tailspin would be too great to allow me to get out of the airplane. I knew their objections were not valid because of my previous experience on the wings of this same Waco 9 in those two tailspins on my John Day experience. However, probably very few people have ever had the experience of climbing around on the wings of an airplane while it was in a

Ted Barber, OX5 Waco 10, Bend, Oregon, 1931.

tailspin. It is not something anyone would do just for fun. Anyway, we did not get to put on our grand finale for my Waco 9, and we refunded the money to the people who had bought tickets to see it.

The State of Oregon was just organizing the Oregon State Police. A friend of mine, R.D. Davis, an Oregon State policeman, had some flying experience. He bought a wrecked OX5 Waco 10 and asked me to rebuild it for him. When I was rebuilding the Waco 10, I sold the Waco 9 to one of my students, Cy Ralston, for $500. When I finished rebuilding R.D.'s Waco 10, I flew it for him. We had no written agreement. I just operated it as though I owned it. Any time I saw R.D., he would ask me how much money I had. I would take the money out of my pocket and count it. He would tell me how much of it he wanted, and I would give it to him. That was our bookkeeping system. We kept no records.

I knew R.D. had some flying experience, so I expected him to want to fly his Waco. Every time he came out to the field he would ask me if I had had any forced landings, and I would always tell him no. I would ask him if he would like to fly his airplane, but he always said "some other time."

Finally, one day he came out to the field and asked me if I ever had any forced landings, and again I told him I had not had any forced landings. He said, "OK, let's go for a ride." He wanted to ride in the front cockpit, but since I knew he knew how to fly, I insisted he get in the rear cockpit and fly the plane, so he did.

We were not more than five miles from the airport when the engine quit. R.D. threw up his hands and said, "She is all your's, Ted." So I took over and set it down in a farm field. That was the first and last time R.D. ever flew his plane. Later, he was transferred to another part of the state, and I bought the Waco from him.

Now I was flying a later model airplane, and it was in very good condition. I put a Hamilton Standard metal propeller on it and was pretty proud of that airplane. There were still the regular operational problems of those days but nothing unusual for that day and time.

About a year later, I met Cy and asked him how he was getting along with my old friend, the Waco 9. He said, "Not very good." Some time back he was making a takeoff up in the Long Creek area, and when he came to a bunch of willows, he "zoomed" over them. Then he came to another bunch of wil-

Four of my students (left to right)—Donald Beatty, Willis Stacy, Harold Freund, Al Mansfield—OX5 Waco 10, Redmond, Oregon, 1931.

lows and he "zoomed" over them, and when he came to his third bunch of willows, he ran out of "zooms." The plane was pretty badly damaged. He dismantled it and had it stored in a farmer's barn. This was one of the chronic problems of a barn-stormer. When you had an obstruction in front of you, and you were fresh out of "zooms," you were in trouble.

ACCIDENTAL TAILSPINS

In the fall of 1932, about two weeks after Margaret Varnes and I were married, I was riding with one of my advanced students, Al Mansfield, from the Redmond airport in the OX5 Waco 10. He was practicing spirals to a landing from 2,000 feet. The object was to close the throttle at 2,000 feet above the ground just beyond the downwind end of the field and see how many 360-degree turns could be completed in a gliding spiral before straightening out for a landing.

There was a south wind blowing about 20 miles per hour. Our takeoffs and landings were into the south. Al's entry into the maneuver was satisfactory, but at the point where he should have recovered from his spiral and straightened out for a land-

Ted Barber and wife Margaret, September, 1932, two weeks after we were married. OX5 Waco 10, Bend, Oregon.

ing, he decided to make one more turn in the spiral. I could see he was too low, especially because he was not using a steep enough bank to complete the turn on his limited altitude.

When he had completed about 90 degrees of his last spiral, I took over and steepened the bank and tightened the turn. When we had completed the next 90 degrees of the spiral, the controls did not feel normal, so I applied full power. It seems we had just entered a tailspin, and I had not become aware of it yet so I did not go forward with the stick as I opened the throttle.

There were several eye witnesses standing near the end of the field. They were unanimous in their opinion that we entered the spin about 150 feet above the ground, which is hard to believe because this plane normally fell about 200 feet per revolution in a power-off spin. In a full-power spin, it would wind up much faster. We completed one and one-half turns in the spin.

As soon as I recognized the spin, I lost no time in going full forward on the stick and applying full right rudder, leaving the power full on. I was in the front cockpit, and as I went forward with the stick, I knocked some skin off my knuckles on the gas tank in front of me. There is no question that the stick was all the way forward. What a difficult thing to do! We were spinning rapidly and were very close to the ground. To have hopes of pulling out of that spin before plowing the nose into the ground was to believe in miracles.

Normally, there is a certain radius of arc that is followed in recovering from the dive after the spin stops. If the nose is brought up faster than this, it is quite common for the plane to fall off into another tailspin, usually in the opposite direction. However, in this case, after I had stopped the spin, we were too close to the ground to give consideration for any certain radius of arc.

In the process of doing the 2,000-foot spiral, the wind had drifted us out over the juniper trees that surrounded the airport. The juniper forest was thick as juniper forests go, but there was considerable space between some of the trees, and we luckily dropped down between trees where there was some space. Someone upstairs had managed the recovery so we were headed due south into the wind. Without these two points in our favor, it would not have been possible to have made a recovery.

118

Because of our closeness to the ground after the spin stopped, I had to bring the nose up very abruptly. The added lift the headwind gave us was a big help in making this abrupt recovery possible. Another factor that helped on this score no doubt was the compression of the air between the bottom of the lower wings and the ground. This is called ground effect, and it gives some additional lift when the wing is really close to the ground, such as five feet or less.

I do not believe our wheels touched the sagebrush but they were close to it. Because of the rapid recovery, we were just clearing the sagebrush with no reserve airspeed, and there were trees on all sides of us. There was not enough room to land and get stopped before hitting a tree that was directly in front of us, and we probably could not get enough lift between where we were and the tree to get over it.

There was no time for mathematics or a conference. A decision had to be made at once. In such a case, if you do not make a decision immediately, it forces a certain course of action anyway. In cases where you are not able to make a conscious decision in the time allotted you, your subconscious mind makes the decision for you. The decisions of this nature are more apt to be correct than the ones from your conscious mind. This was one of the subconscious decisions. It looked to me like I was going to lose either way. Being unable to make a decision, I left the throttle open and held the nose down all I could and still keep out of the sagebrush, in an effort to build up speed before reaching the tree.

It would have been a mistake in a situation like this to attempt to get altitude any sooner than was absolutely necessary in order to miss the obstruction. I lined up to the left of the tree so the right wing would hit it. I figured that would put our left wings into the ground on the other side of the tree, and our chances of survival would be better than if we hit head on and went into the ground on our nose on the other side of the tree.

As we approached the tree and reached the point where something had to be done about it, I pulled up for maximum lift. I was so sure we would not clear it I did something I am sure is not recommended. I had done this same thing once before but have never done it since. Just as I expected to hear and feel the splintering crash of the tree top ripping through our right lower wing, I closed my eyes.

Then I waited until it should have happened, but it didn't. I

119

opened my eyes and we were in the clear with the tree safely behind us. How it got back there, I will never know. Maybe it ducked.

In this go-around there was another experience or sensation I had had only once before and never again. Just as I had gone full forward with the stick for the spin recovery and before the plane stopped spinning, I experienced a very definite tingling the full length of my spine, and I could feel every hair root in my head as though my hair was trying to stand on end. I had a tight-fitting leather helmet on my head, so my hair could not have really moved.

We all know it is not possible to have a one-and-one-half-turn tailspin from 150 feet and recover before hitting the ground, so I do not guarantee these numbers, but these are the numbers that came out when we were discussing this incident. What this really means is that after a hair-raiser like this, no one is very sure of "exactly" what did happen. Just still being counted among the living is the important thing, and realizing I am still capable of making these kinds of mistakes is the sobering thing.

EMERGENCIES

Emergencies were not uncommon almost any time, any place. They were just part of the price of admission into the flying business.

Once I watched one of my solo students take off from the Prineville airport in my OX5 Waco 10. He gained about 75 feet of altitude as he pulled out of the south end of the airport. He was climbing over thick juniper trees. All of a sudden the engine quit. We saw the plane go down out of sight among the trees, then a large cloud of dust boiled up. There were eight or 10 of us watching this, and our blood pressure raised about 100 points. We made a scramble for the cars.

Some of us got in the cars and some just stood on the running boards. We raced down there and found the plane right side up, not a scratch on it. The student had found a narrow, clear place between the trees. We never were able to determine what had caused the power failure. It could have been ice in the carburetor or in a fuel line. This was long before I had learned about ice in carburetors.

120

At one time, one of my solo students was making an approach for a landing at the Redmond airport with a tailwind. The windsock was really hanging out. This field was only 1,800 feet long, so naturally, he overshot and had to go around again. The next time he came in headwind and made it okay. I said, "Harold, why didn't you look at the windsock before you made that tailwind approach?" He said he did look at it, but he couldn't figure out which way the wind was blowing through it.

I have not kept a record of all the forced landings I have had. One week I had seven forced landings, one of which resulted in damage to the airplane.

I had one passenger in the front cockpit on that flight and when I had gained about 200 feet of altitude after takeoff, four cylinders cut out on my eight-cylinder engine, which probably means the carburetor iced up. We were over tall pine trees with no respectable place in sight to land. A grain field was about two miles away, and the engine was still putting out some power. I headed for the grain field into a 10-mile-per-hour headwind. We did not get very far until we were well below the tops of the tall pine trees, weaving to one side then to the other to miss them.

As we were getting very close to the ground, we approached a small grain field that was only about 250 feet across. Without closing the throttle, I touched the wheels on this field, but there was no chance of getting stopped before hitting the fence that bordered the field. I left the throttle open although there was no assurance of even getting over the fence. However, I took a chance on that and did clear the fence.

Next there was a field about a quarter of a mile long and a little downhill, which helped, but it was too full of stumps and things to land on. Along the lower side of this field there was a road with a barbed-wire fence on each side. Above the fence closest to me was a farmer's telephone line that was about twice as high as the fence. Above the fence on the other side of the road was a Forest Service telephone line about twice as high as the farmer's line. Further on was the nice large grain field I was headed for.

As we passed over the field of stumps, I held the nose down to where I was clearing them by a very small margin.

At the point where I had to pull up or hit the first fence, I gave it everything it had and cleared both the fence and the farmer's telephone line. Upon reaching the Forest Service line, I was in a complete stall and the wire caught the wheels. This wire was very heavy and was not attached to the insulators. The insulators were round like doughnuts and the wire merely went through them.

Instead of the wire breaking where I hit it, it broke a long distance from there and just strung along with me, hanging onto the wheels and pulling the nose down into the ground. What little power I still had was still full on as I reached for the stabilizer control with my left hand and applied full back stabilizer as well as full back stick with my right hand. It was not enough, and the wood propeller started churning into the ground with splinters flying in all directions.

When the wheels contacted the ground, the oleo shock struts folded up, and both wheels rammed their bald faces up through the bottom wings as the plane proceeded to skid out across the field on its belly in about two inches of fresh snow.

I was too busy to take my goggles off before the crash; in fact, I didn't think of it. The power stall into the headwind and the slowing-down effect of the telephone wire caused the plane to contact the ground much slower than you would expect. My passenger wasn't even thrown off the seat—and he didn't have his safety belt on. Neither one of us was injured in any way.

As I walked around my wrecked airplane and surveyed the damage, the thought occurred to me that there was not a sad-

The wood propeller churned into the ground, splinters flying in all directions. Both wheels rammed their bald faces up through the bottom wings as the plane skidded across the field on its belly, in 2 inches of fresh snow.

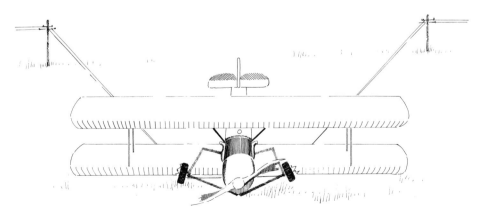

der-looking thing in this world than a wrecked airplane. It is like a crippled bird shivering and shaking in the willows with a broken wing.

This was early in the morning. The snow on the ground was fresh and crisp. The air was also crisp. I swished my hand through the air, and it seemed very light. How this outfit ever got into the air in the first place is probably more of a mystery than what made it come down.

The wheels came up through the lower wings ahead of the front spars, and the spars were not damaged although they did have tire marks on them. I was able to repair the lower wings without removing them from the plane. Some welding fixed the shock-absorbing struts and the landing gear, and the bottom and nose cowlings needed some hammering out. I had to borrow $50 to buy a new propeller—and had to pay back $60 with interest. That is what really hurt. With all the tough breaks a fellow gets with an airplane, one does not feel too badly about it because, if the cards are played right, you can nearly always see how it could have been much worse.

STREET LANDING

It is common for a pilot to believe that after a certain number of years of flying along with a certain number of hours in the air, he has developed the "feel" of flying. Therefore, his technique has reached perfection. I do not agree with this. On one occasion I was riding in a Travelair 6000 with a well qualified pilot, but on every turn he made he was skidding and the ball rolled to a position between the five and 10 on the high side.

During World War II I had the experience of being an instructor on a flight- instructor re-rating course. In order for pilots to teach in the war-training programs, they had to go through this re-rating course. The majority of these men had a poor understanding of the elementary fundamentals of simple control coordination. This wasn't surprising to me because I knew how much time and study it had taken me to acquire this information, and I figured there were still some important things unknown in flying.

I had seen plenty to convince me that the "seat-of-the-pants" type of pilot, or the instructor who teaches his students to fly by "feel" without first teaching the mechanics of flying, is as obsolete as grandma's spinning wheel, but there is, or was at that time, still too much of this going on.

If a person always flies conservatively and never does maximum performance maneuvers, he will never learn of the many pitfalls that are associated with them or how far he can go safely when an unexpected emergency puts him in a position where his life may depend on his ability to skillfully perform.

Sometimes only an emergency can give us the boldness we require to do things we have considered too hazardous. If we live through such an experience and spend some time analyzing it and further practicing it, we lose our fear of it and eventually it becomes part of our normal functions.

In my early flying days, 500 feet was considered a nice width for a runway, and wider was better. The planes had no wheel brakes, and they had an iron tailskid instead of a tailwheel. This left only the force of the wind on the rudder for directional control on the ground. Also, we learned tricks for using the elevators, ailerons and throttle to assist in steering on the ground. Even with all the skill that could be applied, in some situations, directional control on the ground was a difficult thing to maintain.

Losing directional control of an airplane on the ground is called groundlooping. Even famous-name pilots have been known to groundloop airplanes. In some cases when an airplane is groundlooped, considerable damage is done to the airplane and also to other objects the airplane might run into. Perhaps no other part of flying requires more skill than learning how to prevent an airplane from groundlooping. Some airplanes are worse than others for this bad habit.

In the days of the OX5 Jenny, it was common practice for a ground-crew member to walk along, holding a bottom wing tip, to help the pilot steer his plane until he got to the place where he would open the throttle for the takeoff. As boys, we used to argue about which one of us would have the privilege of holding onto the barnstorming pilot's wing tip while he taxied out into takeoff position. Most planes of those days had poor forward visibility while on the ground. Modern planes have tricycle landing gears which eliminate the groundlooping problem and give good forward visibility for taxiing.

Even after I had several hundred hours of flying experience and had experienced several forced landings, I had never attempted a landing on anything as narrow as a road. A friend of mine had landed on a road, making the landing okay, but on the takeoff he got off the road into a ditch and hit a fence, doing quite a lot of damage.

One day in the early 1930's, I was flying over Bend at 1,200 feet in a light rain with a strong north wind when the gas line broke. The engine lost all its power immediately. One of my students was in the rear cockpit doing the flying. I was crowded up in the front cockpit beside a passenger. This limited my use of the dual controls.

I took over as soon as the engine stopped. A metal Hamilton Standard propeller had recently been installed on the plane, and I was concerned about the safety of that nice, shiny, new propeller. I pulled up near a stall to lose airspeed, and held it there until the propeller stopped turning. It stopped almost vertically. In this position, it would be sure to be damaged if we nosed over or if the landing gear folded up on the crash landing that was looking us in the face. I put the plane in a dive and created enough wind to turn the propeller to a cross position. Then I pulled up to a normal glide and proceeded to figure out a plan for the deadstick landing.

I had made several deadstick landings before this, and they had all turned out pretty well. So I had confidence—but anything can happen on a deadstick landing. I considered landing in the river but did not like that idea, so I headed for a playground beside the river. There was no one in the playground. I was down to about 500 or 600 feet from the ground when I realized I was approaching it with a tailwind.

After waking up to this fact, I knew I could never get into the playground with that strong tailwind, but I still did not like the river idea. So, with the limited time I had left for making decisions, I located an open-looking street and headed for it. There could be wires crossing the street, but I figured I could duck in between them.

To give me a wider choice of a place to drop in between the wires, I lowered the nose and increased the gliding speed as we came in over the wires. Then I leveled off and started looking for a hole to get through. As I was losing the excess speed, I had never seen such a maze of wires. No holes were available. I continued to pull up as we floated down the street just above the wires.

Finally, I had pulled up all I could and had lost flying speed down to a bare minimum for maintaining control. Gravity did the rest. We went down because to pull up more would result in a stall and possibly a serious crash. So down we went, not at any particular place I had selected, but at the place that had to be used to maintain control of the airplane. To my surprise, we only hit one wire, and it broke and let us through.

As we dropped to the street, I brought the stick back the rest of the way, and we made a smooth landing. The street was a little downhill, and we did not lose speed very fast, having no wheel brakes and only an iron skid on the tail. The crosswind hitting us from between the houses and trees made it difficult to maintain a straight course.

After rolling about a half a block, the plane swerved to the left. I applied full right rudder as well as having the stick all the way back but could not bring the plane back on course. If I could have applied full left aileron, I might have gotten it back, but I could not move the stick to the left because of the passenger sitting there.

Bend, Oregon, 1931, OX5 Waco 10. It was one of those days—a combination of a power failure, street landing and a power pole. Ted Barber in semi-white flying suit, passenger with helmet, student with tie.

126

When we left the street, the left wings hit a power pole and were completely sheared off. Then the plane rudely jumped over a concrete sidewalk and turned about 120 degrees to the left and came to a stop. The silence that followed was broken only by my passenger taking our safety belt off, jumping out of the plane, and running at top speed about a block before stopping and looking back to see if it was going to explode. After he stopped and started walking cautiously back to the plane, my student and I climbed out and started looking over the damage.

None of us had received the slightest injury, and the plane did not have a scratch on it except that both left wings were sheared completely off just beyond the propeller, which was still standing crossways. Apparently the speed I had gained in the fast glide did not move it. I was too much concerned about other things right at that time to notice what the propeller was doing.

We came to a stop only about three blocks from my home. My mother was in the back yard hanging up clothes, and she had seen us coming down until we got so low the buildings and trees were between her and us. She said she knew I was having trouble, but she was not worried about my safety because she figured I could get it down okay.

Mother used to worry about me when I first started flying in Bend. Then one night she had a dream that she saw me crash. They all ran to the crash, then she saw me crawl out of the wreckage and start putting it back together again. She said she never worried about me after that dream.

By the time we had surveyed the damage, people were running toward the plane from all directions, and cars started approaching in a steady stream. The screams of sirens from police, fire engines, ambulances, and a hearse filled the air. Over 100 people swarmed around the plane asking all sorts of questions.

I walked over to my home to get some tools to start dismantling the plane so I could get it back out to the airport. While I was after the tools, the ambulances and hearse, unable to find any customers, drove away. When I returned to the plane with the tools, the people still standing around were surprised to see me. They thought I was dead. They had seen the hearse leave, and I was not there, so they supposed I was in the hearse.

We dismantled the plane and hauled it to the airport. I ordered spruce from a spruce mill in Portland for all four spars. I built a wood rib jig and made new ribs from the spruce that was in the broken spars. I had recently purchased a crashed plane which was the same model as mine, so had extra internal wing fittings to replace the damaged ones. For covering the wings, I used unbleached muslin sheeting from our local drygoods store at 10 cents per square yard. My students helped and within six weeks I was flying again, with my new home-built wings.

FLYING

The sun was shining brightly
    And all was clear and still
It was a day for gliding
    Beside a rising hill.
The rope was stretched out quickly
    And fastened to the hook
The final orders given
    And all the places took.
When everything was ready
    The pilot said, "Let's go."
The driver who was waiting
    Let out the clutch in low.
At first the wings seemed heavy
    And tipped from side to side
But as the car went faster
    Began an even ride.
The stick went back a little
    The glider left the ground
And started up a climbing
    Without a single sound.
The pilot gave the signal
    The rope dropped off the nose
The wires began to whistle
    And up the ground arose.
But then as he got closer
    He pulled back on the stick
Compared to all the others
    The landing sure was slick.

Cloyde Artman

Experiences such as this can make a person leery of landing an airplane in narrow places; and something else that bothered me was that I had planned to make a deadstick landing on that playground with a tailwind, which would have been a tragic mistake.

About 20 years after this experience, in the 1950's, a pilot was flying a four-place plane at about 10,000 feet a few miles west of Denio, Nevada, when the crankshaft in his engine broke. The pilot selected a suitable place for a landing, on flat ground, just weeds and grass, where a landing could have been made with no damage to the airplane. There was a very strong wind, and he came in with a tailwind. He got his plane on the ground okay, but used up all his landing area, then came to a dry wash that had vertical walls and he was still traveling fast. The plane hit the wall across the wash and turned upside down. There were four grown people and a baby in the plane, and they were all killed.

One of the things I have been dealing with in my life in the aviation world is realism, not sensationalism or mistakes glossed over. My thought, and attempt, to land on that playground with a tailwind was a real boner, and of course the five lives lost, along with a valuable airplane being destroyed as a result of the tailwind deadstick landing west of Denio was even a more tragic boner. The point is that pilots, including myself, do not always make the right decisions. The unanswered question here seems to be, "How is it decided who survives and who does not survive, after such a boner has been made?"

CLOYDE ARTMAN

I had continued exchanging letters with my friend Cloyde Artman after he moved to Washington. Among other things I kept him posted on my fishing-pole glider progress. Some years later, after I started flying in central Oregon, he decided to build a primary type glider, using wood construction.

This glider had a skid that slid along the ground; he sat in a seat with a safety belt, and the glider had regular airplane-type controls. Cloyde sent me pictures of it as it was under construction in his back yard and sometimes he asked me for advice on certain parts of it.

In one letter from him, he had finished the glider and had

tried to fly it, pulling it behind a car. He gave me details of design and construction and asked me what he had done wrong, because at 45 miles per hour behind the tow car, it would not lift him off the ground.

After having Tex Rankin's schooling behind me, I was experienced using nitrate dope to make aircraft fabric airtight. I explained this to Cloyde and suggested that if he would put several coats of nitrate dope on the cloth of the wings and control surfaces to make it airtight, he would get a lot more lift.

When I returned to Bend from the Denio Fourth of July celebration, there was a letter waiting for me from Cloyde. He was very happy. After doping the fabric, his glider lifted him off the ground at 30 miles per hour, and he had taught himself to fly it. He was really having a ball with it.

He sent me a picture he took of himself while he was airborne. He fastened a camera out on the wing and ran a string down where he could reach it and while he was flying he pulled the string and took his own picture. Cloyde also sent me a copy of a poem he wrote about gliding.

Although much of my time was spent on the barnstorming trail, Bend was still my home base. On one of my returns to Bend I received another letter from Cloyde. His first flights with his glider were behind a tow car. Now he was flying it from the top of a hill, using shock cord to launch it. He sent me a newspaper clipping with a cartoon showing a monkey riding on top of a glider playing a harmonica. The clipping read:

AVIATOR PROVIDES TUNEFUL MELODIES
WHILE HE GLIDES

Citizens of Oroville, Washington, were amazed the other day to hear a heavenly music in the skies. It grew louder and louder until two-score men, women, and children were in the streets, craning their necks as they peered upward. One man fell into a bed of mortar.

The music, it was discovered, was played by Cloyde Artman, 19-year-old glider pilot, as he soared over the streets of Oroville. Artman is a harmonica player. He has made 80 successful flights in his home-made glider and likes to play tuneful ditties as he flies.

The congressman in Cloyde's district told him he believed he could get him an appointment at West Point after he finished his education.

130

Cloyde decided to design and build a more advanced type of glider that would have a full cantilever wing. This new glider would have a better gliding angle that would permit him to make long soaring flights, and it would carry two people. He had already started construction of the new glider.

I felt very good about Cloyde and his prospects for the future. Somehow, as for me, some of the glamour seemed to be evaporating out of my life, as I seemed unable to solve some of my financial and operational problems. I could see that Cloyde was taking a more sensible course than I had taken. He was going ahead with his education, and by the time he finished his schooling and West Point, as well as his gliding experiences, he would have a brighter future ahead of him than my life was developing into.

In another letter I had received from Cloyde, he had finished his new high performance glider and he believed he had set a new world's record for endurance by remaining aloft for more than three hours.

After I had discontinued my flying business in John Day and returned to Bend, I received a letter from Cloyde's sister. On his last flight the wings collapsed and he was killed.

Although I had not seen Cloyde since he had moved to Washington, I always considered him one of my real friends. We were friends by choice, by mutual interest. To me, what Cloyde and I were doing, or trying to do, was what this country is all about.

Even my family showed only a passive interest in the things that were vitally important in my life. No members of my family were ever present when I flew my fishing-pole glider. If Cloyde had been in the area, he would have been there, and he would have had an invitation to have flown it. My mother had a certain interest in what her youngest son was doing. She came out, with her camera, and took the only picture I have of my fishing-pole glider after it was finished, but for some reason or other, I was not able to fly it that day.

It is hard to understand why some people are allowed only one mistake. I don't have fingers and toes enough to count the really tough spots I have survived.

The Lord gave me enough wisdom, but just barely enough, so I made the decision to learn to fly factory-built airplanes instead of continuing with my home-built ideas, but He didn't give me enough wisdom, skill, or judgment to keep me from blundering into impossible predicaments. However, it seems He did give me some strange powers to recover from these situations after I found myself in them.

I was almost reaching the point of believing what Tex Rankin had told me on several occasions, that the Lord had His hand on my shoulder. If the Lord had that much interest in protecting me, why didn't He make me smart enough to keep me from pulling so many blunders?

I am not alive today because I have always used good judgment, or even proper skills, in many situations. I have never backed away from adventure in an airplane. My attitude all along has been that airplanes were made to fly and I was made to fly them. That in itself could explain how I got myself into so many tight places, but it does not explain how I got out of them.

Here's one I took of myself as you can see. I was about 150 feet up and still headed up, as you can see the towline. I was plenty busy just then as the glider was almost stalling. (The car was missing) and I had just thrown out a small parachute and lost my cap and then took the picture, followed with a release and a sharp right turn and landing.

I made another flight from the mountain—4 minutes, 45 seconds, and took 5 aerial pictures with a big camera and they all turned out good. I'll send you the best one in my next letter.

Cloyde Artman

11

GOVERNMENT INSPECTORS

Looking back over the OX5 flying days, I can see now that a proper method of eliminating carburetor ice and a flexible gas line would have eliminated 90 percent of my power failures and would have contributed greatly to a more successful operation. In those days, no one seemed to be able to come up with a solution to these two problems.

The only times my OX5 Waco 10 was damaged, the forced landings were caused by: first, ice in the carburetor and second, a broken gas line. The broken gas line could not have been caused by the propeller being out of balance. I was using the Hamilton Standard metal propeller, and there was no better propeller for an OX5 engine.

It was normal for those copper tube gas lines to crystallize and break occasionally, so I developed a habit of replacing them with new lines at certain intervals. The gas line that broke and caused the street landing in Bend was making its first flight, so that forced landing could not be attributed to careless maintenance.

There was another factor regarding propeller vibrations that I did not learn about until several years later, and that was—even a propeller that is perfectly balanced can develop a vibration in a certain limited RPM range. This could have caused the street landing in Bend, and also the dangerous gas line vibration I observed over the Cascade Mountains as I looked down into the engine compartment.

In 1932 I was making a desperate effort to get my flying business on an "eat-as-you-go" basis. My regular price for both dual instruction and solo flying was $10 per hour. To students who would pay in advance, I was selling a complete 50-hour flying course for $275. That was only $5.50 per hour. Gas cost only seven cents per gallon, so the gas and oil were costing less than $1 per hour. My total operating cost was less than $2 per hour, and I would rather be in the air than on the ground. There was no way to make any money with an airplane while it was on the ground.

My home base was Bend, but I had students in Redmond, Prineville, Madras, Sisters, and on the Warm Springs Indian

Ted Barber, Waco 10, 165-horsepower Comet engine, Bend, Oregon, 1933.

reservation. I spent one day a week in each of these towns.

Efforts were being made to outlaw commercial flying with state-licensed airplanes, so I was looking into the possibility of operating under federal regulations but was not making much progress on that. I was told dual ignition was required on engines operating under federal rules, and the OX5 had single ignition.

I thought this problem was solved when I bought a 165-horsepower, seven-cylinder radial, air-cooled Comet engine from a wrecked airplane. It had dual ignition, was lighter, and had 75 more horsepower than the OX5. I installed the Comet engine on the Waco 10, using the steel tubing from a wrecked Waco 10 to weld up the new engine mount.

In making the new engine mounting, I placed the Comet engine far enough forward to move the center of gravity of the Waco further forward than it was with the OX5. When the installation was completed, the airplane had much better longitudinal stability. It would now come out of a seven-turn, full cross control, tailspin and assume a normal glide, hands off. I had never flown a Waco before that would recover from a tailspin hands off.

I figured there was not an airplane in the country that balanced any better or had better performance than my Comet-powered Waco 10, but I was no closer to getting a federal license than before. The inspector said my homemade engine mount was not acceptable because it did not have the necessary engineering. It was light and strong and a good engine mount, but they would not accept it.

The federal inspector would not accept the spruce in my left wings that I built after the street landing because they did not have the little rubber stamp on them that would be proof they came from the aircraft factory. They were made of the best spruce available, from a mill in Portland. They would have passed any kind of a test, but the inspector would not accept them. The cloth I covered the left wings with was also not acceptable. It came from our local J.C. Penney store. This fabric would have passed the same strength requirements for regular aircraft fabric. I figured if they did not have these objections to putting a federal license on my plane, they would have found some other reasons.

Maybe an important factor regarding the inspector's attitude toward me was that I was a long way from Portland and the Willamette Valley. I was a long way from population centers; central Oregon was more wasteland than anything else. If I had been licensed under federal regulations, it would have placed quite a burden on the inspectors to monitor my operations.

Also, it would have been impossible for me to operate under federal regulations unless I also had a federal aviation mechanic license. In practice, I was well qualified for this, but was technically not qualified because I would have been required to serve two years as an apprentice working under a licensed aircraft mechanic. Nevertheless I had plenty of experience maintaining and rebuilding airplane engines and airframes. But I was not given credit for this. However, there was nothing unairworthy about my Comet-powered Waco 10.

Four years prior to this, I was operating a full-scale commercial flying business that began when my total flying experience consisted of 55 hours in the air, both dual and solo. During this time, I had been "run through the mill" with some very rough flying, accumulating around 1,500 hours in the air, and never injuring anyone in an airplane and having never had a student damage an airplane.

There had been a few crash landings caused by power failures, but when you take into consideration the type of flying I had been doing and the times I didn't crash when there was a pretty good excuse to, this was a good track record. I thought the government was being unfair to deny me a federal license to continue the same business I had been operating successfully. I was now flying an airplane that was many times better than the airplane I started out with.

Even with all the mechanical problems, financially speaking, I could have survived the Great Depression, especially since installing the Comet engine in the Waco 10. This engine had provisions for eliminating carburetor ice, and it had a flexible gas line. It was the changing of the laws that made it illegal to do commercial flying on a state license that was shooting me down.

FIREWORKS

When my flying operations became illegal, I had no way to earn a living, so, illegal or not, I felt compelled to continue operating my flying business. By no stretch of the imagination could I see myself as an outlaw. I was only trying to make an honest living at the trade I understood and loved and had exerted so much time and effort to get into. I probably became one of the most notorious flying outlaws in the country, and to the aviation officials I was public enemy number one.

When our daughter, Beverly, was born the latter part of June 1933, we did not have the money to pay the doctor bill—but you cannot stop nature with a poor credit rating. The rent on our small modern home was $7 per month, and we were not always able to pay that when it was due.

About a week after Beverly was born, Margaret had a very serious setback. She was in the Bend hospital with a temperature of 106 degrees, and it was reported on the streets of Bend that she had died. My brother, Cordis, called from Klamath Falls and asked when the funeral would be.

This was the situation that existed as the Fourth of July approached. The committee in charge of the celebration offered me $10 if I would fly over town at a set time that night with fireworks on my wings and put on a stunting exhibition as the floats were drifting down the river through Mirror Pond. I was

FLY OVER BEND

WHIRLWIND RYAN

SISTER SHIP TO LINDY'S

TED BARBER CHIEF PILOT

TED'S FLYING SERVICE

BEND OREGON

in no position to turn down $10 worth of cash business, so I agreed.

The committee planned this as a surprise part of the program. They did not have this act printed on their program sheets, so no one knew about it until they saw the plane overhead with flares on the wings doing all sorts of stunts. I really gave them a show. It attracted more attention for those few minutes than all the rest of the show. Part of the people thought I was just up there on my own showing off, and someone signed a warrant for my arrest for stunting over town. I have never been able to find out who signed that warrant.

Public sympathy was on my side. When I went before the judge, I pleaded not guilty and demanded a jury trial. I refused to sign a confession of any kind. A spokesman for my side told the judge that if I were punished, he would get a warrant out for the arrest of everyone in Bend, because everyone violated some sort of a law during that celebration. In fact, the city put on an elaborate display of fireworks; all the fireworks shot off that night were in violation of a state law, and a small boy was quite seriously burned while the fireworks were being set off. My case was postponed, and today, over 50 years later, I have never heard any more about it.

WHEN THE LAST LONG FLIGHT IS OVER

When the last long flight is over
    And the happy landing's past,
And my altimeter tells me
    That the crack-up's come at last,
I'll swing her nose for the ceiling,
    I'll give my crate the gun,
I'll open her up and let her zoom
    For the airport in the sun.
And the great God of flying men
    Will smile at me sort of low,
As I store my crate in the hangar
    On the field where flyers go.
And I'll look upon his face,
    The almighty flying boss,
Whose wingspread fills the heavens
    From Orion to the Cross.

Anonymous

12

WILD HORSES

Soon after the fireworks exhibition in 1933, I was approached by Art Seale and Bill Blakely to fly to Nevada and help them catch over 1,000 horses they had just bought from Fred Gorham. At this time, I knew nothing about corralling horses with an airplane, but Art and Bill said they knew all about that part of it, and they would show me how to do it.

If anyone was making a living with an airplane during that period, I did not know who it was. Even Tex Rankin went out of business. He survived this lean period by going to Hollywood and teaching Edgar Bergen and some of the other big-name Hollywood stars how to fly.

I was in desperate need of money. The few people who had jobs were lucky; there were no jobs for the millions who were out of work. I was eagerly searching for any way to make an honest dollar with my airplane.

Art and Bill said it was almost impossible to catch these horses with saddle horses, but they believed they could be corralled by using both saddle horses and the airplane. They had a buyer for the horses in Portland at one cent per pound. They thought the horses would average about 800 pounds each. That adds up to $8,000 when you count your horses before they are in the corral. The only trick to this puzzle was to catch them. They had the Double-Square brand.

The Double-Square horses had been an important source of Army horses in World War I, but after the war, there was no market for the horses. For about 15 years, these horses had the free run of the range and multiplied so fast they monopolized the range grass and water holes. There was not enough feed and water left for the wildlife such as deer and antelope, or for the cows and sheep that used that area.

A few years earlier, the counties and ranchers had pooled their resources and had hired men on horseback with rifles; I was told they had killed 8,000 of these horses just to get them off the range. They were thinking about doing that again unless we could catch them. This is what led up to the deal where Art Seale and Bill Blakely bought the horses they wanted me to help them catch.

They offered me a percentage that would make a fair deal, especially when they said if things went wrong, or if we were not successful in this venture, they would guarantee me $10 per hour and I would have a lot of flying to do.

I was not very much interested in the horse-running offer, because I had never heard of anyone succeeding at corralling horses with an airplane. The first pilot I knew of who ever tried it was a young man I had taught to fly, Cy Ralston. He was barnstorming in southern Oregon with an OX5-powered Waco 10 in 1930. A rancher, Mustang Smith, hired him to try to corral some horses he could not catch with saddle horses.

The rancher rode in the open front cockpit and used a six-shooter to try to scare the horses and make them run the way he wanted them to go. At one point in this chase, the horses were running up a mountain that was steeper than the airplane could climb. Cy landed on the side of the mountain in the sagebrush and rocks. The rancher had shot several holes in the wings, and the plane had some damage in the mountain landing. They were able to turn it around, get it pointed down the mountain, take off, and fly back to the ranch, but they did not catch the horses.

When I considered my overall situation, however, I didn't have much to lose because I was not making any money in Oregon. On this horse job, I might clean up some much-needed money real fast, enabling me to purchase an airplane with a federal license.

I accepted the offer and took off for Winnemucca, Nevada, where I was to receive more detailed instructions on the location of their mustang camp, about 80 miles northeast of Winnemucca. Pete Pedroli met me at the airport and gave me instructions on how to get to the horse camp, on the south end of the Owyhee Desert.

In flying out that way, an exhaust valve broke in my engine,

140

and I had a forced landing on the Lower Clover Ranch, owned by John G. Taylor.

The new exhaust valve was very slow in coming. After I waited four or five days for it, I became impatient and made a barnyard type repair on the broken valve stem. It was a hollow stem. I threaded the inside of it with a $5/16$-inch SAE tap, borrowed a bolt from one of my wing struts, threaded it into the valve stem, and screwed the upper part of the broken stem onto the bolt. I removed a bolt off a mowing machine to replace the bolt on the wing strut. It worked like new, and I took off and flew to the mustang camp.

The year before, 1932, Fred Gorham had 50 cowboys and an airplane out there to catch these horses. After a few hours of flying, they had about 500 horses bunched up on the desert, and the horses were surrounded by the 50 cowboys. They were going to drive them to the Humboldt Ranch, about 10 miles away, and put them in a large field. But the horses had different ideas, and they started breaking out between the cowboys. The cowboys started chasing the individual small bunches as they broke out, and they ended up losing all of them. They were not even able to rope any of them.

This was a typical horse-running story. A lot of horse-running efforts ended up with no horses being caught. It is a fairly simple job to move horses with an airplane. It usually is not too difficult to make them go where you want them to go as long as it is on their regular range, and they do not see riders or suspect a horse trap. After they see riders or the trap, they make a break for safe country, and even the airplane cannot turn them.

This type of situation became my biggest problem, and I spent a lot of time trying many different things to solve it. The story about 8,000 horses being shot on this range was not hard to believe, judging from the large number of animal bones lying all over the area.

DRY CREEK

We camped on Dry Creek (it was really dry), and we stayed in a one-room rock cabin that was built in 1873. It featured a stone fireplace in the north end where we did the cooking, a dirt floor, and three windows with very little glass. There was a large crack in the east wall that was caused by the earthquake of 1915. In earlier days, this cabin served as a stage stop, hotel, bar and store. I was told the man who built it still lived in Winnemucca. We were almost rubbing elbows with the days of the early west. Today, this cabin is just a pile of stones.

Our ground crew consisted of Art, Bill, Fred Lee, and Shorty. Fred used to be the buckaroo boss on this ranch. He said that in the 1920's the ranch, which can hardly be distinguished from the rest of the desert, sold for $150,000. The area was more thickly settled at that time.

There was a large field, perhaps 80 or 90 acres, down Dry Creek, north of the cabin. This field was long and narrow, following the creek, so the north boundary was about half a mile down the creek from the cabin. The fence around the field was very old and many of the wood posts were rotten. We hung rags, tin cans and sagebrush on the barbed wires between the posts in an effort to prevent the horses from hitting the fence. It was obvious that if they hit it with any speed, they would go right through it.

Our 1933 mustang camp on the Owyhee Desert, on Dry Creek, in Nevada. This rock house was built in 1873 and served as a stage stop, hotel, bar, store and post office. The man who built it still lived in Winnemucca at the time we camped in it. It is just a pile of stones now.

In the southwest corner of the field there was a good pole corral the cattle ranchers had properly maintained over the years. There was an old hand-dug well near the cabin. By moving some boards back, we could get water by letting a bucket down on a rope about 20 feet. We probably would not have used that water if we had known how many dead things were down there. When you get thirsty, you can drink almost anything that is wet. Maybe this explains why buckaroos drink so much really strong coffee, and so much beer and whiskey in bars. Straight water in many buckaroo camps is not very appetizing, and they get out of the habit of drinking the stuff.

My instructions were to get several bunches of horses together and bring them in through a hole in the fence at the north end of the field. Then I was to fly away, and the riders were going to put the horses into the pole corral. In a couple of weeks, a month at the most, we would all have our pockets full of money and head for home.

We thought it best to bring in a small bunch to start with, just to see how everything would function. For instance, could the horses be brought in with the airplane? Would they go through the hole in the fence? Would the fence hold them? And could the riders move them successfully from the field into the pole corral?

We only had three riders. Shorty was the cook, fence builder, and general roustabout. I wasn't sure how effective Art Seale would be on any rough riding. He had a silver plate in his skull, and he had some kind of an artificial bone in his right wrist that was installed with screws, and the screws were working loose so you could feel them.

I didn't have much trouble bringing in a small bunch of six horses. However, they would not go through the hole in the fence. Two riders appeared from behind a sagebrush ridge to help me force them through the hole in the fence. As soon as the horses saw the riders, they took off in earnest with the riders chasing them and me trying to turn them. After the horses made their break, I could not turn them, and the riders could not catch them, so we lost those horses.

On the ground again, we all went into a huddle and decided to make the hole in the fence larger. The next bunch went through the larger hole in the fence okay, and they stopped when they came to the fence inside the field. But when the riders showed up to put them into the pole corral, they took off

143

at full speed and didn't even slow down when they came to the fence on the other side of the field.

They crashed the fence at full speed. Some of them went end over end, but they got to their feet and headed for Snowstorm Mountain. I was off in the distance watching, and I flew back to the horses and tried to turn them but could not. The riders were chasing them, but they could not catch them, so we lost those horses also.

Art figured I could bring horses back after they broke back if one of them flew with me and used their sawed-off 12-gauge shotgun on them. So Art rode with me and used the shotgun when the horses would not turn from the plane.

The Waco 10 was a biplane, with struts and wires between the wings, so it was like shooting out of a bird cage. The wires and struts were hit with some of the shot, and some of the shot went through the fabric of the wings. In one respect I was lucky; Art never shot the propeller. The gun kicked so hard it pushed the hammer back into his right hand. Finally Art's right hand was so badly damaged he had to give that up. Bill tried the shotgun part, but he got too airsick to stay with it. Fred and Shorty wouldn't get in that flying machine, period.

The shooting didn't do much good anyway, because even with the shooting, I still could not bring the horses back after they had broken through the fence and had been chased by the riders. In desperation, I tied a 40-foot lariat rope on my landing gear and put some tin cans on the other end of the rope. Then I fixed a small rope near the plane so I could pull the long rope in before landing. Sometimes I would drag the cans through the sagebrush beside the horses, and sometimes I would hit the horses with the cans.

This system was more effective than the shotgun, and I considered it less dangerous, although there were some hazards associated with this idea, too. When I hit the horses with the cans or dragged the cans into a rimrock, sometimes the rope would stretch, and if it did not break, it would finally come free and fly back at the plane like it was made of rubber. Sometimes it would wrap around the wings or tail and partially foul up my controls, and sometimes the cans would tear large holes in the fabric of the plane, but this was the most promising idea I had tried. I kept experimenting with it, trying different things on the other end of the rope.

144

One bunch of eight horses that crashed through the pasture fence went three different directions. Art took after the three that went west, Fred gave chase to the two horses that headed southwest, and Bill gave chase to the three that headed south toward Snowstorm Mountain. These three were the largest horses of the eight, including the large roan stud. I could not stay with all three groups, so I stayed with the three larger horses.

I was dragging the rope and cans. I could not control them completely, but the rope and cans gave me an advantage I never had before. When on level ground, I would come in from maybe 400 yards directly in front of the horses with the cans dragging in the sagebrush most of the way. This really worried the horses and slowed them down. Sometimes they would completely stop as I got close to them. This gave Bill a chance to gain on them, but it split the three up, and they went three different directions.

I stayed with the large roan stud. For a long ways, Bill would get almost within throwing distance, whirling his rope over his head as he raced through the brush at full speed. Eventually he made several throws, but missed. We both stayed with this stud, and finally Bill got a good throw and roped him.

Art Seale roped left handed and was good at it. I snapped this picture at just the right time.

When Bill got his rope on the stud, his horse stopped, but the stud kept right on going. Bill had his rope tied to the saddle horn. When the rope came tight, the stud pulled Bill's saddle off his horse. When the saddle hit the sagebrush, Bill was still in it, upright, with his feet pointed forward, digging into the ground and bushes. The stud dragged Bill through the brush 100 feet or so, then he stopped and fell down. Bill got to his feet and walked up to the stud. The stud was dead.

I flew over Fred, who by now had given up on his chase and was riding back toward camp. I dropped him a note and directed him over to Bill so they could catch Bill's saddle horse and get back to camp, several miles away.

This and many things like it were the norm for each day as the days passed. Eventually, after I had put about 100 horses into this field, we had only four horses in the pole corral and we had to come to the conclusion that, as far as that setup was concerned, we were defeated.

RODERE FLAT

About 12 miles west of Dry Creek, on the south fork of the Little Humboldt River—a creek you could jump across almost anywhere—there was a large deep canyon. At the lower end of the canyon was a natural horse-crossing trail. We put a fence across the canyon about a half mile up from the crossing, and one across the canyon close to the crossing trail. We left a large opening for the horses to enter, that could be closed when we were not bringing horses in.

The canyon walls were rock and too steep for the horses to get out, but there were a few places on the sides where a little fencing was necessary. There was real water in this creek, and there was good grass in the canyon. The horses could stay in good condition after we caught them. At the Dry Creek location, the water was in a barrel and the horses were fed baled hay.

Wild horses do not know how to eat baled hay. It takes them two or three days in a corral before they learn to eat it. At first, when they get a mouthful of loose hay, they give it a hard pull trying to break it off at the ground like they would bunchgrass. The other end of the hay is loose and freely comes without the resistance they are used to with grass. This seems to confuse them, and they have a hard time trying to figure out what to do about it.

A short distance below our new trap canyon there was a sagebrush flat called Rodere Flat. At the upper end of Rodere Flat we set up one small tent to cook in and to store our food supply. We burned sagebrush for fuel—there was plenty of that around. We lived and slept in the open, under the sun and the stars, also in the wind, rain, snow and dust.

We found level ground and put some fluffed up baled hay on it to put our bedrolls on. We each selected our own location for this. We were well-grouped, close to the tent so the smell or sound of bacon frying in the pan would get us out of bed in the morning.

One morning as I rolled the covers back to get out of bed, I discovered a large scorpion in bed with me. I can think of a lot of things I would rather sleep with than a scorpion. (In 1985 in southern Nevada northeast of Las Vegas on the freeway, a man was found dead in his sleeping bag. A large scorpion was found in the sleeping bag.)

Sometimes saddles and related gear were kept in the tent, or in the cab of the pickup, for protection against weather. Sometimes the whole crew would crowd into the tent for protection against the weather. These accommodations were far inferior to Buckingham Palace.

With axes, we cut sagebrush on an area of Rodere Flat 30 feet wide and 675 feet long for my airport. The ground elevation was about 5,000 feet above sea level. This was not a very large airport for an airplane with no wheel brakes and an iron tailskid, but it was large enough considering the fact that our axes were dull.

This landing strip was down in a hole, with high ground all around. I had to stall in over a high ridge at the east end and drop in short to land on it, heading west. I could land headed east, but all takeoffs had to be to the west. The ground rose too much at the east end of the runway for a takeoff to the east. After a takeoff to the west, there was plenty of room for getting altitude before coming to the high ground west of Rodere Flat.

It dawned on me years later that these characters on this horse job didn't know any more about catching wild horses than I did. All three of them were top hands as cowboys and rodeo performers, but catching wild horses is a different breed of pups. Nothing else qualifies you for catching wild horses except experience catching wild horses. I considered myself pretty handy with an airplane, too, but that in itself did not qualify me to catch wild horses. However, we had gone through an extensive training period at Dry Creek, and an expensive one at that. It began to look like we might really catch some horses at this new set-up.

We did catch some horses, but our techniques for doing it were still largely experimental. Less than half the horses I brought in to this box canyon got caught. I lost track of how many times I received the news that last night someone cut the fence and let some of our horses out, or the horses broke down the fence and got out. To this day, I am not sure which it was. At Dry Creek I never heard any talk about anyone sabatoging our operations. We never caught enough horses there for anyone to get excited about, but at Rodere Flat we were really catching some horses.

Fred Gorham and his right-hand man were camped out on the desert a few miles from our camp. They were not always at the same place, but most of the time they were in the general area where they could see what we were doing. The rest of the crew figured Fred might be worried because we were catching horses. He had his $1,000. Maybe he didn't want us to catch them, so he could sell them to someone else for another $1,000. This was all just speculation.

Any mustanger worth his salt knows horses are harder to catch after they have gotten away. All the horses that got away from us at Dry Creek, plus all the horses that were getting out of our canyon trap, just compounded our problems of bringing the next horses in.

There was an old abandoned Model T Ford lying in the tall sagebrush just beyond the west end of the runway. One day I took the four connecting rods out of it and tied them to the other end of my rope. I figured something other than tin cans would be better, but it didn't take me long to discard this idea. On the second horse run out with the connecting rods, I ran them directly into the face of a cliff and the rope broke, so I went back to the cans.

The propeller of my plane was called a Micarta propeller. It had a steel hub with Micarta blades, which were layers of cloth bonded together under pressure with some material that resembled plastic. The summer and fall of 1933 was very hot and dry, and where the Micarta blades were inserted into the steel hub, they shrank. When I tightened the two bolts that held the blades firmly in the hub, the blades were still loose. I tightened the bolts too tight and stripped out the threads on one of the nuts.

I went back to the Model T and took a nut off a main bearing cap. It was just the right size. The hub end of the propeller blades still had to be made larger. We had a small can of red enamel paint in camp. I painted the hub end of the blades with the enamel and let it harden overnight. The thickness of the paint made the hubs larger so they fit tight. Then with the Model T main-bearing nut, this problem was solved, horse camp style.

Another time, a sagebrush stump went through one of my tires and caused a flat tire. We had a jack and a tire pump in camp, but no inner tube patching material. I borrowed an $8/32$ machine screw from my instrument panel and forced the head of the machine screw through the hole in the inner tube. I stretched the hole enough to get a small flat washer through it. Then I put a small flat washer and nut on the machine screw. I held the outer end of the machine screw with pliers while I tightened the nut, squeezing the two flat washers against the rubber. Then I filed off the outer end of the machine screw flush with the nut. Another problem solved, horse camp style. I never did replace that tube repair.

Fred and Shorty told us about an incident that happened on Rodere Flat a couple of years earlier. Sheriff Graham Lamb of Humboldt County was pursuing an outlaw, and he found the outlaw in his tent about 100 yards south of where the Model T lay. Lamb shot the outlaw and killed him while he was eating a plate of beans in his tent. No doubt, there are a lot of details we do not know. Anyway, our crew felt the sheriff should not have killed the man under those circumstances.

Before this horse job was finished, I had an occasion to meet Sheriff Lamb, under circumstances where he could have been a problem to us, but he proved to be a real friend. He was shot and killed three weeks after our go-around with these horses.

While we were camped at Rodere Flat, a large band of sheep moved slowly through our horse-running area. The herder told us a bank had foreclosed on the owner, and the bank was taking the sheep. After they went past our camp, Art found two old ewes that had been left behind. I do not know if they were old and weak and could not keep up with the band or if they just became lost from the band. Anyway, we ate mutton for quite a while. It would not surprise me if Art had run them out of the band while the herder was not looking. No one in our camp would have figured stealing a sheep from a bank was as big a crime as stealing it from a rancher.

Mutton was not one of my favorite dishes, but we ate many things in this horse camp that would not have rated very high in a cooking contest. One of the things we ate out there was called "sonofabitch." I never was able to find out what was in it, but it tasted okay.

13

MOUNTAIN CRASH

After about 300 horses had been put in the trap canyon, they all had gotten out except about 130 horses. One morning, leaving on my early flight, I told the crew I was going to fly north and bring horses in from the Owyhee Desert. But after I was in the air, I saw several large bunches of horses south of our camp on the lower slopes of Snowstorm Mountain. I changed my mind and headed south.

I selected a bunch of 14 and went after them. Obviously they were some that had gotten away from us, because they would not turn. They ran south toward the top of the mountain instead of north toward our trap canyon.

By this time, I was beginning to develop some horse psychology, so I just let them run to the top of the mountain. I had learned it is easier to turn tough horses after they get to wherever it is they are headed. These horses would probably turn easier after they reached the top of the mountain. However, on the way up, they split up into groups of six and eight, so I stayed with the eight.

As they reached the top of the mountain, I went in on them and hit the leader with the five-gallon square kerosene can that was on the end of my rope. Then I pulled up under full power and was getting into a position to come right back on them when, at the top of my climb, the engine suddenly quit. This was my first power failure since the valve stem broke, and even then there was still power on six cylinders. This time I lost all of my power, suddenly and without warning.

I was on the south side of the top of the mountain. There was plenty of ground south of me that could have been reached with a dead engine, but in the very limited time I had to make a decision, this low ground looked broken and rough. The smoothest place was the ridge right on top of the mountain, so I headed for that. Under the circumstances, I had no time to pull in my rope. Down I went, but under control.

There was about a 10-mile-per-hour tailwind I did not know about. As I maneuvered for my chosen landing place, I began to suspect this and did several violent fishtails, which helped, but I still came in too high and too fast. The rope and can hit first and were dragging through the rocks as I pulled the stabilizer control and stick all the way back and put the tailskid on the mountain while the wheels were still in the air.

This was the slowest possible landing in these conditions. The air at 8,000 feet is very thin, which increased the landing speed, and the tailwind increased it even more. I was really traveling when the plane contacted the mountain. I turned off the gas and switch, hoping to avoid fire.

The top of the mountain was made of rocks. As the plane contacted the mountain, the right tire blew out. If I could have made a slight left turn after landing, I could have stayed on top of the mountain; but with the right tire flat, a tailwind, an iron tailskid and no wheel brakes, even though I applied full left rudder, full right aileron and full back stick, the plane was still turning to the right.

Someone had built a rock monument on top of the mountain, and the plane was headed directly for that. It was plain to see we were going over the top of the mountain and down the other side. It was the down the other side part I did not like. The north side of the mountain was very steep. There might have been a rimrock on that side, but I was not sure about that. Anyway, I quickly decided I did not want to be in the plane when it started down the other side.

Just before the plane hit the rock monument, I unbuckled my safety belt and wasted no time in jumping over the left side of the cockpit, head first, like a bullfrog. The plane was still traveling about 30 miles per hour when I left it.

I had on a heavy leather jacket, heavy gloves, leather helmet and goggles. Pilots then were advised to remove their goggles in case of a crash to protect their eyes from shattered glass, but you do not always think of everything in a situation like that. I forgot to remove my goggles, but they were supposed to have shatter- proof glass. The glass over my right eye was badly bro-

Pre-crash leap on Snowstorm Mountain.

ken, but none of it got in my eyes. Maybe they were closed. If I
had removed the goggles, the rock that broke that glass might
have done some serious damage to my right eye. I still have
that shattered glass as a souvenir.

The heavy clothing helped shield me from the rocks. My
hands and arms hit first and took some of the strain. When my
head hit the rocks, I went out like a light. When I regained con-
sciousness, all the noise had died down, and I had never experienced such silence. There was a large pool of blood on the
ground, and I was bleeding badly from my nose and mouth. I
became concerned and weak from loss of blood.

I slowly made my way to the edge of the mountain and saw
the plane lying upside down on the north slope of the mountain. There was no rimrock there, but it was very steep and a
long way down. Making my way to the plane, I crawled up inside the rear cockpit, removed the first-aid kit, broke the glass
tube that keeps people from fainting, and smelled it while it
lasted. That pepped me up some. Then I poured something
from a bottle into my mouth and nose. I was still bleeding badly
and was beginning to wonder how much blood I could lose and
still remain operational.

The north side of the mountain faces slightly east, and the
early morning sun was warm there at the plane. There was no
wind as it was coming from the other side of the mountain. I
lay down on the under side of the upper wing and went to

sleep. I figured keeping quiet would do more than anything else to stop the bleeding, and it would keep me away from the rattlesnakes and scorpions.

When I woke up, the bleeding had stopped. I felt a little better, but was very weak and thirsty. There was no water available.

After analyzing the situation, I figured if I had stayed in the plane, with my weight in the rear cockpit, and the fact that I would have naturally held the stick all the way back, the plane would not have turned over where it did. Remaining upright on its wheels, it would have gone all the way to the bottom of the mountain, gaining speed all the way and even possibly becoming airborne again. So I still figure jumping out before it went over the top was the right thing to do.

The ground crew and I had an understanding all along that if I ever crashed on a horse run, I would build a fire, if I was able, so the crew could see the smoke and know where to come after me. There was nothing up there to build a fire with except to burn the airplane, and I didn't want to do that.

Our horse camp was about 10 miles north. Four hours after I

It was one of those days. Waco 10 with 165-horsepower Comet engine on 8,000-foot Snowstorm Mountain, on Nevada mustang job, 1933.

took off, the crew would know I was down somewhere because my gas supply would have been exhausted. I had told the crew I was going north but had gone south, so they would be looking for me in the wrong direction.

I started walking off the mountain. About halfway down, there was a tight mass of mesquite brush that was higher than my head. Right in the middle of this brush, I started a fire and sat down to relax a little.

When I realized how fast the fire was spreading, I was not sure I could get out of the brush ahead of the fire. As I was trying to beat the fire out, I was bothered by the thought of becoming unconscious and not being able to get out in time.

After getting out of the brush, I was more thirsty and feverish than ever. There was no water around, so I continued slowly on my way. I figured the crew at camp would see the smoke from the fire, as this side of the mountain faced toward our camp.

Finally I reached the bottom of the mountain and was in tall thick sagebrush when I saw an animal headed my direction. I did not have a gun with me and did not feel in condition for any hand-to-hand combat, so I hid myself as well as I could. As it

Snowstorm Mountain crash. The rope seen going over the fuselage had a square 5-gallon kerosene can on its outer end.

came nearer me, I could see it was a large coyote. It went by without detecting my presence.

After three hours of walking, I was about three miles from the plane when Bill Blakely rode up to me on his saddle horse. I was weak and thirsty. Bill said the crew saw me head south so they had known which direction I went. All morning they had seen the sun reflecting off the silver wings of the plane up on the mountain. At that distance however, they were not sure it was my plane. After they decided I was down, they started riding that direction; then they saw the smoke from my fire.

It had been a long time since I had been on a horse, but I got on behind the saddle, and we headed for camp. I do not remember anything that was more torture than that seven-mile horseback ride. There was no drinking water between us and camp, but riding was faster than I could have walked.

Since I had not shaved for a couple of weeks, I was a bloody looking mess when we reached camp. About four days later, we drove to Winnemucca, and I went to a barber shop and a doctor. The barber did more for me than the doctor. My only injuries seemed to be loose teeth and a combination of pain and numbness on the right side of my face. There was nothing for the doctor to fix. The right side of my face is still partially numb from that experience of 53 years ago.

We had about 130 horses in our canyon, and the crew started making preparations to drive them 80 miles to Winnemucca where they could be shipped to Portland in railroad cars. One front leg on each horse was tied up the first day so as not to lose them. This was hard on the horses, and some of them died on the way to Winnemucca. It was also hard on the crew to rope all those horses and tie up one front leg; later, they had to catch them again and untie their legs for the second day of travel.

It required four days on the trail to reach Winnemucca. My job was to drive the pickup and have the camp supplies at each overnight location. The day the horses arrived in Winnemucca I drove the pickup into town ahead of them, and was parked near the main street, sitting in the pickup writing a letter to Margaret. The pickup did not have a license on it, and I was a little nervous about that. It was loaded with miscellaneous horse camp gear and had several saddles on top of the load.

Sheriff Lamb and his deputy drove up and parked right in front of me. They got out of their car and walked back to the pickup and started looking it all over. Then the sheriff asked me who I was and who owned the pickup. I had never met him, but he knew all about our horse-running project. He said the night before someone had stolen two saddles. He was satisfied the saddles on the pickup were not the saddles they were looking for. We had a nice long visit, and he was interested in hearing more about our experience with the horses. When they left, they had not even mentioned anything about the pickup not having a license.

Of the 400 horses we had corralled, only about 120 were shipped. A lot of them had gotten away. The 120 that were shipped sold for one cent per pound, bringing about $7 each.

The horse buyers had already advanced Art and Bill some money, and obviously there was not enough money to go around. I never received a dime. After the horses were shipped, we all went back to camp.

After deducting the airplane operating expenses, such as gas and oil, Art and Bill still owed me over $1,000 if they were going to live up to their agreement. I had certainly lived up to my part of the bargain, but they did not have the money to pay me.

They said the Sletcher Brothers in Portland who bought the horses were really the ones who owed me because they were financing the whole operation. They had a slaughterhouse and meat packing plant there.

When we returned to camp, Fred drove his pickup out, so we had two pickups in camp. They were all going to help me get the Waco off the mountain, but they wanted to go to Elko first. I had no interest in Elko, so I stayed in camp alone as they left in the two pickups. They said they would be back the next day.

They did not return the next day or the next, and I was getting fed up with the situation. I did not believe they had much more money with them than I had, and I didn't have any, not a cent. Maybe they took their sawed-off shotgun with them and held up a bank. After all, what did I really know about these men?

HITCHHIKING

On the fifth day at nine o'clock in the evening, I decided that was enough. Without money or transportation, I started walking toward the Bullhead Ranch which was 28 miles west of our camp. In the middle of the night an animal, right at my feet, jumped up, loudly rattling the bushes, and scurried away through the brush, but not before I jumped about 10 feet and grabbed my German Luger out of the holster and prepared to defend myself. It was probably a porcupine and probably was more scared of me than I was of him—if that were possible. I arrived at the Bullhead Ranch at 6 a.m., just in time to enjoy a real ranch breakfast—eggs, fried potatoes, beefsteak, coffee, and sourdough biscuits.

After breakfast, the foreman, George Able, drove me to Winnemucca. I borrowed $5 on my German Luger from a friend, Hap Hapgood, who owned the auto wrecking yard there, and started hitchhiking toward home.

When I reached our home in Bend, Margaret and our baby daughter were not there; they were with Margaret's mother in Salem. I wanted to try to get my $1,000 from the Sletcher Brothers, so I continued on to Portland.

When I reached their office, I sat in the waiting room with their stenographer while I waited to get in to see Mr. Sletcher, who was in the next room talking to a con-man type who was trying to convince him he should join his "protective association" for $500. The wall was thin so I could hear everything they said.

If Mr. Sletcher joined his protective association, he would be assured that when he shipped a carload of meat to Chicago the

Homeward bound after mountain crash in Nevada. My mother, wife Margaret, and one-year-old daughter, Beverly.

boxcar would be promptly parked where the meat could be quickly taken care of. If he did not join this association, the boxcar might get parked on a sidetrack, and the meat might spoil. When this man left, the stenographer issued him a check for $500.

I explained my problems to Mr. Sletcher, but he accepted no responsibility there. He said I would have to collect my money from Art and Bill. I have never collected a penny of it.

I continued hitchhiking on to Salem and got a ride from Swan Island to Salem with Lee Eyerly in his new Stinson Monoplane. When I reached my family, I had traveled about 900 miles since leaving Winnemucca with $5 in my pocket. I still had $4.

RETRIEVAL FROM SNOWSTORM MOUNTAIN

I was finally becoming aware of the fact that things were not developing into exactly what I had in mind when I ventured boldly forth with a freshly won pilot's license in my pocket. After this Nevada mustang experience, I was probably suffering from battle fatigue from all that had gone before and still had to face the uncertain depths of our Great Depression. My main concern now became supporting a family under what seemed to be an impossible situation.

Now, once again, there was no airplane in all of central Oregon. I did what work could be found such as picking up potatoes for a farmer. Even he could pay me no money. I had to take potatoes for my work, and there was no market for the potatoes.

One of my better jobs during this period was working on a government WPA project for $15 per week. We could live on that, but it left no money for retirement plans, doctor expenses, or money for retrieving our wrecked Waco from Nevada, and rebuilding it.

Early in November, one of my students, Fred Bembry, and I left Bend for Nevada in our 1930 Chevrolet sedan to get the Waco off Snowstorm Mountain. I had very little cash, so we took along all the 100-pound sacks of potatoes the Chevrolet could handle. Some of them were tied on the fenders.

As the trip progressed, we sold some of these potatoes for traveling money and traded some for gas. On the second day, we finally reached George Reed's ranch in Paradise Valley, which was about 40 miles from where the airplane lay upside down on the mountain. Because of Reed's hospitality and his interest in airplanes and mustangs, his ranch became our base for airplane salvage. The ranch was mortgaged for more than it was worth, and the payments on the mortgage were past due. He couldn't even pay the interest, but the man who held the mortgage was very patient and took what he could get over the lean years in hopes of collecting more later. That fall, of 1933, steers sold for five cents a pound.

George outfitted us with a grubstake. We borrowed the light spring wagon his mother and father had proudly purchased new in 1910—their most cherished possession for many years. He also loaned us two stout, gentle horses that even we could handle. Off Fred and I went on a 40-mile trip with the team and wagon. Neither one of us were horsemen in any sense of the word. Forty miles of this kind of travel was a big adventure for us.

Nightfall found us camped at the old Leighton Place, perhaps a little farther than halfway to our destination. This place consisted of a one-room stone cellar, some trees, and a spring with some green grass around it.

The story that goes with this place is that a Mr. Leighton lived here all alone and he spent a lot of time prospecting. Every time he went to town, he had an abundance of gold to buy whatever he needed. No one was ever able to find out where he got it, and when he eventually died, his secret went to the grave with him. We didn't find it either. Forty years later a prospector hired me to fly him over that area in a Supercub, hoping he could see from the air the place where Mr. Leighton might have gotten his gold.

The next evening, we camped on a creek at the foot of Snowstorm Mountain about three miles from the plane. This was the night of November 15. I had made my crash landing up there on September 15, and since it had been there two months, I was concerned about its safety. Almost anything could have happened to it in that length of time. After we made camp, there was almost an hour of sun yet, so I decided to walk up and have a look. There had been a clear sky and a full moon the night before, so I figured I could get down off the mountain in the moonlight. Fred stayed at camp to have something ready to eat when I got back.

It got later than I had expected. The sun went down a good half hour before I reached the plane, and instead of a clear sky, a heavy dark overcast was forming. It was rather dark when I reached the place where the plane lay, but I was pleasantly surprised to find it exactly as I had left it. The wind had not moved it, and there were no signs of anyone having been there.

It was getting so dark I didn't think it was safe to try to get back to camp before morning as there were cliffs to stumble over in the dark. At one place, there was a choice of three ridges to take. Only the middle ridge would lead me to camp, and I could not see which ridge to choose in the dark. The German Luger was with me but I only had seven cartridges for it. The sagebrush up there at 8,000 feet was too short for firewood, and it would get very cold before morning.

I was just lying there on the side of the mountain beside the airplane, trying to decide what to do when suddenly I jumped to my feet and grabbed the Luger out of the holster, trying hard to look into the darkness to see what had spooked me. I did not hear or see anything but just suddenly became frightened. As I stood there peering into the darkness, I became nervous and started walking slowly toward camp. I had gone only a few yards when I heard padded footsteps in the rocks near me. As soon as I heard this movement, I stopped. I did not know from which direction the sound came, so I started walking again, and again I heard the footsteps. They were following me. So I stopped again, and this time the footsteps did not stop when I did. They kept right on stepping; then they stopped again. This gave me the direction they were coming from.

I had heard a lot of wild campfire stories about this country, but I didn't really know what to expect. I figured if it was a pack of wolves, I didn't have enough cartridges to hold them off. If I never knew it before, I learned right there I was not cut out to be a hero because I was really scared. Nevertheless, I figured we might as well have it out right there. Knowing where the footsteps stopped, I ran directly toward whatever it was, yelling like a wild Indian. I had progressed only about 50 feet when there it was, standing before me broadside. As soon as I saw it, I stopped.

The Luger was in my hand, the safety was off, and it was ready for instant action. The animal looked like a large mountain lion. Not knowing for sure what it was, and not knowing how many partners he might have out there in the darkness, and only having seven cartridges, I figured I couldn't risk wild shots in the dark, so I stood there and held my ground. I was waiting for him to make the next move. If he came at me, I would shoot to kill, and if he went the other way I would let him go.

In a short while, he walked slowly away from me and disappeared in the darkness. This gave him the advantage of a surprise attack from some other direction when I might not be looking, but I decided to take that chance. I also decided to head for camp regardless of the consequences. I slowly and cautiously started feeling my way in the dark along a three-mile journey off that mountain.

The first barrier was a large snowdrift on the steepest part of the mountain. The next obstacle was a large patch of very thick mesquite brush that was higher than my head. This really bothered me because an animal could spring on me from close quarters as I was crawling through this brush on my hands and knees part of the time.

Finally I stood at the base of the mountain where there was the choice of three ridges. Only the center ridge would lead me to camp. As I stood there on what I believed was the beginning of the center ridge, I decided to risk a shot. So I fired once in what I thought was the direction of our camp, in hopes of Fred hearing it and answering back with another shot, but he did not hear it. He told me later he figured the horses heard the shot, because they almost broke away about the time I had fired the shot.

After receiving no answer from the shot, I decided to take a guess on which way camp was, so I headed out where I thought the center ridge would be. Instead of coming out on the center ridge, I ended up in the bottom of a deep canyon.

I figured I could not be very far off on my navigation, and that the ridge I wanted was either on my right or on my left. There was no way of figuring which one it was most likely to be. For lack of any better idea, I decided to climb out of the canyon on my right. When I came to the top of the ridge, I followed it.

When I came to the end of the ridge, it dropped sharply off into the big gorge our camp was in. I still did not know if our camp was straight ahead of me or to my right or my left. I had not seen any more of my animal friend, so I decided to risk another shot. I fired directly across the main gorge, and in a very short while I heard an answering shot directly ahead of me. By the time I moved another hundred feet, I saw the campfire directly ahead of me.

This was a welcome sight, and I tried going a little faster after seeing the campfire. The steepness of the slope made any speed impractical, and the light from the campfire destroyed some of the night vision I had acquired earlier. At one place, I lost my footing and slid and rolled a long distance down the slope before I could grab a bush and get stopped. I got a few bruises and tore my clothes, but made it to camp okay, took on some nourishment, and went to bed.

The next morning, I looked up to where I had lost my footing and saw that if I had been a few feet more to the south, I would have gone over a cliff of considerable height.

We got an early start that morning and drove the team and wagon right up to the top of the mountain from behind, on the south slope. The plane was lying upside down near the top, and we had a rope long enough to pull it to the top of the mountain.

We started dismantling the plane so we could get it right side up. We took all the tail surfaces off and had both left wings off. Then we managed to turn it over with the help of the horses and got it right side up with the tail pointed up the mountain.

We fastened the rope to the tail and had the horses on top of the mountain at the other end of the rope. Fred drove the horses, and I was going to steady the plane as we pulled it to the top of the mountain where it would be easier to finish dismantling it.

As the horses started pulling, the rope tightened, and the plane moved up the mountain a few feet. Then the rope broke, and the plane started down the mountain. I tried to hold it, but it was too much for me, and I took a beating, tearing my clothes again in the process. I was forced to let loose of the plane, and it gained momentum rapidly as it sped down the steep mountain slope.

The farther it went, the higher the tail went until it finally nosed over completely. Then it did another 'flip and stood directly on its tail, pivoted 180 degrees, flopped down with a loud thud, and stopped. I had just seen an instant replay of approximately what would have happened if I had not jumped out of the plane on that crash landing before it went over the top of the mountain.

This really wrecked things and caused a great deal more damage than the crash landing had. Now the plane was way out of reach of our rope, which was not strong enough anyway. We could see no possible way to overcome the obstacles that confronted us. We loaded the small parts we could get on the wagon and headed back to the Reed Ranch, following the same tracks we made coming up.

George thought we could still get the plane off the mountain by using a long length of steel cable he had on the ranch. Fred had more important things to do. He had a date to get married back in Bend and could not spare the time to go back for another try. I let him take the Chevrolet back to Bend. George, his father-in-law, Ransom, and I headed back for Snowstorm Mountain in the spring wagon with a fresh grubstake and plenty of steel cable. Ransom rode a saddle horse.

With George's wider experience at such things and his greater enthusiasm for salvaging what was left of the plane, we succeeded in getting it to the top of the mountain. We tied the wings on the sides of the fuselage and started trailing it off, with the tail end of the fuselage up on the back of the wagon.

With the airplane behind the wagon we could not go down the mountain on the same tracks we used going up because there was one place there that had too steep a side slope to pull the airplane over, so we chose a different route to get the airplane off the mountain.

We approached a very steep ridge we had to go down. I did not believe it was possible to go down there with that load behind the light spring wagon. I tried to talk George and Ransom into abandoning the plane there and just leaving it; it was not worth losing a life over or wrecking the wagon and possibly killing the horses. George's interest in salvaging the plane was greater than mine at this point. He insisted it could be done.

Ransom was on the saddle horse. He tied his horsehair rope on the back of the wagon and had some turns around his saddle horn. He said the horse he was riding was one of the best horses he had ever seen for holding back on things like this. There was no road or trail of any kind to follow. A horsehair rope is more slick than other kinds of rope, making it harder to hold the turns on the saddle horn. George warned Ransom to get a good hold on the end of his rope because he would not be able to stop after starting down the steep part.

As we started down the steep part, Ransom was holding back all he could. George had the brakes set hard and was on the seat handling the horses. I was holding onto the wagon and dragging my feet into the ground and bushes. Part way down, Ransom's rope slipped out of his hand. With great effort and skillful handling of the horses and with my help, George got the load stopped. I quickly handed Ransom the end of his rope, but before he could get his turns on the saddle horn and a good hold on the rope, the horses could hold it no longer, and it started to roll again. By the time it had gone another short distance, Ransom lost his rope again.

I was still sliding my feet into the ground and bushes, but the wagon kept gaining speed, and I had to let loose. This time George could not hold it, and it rapidly gained speed as it plunged down the steep slope. The only hope George had to avoid a tragedy was to get closer to one—he had to keep the horses ahead of the load.

He stood up in the wagon swinging his whip and yelling orders to the horses to get their highest possible speed all the way down in an attempt to keep them ahead of the heavy load that was pushing them. If either of the horses had stepped in a badger hole or stumbled for any reason, the results would have been tragic. I have never before nor since seen such a sight as this. When George reached the bottom and came to a stop, everything was still right side up.

After that go-around, anything else that could have happened would have been tame. The rest of the trip back to the ranch was relaxing and uneventful.

When the dew is on the runway
And the altitude gets rare,
Keep an eye on the gauges
And watch the outside air.

14

ODD JOBS

After returning to central Oregon with my Nevada mustang experience behind me, a wrecked airplane I could not afford to rebuild, and a family to support, with no work of any kind available, I began to develop a feeling we were not living in the utopia our forefathers had in mind when they laid out the blueprints for this country.

Millions unemployed. Countless breadlines. Big financiers in our eastern cities jumping out of skyscraper windows. Banks going broke all over the country. It seemed the only people making any money were the bankers themselves as they skedaddled out the back door with their satchels full of money, while their employees were locking the front door.

I became disillusioned at the fare our society was dishing out to us, although we probably fared as well as or maybe even a little better than some. It was still far from the life I had looked forward to, and it caused me to question the wisdom or integrity, or both, of the people we hire to run this country.

If our newspaper editors knew any important answers, they preferred to ride on their prerogative of "freedom of the press" and continue to ignore the people's right to know the truth. They continued to feed the public their usual meaningless chatter that only deepened the mystery of what could be done to improve things.

Finally, a very forceful leader, actually a dictator, by the name of Franklin Roosevelt, came along under the banner of democracy. He got things in this country moving again, but his course of action put us in World War II. We really do not know yet if he was an asset or a liability to us. Some day we might decide he merely handed the control of our destiny from one bunch of crooks to a different set of crooks, because something very serious still appears to be wrong with the management of our world, and we seem to be no closer to solving the problems that confront us today than we were to solving the problems that confronted us in the depths of the Great Depression.

I remained solidly earthbound for the remainder of 1933. In the spring of 1934 a man in Redmond, Selby Towner, bought a 45-horsepower Curtiss Pusher in Reno, Nevada, for $400. I went with him to Reno and flew the plane back to Oregon. I obtained a federal pilot license and taught him to fly; I operated the plane commercially for two years during any time I could spare while still doing any other kind of work I could find to do.

During my Curtiss Pusher flying days I landed a job driving a lumber carrier (some people called them straddle bugs) at a lumber mill in Redmond, for 50 cents per hour. That put us in the "chips," and we bought a 40-acre farm a couple of miles west of Redmond. I was flying all I could— early mornings, evenings, weekends and holidays. There was not enough flying to make a living, but it kept me involved in aviation and supplied some income in addition to my other work.

When the lumber mill built a shop for maintaining its equipment, I took the job of operating the shop. With two employees working under me, I accepted the responsibility of keeping the lumber carriers, planing mill, lumber mill, and trucks in operating condition. I bought a new lathe and learned to operate it

The Curtiss Pusher with a 45-horsepower Zekeley engine that I flew for two years, 1934-1935.

on the job. We did all the mechanical work, welding, and lathe work to keep things operating.

Eventually Selby sold the Pusher to a man in Idaho, and bought a new 40-horsepower J-2 Cub that was just coming on the market. I flew the Cub commercially for about a year, after which I organized a flying club in Prineville. The club members put in enough money to pay $1,395 cash for a new 50-horse-power J-3 Piper Cub that was Piper's latest model at that time.

My main interest was flying, and when I finally had the Prineville Flying Club going, we sold our farm, moved to Prineville, and went whole-hog into flying.

I taught the club members to fly and did any other flying jobs available. During this period, our daughter, Beverly, started first grade at the Prineville school. Her teachers asked all the first graders what kind of work their daddies did. Beverly said, "My daddy doesn't work. He just goes up to the airport and plays around with the airplane."

Eventually this flying activity slowed down enough that I located a job driving a lumber carrier at a Prineville sawmill, for 50 cents per hour (which was good money for those days), and I still did all the flying there was to do in the area.

From this we took on the job of operating the cookhouse

Our daughter Beverly, the Curtiss Pusher and me, 1934, Redmond, Oregon.

there, feeding the mill employees four meals a day, which included a midnight meal. This was Margaret's burden. She held up under it surprisingly well, with two small children to care for. I quit my job driving the lumber carrier, established a grocery store and meat market there, and became a meat-cutter, self-style.

As Hitler's war in Europe was building up steam, our government decided to take flight training seriously. A program was started that required all flight instructors to take a re-rating course at government expense in order to continue as instructors. I went to Seattle and took the re-rating course, then went back to the Washington Aircraft Company at Boeing Field as a flight instructor.

CARBURETOR HEAT CONTROL

During my Curtiss Pusher, J-2 and J-3 Cub flying days, I had learned about carburetor ice and how to control it. This had been one of my most serious obstacles to having a successful flying business in my OX5 Waco flying days. Even as we were learning how to control this problem, it was still the cause of many forced landings and crashes because controlling it required the pilot to understand how to control it; and it required the pilot to remember to apply carburetor heat every time he closed the throttle.

Ice can form in the carburetor when the outside air temperature is warmer than freezing. When ice first starts forming in the carburetor, you are not aware of it; it is necessary for a large amount of ice to accumulate before the engine begins to malfunction while you are using cruising or full power. However, even before there is enough ice in the carburetor for the pilot to become aware of it, the engine will stop on idle if, for any reason, the throttle is closed. This will happen if the throttle is closed for training maneuvers like stalls, tailspins, or approaches to landings. Therefore, any time you are airborne it is important to always apply carburetor heat just before closing the throttle, to melt any possible ice formation out of the carburetor.

One day at Seattle I was out with a student in a two-place Aeronca. We were flying between Seattle and Bremerton, over Puget Sound, with nothing but water under us. At 4,500 feet, I decided to give my student some instructions on tailspins—a dumb thing to do over water. We both forgot to apply carburetor heat. Right in the middle of our tailspin, the propeller stopped. This plane did not have an electric starter. We both had parachutes on, but it would not be any fun to land in water that possibly had sharks in it, with a parachute, miles from shore without any kind of a life preserver.

In my OX5 flying days, just to give the spectators a thrill, I would stop the propeller 1,200 feet above the ground; then, by making a steep dive the propeller would start rotating again at the bottom of my dive right in front of the spectators. These OX5 engines had low compression and an eight-foot propeller, which made this an easy and safe maneuver to perform.

I had never tried to start a 65-horsepower Continental engine this way; these engines had higher compression and smaller propellers, so I was not sure this stunt would work on them. However, this was our only way out of this situation, so I really pointed the nose of the plane for the center of the earth. The airspeed needle went way past the red-line, but the operation was successful; the propeller started turning and everything was OK. (A word of advice to anyone trying this: Turn the switch off until the propeller starts turning; otherwise it might kick backwards, requiring a longer dive.)

This experience gave me the incentive to get serious about

Ice in the carburetor gave me a deadstick landing. This is where I landed.

figuring out a method of having the carburetor heat applied automatically every time the throttle was closed. I figured out a mechanism that would automatically apply carburetor heat every time the throttle was closed, and automatically put cold air in the carburetor when the throttle was opened. Cold air is very desirable when you need full power, like for a takeoff. Also, my mechanism permitted the pilot to have an overriding control so he could apply hot air when the throttle was open, when he needed it under certain icing conditions.

I applied for a patent on this mechanism, built several units, and installed them on a local airplane for test flights. It proved to do the job very well. Then I needed to locate someone who would take this idea, do further development work and engineering on it, and go through the necessary testing to obtain federal approval to use it on federally licensed airplanes. I did not have the money, time, or facilities to do this myself.

We lived on the west side of Angle Lake, a few miles out of Seattle, in a real nice log house that had appropriate shrubbery and a fish pond and a sloping yard down to the lake where there was a boat dock and diving boards. It was beautiful even

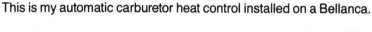

This is my automatic carburetor heat control installed on a Bellanca.

in the winter when everything was covered with 10 inches of snow.

FLIGHT TRAINER

Perhaps the thing I enjoyed most about our home at Angle Lake was my workshop in the basement where I spent my off-duty tinkering hours developing the automatic carburetor heat control, and at the same time I was making progress on developing my ideas of a primary flight trainer. This was a machine a student could sit in on the ground and learn a large part of what he would need to know to fly an airplane.

Such a machine already existed for teaching instrument fly-

Beverly and Curtis in front of their playhouse at Angle Lake on Beverly's eighth birthday, June 22, 1941.

ing. This was the "Link Trainer." It was a very good machine and was widely used, but it had no value as a primary flight trainer. We needed something beginners could use to help them learn flying in their primary stage of learning. I began on paper to design such a machine while we still lived in Prineville and continued working on this idea after we moved to Seattle.

My first machine, in Seattle, resulted in a simple machine that gave students practice on coordinating the rudder and aileron applications only. It did not give instructions on controlling banks and turns or climbing and gliding or pointing out the differences of rudder and aileron coordination at different airspeeds, which I considered important. So I continued development work on this flight trainer until it did all of these things.

I had purchased a 10-inch Atlas metal-cutting lathe and had other shop equipment such as electric grinders, drills, etc. I could not afford these kinds of luxuries in the OX5 flying days.

This was my early model trainer for students to practice rudder and aileron control coordination. In just a few minutes it could be changed from wheel to stick control. The lever at right rear was for the instructor to apply rough air. Boeing Field, Seattle.

For the first time in my life, I was receiving a monthly paycheck for flying, had a nice place to live, and had a few hours each day and a few days each month to call my own.

I was flying six days a week and making more money than I had ever made before. My base pay was $300 per month. I did a little extra flying besides what I was specifically hired for on the flight training program and was paid extra for that. Our country was finally recognizing the value of the talents I had acquired while practically making an outlaw out of me in my home community.

While I was on the job in Seattle, the Japanese attacked Pearl Harbor, and we were suddenly in a full-scale war. Seattle became a major ship-building area, as well as a major airplane producing area, since that was the home of the Boeing Aircraft Company.

My employer, Washington Aircraft and Transport Corporation, was much involved in flight training, aircraft sales, service, and maintenance. Elliot Merril, who was part owner, had an illustrious background in aviation himself, was getting involved as a test pilot for the Boeing Aircraft Company and later became Boeing's chief test pilot.

The company was not interested in becoming actively involved with developing, manufacturing, and marketing my carburetor heat control or my primary flight trainer, although I was encouraged to continue development work on them.

I contacted another company in Seattle, C & H Supply Company, owned by Phil Coffer and Kay Houston, which was interested in getting involved in manufacturing and marketing both units. I joined them, and we moved to Glendale, California, where we set up a factory to produce these items. The war greatly interfered with our ability to purchase the needed materials and caused extra hardships and delays in getting into production.

In the process of developing the flight trainer, I gave a lot of study to rudder and aileron control coordination. The explanations in books on this subject were not completely satisfactory. It seemed there were some important things about rudder and aileron control coordination, and also about quick stall recovery, that were not understood.

As a result of my study in connection with developing the flight trainer, along with my actual experience teaching those

174

subjects on flight training programs, I finally started coming up with some answers that explained why an airplane will sometimes "spin over the top" from a stall in a steep turn, and at other times will spin in the direction of the turn, also how it can be prevented from spinning in either direction.

This was important because it is common knowledge among pilots that a plane can rather easily be prevented from going into a tailspin if it is stalled in level flight, but it nearly always goes into a tailspin when it is stalled in a turn.

A government inspector at Boeing Field flunked one of my students on a commercial flight test because he was "skidding" on his 720-degree power turns. The inspector admitted the "ball" was centered, but he said, "To hell with the ball. You had your controls crossed. You were using top aileron and bottom rudder." Therefore he flunked him because "everybody knows your controls should be in neutral in a turn."

It seemed incredible to me that as late as 1941 there were pilots, including government inspectors, who were actually very good pilots, with a lot of flying experience, who did not understand proper rudder and aileron control coordination.

The inspector required me to give the student five more hours of dual. I simply instructed him to make his turns the way the inspector wanted them. Then he took his flight test again and passed it. He could have passed his test the first time if I had known the inspector wanted him to "slip" all the way around on his 720-degree power turns.

I had known this inspector personally for several years and knew him to be a "top pilot." He could really make an airplane do what he wanted it to do. He was an old army pilot. One day in the early 1930's I just happened to be at Pearson Field, Vancouver, Washington, when a small group of army pilots were flying a military plane the army had recently acquired, a Consolidated PT-3 that the army used for flight training after they discarded the Curtiss Jenny.

This man was far superior to any of the other pilots in the group. He was showing the rest of them how to really handle an airplane. So I always looked up to him, and had a lot of respect for his flying ability.

At this time I was just sort of a renegade civilian barnstormer operating under state laws, trying to avoid federal laws, and trying to make a living with my airplane. I envied those who were lucky enough to be able to fly the nice new army flying machines at taxpayers' expense, and even got paid for doing it.

But when he flunked my student on that commercial flight test, I found out he didn't really have the "feel" of an airplane, and that he did not properly understand rudder and aileron control coordination. The frustrating thing to me was that I knew I was right, but at that time I did not understand it well enough myself to properly explain it to a veteran pilot. Anyway, who was I, a "Johnny-come-lately," to be telling a veteran like him how to fly an airplane?

At the time of this incident, my flight trainer was not perfected, but I was working on it. At the request of the Navy Department I took this machine to the Anacostia Naval Air Station in Washington, DC, demonstrated it, and talked to the men who represented the top airmen of our nation. These men liked the general idea of my primary flight trainer, but none of them agreed with me that there was any difference between coordinating rudder and aileron controls at low airspeeds than at higher airspeeds.

It seemed I had discovered something that was not widely known. In performing the maneuver we taught in the flight training programs called the "lazy eight" with a high degree of skill—in other words, in order to keep the "ball" centered throughout the maneuver—it was necessary for the pilot to master what I was preaching. But it seems no one had ever attempted to put this into words before, to actually understand it, and to be able to explain exactly what was happening, and why. At this time, I had only flown with two pilots who were really "on top of it" throughout this maneuver.

It seemed that the men holding the nation's highest positions in aviation did not understand the finer points of flying an airplane. Maybe the attitude of the military was that this was something you did not have to know to fly an airplane, so why bother with it? We have a war to win. Nevertheless, they did like the general idea of my primary flight trainer. They just did not agree with me on the finer points. I considered getting all pilots standardized on their understanding of control coordination work the most valuable part.

Regardless of our differences of opinion on rudder and aileron control coordination at different airspeeds, the Navy Department decided to order 10 of our flight trainers as a starter, to use experimentally and order larger quantities later on.

I priced these machines to them at $1,200 each. The Link Trainer, which was widely used in the military and airline training programs for teaching pilots to fly on instruments, sold for $14,000.

This flight trainer I had in Washington, DC, was the only one we had. I wanted to ship it back to Seattle because I did not have a complete set of blueprints for all the mechanisms in the machine; however, I did have rough shop drawings for everything.

These men insisted that I leave this flight trainer there. They said they realized it cost more to build the first one than it does to build regular production models, so I could set any price I wanted on it, but they insisted I leave it there.

They thought $25,000 would be a reasonable price for this first machine. I have never won any prizes for being a good business manager, but my idea was to make our money on production models, and for us to absorb the cost of producing this first flight trainer. So I suggested we price this machine at $1,500, and my Seattle associates agreed with me.

The Navy suggested I get right back there to Seattle and get started building these first 10 flight trainers. They said the paper work would follow. So I left our flight trainer there, got on the train, and headed for Chicago, where I met one of my Seattle associates. We spent the night celebrating our success with the Navy by nightclubbing in Chicago; then I flew from Chicago to Seattle on a DC-3 Mainliner.

On the train ride from Washington, DC, to Chicago two rather young, well dressed businessmen approached me. They were thoroughly familiar with our flight trainer and what we were trying to do with it. They told me the company they represented wanted to take over the flight trainer and pay me a small royalty on all sales. They said their company was in a position to develop this into a multi-million dollar business. One point they stressed was that "nothing" gets approved in Washington, DC, unless it goes through "their" company.

We had the only primary flight trainer in existence and it had been my baby from the very beginning of the raw undeveloped idea to where we had it now. I could see nothing but success in the path ahead.

At this point I was so elated over our product and prospects of the future we faced with it that I was more interested in pressing forward with our own plans than I was in turning this project over to a group of strangers and taking a back seat on it myself. I felt fully capable of managing the production of this flight trainer and carrying on with the engineering improvements on it. So I turned their offer down.

As soon as I arrived back in Seattle, we started production on these first 10 flight trainers. During this period, a high-ranking Navy man flew out to Seattle from Washington, DC, and contacted me. He said the Navy Department was setting up a synthetic training department and asked me if I would be interested in joining the Navy and taking charge of this department. He said I would start as a Lt. J.G. This made sense and I wanted to do it, but my business associates in Seattle had considerable investment in our projects by this time and they vetoed my wish to accept this offer. They said I was worth more to the war effort by staying with the further development and production of these flight trainers and the automatic carburetor heat control, and of course that made sense too.

C & H decided they wanted to set up a manufacturing plant in Glendale, California, to produce the automatic carburetor heat control unit and the flight trainer. When they were making preparations to set up for manufacturing in Glendale, they figured all these plans would be seriously set back if I accepted the Navy's offer, so I reluctantly turned it down.

We had the 10 flight trainers about half finished before we started getting concerned over the fact that the "paper work" had not arrived from the Navy. We discontinued further work on them and made the move to our new manufacturing location in Glendale. We went forward with producing and marketing my automatic carburetor heat control and did further development work on the flight trainer.

I made some major improvements on the flight trainer, over the machine I left with the Navy. We completed just one of these new model trainers and moved it to a training field in Safford, Arizona, at the request of the Navy Department.

A new group of Navy cadets arrived. Five cadets were assigned to each flight instructor. I was signed in as a regular flight instructor and had my five cadets. Our flight trainer was set up in a room. I was the only flight instructor using it, and I used it only with my five cadets. Each of the other flight instructors had instructions to transfer their weak cadets to me in exchange for my best cadets. So as the flight training progressed, I kept losing my best cadets and getting the poorest cadets in the whole class. I gave my cadets a lot of training on our flight trainer.

There was a rule none of us could violate. If any cadet received 12 hours of dual instructions and had not soloed, he was automatically washed out. I still figure someone was playing tricks on me, because I had two cadets transferred to me who had over 11 hours that were not even close to making a solo flight. I gave these cadets a workout on the flight trainer and succeeded in soloing every cadet. They all made very satisfactory solo flights. This whole class completed their primary flight training without any washouts, and they graduated to their next stage of training.

This could not have been accomplished without our flight trainer, which should have been obvious to everyone con-

This is my latest model flight trainer that I completed in our factory in Glendale, California, in 1942. I used this trainer on the flight training program at Safford, Arizona.

cerned. In my final talk with the manager of the base, he congratulated me on our successful work. However, he was still undecided about how much credit to give our flight trainer. He said there is sometimes a lot of difference between the abilities of various flight instructors, and he figured maybe I could have done the same thing without our flight trainer. This attitude really floored me. There could be no question about the value of our flight trainer. It was just a matter of butting our heads up against a stone wall to get cooperation from the people who had the power to say yes or no.

Finally the Navy shipped our number one flight trainer back to our factory in California. Maybe there really was something to what those fellows told me on the train: "Nothing gets approved in Washington, DC, unless it goes through "our company." I was beginning to feel like I was a cottontail rabbit among a bunch of hungry coyotes, except that a cottontail rabbit has an advantage I did not have—the rabbit recognizes his enemy when he sees him; I did not know who my enemy was.

If you tie two cats' tails together and hang them over a clothesline, they immediately fight one another; they do not go after the person who tied their tails together and hung them over the clothesline. We finally found ourselves in approximately the same position.

We didn't know who tied our tails together, but something was beginning to hurt. I figured my associates were not doing right when they expected me to handle the business contacts by myself. I figured they should back me up with a proper staff that would be better qualified to handle that part of it. I felt well qualified to handle the inventing, designing, engineering and flying, but I did not have confidence in handling the kind of business contacts that were required to make this thing go.

We had two perfectly good and proven products. As I saw it we were short of business administration. I believe they were losing confidence in our flight trainer. By now, the war was nearly over, and the flight training schools were closing down. We exerted considerable effort to get our flight trainer accepted in the public schools, but without success.

We had sold over 500 of our automatic carburetor heat control units, and it was a very good product. But we were not showing a profit, and Phil and Kay wanted to close shop and hang onto the profits they had made during the war. So we closed shop.

180

When Kay first asked me to move to California and set up for manufacturing these units, I was not very anxious to make that move. He told me that if I would agree to the move, they would back me all the way on our two products; and if they failed to get this business on a paying basis or if they gave it up for any reason, they would return all the rights back to me free and clear with no strings attached. Both products were my inventions, all patents were in my name, and no one else had any claims on the ideas and mechanisms in them.

Kay told me that for every dollar they spent on these projects it only cost them 10 cents because they were making so much money selling supplies to the Boeing Aircraft Company and the shipyards; 90 cents of every dollar their books showed as profit were paid as income tax. When I traveled, they insisted on me traveling first class and staying at the best hotels.

After we closed shop in Glendale, I wanted to carry on, either alone or perhaps with some other partners, but now Phil and Kay said in order for me to go forward with either or both of these products, they would require me to pay them $50,000 that their books showed they had spent on them. Considering an actual cost to them of 10 cents on the dollar, this whole project had cost them only $5,000, not $50,000—but this shows the kind of people I was dealing with.

This $50,000 burden destroyed any chance I might have had to carry these products forward. Now, many years later, my patents have long since expired, and my beautiful flight trainer sits in our basement, gathering dust and cobwebs—a memento of bygone days.

When the government flight training programs ended, C & H decided to get out of the manufacturing business, and I went to work in a machine shop in Burbank.

The loss of money we might have made from these projects isn't of as much concern to me as the loss the aviation industry has had from not having had the benefits the widespread use of these products could have provided. There are several primary flight trainers on the market today. I do not know if any of these new machines have the control coordination features built into them that mine had, but we were first, by a wide margin, with a very good primary flight trainer. And my automatic carburetor heat control still is not available to aircraft on today's market.

15

CORRALLING MUSTANGS

We moved to Nevada in the fall of 1947. Margaret's brother Al and his family joined us in purchasing 760 acres of undeveloped sagebrush land for $1 per acre. All our buildings were quonset huts except the little two-holer building made of rough lumber that was almost too far from the house. We had to put up the buildings, fence the land, clear the sagebrush, level the ground, and dig an irrigation well. By the spring of 1948 we had 50 acres planted under irrigation.

That fall we went to the annual rodeo in Winnemucca. While we were watching the rodeo, a helicopter flew over. Someone said the helicopter was being used by its owner to corral wild horses for Marvin Myers.

When we moved to Nevada, I had no intentions of doing any more commercial flying, and least of all to ever run any more wild horses with an airplane. I still remembered 1933 and had found better ways to make a living than trying to corral wild horses.

We owned a 65-horsepower Interstate, and I just wanted flying to be a part of my life. I had already experienced enough wild adventure with airplanes to last a lifetime. I was merely interested in a practical, safe, way to make a living and to work on some development projects I had in mind. I had never lost confidence in my Automatic Carburetor Heat Control or the Flight Trainer, but seemed to have run into a stone wall as far as knowing how to go forward with them.

In the spring of 1948, Marvin Myers came to our farm and said he had heard I had experience corralling wild horses with an airplane. He said he had been running wild horses for several years with an airplane and also with a helicopter. Marvin was not a pilot, but he had several different pilots fly for him. At that time he had a corral out on the Owyhee Desert. Four men were living out there in tents; he had saddle horses and pratha horses there and was all ready to run horses. Pratha horses, the way Marvin used them, were three or four gentle horses that were trained to lead the wild horses into the corral.

Marvin was in desperate need of a pilot. He had a 65-horse-power J-3 Cub and offered to pay me $4 per hour for flying if I would accept the job. Marvin was very persuasive, and he promised me the $4 per hour whether we caught the horses or not. He would stand all costs such as groceries, transportation and repairs. I would be taking no financial risk. This was a great deal less risk than I took in 1933. The only risk I was taking now was with my life. That was a very small risk because I figured I knew enough about handling an airplane that I could set a J-3 Cub down almost anywhere and walk away from it. I did not see how I could lose on such a deal, making $30 to $40 per day clear with no financial risk, so I accepted the job.

Marvin had his camp all set up so when I arrived, we were ready to start. He was very good with horses and knew much more about how to handle wild horses than the men on my first horse job.

This was the Owyhee Desert area, the same area where I had run horses with Art Seale and Bill Blakely in 1933. Our old trap canyon, camp site and landing strip on Rodere Flat were about 15 miles south of Marvin's setup.

The ground crew cannot catch horses if the pilot does not bring them in. Also, the pilot cannot catch horses if the ground crew does the wrong things after he brings them in. We would have made a profit on our 1933 horse job, even at one cent per pound, if Marvin's crew had been handling the ground operations. I doubt if there is any other occupation in the world with more room for different opinions on how to accomplish a specific result than there is, or at least was at that time, on how to catch horses.

Our efforts were not successful at first. This didn't surprise either one of us very much. We both had the ability to sit down after each unsuccessful run and discuss what had happened and listen with an open mind to each other's ideas on what should be tried next.

Marvin's idea was to send the cook out with me and have him

shoot at the horses with a long-barreled, 410-gauge shotgun. The small-gauge shotgun didn't really do any damage to the horses, when I stayed back from them, but it stung their hides and was pretty effective in helping to turn them if the leader was hit.

The cook kept getting sick in the airplane, and even when he wasn't sick, he couldn't place his shots where they would do the most good. It doesn't to any good to hit any horse back of the leader; horses are going to follow the horses in front of them anyway.

The ground crew had a 410-gauge shotgun pistol they used to shoot on the ground just before the horses went through the corral gate. I suggested they use the long-barreled shotgun on the ground, give me the shotgun pistol, and leave the cook on the ground. I figured I could place the shots where I wanted them, and it would do a better job of getting the horses to go where we wanted them to go.

I could fly the plane with my left hand, operate the throttle with my left elbow and shoot with my right hand. Then after I pulled up and was making my turn to come back on the horses, I could use both hands to reload the shotgun. Also, getting the cook's weight out of the small 65-horsepower airplane increased my maneuverability. This was another advantage in tight maneuvering.

I told Marvin about my experience dragging tin cans under the airplane on a rope in 1933. I also rigged this up on the Cub. With these changes made, we started catching horses.

Fourteen days after I arrived at the horse camp, I flew home, and Marvin had shipped 348 horses. He was very happy about the job and said it was one of the most profitable horse jobs he had been on. He told me he knew where he could get more horses to run, but he would not take on another horse job unless I would agree to fly for him. He offered me $5 per hour for the new job, so I accepted.

Marvin went with his crew; they established a tent camp at a spring and built a trap corral. When one of the crew members called me on the phone and said they were ready for me to fly out there and start corralling horses, I asked him if there was a place where I could land the plane. He said I could land there and that they had driven the pickup right up to the camp.

When I arrived, they were ready for action. Thirty days later

I flew home and Marvin had shipped 1,000 horses from this location. By this time he had another horse job lined up which was even bigger than the job we had just finished. On this job, he raised my pay to $6.25 per hour.

Ten-hour days were not uncommon, and there were days I put in over 13 hours in the air, eating breakfast in the dark, eating lunch while flying, and eating supper in the dark. That is a long day for that kind of flying, but I was younger then and could take it.

I had no duties to perform except to keep the airplane in flyable condition and to keep it in the air as much as possible, because we were not making any money when the horses were not coming in. No one cared anything about what the airplane looked like, or what the pilot looked like, or whether I shaved or had a clean shirt, or anything about the flying techniques I used. The only thing that scored in those horse camps was catching the horses. This gave me a lot of leeway to experiment with various techniques of maneuvering the airplane and to try various things on horse psychology.

I do not know anyone else who has ever been paid as much for flying a 65-horsepower J-3 Cub as I was during the 18

The Cowels horse job, southwest of Gerlach, Nevada. Marvin Myers on right; Vern Ryan and Bill Garaventa on left. 65-horsepower J-3 Cub, 1949.

months I flew for Marvin. He shipped over 6,000 horses during this period.

I figured Marvin was making 10 times as much as he was paying me. I suggested to him that I buy the airplane from him, and we take on other horse jobs on a 50-50 basis. But he was not interested in that idea.

We had used up all the financial resources we had come to Nevada with. Our farm was not making any money, and it soaked up money like a one-way sponge. We seemed unable to squeeze it any way that would get any money back out of it. I did not like horse running, which was a hard life in many ways, but I could not figure out any other way to earn the money we needed to get our farm on a paying basis. Margaret helped out by taking a job teaching school, beginning at $2,400 per year. This was 1949.

In December 1949 I began a horse running partnership with a neighboring rancher, Chug Utter. He had never done any flying, and he had never seen horses caught with an airplane, but he understood livestock in general and was good with a saddle horse.

We built a portable corral and bought a 65-horsepower J-3

Beverly was closing the gate when I snapped this picture.

Cub in good condition for $500. We decided to spend a few days on a scouting flight before making a decision on where to make our first setup.

We had hoped to find an area where we could run 400 or 500 horses into one corral. The first area we looked over, directly east of Mina, should have had over 600 horses. A Mr. Stinson, who lived in Carson City, had put cattle in that area in the last few years, and he had shot all the horses he could to preserve the feed for his cattle. We looked the area over and saw only about 30 horses.

We looked at and landed on a dry lake in the Mina area with the idea of roping horses on it, but it was too small.

We stayed in Tonopah the second night. The Forest Service controlled much of this southern horse country and wanted all the unbranded horses out. The ranger in Tonopah told us of an area about 20 miles east that he figured had over 150 horses. He had already told Harold Johnson he could run horses in that area. He was not sure when Johnson intended to start, or if he would get very many of the horses. The ranger said that on all grazing land not controlled by the Taylor Grazing Act, which is

When the cans hung up on a horse or a rimrock, the rope would stretch, and if it didn't break, the cans would fly back toward the airplane and make large holes in the fabric wherever they hit. I used a 3/4-inch rope. One time the cans broke the windshield out of my J-3 Cub. Another time they broke about one inch off one propeller blade. It could have been worse.

called public domain, that the man with the largest six-shooter had the most power.

Chug and I made money, but we finally decided to go our separate ways. After this association ended, I ran horses entirely on my own. I built a portable corral, had my own saddle and pratha horses, and hired riders and other ground help. I even had my own truck for hauling horses to market.

For a while, in the summer of 1952 during school vacation, our son and daughter, Curtis and Beverly, were my buckaroos, and my wife Margaret was the cook and gate-closer, a real family operation.

POLLY, THE PRATHA MARE

One of my favorite memories is of a pratha horse we used for a long time, named Polly. As mentioned earlier, a pratha is several gentle horses that are trained to lead the wild mustangs into a trap corral—in other words, decoy horses. In all the long history of mustanging I don't believe there has ever been another pratha horse as good as Polly. She was a two- or three-year-old palomino filly when we caught her with mustangs. She was such a beautiful horse I decided to keep her, and asked one of my buckaroos to break her so she would be a gentle riding horse for my wife to ride.

Well, he broke her, but intentionally or not, he made a bucking horse out of her. She bucked hard with every man who ever got on her, and she threw most of them off. No woman ever attempted to ride her. I had three other buckaroos try to break her from bucking, and they all gave her up as impossible.

Because of her bucking habits, I decided to use her with the pratha, and she took to that job like a fish takes to water. Throughout the remainder of her life she objected violently when anyone attempted to ride her. She would buck, squeal, bite and kick. She was almost as wild as the mustangs around the corral, but if you just kept your hands off of her, and let her catch mustangs, she was easily handled and seemed to be very happy about it. Polly just loved the pratha job and became my best pratha horse.

Sometimes I think Polly was the smartest ground-crew member I ever had, and I do not know for sure how she got that way. She seemed to know exactly what we were doing and what we wanted her to do, and she did it with great enthusiasm. On a pratha run she would slow down and sometimes even stop and wait for slow horses, to allow them to catch up with her, and I have never seen her let a fast horse get ahead of her for very long. She would not even allow any of the other pratha horses to get ahead of her.

After every pratha run all the pratha horses were hand fed a pan of oats—"if we caught the horses." If we did not catch the mustangs, they did not get the oats. They soon learned about the importance of catching the mustangs.

To show how helpful Polly was in capturing wild horses—as well as to give a little flavor of a typical day's activities during that period of my life—here is a short excerpt from my diary of January 1, 1953.

Now I am about a mile and a half from the pratha ground and they are almost stopped; I know they are not tired, just smart. I just stung the stud with some #5 shot, from a safe distance, so as to not really hurt him, and he has taken off at full throttle. The rest of the horses cannot keep up, but they are trying. I can see the pratha is in position and waiting for the signal to go. I climb for altitude and keep my distance to get the stud to slow down so the rest of the horses can catch up with him. They are together again and making better time now.

I gave the pratha signal extra early because these horses might take off like a bullet when they see the pratha. Polly led the pratha down the ridge, then stopped and looked 90 degrees to her left for the mustangs; but because I gave the pratha signal early this time, she could not see them yet because they had not quite got around the turn where she could see them. So Polly stopped and waited, and the other two pratha horses and the mule also stopped behind her.

As soon as the mustangs come around the bend where they can see the pratha, they start to shy away, but right at this time Polly takes off and leads the pratha down the trail.

I swing in low, to the left of the mustangs and drag my tin cans in the brush beside them, and by the time I pull up and make a turn and look back, the pratha is running at full speed. The mustangs are also at full speed, about 100 yards behind the pratha.

Then I keep my distance, and Polly slows down just enough to let the mustangs drop in close behind her. If the mustangs are real slow, Polly runs accordingly, and if the mustangs try to pass her they really have a lot on their hands, or I should say feet, because that is what they have to use a lot.

Now the riders are coming off the ridge, to drop in behind the mustangs. The pratha and mustangs are slowed down to a fast trot, and I am keeping my distance as the riders close the gap between them and the mustangs.

The stud turns around and sees the riders coming up from behind. He turns around toward the bunch and swings to the left enough to get around the other horses and puts on all the speed he has. Polly is not asleep. She sees him coming and opens up, and he cannot pass her, so he drops in behind her. All the other horses, mustangs and pratha mixed, put on all the speed they have in an attempt to not get left behind, but of course little Fluffy (a pratha filly colt) cannot keep up at this speed so she is the first to drop behind. The mustang colts drop behind and string out ahead of Fluffy.

I keep my distance as long as all goes well, but try to hold a

This is the critical moment, as Polly leads them in. A family operation: our daughter Beverly on the right, our son Curtis on the left, and my wife Margaret hiding in the bushes, ready to close the gate. The 90-horsepower Franklin Interstate. The cans can be seen under the airplane.

position where I can get down there in an instant if the mustangs make an attempt to leave the pratha. Because I know we have lost these horses before, I am expecting anything to happen. I am hoping it will be something we can correct before it is too late.

Things can happen fast from here on in, and there is not much time for corrections. Now the horses are heading up the steep ridge, and another 75 yards will put them between both sack wings. This is the first horse run since the right sack wing was built, so this is a tense moment.

The two riders are at full throttle now in an attempt to get up close in order to be in a position to press the horses hard for the next 1,200 feet into the corral, but they are much too far back to suit me. Because this is an educated bunch, they are putting on everything they have. The riders are giving their horses all they will take. They might still be able to close the gap in time.

Polly is still holding the lead as they approach the top of the ridge. She swings her usual 90 degrees to the right to avoid the left sack wing, but at this point she sees the new right wing and swings back toward the pratha trail.

This slight delay gives the riders a chance to make a small

A typical good arrangement that caught horses in Central Nevada.

191

gain. Supie is in the lead on Smokey; Boyd is close behind on Rambler. Now all the horses are on the trail and halfway to the corral, between the two sack wings. Polly still has the lead. Everything is full speed.

I am trying to hold my quick-dive position. This is where I become an artist at slow flight. I don't want to go anywhere. I just want to hold this position. But I realize I could not get down there in time now if the mustangs make a break for the sack wing that is only 20 feet from them, and if I dive at their left side needlessly, I might spook them through the right wing. So I just spit out my chewing gum so I won't swallow it and do my best to hold a position where I can dive and shoot just as the horses are within about 100 feet of the gate, so they won't turn back. It looks now like the riders are too far behind to push them as they reach the gate.

Then suddenly one old bay mare makes a break for the left wing. I cannot possibly get there in time to do any good, but I have a bird's eye view of the show. The rest of the mustangs all swing to the left to follow her. Then she comes face to face with the sack wing. She suddenly puts on all four brakes and slips on the snow and ice and falls down. She gets up rapidly and heads back toward the pratha, which has now gained a little lead

Ready for a horse run in Newark Valley, Nevada. Garley Amos on the right.

over the mustangs. All the mustangs follow her and put on extra speed to get back to the pratha.

This incident has given the riders a chance to gain a little distance. Now the pratha slacks off a little, and the mustangs catch up with them, as the riders also get their proper positions and start firing their blank revolvers. I swoop down and fire my 410 pistol. Everything goes in the corral, and the riders are right there to close the gate.

This was a run that had everyone's nerves on edge and put everything to a full capacity test, but it was really no more strenuous than many of the three or four runs we make almost every day. The important difference is that we caught these horses, and we know these are horses that have gotten away from us before. This run did a lot to build up our confidence in the runs to follow.

A few years later, Garley Amos and I were corralling mus-

I put the Interstate on its back in Idaho after I had landed in a farm field during a very high wind. This is the way I brought it home. I had landed and had come to a stop. Then in trying to taxi over to a fence, so I could tie it down, the wind flipped it up on its nose, breaking the wood propeller.

As it sat there with its tail pointed toward the sky, I got out and roped the tailwheel. I was pulling on the rope trying to pull the tail down as two men drove up in a car. One of them said, "How far did you fall?" Even with their help, the wind flipped it the rest of the way over on its back.

The 90-horsepower Franklin Interstate was a good mustang airplane. But every 700 hours it broke a piston, and two times it wasn't any fun, but I got it down without damage.

I was headed for the airport at Sparks, Nevada, where I had my extra Franklin engine all majored, ready to install in the airplane. My engine had 700 hours and was due to break another piston, so I figured I would put the majored engine in the plane before the next piston broke. I was over high mountains when a piston decided not to wait until I got to Sparks, and it broke right there.

The engine was still running on three cylinders, but I had a severe loss of power and the engine was running very rough. Oil was covering the windshield and cowling, and the cabin filled with smoke. I opened the windows to clear the air.

There was a dirt road where I could have landed, but the plane would have been a long ways out in the country where it would have been very unhandy to get to and install the other engine. So I decided to try to coax the plane the rest of the way into the Fallon, Nevada, airport, where it would be much easier to change engines.

With full throttle I was losing altitude, but at the beginning of this ordeal I had extra altitude to spare. As I reached lower ground, I was following a highway. A highway patrolman was following me, as he could hear my engine clattering and banging and could see the smoke trail I was leaving behind.

Finally I was down to about 200 feet and still sinking, when I remembered I had two five-gallon jeep cans full of gas on the back seat that I had intended to land and put in the gas tank so I could get to Sparks. I opened the right window and tossed these two cans of gas overboard. They fell into the sagebrush about 100 yards to the left of the highway. After getting rid of this extra gas, I could hold what altitude I had left but could not gain any more. I was able to fly on into the Fallon airport to change engines.

tangs in the central part of Nevada. My portable corral was set up in an area of rather thick juniper trees, which made it easy to have it hidden as the horses approached it.

On one horse run, the mustangs turned back at the corral, and I fought them in a running battle for about two miles before I succeeded in getting them stopped. The juniper trees complicated controlling a tough bunch like this.

After getting them stopped, it was very difficult for me to move them back toward the corral. They would willingly go just any direction except back toward the corral, but I was persistent and made progress slowly.

Garley could see what my problem was, so he and his partner brought the pratha out to meet me. When they finally had the pratha behind the mustangs and turned them loose, the pratha got with the mustangs, and everything headed for the corral through the juniper trees. We were about half a mile or more from the corral when this chase started. It was a good solid bunch with Polly in the lead and the mustangs behind.

Beverly and Boyde looking them over. We didn't sell every horse we caught.

The juniper trees were thick, and Polly had never made a pratha run from this direction. Our south wing fence ended at a large juniper tree. Polly went on the wrong side of the tree, and she hit the wing fence at full speed with everything else close behind her at the same speed.

Polly tumbled and fell on her head on the other side of the fence. The wing fence was broken. In the following confusion, some of the other horses followed through behind Polly, and some of them went around the tree on the left side, where there was no fence. I had a ringside seat with a bird's eye view of this whole mixup.

By the time everything had gotten around the tree, on one side or the other, Polly had gotten to her feet, and led the horses into the corral. We caught all eight of them, but before they could get the gate closed, Polly fell over dead, with a broken neck.

That seemed, and still seems, incredible. Sometimes I wonder if a dead horse led those mustangs into the corral. I had worked with Polly throughout her captive life, and we didn't think of her as a wild horse. She was just part of our family. Except for her bucking when anyone tried to ride her and her

A good setup in northern California.

reluctance to allow anyone to put their hands on her, she was always treated well and with respect. I believe she enjoyed her life as a pratha horse more than she would have enjoyed her "freedom on the range." We felt we had lost a friend and a valuable asset to our business the day Polly died.

When getting this close to the corral, I liked to make two or three quick passes at the horses.

As the horses approach the gate, one rider can be seen close behind them. Another rider is farther back. The rear rider will have a chance to rope one if any horse turns back at this point.

The airplane was shuddering in a stall when I snapped this picture, causing the picture to blur a little, just as the horses were entering the corral. The Owyhee Desert job.

This deserted ranch house was used as a cow camp, and we used it as a mustang camp. Left to right—Margaret and Curtis Barber, Mabel and Harry Wilson, Dave Bebe and Clarence Maxwell. Mabel was a good cook. The Alkali job.

Getting close. The left wing fence was camouflaged with sagebrush.

This is the Virgin Ranch job, in Virgin Valley, Nevada. Four of the same crew we had on the Alkali job.

All the essentials for catching horses—the corral, the truck, the airplane and my airport.

Alkali Ranch corral. Sometimes they roped the horses, got them down and clipped their hair to check for brands. Clyde Reborse on dark horse. Harry Wilson on light horse. One large stud jumped over this corral and got away from us.

16

NEVADA MUSTANGS

Corralling ownerless horses on our federal range lands is a deep, involved, and "emotional" subject. The opposition would have you believe horses are wild animals that have the same inherited rights on the range as animals such as deer and antelope, and that aerial mustangers are an unscrupulous, inhumane bunch of outlaws who move around in the back hills, mostly by moonlight, and steal horses.

These people want you to believe it is inhumane to catch horses and sell them to someone who is going to slaughter them for making pet food. They see nothing wrong with horses becoming snowbound during periods of deep snow and slowly starving and freezing to death on open range lands.

Horses are not wild animals in the same sense that deer and antelope are. The horses that escaped or were turned loose by early settlers became the wild mustangs that were so numerous on our western plains. These were not "wild" horses. They were "feral" horses. A feral horse is one, or the descendant of one, that has formerly been domesticated. So, it is "feral" horses, not "wild" horses, that populate the West. They are commonly referred to as "wild" horses simply because they run wild and are hard to catch. They were put on the range by man, so they do not belong to the public as deer and antelope do. They have no natural predators and their numbers increase rapidly to a point where they take over the range unless their numbers are controlled.

There have been periods of high demand for horses. This was true during World War I. At such times ranchers were encouraged to breed their horses up to better grades and to keep all their horses branded. As the demand grew and prices rose this encouraged mustangers to operate, and it kept the wild horse numbers within reasonable limits.

When World War I price levels declined, ranchers permitted their herds to go unbranded and join the other feral horses on the range. Mustangers could no longer make a living, so unlicensed horse numbers increased again to unacceptable levels. The mustangers and cattle men had never been able to remove these horses as fast as they increased.

Following the big buildup of horses after World War I, most of the horses out on the range were horses ranchers and mustangers were not able to catch. Mustangers, including myself, were running smart horses that knew all the tricks of getting away. This was especially true of the studs because it was usually the studs that got away.

There has never been a time when there was the remotest possibility of completely cleaning the range of "wild" horses. There has never been any danger of wild horses becoming extinct. If they did, their numbers could easily be replenished with domestic horses.

The initials BLM stand for Bureau of Land Management. Their job is to manage our federal land. However, the question is—whom are they managing it for—the city folks who are represented by such groups as the Sierra Club and the Wild Horse Protection group, or ranching interests and meat producers who feed all our citizens and contribute to the economic well being of our country? Is the BLM giving proper consideration for our taxpayers' interests? Or do they set policy according to the interests of pressure groups who swing a lot of weight with the news media, giving them political and vote-getting power, from a public that is grossly misinformed on this subject? If this is so, then are we to assume the rest of our country's problems are handled in a like manner? If this is so, then we have just taken a big step towards understanding how, and why, our national debt is approaching and probably will have passed two trillion dollars by the time you read this—because we have no method of injecting common sense into government decision making.

I do not know what has happened to the idea that we have, or had, a government of, by, and for the people, but our present wild horse situation is proof we do not have such a gov-

202

ernment now. If they were properly informed, the "people" would not permit wild horses, at taxpayer's expense, to acquire the same status which they now have in this country that the "Sacred Cows" have in India.

Our wild horse situation is a good example of bureaucratic boondoggling. Instead of following a sensible program for controlling the number of wild horses, the BLM concentrated for several years on reducing ranchers' range permits because they needed the grass to feed the wild horses. After a few years under the wild horse protection laws, the uncontrolled buildup of wild horses caused the law to be changed to permit the BLM to remove "surplus" horses by using helicopters to corral them.

For a long time these horses were given away free to anyone who wanted them, if they could convince the government they would take good care of them. The new horse owners did not really own them. They were not free to sell them to anyone else. Eventually the law was changed so that after a certain length of time, they did receive a title to the horses. But even with this system the older, crippled, or sick horses were killed and buried. The buzzards and coyotes were not even allowed to eat them. Anyone could tell our lawmakers it would make better sense to butcher these horses that cannot be given away and make pet food out of them.

No doubt you could test any one of our lawmakers and discover they are almost as intelligent as we are. But when you get the whole lot of them together they get to playing a game; it is called "You scratch my back and I will scratch your back." Then the horse-trading really begins. At this point their level of intelligence, and also their level of integrity, can drop to very low levels. The whole idea behind the theory of a democratic form of government breaks down, and the goals of minority pressure groups replace the commitment to the common good.

An easy-to-see result of this is our present wild horse protection laws; our system of government does not provide a satisfactory method of correcting this situation. The proper answer to this question is simple, but getting it past our lawmakers is impossible.

As soon as these horses are caught, they should be sold to the highest bidder, all of them, with no strings attached. With proper management, the government should be able to recover all the money it costs to manage the wild horse program, and maybe even show a profit. We did.

The 17,000 horses I have corralled over the years did not cost the taxpayers anything. With each horse valued at $500 each, which I am told is about what it costs our taxpayers now to remove each horse from the range, this saved the taxpayers $8,500,000. We made a profit selling these horses for $30 to $50 each and generated money that helped the economy of our country—as well as our own—and we kept the wild horse numbers under acceptable control. We operated within the framework of "free enterprise," not under repressive, dictatorial, federal laws.

As long as our present wild horse situation goes uncorrected, our taxpayers will continue to spend millions, and eventually billions, of dollars to control a situation that could be handled at no expense to the taxpayers. I am retired now and would not run horses again for anything, but I would like to see some common sense used to correct this situation. I know of no way to penetrate the inner sanctums of our lawmakers with common sense.

Some of the people who write extensively about wild horses seem to have a vested interest in distorting the facts. This has resulted in giving the public a false picture of the problems that are created by having too many wild horses on our western range lands. The books and magazine articles on this subject never even touched the real story of wild horses and the men who worked with them. Occasionally, movies were made that attempted to cover wild horses, but these also were dismal failures regarding the realities.

Eventually, I decided to keep a sort of a blow-by-blow diary of our daily activities in our various horse camps. That way I would at least get some of the essential facts on paper. I have hundreds of pages of these papers written both in the air and on the ground.

Critics say my notes make monotonous reading because there is too much of the same thing day after day. That is the way life is in a mustang camp, and we cannot change that. Life in a mustang camp is totally lacking in Hollywood-type, melodramatic excitement. Mustanging was just a job that had to be done. It was a tough job and required highly skilled operators, and sometimes the best performance available was not quite good enough.

GHOST MARE

A man from California left several high-class mares at a ranch on pasture for the purpose of raising some well-bred colts. The first colt that came was a pure white filly. When the owner of the horses came to get them, this colt was about six months old, and the man who owned the ranch wanted it. He stole it by turning it out on the range, so when the owner took his horses, he took them without this white filly colt.

The rancher planned to rope this colt and bring it back in after the other horses were gone, but he did not see it again for several months; then he could not catch it. It was not branded.

This filly grew into a fine looking animal. As the years went by, the rancher spent a lot of time trying to catch this beautiful white horse. He tried to run her down and rope her, but he never had a saddle horse that was fast enough to catch her. He tried many times to trap her, but she always outsmarted him.

He was not the only man who wanted this beautiful white horse. She was running on the open range where many hundreds of other wild horses ran and she drew the attention of many buckaroos who tried all sorts of methods to catch her. She became known as the "Ghost Mare" because she was pure white and no one could catch her. They had even tried to catch her with an airplane without success.

The day I started running horses on Seven Troughs Mountains, I was told about the Ghost Mare and her bunch and was told approximately where I would find her. She was now over 20 years old, and over all these years she was still out there and had become a legend.

The second day, I located this bunch of 10 horses. I had never seen a wilder bunch of horses. They were within eight miles of our corral. Because of the Ghost Mare's age, there were other horses in the bunch that were more powerful and faster than she was. Most of the way in, some of the younger horses took the lead. Even at that, the Ghost Mare took the lead part of the time. She was large and well built, but I could see her age was against her.

We probably would have lost this bunch if I had brought them in the first day. By the second day, we had our technique worked out pretty well, and all of the crew did exactly what they were supposed to do at just the right time. These horses ran into the trap, and the ground crew had the large canvas pulled behind them before they realized they were in a trap.

As soon as they saw they were trapped, the Ghost Mare definitely became their leader. She led the bunch at high speed, head on, into our corral fence several times. The fence weakened, and several of the posts broke and bent over at an angle. But the fence held, and after a while they decided they could not get out and settled down. The ground crew succeeded in getting them into the small corral with the help of the pratha.

If the Ghost Mare had been 10 or 15 years younger, we could not have held them. We let them stand in the corral overnight, and the following morning water and hay were put in for them. All the horses except the Ghost Mare drank and ate. She would not touch either hay or water. She was thin and looked bad. We were afraid she would be too weak to ship. The next day, she started drinking water and eating hay. Because of her weak condition we did not ship her in the first load. By the time the second truck arrived two days later, she was in better shape than when we caught her. So we loaded her in the truck and sent her down the road.

It is doubtful if she would have survived another winter on the open range. We figured this was a better ending for her than a slow starvation, freezing death on a cold winter range.

LARRY'S LEG

The winter of 1958-1959 in northeastern Nevada near Contact:

A mile or two out from the pratha location, the mustangs had to cross a creek. Because of the cold temperatures, this creek was frozen over where I wanted to put the horses across. I had discovered it was easier to get the horses to cross the creek if a rider would ride up there and break a trail across the creek with his saddle horse before the first run each day.

10:53: I see Larry breaking the ice. I hope these horses don't see him. They still have a ridge to go over before they can see the creek. These are faster horses than the bunch of 11 yesterday.

10:55: I see Larry leaving now, so this is working out just right. The horses are nearly to the top of the ridge.

10:57: They are over.

11:03: Just called Bud on the radio and reported that they

crossed the creek without a fight. The large bay mare that was leading crossed about 50 feet below the trail Larry made, and the others crossed about 50 feet above the trail. Well, so far, this part of the run is just routine. The tension part comes up pretty soon now. None of this part counts if we lose them on the last part.

11:26: They are in the corral, all six.

Larry's horse fell as he went through the gate. The horse got up, but Larry is still lying on the ground. Bud is waving wildly at me so I know Larry is hurt. The mustangs are trying to get back out of the gate right where Larry is lying, so I can't land yet. I keep circling to keep the horses in the lower end of the corral. Finally Bud gets them in the center corral and closes the gate.

The gate where Larry is lying is just wires with sacks on them. As soon as the pole gate is closed, I start getting into position to land. Then Bud turns on the corral radio and tells me Larry's leg is broken.

As I land, I see Frances around Larry with blankets. No one else is in camp except LaRena, their small daughter. I land and get one tiedown rope on the plane and get up there as fast as I can. Larry is still lying where he fell.

We consider flying him to Twin Falls, Idaho, but his leg below the knee seems to be very badly broken. Getting him in and out of the plane and even just riding in the cramped up position required in the back seat of the SuperCub would be very painful for him. We decide it is best to move him in Bud's car. Bud and LaRena carry him to the car while Frances helps with the broken leg and opens gates, etc. I am busy trying to get vehicles started.

It is cold, and Bud's car needs towing. Luckily, Bud and Larry had built a fire under the truck engine earlier in the morning and had it running. I towed Bud's car with the truck and got it started. As we were getting ready to tow Bud's car, Larry's father, Walt, drove up from San Jacinto Ranch.

Bud, Frances, LaRena and Larry head for Twin Falls Clinic while I go back and tie the plane down with both ropes. Walt removes the saddles from the riding horses and gets them out of the mustang corral. Then I ride with Walt to his house at the San Jacinto Ranch where we pick up Mrs. Schroder, Larry's mother, and we drive to Twin Falls in Walt's car.

On our way out from camp, we met a pickup with three or four people headed for our camp. These are the same people who have been up there several times. They say they want to buy a colt, but the price isn't right so they just keep coming back. I don't know who they are or what they really want. We do not have anything to hide so it doesn't bother me.

We spent the rest of the day at the clinic. The X-rays show a very bad break, broken in three places. About five p.m. they put Larry's leg in traction. About seven or eight p.m. they are going to X-ray it again. We had our lunch between five and six at a drugstore, bought some groceries, then checked back at the clinic. We finally drove back out to the Horseshoe Club at Contact and got a room where we can get a much needed bath.

I am in need of some of this new insulated underwear, but I can't get any on Sunday. Walt is going back to Twin Falls tomorrow; he said he would get some for me.

The temperature last night at San Jacinto Ranch was 15 degrees below zero. The night before it seemed even colder to me. I sleep cold and am cold most of the day except when I am sitting close to a stove. Mustang flying requires flying with the door and windows open much of the time, in all kinds of weather. The main reason I want the insulated underwear is not just for comfort. If I should ever have to spend the night out in these mountains, survival would be a very serious problem in this kind of weather. Nobody realizes more than I do just how easily or quickly that could happen, and I could even be in worse shape than Larry was in and much farther from help.

When I get to thinking about such things, I can get some relief by looking back at my record—quite a few thousand hours of this kind of flying with no serious mishaps, yet, but that does not make the mountains or rocks any softer if I should have to hit them.

Sometimes this horse running makes me feel like I am playing a cat-and-mouse game. I am the mouse. Fate is the cat, just waiting until he is ready to spring on me. Could do it any time, but just waiting, for what I don't know. Common sense should tell me I cannot do this kind of work forever and get away with it. But it doesn't.

Monday, January 5, 1959.

10:30: In the air on a horse run. The sky is gray with strong surface winds. We ordered a truck for today. Have 28 horses in

208

the corral. Then we learned on our way to camp that the brand inspector is away on a job and might not be back until this afternoon or late tonight.

Don't have much enthusiasm for running horses today. Larry's brother, Vern, is helping Bud today. Roger and Walt drove up this morning to take some horses and colts, but we don't have anything they want so they didn't take any.

Guess I will look the east area over this morning. Yesterday it was 15 degrees below zero. This morning it was 22 degrees above. The wind is very rough, and it looks like a storm is moving in. I left before lunch so am munching a large almond Hershey bar as the snow-covered mountains pass slowly beneath me. As I let down over the large juniper slopes of our east area, I wonder just how crazy a man really has to get to do this kind of work.

No more time for practical thinking as I spot a bunch of seven at 11:47, and I recognize Blacky as their leader. I know I am in for a rough time if we get him in our corral again. He is the stud that went through our wire-and-sack gate after we had them in the corral.

BUD'S FALL

Day followed day on these horse jobs. In a way there was a lot of monotony. In another way there was never any monotony.

We have cold winters in northern Nevada. The first thing out of bed I put a small oil stove under the engine. When we had finished with breakfast, it was warm enough to start. It was the pilot who was cold the rest of the day, with the windows open on much of the flying.

We never knew what was going to happen next, knowing full well something would. There was no real theme running through our days like there is in a John Wayne movie.

There were no clearly visible villains or any clearly visible heroes, and there seemed never to be a really satisfying climax. When you watch a TV program, you know there is going to be a sort of a "lived-happily-ever-after" conclusion at the end of the hour, but this sort of thing never happens in a mustang camp. Each day just wins you the privilege of going through another day, with just as many uncertainties ahead as there were behind.

One other day, on our Contact job, went like this.

1:07: Across the creek about one mile below camp. This is a lucky break, but now three are running ahead. The mare and colt can't get up over the steep frozen creek bank where they crossed the creek. They finally made it, but the other three are about half a mile ahead now.

1:15: I have the three stopped now and they are all together again. Looks like I forgot to wind my watch last night, it stopped.

From here on they are slow, but they handled well until I had them about 20 yards from giving the pratha signal. They set up solid in their tracks and looked directly at the pratha location for about five seconds, then did a quick 180-degree turn and headed back on the tracks they just made.

I am sure they couldn't have seen the pratha from where they were, but they could have heard something or smelled something. I called Bud on the radio. He said the wind was blowing toward the mustangs, so the horses must have smelled something.

I have them stopped about a mile from where they turned back. Will try to get them between the pratha and our corral. This is working. Have them on the first ridge the pratha runs over, and asked Bud to turn the pratha loose. The mustangs see the pratha as it approaches them, and two of the mustangs are running southwest to meet the pratha. Looks like the mare and colt.

I see Bud coming up on his horse, Polly. (Bud's Polly is a gelding—Bud's favorite riding horse—and is not Polly the Pratha Mare.) When the two mustangs heading for the pratha saw Bud, they took off north, over the ridges and through the trees, and I couldn't turn them. The other three got with the pratha. At the second ridge these three left the pratha. With Bud and I both working on them, we got them headed back on the pratha trail. The pratha was well in the lead.

Vern comes out on his horse from his hiding place, and we push them. Just as they are about to get with the pratha, the black mare turns right. I make a close pass at her, but she won't yield, and she goes through our right wing fence. We caught the other two—the largest ones.

Now I am looking for the mare and colt but can't find them. I go back and find the black mare that crashed our right wing. She is very hard to handle. I hold her in a pasture fence corner for a while. Finally she spooks and goes through the fence. I fight her to a standstill on top of the two ridges and hold her there as Bud and Vern get the pratha in position.

They turn the pratha loose, and the pratha and black mare get together. They run together for about 100 yards; then the black mare turns right and leaves, and I can't turn her or stop her. As Bud and Vern go into the chase with their ropes ready, I get her slowed down enough that Bud gets up close.

As Bud approaches her, she swings into his saddle horse; and

Wild Horse Smith forgot to tie.

211

instead of hitting shoulder to shoulder, the black mare ducks her head and goes under Polly's belly, between his legs. This upsets Polly. As Polly is falling, and as Bud is sailing through the air, over Polly's head, the black mare's head is sticking out from under the right side of Polly; Bud threw his rope and got it on her.

I saw Bud hit the ground vertically, square on top of his head, out in front of Polly, as Polly tumbled. No one has ever seen anything like that before. It looked to me like Bud bounced once before anything hit the ground but his head. Then he came down in a heap and lay motionless. Bud was tangled up in Polly's legs as Polly was kicking and scrambling to his feet.

Polly took off down the ridge as the black mare took off up the ridge. In this confusion I had lost track of Vern; he was somewhere in the trees. As he came riding up to the scene, Bud got to his feet and went around in circles, rubbing his neck.

Bud asked Vern to catch Polly for him, and I pursued the black mare. She was dragging Bud's rope, with one foot through the loop. Bud is one of the few mustang ropers I have met who ties hard and fast. Most ropers consider this too dangerous. Bud seems to be well educated, but I don't think he ever found out what the word "danger" means. Anyway, under these conditions he didn't have time to get his rope tied to his saddle horn.

I see both Bud and Vern following the chase, so apparently Bud is not too seriously hurt. For the first time on this job Bud holds back enough that Vern is leading the chase. Vern seems to be riding a better horse than usual, as he pulls right up to the black mare. But it seems his horse is afraid of the dragging rope and won't get close enough to give Vern a throw.

I circle back to see what Bud looks like. His face is a solid mass of blood and Polly is all bloody in front. So Polly got hurt too, but they are both following the chase.

After a long chase, Vern is not able to get close enough to throw his rope, so he gives his rope to Bud. Then they both pull in close as I swing the black mare back toward our corral. We got her right against the right wing fence, and Bud pulls in above her. She tries to get through the wing fence, but she doesn't have the speed or power to do it. So she bounces back and Bud gets a throw. It is a long throw, but the loop goes over her head, and the chase is over. They lead her into the corral as I land.

The left side of Bud's face is badly skinned and peeled. Bud is in the barn putting a bandage on Polly's left front leg as I walk over there. Polly got an artery cut and lost a lot of blood. Bud has the bleeding stopped as I arrived. After Polly was taken care of, Frances tried to get Bud to come in the house so she can clean him up and take care of his cuts and bruises. But three men are here to buy some horses.

One of these men has a sheriff's posse in Idaho, and they buy five or six of our good-looking sorrels and buckskins. We are glad to see those horses find a good home. They have color, conformation and gentle dispositions. These horses are really something special to come in with mustangs. They have good breeding.

For $90 these men took one mare that will weigh about 1,000 pounds, and she will have another colt soon. Bud got a rope on her and looked at her teeth. She is six years old, and as we load her, she acts almost gentle.

After the work is all done, the pratha and saddle horses taken care of, Bud goes in the house. Frances washes him up and pops some joints in his back and neck. I don't know what shape he or Polly will be in tomorrow.

A stud bit Bud's foot, and he still soaks it in hot water at night. Some time back when Bud roped a large stud, the stud was highly insulted when he got roped. Instead of pulling back at the end of the rope, he came forward and bit Bud's foot that was extending forward out of his stirrup. The stud clamped his teeth down hard on Bud's foot and wouldn't let go. Two other riders there with Bud had a hard time to get the stud to let go of Bud's foot. Finally they succeeded.

That evening when Bud took the boot off his injured foot, there was a lot of blood in it and some toenails that were no longer attached to toes.

IMMELMAN TURNS

I have never been in a mustang camp before where there were so many injuries and where there were so many hard-to-catch horses. Having our wing fences and pratha-run on sloping ridges with all those trees complicates things a lot for catching horses.

All the merry-go-rounds didn't happen on the ground. Some of them were in the air.

One other day went something like this—

I was in the air again at 2:03. That was a rat race. This bunch was smart to our setup. They took out the left outer wing fence on the first try. Then I brought them back, and they went through the same wing a little further back. Two came back through and we caught them.

The riders brought the pratha back out, but these two horses split up. I stayed with one, and they brought the pratha out where I had it. It wouldn't take the pratha, so after a long run, Bud roped it. I don't know where the other one went, so I looked for a new bunch.

I landed and put in about seven gallons of gas without turning the engine off.

At 2:10 I saw five horses on high mountains east of camp. I also saw the three that were with my four a while ago. All eight, plus about a hundred deer are headed for camp, but not together.

At 2:40 I tried to contact camp on the radio but no luck. I guessed they haven't got in yet with that roped horse. They also had a lot of wing fence to repair.

At 3:10 I crossed the creek. I called Bud at 3:00 and 3:10. He was taking the pratha out. I thought those horses were slower than they were tired. That would mean they knew our setup and just didn't want to go that direction.

At 3:30 I gave the pratha signal. We missed all of them. They didn't seem to be wise to this setup, but they were wise to a pratha. Another rat race. On the second try the mustangs got the lead in the wings and kept trying both wings. Finally one crashed the right wing and got out. We caught the other four.

Tuesday, December 30, 1958. There was almost an inch of snow on everything. At 8 a.m. I was in the air solo, headed for the brand inspector's ranch.

We have about 29 horses in our corral, and a semi truck is due here today to haul them to Twin Falls. There were too many clouds in the mountains to run horses.

On that last run yesterday the maneuvering in the wing fences was so violent that I got the plane completely upside down within 50 feet of the ground and had to push my joystick all the way forward and do a half of an inverted snap-roll to recover.

When I learned to fly, the course of instruction called for teaching students to do Immelman turns. An Immelman is half of a loop with a half-roll from the top of the half-loop, which puts you right side up again and going in the opposite direction. This half-roll was always thought of as being half of a slow-roll, or aileron roll. The planes at the flying school were OX5 Waco 10's, and they were not capable of doing half a slow-roll from an inverted position on top of a loop. I spent several hours of my solo practicing Immelman turns, and finally got so I could do them by doing half of an inverted snap-roll from the top of a loop.

When I was practicing this maneuver with the planes at the flying school, I was always several thousand feet above the ground. When I got in trouble, as I often did in the upside down positions, the airplane would sometimes tumble and fall a great distance before I could manage to get it back under control again.

Yesterday was the first time I ever had an airplane upside down within 50 feet of the ground. This was not just practice. My life was at stake. This was the real thing, and I only had one shot at it. I was in a situation doing a precision maneuver that acrobatic pilots do at airshows. Even they do not do this maneuver within 50 feet of the ground.

They are highly skilled and continually do a lot of practice before the shows, so they will be at their very best right at show time. I was just a very bushy bush pilot faced with doing a precision maneuver I had not practiced for over 25 years. I could not have recovered from that predicament without having had this previous experience.

The doors and windows were open and the 32 blanks, 410 shotgun pistol, shells, and other things from the floor in front of me all floated in the air as this maneuver progressed. I think God took over along about there. Of course, I know now how to do an inverted snap-roll, but did I know it then, in the heat of the battle?

Some of these free-floating things went out the open door and windows, some of them ended up in the luggage compartment back of the back seat, and some of them ended up in the extreme tail end of the fuselage and are still back there. Luckily I didn't lose the 410 pistol or the 32 revolver that shoots blanks.

An error in judgment, such as the one that caused this predicament, requires only a fraction of a second and can result in a permanent ending of a person's existence. Sometimes I wonder how many reprieves I will be allowed for such errors. Some pilots don't get any. I have lost count of how many reprieves I have already had in my flying career.

TAKING PILLS

January 3, 1959, was a Saturday. I took off at 11:40 without my fountain pen. I thought I would write with the pencil I usually carried in the pocket behind the front seat. A few days before, when I was upside down, the pencil and other things in there came out and ended up in the tail end of the fuselage, and they are still back there.

Friday night when I went to bed, I had a sore throat. I had expected something like this, as I was susceptible to pneumonia. I had brought a jar of pills along and took two before going to bed and rubbed my chest with ointment. Saturday morning my throat was worse, and my lungs were sore. I took two more pills and did not try to get an early start.

Finally, by 11:40 I was in the air headed for our southeast area. A strong northwest wind came up and there was some local storming. I picked up the 11 horses I had seen there before and started in with them. I took them clear to the top of the mountain and called camp from the mountaintop at 10,500 feet.

These horses were fairly easy to handle, but it took me almost half an hour to put them across the creek where Larry had broken a trail for them with his saddle horse. Of course, it had frozen over again. After crossing the creek, they moved up to the pratha location okay. I called Bud and told him these horses seemed slow and might not be able to keep up with the pratha; he might have to push them to keep them together.

Like a lot of other things in this business, this was an uncertain situation. If I had let them get too close before I gave the pratha signal, they would sometimes put on extreme speed when they saw the pratha. Then they could get down between our wing fences ahead of the pratha. This sometimes ended up with the mustangs crashing a wing fence and getting away. On the other hand, if I gave the signal too soon on a slow bunch, the pratha got too far ahead and completely out of sight of the mustangs in the trees, turns, and hills on the pratha trail.

All things considered, I gave the signal to turn the pratha loose. The pratha came down the trail as usual, and I dived on the mustangs and put them together perfectly. Then after they got together, the pratha ran too fast for the mustangs, and the riders were too far behind. (This was after I had lost Polly.) The mustangs turned to the left. I dived down and put them back on the trail. By this time the pratha was out of sight, behind trees, around turns, and over a hill. Bud and Larry were behind the mustangs now, and together, with successive and rapid diving and with very good cooperation from the riders, we headed down the pratha trail with them.

The pratha was all the way in the corral before we even brought the mustangs over the hill. The mustangs were running from one wing fence to the other more than they were on the trail. We finally got them all the way down and in the corral, and the crew got the gate closed on them. Even as I landed, I could not tell if we caught all 11 of them or not. The corral radio was turned off, but I found that we did catch all of them.

Roger and Walt were there with Bud. Roger said that was really "some" flying. All the way in with this bunch, I had felt drowsy from the pills. The instructions on the bottle said not to drive or engage in hazardous occupations while taking the pills. There were some juniper limbs and bark in my left wing where I had put it through the top of a juniper tree.

IN THE DARK

Another horse run on the contact job went like this:

Right after 4:40 five horses started giving me trouble. I could tell from their actions they knew our setup because they did not want to go that direction. It just kept getting darker and darker. I could not make them go toward the pratha location, so I gave in a little and took them over the ridge a little higher. Then I got them down to the wash south of the ridge. The pratha was only about one-quarter mile down the canyon from us.

It was too dark for me to see the pratha. Bud explained on the radio that he was near the place on the ridge where I had battled that last bunch, and I could see the ridge.

This was a new pratha location the mustangs would not be used to. I knew from experience it is easier to fool mustangs in the dark than it is to fool them in the daylight. These horses battled me across the wash and started up the next ridge south, and in the dark I had quite a time with them. I finally got them back across the wash on the same side the pratha was on.

When they were approximately even with the point of the pratha ridge, I told Bud about where they were, and if he could see them, he should turn the pratha loose whenever it looked right to him. Finally, in the dark, I could see that Bud had turned them loose and everything was in motion. A couple of times I thought I could even make out the riders trailing behind.

It seemed that if we lost them, it would happen at the place where everything had to make a 90-degree turn to the right to get on the pratha trail that leads down to the corral. I concentrated on looking at that place and tried to keep a position that would permit a quick dive when they reached there. This means a sort of a combination of the edge of a stall and hanging on the prop, using half flaps and plenty of power. In other words, temporarily making a SuperCub act like a helicopter.

I had my red, green and amber navigation lights turned on, as well as the red rotating beacon, all of which made the airplane look like a flying Christmas tree. Along with this an occasional blast of the siren on my wing strut made it pretty effective in the dark.

As I watched this critical location, I saw a mass of black heading the wrong direction. I made a quick pass at them, yelled, fired my 410 pistol, and saw them swing back toward the pratha trail as I pulled up. From here on I could not see what was happening but could see something going down the pratha trail. So I made two or three quick low passes and yelled at them between there and the gate. I couldn't do any more shooting because I couldn't tell the mustangs from the riders.

Then I called the ground to see if we got them. Everyone was too busy to turn the corral radio on. Besides, if we lost them, I would have to land anyway because of the dark. I circled long enough to give the crew enough time to get them in the center corral and get the gate shut on them. Then I came in for a landing.

I stuck my head out the right side for better visibility and held the plane above fence level until I saw the gas barrels go by. Then I chopped the power and let it down with a big bump. As soon as I shut the engine off, I yelled up to the corral and asked if we caught them. We did—all five.

After we ate, I took a couple of aspirin to get back to normal. Bud said when I made that pass that turned them back on the pratha trail, it was so dark he couldn't see for sure which way they went, and he was right behind them. He thought they went that way, so he headed that way on his horse, but he came up on the wrong side of the pasture fence and had to turn back.

NAVIGATION

During much of the time while corralling horses, we were working under a lot of pressure, and things did not always work out the way we planned. However, I was relaxed part of the time and did not always take my navigation seriously.

One day at Tom Pedroli's mustang camp, the weather was too bad to run horses, so I decided to fly home.

The ceiling was low, it was raining, and the visibility was poor. I wanted to come out at the Indian reservation then follow the highway home. There was no map in the airplane, and I could not see anything to use to get my bearings so I could set a course. I just headed south. There was a *Reader's Digest* in the plane, and I started reading. Suddenly I looked up from reading, into the poor visibility ahead, and decided it was a good thing I looked up because south was the wrong direction for me to be flying, and I turned and flew north.

I looked down and saw some cows and calves. Some were lying and some were standing in the sagebrush on the wet ground in the rain. I thought, "Well, at least, even with all their discomforts they know where they are and are not concerned about getting lost." Shortly after this I woke up to the obvious fact that north was the wrong direction for me, and I headed back south again. Then I flew west for a while. Then I decided southwest would bring me out reasonably close. My compass was not compensated, so I did not know what corrections to make for deviation, and I didn't even try to figure variation. An exact heading was not very important anyway because if I was approximately right, I would come out to the oiled highway somewhere in the vicinity of McDermitt and could then follow it south.

I finally decided southwest would be okay, and I took a southwest heading, then went back to reading. Every time I looked up, I was heading 205 degrees. Then I would swing back to southwest and continue reading. This happened three or four times, and with my exact heading not being very important anyway, I just let the plane have its way. I let it fly down this 205-degree groove that I could not seem able to keep it out of and continued to read.

Finally I squeezed in between a high ridge and the clouds, and there I was, right over the Indian reservation. I could not have steered a better course than this on a clear day, and I did it by letting the plane go where it wanted to go while I read my magazine.

When getting this close to the corral, I liked to make two or three quick passes at the horses.

17

BEVERLY'S FALL
CEDARVILLE STRONG WIND

Wednesday, March 18, 1953. Hart Mountain horse job in southern Oregon.

In the air at 8:37 a.m. on a horse run. There is a strong southwest wind, and the sky looks threatening. When I throttle back a little, I can fly backwards. Even the birds stay on the ground in this kind of weather. Our daughter, Beverly, is one of my buckaroos on this job. Beverly and Supie will handle the pratha today.

I found a bunch of four and am headed in with them; they are on the Antelope Refuge. The air is very rough. These horses are slow and a long way out. The air is too rough to work them very close. Sometimes when I am near the ground, a wing drops suddenly, and I quickly apply full opposite aileron and rudder; it continues to drop until I begin to wonder just how crazy does a man have to get to do this kind of work.

11:15: They are getting close to the pratha now. I gave the pratha signal, but the mustangs stopped. The pratha is doing okay. If Supie would drop in behind the mustangs as he usually does, everything would be okay, but he isn't doing it. Now Beverly is doing the wrong thing. She is riding hard, too hard for safety, after the pratha, and she is in sight of the mustangs instead of in the draw where she should be. This has turned the mustangs back. I wish I could tell her to slow down. Smokey fell with her. Hard. Smokey got up, but Beverly is lying motionless on the ground among large thick rocks in the dry creek bed. Almost anything could have happened.

I signalled Supie to ride back to where Beverly is. She is up and limping away before Supie arrived there. Supie got off his horse, Brutus, and offered it to Beverly, but she wouldn't take it and is still limping toward the corral. She apparently is not seriously hurt.

I signalled Supie to bring the pratha back out and hold them on the other side of the ridge this time. I am not sure I can bring these horses back in this wind; they are very hard to turn.

I finally have them going back toward the pratha. This approach from the north is better for a tough bunch like this, especially with this strong southwest wind. It gives me a better chance to dive and pull up without having the tailwind blow me clear out of position.

11:58: They are in place now and I gave the pratha signal. This looks good, they are all headed down the pratha trail.

12:02: They are in the corral.

12:10: On the ground.

When the crew came in from the corral, I learned what happened with Smokey and Beverly. Smokey ran away with her, and she could not stop him. Smokey gets so excited when he hears my pratha signal he is hard to manage. He knows it is time to run and he wants to get in motion. We caught Smokey as a wild horse, broke him for this work, and he loves it.

I took this picture the day we caught "Smokey." He became one of my best riding horses.

12:45: In the air again on another horse run. The four we caught are all unbranded. I have another bunch of four headed for the corral.

2:27: Windows open.

2:37: They are in the corral.

2:45: On the ground.

3:00: In the air on another horse run.

3:17: I have a bunch of three. The wind is still strong and I can still fly backwards. It looks like a full-scale storm toward Cedarville, California.

4:18: Windows open.

4:28: Pratha signal. They are going down the pratha trail okay. We have never missed a bunch yet after they got this far.

4:36: They are in the corral.

This has been another rough day. Over seven hours of flying in very strong wind and rough air. Caught 10 horses, eight of them unbranded.

Beverly is resting fairly well tonight, but she has a headache and several pretty bad bruises from her fall with Smokey. I will get her to a doctor tomorrow if she is not feeling better.

Thursday, March 19, 1953.

9:15: Beverly and I are in the air headed for Lakeview to get her to a doctor. Following the road. Strong headwind and storming south and southwest of us.

The setup at Hart Mountain, Oregon.

9:30: Over Warner Valley now. The weather ahead looks pretty solid; I don't know if we can get through or not.

9:52: Have passed Plush. Following the lower road to Adel. Flying in rain, the outside temperature is 22 degrees above zero. It might be pretty rough flying over the mountains to Lakeview.

10:02: Adel is behind us. Following the oiled highway up a rugged canyon. Rain has changed to snow. Very poor visibility. Temperature 18 above at 6,000 feet. Cannot detect any ice on wings. If ice starts forming, I will turn back.

10:15: Weather is too thick. I turned back. There is nothing sure about even getting back to Adel. If it gets too thick, I can find a place to land on the highway, but even that will not be easy because of the steep canyon walls, curves and wind.

10:32: Back over Adel. The rain at Adel has turned to snow. We are flying through heavy snow as we progress toward Plush. All the ground we can see is white where it was raining a few minutes ago. At least we are out of the mountains.

10:36: Ice is forming on the wings and struts now, and it is getting heavy fast. I hope to make Plush. Don't see any good place to land here. The engine smells of hot oil, but the temperature is under 140, the oil pressure is over 30, and the engine is running smoothly with full carburetor heat.

Some mornings we had scenes like this to contend with before we could get started.

10:45: Landed on a road about one mile west of Plush and brushed the ice off the leading edge of the wings and struts. It was continuing to get thicker. That was a cold job.

10:49: In the air again, headed for camp. Snow has turned to rain east of Plush.

11:04: Ice is forming on the wings again as I climb through heavy snow to get over the Warner Valley rim to get to the Antelope Refuge Headquarters. Beverly is covered with a down sleeping bag on the back seat and seems to be asleep.

11:08: Passing headquarters in heavy snow. Will go to Lakeview in our pickup. The ice is getting thicker; it is a good thing I got the ice off at Plush.

Later we drove to Lakeview in the pickup. Arrived there about 3 p.m. and took Beverly to a doctor. He didn't find anything seriously wrong, but he gave her a prescription for some pills that later relieved the pain and headache.

Saturday March 21, 1953. I flew to Cedarville, California, to see if I could hire Clarence Maxwell to help us here, but he was already employed on a ranch job so he was not available.

Monday, March 23, 1953. 8:35 a.m. In the air headed for our horse camp from Cedarville. Lots of clouds but no surface wind.

I didn't realize the wind was so strong yesterday until I flew over Cedarville. It was directly across the single runway and much too strong for a crosswind landing. Besides, I am a little allergic to crosswind landings since I put my 90-horsepower Interstate on its back a few weeks ago in Idaho.

Several planes were tied down at the Cedarville airport, but no one was out there. I flew over town until I saw a car head north toward the field. Then I flew back out to the field and made an approach directly headwind, across the narrow surfaced runway.

As I made my final approach about 50 feet above the ground, the car pulled up to a stop just off the runway right in front of me. The four doors flew open, and five men jumped out and fanned out across the runway toward me. Two of them headed for my right wing as I sat there in the air waiting for them to get into position.

As they approached, I throttled back enough to settle down. The two men on my right wing had hold of the wing struts before the wheels touched the ground, and the three on my left wing were only a couple of seconds behind them. It was as though they were just standing there on the runway pulling me out of the air.

Such thoughtfulness and cooperation as displayed by these men is of great value to airmen in such cases of emergency. In my past flying experiences I have been assisted several times by quick-thinking and quick-acting men on the ground.

These five men were members of a local flying club. The wind had recently wrecked their Aeronca airplane while it was tied down. They were out in a shed repairing their airplane when I flew over; they were very conscious of the wind and readily understood my problem. They lost no time in coming to my rescue, for which I was very thankful.

RIDER INTERCEPTS HORSES

RIFLE SHOTS

On the Hart Mountain horse job in southeastern Oregon, I had problems with the Taft Miller family. They were a pioneer family in that area and were long-time abusers of the federal range laws. The Bureau of Land Management and the Hart Mountain Antelope Refuge, in attempting to bring them into compliance with their range permit, gave me a contract to gather all the horses that were in trespass on that range. My job was a simple case of fulfilling a government contract. In doing this, I caught some of Millers' horses, and they didn't like it.

Taft Miller was the kind of a man I would want on my side if I was in a gun battle with a band of desperadoes, and he was the kind of a man you would like to have as a neighbor if you did not have some cows out on the federal range that needed some of the grass his over-population of horses were eating.

Before I started making my setup at Hart Mountain, Millers got the word that I was going to corral those horses. This prompted them to corral horses in earnest before I could get started. In the end, they caught more horses than I did. Anyhow, between the two of us we took a lot of horses off the range, and after all, that is what the BLM and the Antelope Refuge management wanted. Nothing less than this could have caused Millers to take so many horses off the range.

Monday, February 16, I was in the air on a horse run at 10

a.m. Millers' pickup had just driven past our camp after I landed, returning from Lakeview. They had a saddle horse in it and parked about one mile east of our corral.

I picked up three horses, one white and two bays, on BLM ground north of Beatty Butte. As I approached the area where Millers' pickup or buckaroos could intercept me, I kept a close lookout for the pickup, riders, or rifle slugs. There was blood on the left hip of the white horse, so I guessed it was one they couldn't catch.

A rider intercepted my horses, coming in fast, between the mustangs and the pratha location. He was on the refuge. He turned my horses back, but I just kept diving and headed them south again. The rider stayed in position so he could cut in between the mustangs and my corral when I swung them back north.

When I first ran the mustangs away from the rider, after he had turned them back, I had seen him reach around to the right side of his saddle as though he was untying his rifle. At this point I had corralled over 9,000 horses and had never had anyone interfere with the bunch I was running.

Obviously, I could not put horses in a corral when a rider was out there to prevent it. If that had developed into a shooting war, they had me outgunned. I had a 32-caliber revolver with a solid barrel that shot nothing but blanks, and a 410-gauge shotgun pistol that wouldn't even sting a horse if I was more than 60 yards away. The shotgun pistol was an illegal gun. I had gone to our district attorney and sheriff and asked for a permit so I could use it legally in our mustang work. They both told me that everyone knows you have it, and no one is giving you any trouble, just go ahead and use it. So I never did get a permit to use it.

Millers had no restrictions on rifles and six-shooters, except that the refuge manager had ordered them to carry no guns on the refuge, an order they did not respect. If I had gotten close enough to do them any damage with the 410 pistol, I would have been in easy range of their superior firepower. I did not have the slightest interest in a shooting war with them, but was not easily bluffed since the law, such as it was, was on my side.

A study of the time and expenses I faced, in order to get the law to do what it was clearly supposed to do, helps us to understand why crime has continued to be such a profitable occupation in this country. The criminal is not handicapped by obscure rules and regulations, whereas the law-abiding citizen is.

My next move was to see what legal steps could be taken to prevent Millers from interfering with me carrying out the terms of the contract I had with the Antelope Refuge to corral these horses.

The refuge manager said he could not keep Millers from riding on the refuge with pickups and saddle horses if they were after their own horses, but they had no right to interfere with my activities.

On February 17 Jimmy Varien, the brand inspector, and I flew to Lakeview to talk to a lawyer. He told us we could expect some action from the Portland Game Commission. We also talked with the personnel at the local BLM office. We then flew to Burns and talked with the BLM there. We met with all the bigshots we could gather in Burns, and on Wednesday, February 25, Mr. Shelton, the deputy sheriff from Lakeview, came to our camp.

That afternoon I flew a horse run with the deputy sheriff in the plane with me. After the horse run he served Don Miller the papers to keep him from interfering with our activities. It took me 10 days to get some action out of the law enforcement agencies. During this time I was not able to corral any horses. The law should have been able to do this in 24 hours, but our law is actually a paper tiger.

On the last day of February it was 18 degrees above zero at our camp and five above in the air. I made a special effort to find oreanas (unbranded horses) because we needed eight or 10 to fill out a load. There was a heavy layer of broken clouds at 6,500 feet. There was frost on the sagebrush and rocks where the clouds had touched the mountains.

About eight that morning I jumped a bunch of six horses and a small colt. Nothing less than a perfect setup would have put these horses with the pratha. They went down the pratha trail with two riders on their tails and were in the corral at 10:52.

11:30: In the air on a horse run. I found a large bunch of 11 horses and no colts. They took off like oreanas, but they were slow. By 2:30 I was just getting them to Guana Slough when I heard something that sounded like a rifle shot from the ground. The horses heard it too and took off on a hard run. I

228

didn't see anyone around, but there were a lot of cliffs and trees where a man could hide.

If someone did shoot, they did me a favor. I had been shooting 32 blanks at the horses but was not able to get any speed out of them. The bullet was probably intended for me.

I would only have been able to hear a rifle shot during a relatively short period when the throttle was closed on various maneuvers in handling the horses. There could have been many rifle shots on this job I did not hear.

JIMMY VARIEN

The management of the antelope refuge and the neighboring ranchers had complained for years that Millers' horses were eating the grass that was needed to support the antelope and cows of that area. Taft Miller was an old-time resident there, and he seemed to think he had squatter's rights to all the grass his cows and horses could find, regardless of how this might affect his neighbors.

My contract called for having a state brand inspector in camp to inspect the brands on all the horses we caught. In fact, I paid half of the brand inspector's wages. Jimmy Varien from Burns was our brand inspector. Jimmy had diabetes and had to give himself insulin shots regularly to keep it under control. Sometimes he would get too much insulin and would pass out. At such times, we would give him a candy bar to offset the overload of insulin.

It was difficult for me to hire the kind of help I needed to handle the ground work on our job. I had flown to Burns, Prineville, Redmond, and Bend and had hired Walt Buchanan in Redmond. He was driving his car from Bend, and we had agreed to meet at the Paisley landing strip on our separate ways to my Hart Mountain mustang camp. At Paisley we loaded Walt's car with groceries for our camp.

As I approached my camp, I didn't see my pickup there, at the corral, or the Flook Ranch. This had me puzzled because I couldn't figure where it would be. I didn't see any sign of life as I flew over my camp. Jimmy's pickup was there. As I landed and taxied up to camp, no one was visible. I supposed Supie and Jimmy had gone to Plush in the Ford pickup to get some groceries.

I landed directly toward the cliff because there was a stiff wind from that direction. I tied the plane's left wing to my house trailer and opened the door. Jimmy was lying there on my bed. I thought he was just having one of his unconscious spells, but he looked very dead. I spoke to him but received no response, and I touched his arm. There was no question about it, he was really dead. No one was in camp to answer questions. I went over to his pickup, started it after several tries, and drove over to the road construction crew about half a mile away.

I was quite nervous when I arrived there. I talked to the road contractor and he already knew about it. Supie had told him, and Supie had headed for Plush in my Ford pickup to call the coroner. I drove Jimmy's pickup over to the Flook Ranch. The road contractors' men were camping and boarding there.

The contractor had just bought a new trailer house. He went into it, brought out a new bottle of whiskey, and opened it. Ordinarily, I am not interested in a straight shot of whiskey, but I took this one with enthusiasm—and a couple more in a short while. I decided I didn't want anything to eat, but Mr. Murphy came to the trailer house and asked me to come in and eat. As the dinner call came, I tagged along and washed up with the other men.

At 6:35 I left the table to go over to operate the two-way radio to get a message through to Burns. The contractor took me over in his Buick. We hurried over and turned the radio on. I heard Burns calling me, and I answered, but our battery was too low and they did not hear me. The road contractor went over to the gravel pit to get a good battery, but by the time he got back with it, Burns and Fields were off the air, and I couldn't get the Sheldon Refuge either, so we gave up.

Before we got back as far as the shovel, we saw lights coming from the Lakeview direction. We waited a little while, then drove up the road to meet the lights. I didn't want my new buckaroo to drive down to my camp in the dark and find a corpse there. He had our camp groceries with him, and I didn't want to lose either the groceries, or him.

When we met the lights, it was Supie and the coroner, so we all went back to camp. The coroner took Jimmy's body back to Lakeview. My new buckaroo drove up while the coroner was there.

1:45 a.m.: Supie and Walt are in bed, but I am not interested in sleep yet. The bottle of whiskey I bought for Christmas was finally being put to some practical use.

Tuesday, March, 1953.

7:30 a.m.: In the air headed for Burns. Three above zero.

9:00 a.m.: Landed in Burns. Reported to Tom Campbell and Howard DeLano, BLM. They called Jimmy's niece, Mrs. Coe. They also called Mr. Knickerbocker, head brand inspector at Salem. He said he would get a brand inspector out of Salem for us. Murl Coe and I flew out to my horse camp. After spending a little time there, we flew into Lakeview so Murl could talk to the coroner and the sheriff and make the necessary arrangements to get Jimmy's body back to Burns. We discovered at the sheriff's office that they suspect foul play in Jimmy's death.

The district attorney ordered a post-mortem. Jimmy's body and his personal belongings would not be released until this investigation was completed. Murl felt as we did that there was no foul play, but as long as there was any doubt, it would be better to get it cleared up than to have anyone under suspicion for a long time.

There were several rather severe bruises on Jimmy's head. If the investigation should show he died from a fractured skull, they planned a more complete investigation. Supie, Murl, and I told all concerned we did not suspect foul play.

The officials had expected someone to get shot in our mustang camp ever since we started that mustang job. They said people were making bets in Lakeview that someone would get shot in our horse camp. My name was the most frequently mentioned on this subject. Anything mysterious connected with a death in our camp looked bad to them.

Ferren Wall, the gas cowboy from Ontario, Oregon, arrived at camp on the brand inspection deal. He talked to Mr. Green. Mr. Green said he will come out from Lakeview and inspect our brands as we need him.

It was after 3:30 p.m. when the post mortem was completed. The district attorney, sheriff, deputy sheriff, two state police officers, two doctors, and coroner took part in it. Mr. Coe and I waited outside. When they reached their decision, they came out and told us Jimmy's death was caused from bronchial pneumonia. There was no skull fracture, and there would be no criminal action taken. The case was completely closed, as the death resulted from natural causes.

I do not recall that Supie ever mentioned anything about Jimmy having a cold. His lungs could have become badly congested while he lay unconscious with his head, arms, and chest on the frozen ground before Supie returned from the corral and found him in that position. The bruises on his head could have been caused by him falling against and opening the trailer door as he became unconscious. An overdose of insulin after breakfast could have caused unconsciousness, and the pneumonia developed after he became unconscious. An involved assumption, but it almost had to be.

Anyway, it is officially settled now, and we can get back to work. Murl and I are staying in town again tonight because Murl is going to take Jimmy's pickup and house trailer back to Burns with him, and he does not want to start out after dark. We will get an early start for camp in the morning.

Now, who was it who said that Ted just loves to run horses? Horse running is not for the meek, who are scheduled to inherit the earth, according to the "good book." Frankly, I do not believe they will be able to handle it. I am not exactly meek, and my very small part of it is too much for me to handle.

SQUAW VALLEY

On March 2, 1969, I flew the Squaw Valley area for the U.S. Fish and Wildlife Service. We were hunting coyotes on sheep lambing grounds. I had done flying in this same area early in January of this year for the Stanley Ellison Ranching Company. On that job their ranch foreman at the Squaw Valley Ranch, Mark Cowley, flew with me. We were looking their range over to see if they had missed any cows and calves when they gathered their cows last fall.

We didn't find any cows or calves, but we found one bunch of 10 horses. These were ranch horses. Mr. Cowley wanted me to bring these horses into the ranch with the airplane. He said he had tried several times to catch them with saddle horses but they had not been able to catch them. I asked him if these horses were branded. He said he was sure most of them were branded, and the young ones that were not branded would be colts from the branded mares.

I told him about my experience corralling horses for Julian Goicoechea and Art Cook. On that job they hired me to help them corral their ranch horses on their leased BLM land. The BLM was threatening to sue them if they did not remove these horses from the range. The BLM said there were no wild horses in that area. Before we finished the job, the Horse-Lover's organization had us arrested for corralling wild horses.

We had a jury trial in federal court in Reno, 230 miles from where I live. We hired lawyers; there were endless trips back and forth over a period of several months. The jury found us not guilty, but it cost us $5,000 to defend ourselves, and we lost a lot of time we could have used for more productive activities.

With this go-around fresh in my mind, I told Mr. Cowley it wasn't worth the risk to get involved with corralling his horses. It seemed to me this was the equivalent of our federal government confiscating private property when they make it against the law for a rancher to corral his own horses.

As we were flying over this area today, we saw these same horses. The whole area has had a heavy snow cover for the last two months. These horses are snowbound in a small patch of large sagebrush. We could plainly see their tracks in the deep snow. They had not moved 200 yards since this snow condition has existed. The horses were very poor and weak, just skin and bones. They had had nothing to eat for a long time except sagebrush, and they had eaten the hair from the other horses' tails.

I talked to Tex Oliver, ranch foreman for the I.L. Ranch, about these horses. He said they would probably all be dead by the time the snow melted. He added that if any horses were still alive, they would die when they started eating green grass again along in April because after having lived this long on heavy sagebrush, their stomachs would be filled with sticks and splinters from the brush. There is nothing anyone could do to save them.

This was a good example of how our present horse protection laws are denying ranchers the right to gather their own horses.

We ran a bunch of five coyotes away from the horses and shot all five of them. They were probably staying with the horses so they could start eating on the first horse that went down, even before it was dead. The coyotes were hungry also. So, how about a movement to feed the coyotes, at taxpayers' expense?

18

PIONEERING

No book of instructions came with the horse-running business. It was not an exact science. Countless people had tried it with varying degrees of success or failure.

In my 1933 horse-running experience I had learned many different ways to handle horses that didn't work, and I had hitchhiked home, leaving my wrecked airplane lying upside down on a high mountain in Nevada. This left me with no desire to ever do that again. My experience running horses with Marvin Myers in 1948 and 1949 was the first real success of corralling horses with an airplane I knew of. It makes all the difference when the crew on the ground knows how to handle that part of it well. Even this job might not have been a success except for some of the things I had learned in my 1933 experience.

Back in 1933 Art Seale and Bill Blakely wanted me to get several large bunches of horses together and bring them all in at once. I could never do this. Sometimes I could get several bunches together, but in moving them a long distance, they would never stay together. A stud bunch would split off and head a different direction, and while I was putting them back in the big bunch, one or two other stud bunches would split off the other side. At one time, on the Beatty Butte job in Oregon, I started in with a good solid bunch of about 150 horses (a mustanger's dream). But it was a long run. I could not keep them together and ended up putting less than 20 of them in the corral on that run. But 20 was a large bunch to corral on one run so I considered the run very successful. I believe about 35 is the largest number of horses I ever put in the corral on one run. I finally gave up on the idea of getting several bunches together and started bringing in one bunch at a time. At least that worked, and we could catch horses that way.

Even on my first horse job with Marvin in 1948, he wanted me to get several bunches together and bring them all in at once. I tried this again and still could not do it. Again I started bringing in one bunch at a time, and that is the way we caught horses.

As far as I know, I pioneered the idea of bringing in one bunch at a time. In buckarooing, when you are gathering ranch stock—either cattle, horses, sheep, or whatever—you always get a lot of them together before you start in with them. It took me some time to learn this does not work when corralling wild horses with an airplane, and it took me some time to convince various ground crews I worked with of this fact.

Also I pioneered the idea of tying a rope under the airplane and hanging cans on the outer end of it. This was used to help convince the horses they should go the direction I wanted them to go. This became my trademark as a mustang pilot. I broke several other mustang pilots into using the rope and cans, but after a little while they all quit using them, saying it was too dangerous. There was a certain amount of danger associated with this idea, but the results were favorable, and I didn't have to do so much shooting when I used the rope and cans.

In 1933 I used a rope 40 feet long, a regular lariat rope. When the cans hit a horse, a cliff or a tree, sometimes the rope would hang up. Of course, the airplane kept right on going. The rope would come tight and stretch. Sometimes it would break. Sometimes it would not break and would come loose and fly back toward the airplane as though it was made of rubber. Sometimes it would wrap around the wings or tail, and sometimes the cans would tear large holes in the fabric of the wings, tail or fuselage. Sometimes it would foul up my controls, the elevators or the ailerons. One time the cans broke the windshield out of the J-3 Cub. Three different times the cans bent the wire gas gauge that is only a few inches in front of the windshield on the J-3 Cub. One time the cans got into the propeller, but only near the outer tip. They broke off about an inch of one propeller blade. I just smoothed it off with a hacksaw and a file and cut the other blade off to make it balance.

Many things were tied on the end of the rope, and I tried ropes of different lengths and sizes. I finally settled on a 3/4-

inch manila rope. When this size hung up on something enough to make it break, it gave the airplane quite a jerk, but it never did put me down, and I broke several of these ropes. I heard some interesting stories from the buckaroos about things they saw: for instance, the rope lifting horses off the ground. If things like this really happened, I never saw them; that was not in my field of vision right at that time. Later I went to a 3/4-inch cotton rope. I have never broken one of these. Maybe I have just been lucky. Shorter ropes caused less damage to the airplane. The best length hung down 10 or 12 feet below the airplane.

Catching horses was the name of the game. If we did not catch the horses, we were out of business, so we just had to pay whatever the price happened to be to catch them.

In a high percentage of mustang flying, I was in a position where a sudden power failure would leave me with no satisfactory options. Not even considering a power failure, a lot of this kind of flying is done under conditions where just a small mistake in judgment could be very unpleasant.

Once, when I was running horses with Garley Amos in the south end of Grass Valley, I had just made a steep dive at the horses and made a sharp pull-up out of the dive. A few seconds later my control stick jammed, and I could not pull it back past neutral. It would move ahead and would move sideways, but I could not pull it back. If this had happened when I was in that dive, I would have gone straight into the ground with no chance of survival, and no one would have ever known what caused the crash.

This happened in my Piper PA-11 90 HP Continental. After a few minutes of level flying, the stick came unstuck and was perfectly free again. I did not trust it as I did not know what had caused it to jam. I reached some tools and removed the bottom and the back of the back seat while circling in view of the horses. Now I could see all the way back to the back end of the fuselage but could not see what caused the control stick to jam. I could not see anything wrong anywhere. So cautiously and with a feeling of apprehension,I flew back to my horses, took them in, and we caught them.

Then I landed and inspected the plane and still could not discover what caused the control stick to jam. Finally I took off and went on running horses, and it never did jam again. When I first bought this plane, it had a steel spring in the back end of the fuselage that held the elevators up in a neutral position when the plane was on the ground. I decided later that the spring might have caused the jam because it was disconnected at the time this happened, and was lying loose back there inside the tail end of the fuselage.

On the 1948 horse job on the Owyhee Desert in the J-3 65 HP Cub, I had almost exactly this same experience. I had just made a sharp pull-up from a steep dive at the horses, and the control stick jammed in this same manner. It would not move back from a neutral position. It also was free to move sideways and forward. I was reluctant to move it forward very far because I was not sure I could get it back even to neutral if I did. In just a short while it became completely free, and I finished the horse run. Then I gave the plane a complete inspection.

I found a piece of broom handle on the bottom of the fuselage just back of the rear seat. This was lying under the walking beam where the elevator cables go back to the elevators. It had vibrated up a fraction of an inch and had become wedged between the walking beam and a fuselage member. I could see the fresh marks on the broom handle that I had made when I was trying to force the stick back while it was wedged in there.

This was my first job with that plane. The pilot who had flown it before me had used the short piece of broom handle as a temporary rear control stick in order to give someone flying instructions, and it had been left in there. After having found this, I knew I had found the trouble, and it would not happen again. However, the PA-11 incident bothered me for a long time because I was never quite sure what caused it. (The pilot who left the broom handle in the J-3 Cub crashed a spray plane in Idaho and was killed about two weeks after this incident.)

On one horse job the top window blew out of a 65 HP J-3 Cub as I pulled out of a dive close to the ground. I did most of this flying with the right door and the left window open. This permitted the wind to blow through the cabin and out the broken top window. This destroyed a lot of the lift on top of the wings, and the plane would not do any more than just barely hold its altitude with full power.

I had to leave my horses and fly back to camp. Of course, we did not have an extra top window in camp, but I found a piece of stove pipe, flattened it out, cut it to fit the opening, and put it in with stove bolts. We were able to continue operating until I had a chance to buy a new top window.

The pilot's seat in the Piper PA-11 is the front seat. Passengers ride in the back seat. For student instruction, the instructor rides in the back seat with the student in front. Usually for running horses I remove the back control stick because occasionally some member of our crew would be riding with me and the rear control stick would be in their way.

One day when I was on a horse run with the PA-11, I had recently given a student some flying instructions and had neglected to remove the rear control stick. Then when I was pulling out of a steep dive at the horses, the G loading completely collapsed my front seat, and I fell into the back seat. Of course, my hand came completely off the front control stick. The only thing that kept me from crashing full speed into the ground was that in falling into the back seat, I fell against the rear control stick, and that finished pulling me out of the dive.

If the back control stick had been removed, as it normally should have been, that would have been my last horse run. I had to leave the horses, fly back to camp, and land. The wrecked front seat had to be removed and rebuilt.

Things like these do not happen very often, but just once can be too many times. The most well-prepared and the most innocent-looking takeoff can end in tragedy as it does for many people. This mustang type of flying is not the kind of flying where you can ever let your guard down. Sometimes a little luck can be very helpful.

Actually I was lucky. The injury to the right side of my face on the 1933 horse job is my only injury in my whole flying career. The ground crew suffered far more injuries than I did.

On one occasion, a stud we had roped in the corral grabbed the arm of one of our buckaroos. The stud clamped his teeth down hard on the man's Levi jacket at the wrist; then the stud reared up and came down on the buckaroo with his front feet. While this was going on, I was going at top speed over the corral fence to get to my 45 automatic which was in a pickup nearby, so I could shoot the stud to try to save the man's life. When the stud came down on the man with his front feet, the arm of the jacket tore off, the man was knocked clear, and the stud was at the end of his rope, so he could not reach the man after he was knocked clear.

All this happened so fast, it was all over before I even reached the pickup. If the man had not been knocked clear, I probably would not have gotten back with the 45 automatic soon enough to have saved him. If the stud had had hold of the man's arm instead of just the jacket sleeve, this episode could have had a sad ending.

CLAUDE BRYSON

Over the years I have had the good fortune to meet and work with some very interesting people who were the best in this line of work. One man who worked for us for a long time, Claude Bryson, was as good as they come. He was born and raised on a cattle ranch in southern Oregon, where there were a lot of wild horses. As he was growing up, the mustangs held his interest more than the cows did, and he spent a lot of time chasing mustangs with saddle horses. So when he came to work for us, he already had a lot of experience with saddle horses and with mustangs.

I asked Claude to write some of his experiences that we might be able to use here. Unfortunately, because of limited space, we cannot use all of it, but here is part of what he wrote, in his own words:

> Some of those studs were a bit ancient and I used several to run mustangs at the trap. They were good runners and tough, but sometimes I never had much control. We would get behind a wild bunch and my mustang saddle horse would run wide open and out of control down a mountainside and over whatever got in front of us. A time or two he went full tilt at a dead run downhill with no control, over a cliff that was a little higher than I care to be on a horse. We lucked out when we hit straight and never rolled over. I guess if it had been 100 feet it would have been the same.
>
> Twice, with Barber and Utter I remember my horse falling in a wash, with me underneath him and the horse not able to get up, and me not able to get out from under him. Once Ted saw me right away from the air and had my partner come and help me by pulling the horse off me. The other time I was pinned under a horse in a wash for perhaps an hour and a half before Ted flew back and spotted me. Chug then rode out to my rescue.
>
> On one horse job Bill Garavanta and I were in camp alone

for a few days. Bill was also a pilot and he had been helping fly horses. We had a new horse that someone had brought for us to use for a while. So with nothing much else to do, I got on him and took him out to try him out for speed and endurance. He had the speed all right, but at top speed he fell, rolled, then ended over, and the saddle cantle hit me in the back, breaking my back. I was alone and knew if I could do anything, I had to do it in a hurry or I never would.

I crawled to my horse, which had gotten up and was standing and staggering a bit, practically knocked out. I reached him, grabbed my stirrup, and pulled myself into the saddle with my arms. This was a gentle horse. I don't think I could ever have done this if he hadn't been so stunned. He never moved while I pulled myself onto him, just stood there shaking. We made it to camp, and Bill helped me inside our trailer and onto a bed, where I just couldn't lie comfortably—my back was killing me.

Bill was afraid to try to take me out in a pickup, as well he should. He went to Boone Springs Station to phone for an ambulance. Ely wouldn't send one because we were just over the county line, and Elko wouldn't because it was too far and closer to Ely.

Bill came back a couple of times to check on me and tell me the bad news. Then he would take off and make another trip. Finally he got hold of Chug in Winnemucca, and Chug put the pressure on someone. An ambulance finally came to take me to Ely, to the Steptoe Valley Hospital, $12\frac{1}{2}$ hours after I was hurt.

While Bill was at Boone Springs these different times trying to get help, there was a fellow there at the station who had gotten stranded. He had wrecked his car. Bill had told him of my predicament, and he got very concerned and really worried about me. Now Bill had quite a sense of humor and really enjoyed razzing someone. So on this last trip he told this fellow, "Hell, I can't get Claude any help and he is in too much pain, so I will just go back to camp and shoot the son-of-a-bitch and put him out of his misery." The guy took him seriously and darn near went off his rocker. I guess Bill had quite a time quieting him down, with the help of the station operator.

Needless to say, my back being broken stopped my mustanging for quite a spell. Several years later Ted and I ran horses again on two different occasions in another state. Soon after that I left the desert country and moved to Emmet, Idaho. I miss the mustangs, as there are none in this area. But it is impossible to do anything with them, anyway—too much protection and no control.

URANIUM

There was never a time when I really enjoyed running horses. I had never lost faith in our farming venture, and running horses was the only way I knew to make the money we needed to get our farm on a paying basis. I figured at each point of the way that we were about to accomplish this. I gave a lot of thought to trying to locate some activity other than running horses to make a living. But it seemed we were always in a situation like a bank robber who needs to rob just one more bank—then he will have enough money to retire.

In 1951 we had a deep 16-inch irrigation well drilled on our farm. With the money that came from horse running and Margaret's teaching wages, we purchased an irrigation pump, diesel pump engine, and a sprinkler irrigation system. We tried to produce a pay crop on our north 80 acres: oats, barley, and corn. The total crop sold for almost enough money to pay for the fuel the pump engine used.

During the big uranium boom that made millionaires out of so many people, I got started using our airplane (a Piper PA-11 90 horsepower Continental) to search for uranium by flying around likely-looking places with an instrument that was supposed to register if we flew close to a uranium deposit. This activity involved flying in mountainous areas. At one point, a small group of prospectors figured they had found a really rich uranium field in Death Valley, California. They called in a scientist from southern California to verify their find. After he looked the area over, he was well impressed with it, but he said the best way to really check it out further was with an airplane carrying his very sensitive instrument. He told these people he knew only one pilot he would ride with on this type of flying, and that was me.

They called me, and I did the flying for them. I became permanently associated with the group until we reached a point where it became obvious we were not able to get our hands on anything that would be profitable mining, and we discontinued our operations.

At one time I had an interest in about 1,000 uranium claims, but we never found one ounce of uranium, and we never made any money from these activities. I could not develop much interest in just making money from investors on worthless mining claims, as so many people did.

We discontinued our mining activities in 1955 and managed to get our south 100 acres leveled for surface irrigation. I had lost confidence in sprinkler irrigation after our 1951 experience. Most of 1955 was spent preparing for the 1956 farming.

SPRAYING

In 1956 we raised corn and grain on our 100 acres. We almost made expenses that year. I still did some flying but was trying to get away from horse running. Margaret had gone back to teaching school, and in 1957 I worked one year as a blacksmith at a mercury mine out of McDermitt, Nevada. I have done a lot of different things, but being a blacksmith surprised even me.

In 1957 one of our neighbors raised 40 acres of alfalfa seed. This was the first alfalfa seed raised in our valley, and it was fairly successful. Quite a few farmers had moved into the Quinn River Valley by this time, and everyone was trying desperately to find some crop that would show a profit. The 40 acres of alfalfa seed looked encouraging, so there were plans for more alfalfa seed to be produced in the valley in 1958.

Alfalfa seed required spraying, and I was persuaded to do the aerial spraying. I did this from 1958 to 1960, using three Super-Cubs. This was a new occupation for me also.

Most of the spray work was for killing various insects that were detrimental to raising alfalfa seed. Alfalfa seed producers, of which we had become one, had to use bees to pollinate the crops. When we sprayed in the daytime, we also killed the pollinating bees. We could spray only about one and one-half hours very early in the morning and about one and one-half hours very late in the evening. We could not cover many acres on this type of a schedule. Then I heard that someone in California had solved this problem by putting lights on their plane and spraying at night.

In 1960 I put lights on our two SuperCubs and sprayed nights. This really solved the problem, and I became one of the pioneers in night aerial spraying. Nearly all spray operators do it now.

242

After three seasons of spraying, I decided that job was even less desirable than horse running. In 1961 we sold our spray business to a pilot who moved from California. He operated one season, crashed and burned one of our planes, then went through bankruptcy. This left us in worse condition than when we sold to him. I did not want to go back into spray work. So I went to California, found another pilot with spray experience, and made a deal with him to come to Nevada, take over our business, and operate from our field using our shop and hangar for the first year.

Alfalfa and clover seed proved to be money makers in Quinn River Valley. In 1963 we succeeded in getting an FHA loan, leveled the rest of our 160 acres, and planted certified alfalfa seed.

Honeybees have been the main pollinating bees for such crops worldwide, for thousands of years. However, we learned there is a wild bee, called a leafcutter bee, that is a much better pollinator than honeybees. Leafcutter bees lay their eggs in small holes (about $7/32$ of an inch) that are drilled in boards. Farmers were drilling about 2,000 holes in a board 3 inches thick by 6 inches wide, by 48 inches long, for these bees to lay their eggs in.

I designed and built an automatic drilling machine that drilled these holes. It drilled 60 holes per minute, automatically, moving the board to its proper position, and it turned itself off when the last hole was drilled. We hired a man to operate this machine and sold the drilled boards to alfalfa seed producers.

Our FHA operating loan budget was worked out on the basis of my continuing to do commercial flying, which consisted of a rather wide variety of flying jobs, since my reputation as a horse runner was spreading far and wide.

SALT DROPPING

Many ranchers in this area had horses on their leased BLM land they couldn't corral without using an airplane. I still helped ranchers corral their horses in situations like this, but had sold all of my horse running equipment. I did some flying for the United States Forest Service, the Bureau of Land Management, the Nevada Fish and Game Department, the United

States Fish and Wildlife Service, shooting coyotes, and considerable flying patrolling power lines. Also, I dropped thousands of 50-pound blocks of salt for livestock in areas where it was too rough to drive ground vehicles.

I developed a bomb rack to mount under each wing and put seven 50-pound blocks of salt in each bomb rack. There was a small nylon cord from each block of salt running into the cabin for releasing the salt. The ranchers wanted only one block of salt at each location; this idea scattered the cows out more and they made better use of the grass on the range. When the salt was put in large piles, as it often was when placed with ground vehicles, the cows bunched up around the salt, overgrazed the area near the salt, and did not range out far enough to make proper use of the range grass where there was no salt.

I perfected a dive-bombing technique and could place each block of salt very accurately. The plane would enter a stall about 150 feet above the ground, with full flaps, then go into a steep dive. I would release one block of salt; then the flaps were put in half position as I pulled out of the dive with just enough flying speed to regain control.

Loaded for a salt run; 14 50-pound blocks, 700 pounds. The 125-horsepower Supercub. Ground elevation, 5,000 feet. This road was my airport.

Also, by developing different release latches for these bomb racks, I flew steel and wood posts, rolls of barbed wire, and other fence-building supplies into mountain areas for fence builders. Otherwise, these supplies would have to be packed in on pack horses.

Twenty years after starting to do commercial flying in Nevada, I was still flying the same SuperCub I had been flying for the last 10 years. I had flown this plane 8,000 hours, much of it very rugged hours, and it was still going strong. Even at that point, the money I earned with the airplane was still essential to our activities. There was no shortage of flying jobs.

I hauled 600 to 700 pounds of steel posts, wood posts, rolls of barbed wire and anything else the fence builders wanted delivered on their fence building job up in the mountains where only pack horses or airplanes could do the job. The 125-horsepower Supercub.

Loading for a flight home. Half a deer under each wing and half a deer in the luggage compartment. Daughter-in-law Fern and grandson Teddy on back seat, Ted in front. Total weight, anybody's guess. Ground elevation, 8,600 feet. We will land at home seven minutes after lift-off.

On the way home.

19

REFLECTIONS FROM THE COCKPIT

A lot of water has gone under the bridges since I was the little boy who looked up at the sky and wondered what goes on up there, and since as a somewhat older boy, I built a glider out of cane fishing poles bought at our local hardware store for 25 cents each.

My specific goal in life was to fly. In my early stages of life this seemed light years ahead of my ability to achieve it. I spent critical years in my effort to accomplish this. This was my "Gettysburg Charge Up the Stairways to the Stars." During these critical climbing years I was willing to settle for nothing less.

There was a long, hard, and sometimes frustrating road to follow before I achieved an entry into the aviation world. Then there followed a road just as long, hard, and frustrating. But at least during this phase I had the satisfaction of living the life I had worked so hard to get into. There were no free rides anywhere along the way.

Just the fact that I have had the privilege of participating in the most exciting venture in the history of our society is very satisfying to me. The fact that I have never made the "big time" disturbs me not at all. I could have made more money over the years if I had gotten a job doing almost anything else, but it would not have been as rewarding.I feel fortunate to have entered this life in the early stages of aircraft development. I have been engaged in aviation as a pilot for a period covering more than 61 years. Of the 82 years that have elapsed since the Wright brothers' first flight, my lifespan covers 78 of those years. Now nearing 80, with great grandchildren, I remember the "good old days"—many of which I would not care to live over unless I was guaranteed that the outcome would be no worse than it was on the first go-around.

As I look back over the years of my love affair with aviation, I realize I have lived through an exciting period of human history; I have seen many, and have participated in some, of the developments that have brought us to where we are today. I am grateful for those who have passed this way before me and have left their vapor trails in the sky for me to follow; and I would like to believe I have also left a few vapor trails for those who follow me.In my youth it seemed to me that conquering the sky was the wave of the future. It presented adventure for all and glory for some, but also hardship, disappointment, and even death for many.

Only after seemingly endless struggles did I succeed in becoming a licensed pilot. Then throughout my flying career, if I achieved any successes, they were sometimes shadowed by the struggles for goals I never reached.

I started with less than nothing and lifted myself by my bootstraps into the life I wanted to live. I feel grateful for the successes I have had, rather than resentment for my failures, which also have been significant.

At college commencement exercises the speaker says something like this: "Whatever you want is out there. Claim it. It's yours." I go along with that and say more power to them, but I did that with an eighth grade diploma. All the goodies of this world are not reserved for college graduates.

I realize any good story has to have a conclusion. For me this presents a problem. As I write this, I have only experienced 78 years of this life. The story of my life still has drama and conflict, crises and climaxes, but the conclusions have not been pinned down yet. The drama and conflict in my story are the drama and conflict of life itself. May I survive long enough for it to tie together and make sense.

A very wise person once said, "Life is a disorderly journey; we hardly ever get where we are going, but there is adventure in putting into strange harbors." I agree with this statement. I did not get where I was going; I have had a disorderly journey; I have put into strange harbors, and there has been no shortage of adventure in my life.

It seems to me that an unreasonable amount of my life was spent just looking for the sky. I knew it was out there all along, but I did not know how I could get into it. When, after it seemed forever, I did get into it, I had 50,000 square miles of it to call my own. I didn't fight off intruders like hawks and eagles do. I welcomed other adventurers into this vast sky. That was more than I could handle anyway. At times, I felt a little lonesome out there all by myself, and I figured I needed some help to get this sky tamed and domesticated. That became my business in the years ahead—to introduce others to this vast, untamed sky.

This sky had many faces and moods. Sometimes it was a lonely sky, filled with wonderment and adventure for a young inexperienced pilot who was not only inexperienced regarding flying, but also in the ways of the world. Sometimes this sky was friendly and inviting, sometimes it was hostile and threatening, and sometimes it was downright vicious. It could throw large hailstones and bolts of lightning as easily as it could smile. Eventually, I learned not to provoke it when it was having one of its moody spells.

It was scheduled to give me a lot of education in the years ahead. I had already matured considerably, but I was going to grow a great deal more in this big, wide-open sky that lay ahead. It was not only going to teach me about flying; it was also going to teach me about how our society operates. Even more than this, it was going to teach me about how our society does not operate.

Sometimes, when flying through poor visibility, I could feel the presence of the ghosts of the early aviation pioneers, not just the famous names we are all familiar with, but also the little guys and gals we never heard about who were invisible to our aviation history writers. They were also an important part of progress in the aviation world, and just as interesting to visit with. Sometimes I thought I could see the faces of future generations, but the crystal ball I used as a guide for the pitfalls of daily activities was often cloudy and had limited visibility.

I had no compass in my airplane that would guide me through these types of obstacles. Neither our public school system nor Tex Rankin's Flying School taught me how to navigate through these kinds of waters.

As I look back on these experiences, it seems to me now that many of the problems I had in earlier days (except for those caused by my poor judgment and general lack of knowledge that all, or most, pilots of that era possessed) were caused by lack of mechanical refinements in the engines. I did very little flying behind engines other than OX5's until well into 1933, and the other engines of that period were not much better.

As for real flying ability, no one had that until they had succeeded in living through several years of strenuous flying experiences. If they were too cautious in doing this, they never really learned the limits a pilot has to keep his airplane within for safety. I have been told, "There are old pilots and there are bold pilots, but there are no old bold pilots." However, a certain degree of boldness was required to be a successful pilot.

Even when a proper balance between caution and boldness was exercised, only a certain percentage of pilots survived, because you had to play close to the edge of recklessness to really live with this thing, to really learn it. You could lose your life even when living up to all the safety rules. Judgment, seasoned with years of experience, was the best insurance you could have. Your first few years were without very much insurance.

Overconfidence can be fatal in the flying business, but also, so are a lot of other things, such as fear and lack of confidence. If I had my early flying days to live over again, I doubt if I would do things very much differently. I was never one to back away from adventure in an airplane.

Fifty years back, the average pilot did not understand flying very well. When I think of all the things I have learned about flying since I became a licensed pilot, it makes it seem like a joke that I considered myself a pilot the day I received my pilot's license. A pilot's license is merely a permit for you to go out into the world and learn "the rest of the story."

Over the years I was destined to learn many things I did not learn from books, or even from my flight instructors. It seems that during a good part of my life I have been facing the unknown, trying to figure out how certain things really are, as compared to how they seem. I have discovered that in the earlier days of aviation we were dealing with many misconceptions and unknowns—at least I was.

Although I have always had high confidence in my ability to fly, I have never mastered all the elements of aviation I have come face to face with, which brings me around to say that flying is something that is never completely learned. No one person will ever know all there is to know about flying. Some of the skills that were essential to pilots of earlier days are escaping our modern pilots. However, our modern pilots are developing skills that evaded pilots of earlier days. We old-timers are rapidly becoming an endangered species.

In my early flying days, Bend, the largest city east of the Cascade Mountains in central Oregon, still was only a small jump from the early-day pioneer town it had been. I knew most of the people there, and the ones I didn't know knew me, as I had the only airplane, an OX5 Waco 9, and operated the only flying business in that 50,000-square-mile area.

In the 1920's and much of the 1930's aviation was not recognized as a respectable occupation. The powers in control of things could not believe aviation would ever play a very important role in our national security, or that it would, in any important way, affect our civilization.

In reading accounts of World War II, we learn that one of the greatest national assets this country has is the intelligence and adaptability of our youth. When this intelligence and adaptability of youth was available in my earlier years, it was not recognized as a national asset. In fact, our government aeronautics inspectors considered it a liability. Our young pot smokers of today receive more consideration from our government than young people did in my youthful days.

In the earlier days of aviation there were no specialized experiences to draw from. Aviation was made up largely of pilots like myself. The only thing we had to offer was our strong interest in flying. The records of this period speak for themselves, and they show in no uncertain terms that no phase of aviation was an easy money proposition. It was not in any sense of the word a get-rich business. Although I am sure all of us had a desire to make a lot of money, just as soon as we could get a few uncontrollable things under control.

There were times when I actually had a few hundred dollars in my pocket. But along about this time a power failure would result in a crash landing. Before I was back in business, I would be scraping the bottom of the barrel again, and sometimes selling flying instructions at reduced prices in order to get payment in advance, so I could get going again.

This is briefly the picture of barnstorming in the late 1920's and the early 1930's, when the best planes available were the

OX5-powered Wacos, Travelairs, American Eagles, Birds, etc. We tried many things in those days,and we considered a lot more than that.

There were meetings with big stockbrokers from the East to introduce plans for starting airlines with Tri-motored Fords that cost $50,000 each. Why not? We might develop into a big prosperous airline. (That is how and when our big airlines of today got started.) But there were conservative members on our board of directors who dragged their feet and were too timid to incorporate for enough money to take such a gamble with investors' money. So these ideas died on the vine and we fell back on more OX5 barnstorming days.

The Great Depression of the 1930's was on us and getting worse. Finally, instead of being the big wheels of a large corporation and airline, it was WPA for $15 per week and more barnstorming to try to keep on eating.

One day I landed my Waco 9 on Swan Island in Portland on a charter flight, and there was a twin-engine Douglas plane there. I was told this type of plane was going to replace the twin-engine Boeing 247 that was very popular on the West Coast airmail and passenger runs.

I had never seen an airplane as large as this before. It was called a DC-2. I walked all around this plane and looked it over as well as I could. I doubted its value. It looked too large and heavy to be practical. I was sure it would have no value for the kind of flying I was doing. The kind of fields I flew from couldn't accommodate a plane this large.

The crystal ball I used to make judgments like this could have had some flaws in it. This seems apparent now when looking back 50 or 60 years and realizing the next model Douglas came out with was only a slight improvement over the DC-2. It was called the DC-3, which became the world's most famous airplane. It played a very important role in helping us win World War II, and many planes of this model are still flying today.

I stayed with flying and was instructing on the war flight training programs at Boeing Field in Seattle when Japan attacked Pearl Harbor. After the war I did a great deal of flying in the western states; and as I have reached the age of 78, I have accumulated over 25,000 hours of flying time. During my commercial flying days I never had a student damage an airplane and have never injured a student or a passenger in an airplane. I became a member of the Veteran Air Pilots' Association over

252

40 years ago and am a member of the OX5 Aviation Pioneers.

Now, retired on our farm in northern Nevada, I remember the "Good Old Days" when Lindbergh was the brightest star in the sky and I was naive enough to see no limits in the path ahead. Although there have been some rough spots and uncertain times, it has been a good life, hopefully with more still to come.

When remembering back to the period covering my early years of flying, the parts that come to mind first are the power failures, the crash landings, and that sort of thing. However, these sorts of things did not add up to one percent of the flying I did. If the details of the other 99 percent were as easily recalled, those years were not so bad.

I was living the life I set out to live, and I was enjoying it. The bad spots were actually products of the times, over which no one had much control. But these facts in no way lessened the frustrations at the time. The causes of many of the countless power failures were not understood until years later. Also, we did not know as much about flying as we thought we did. We thought we were pretty hot pilots.

They say all the world is a stage, and we are the actors, and most of us are under-rehearsed. I certainly was under-rehearsed as I stepped out on the stage of life. It would be an understatement to say we were not very smart in those days. However, eventually we did learn how to fly airplanes. Today, students have to spend so much of their time trying to learn how to handle their fancy electronic and navigation equipment they never have time to find out what they can do with their airplanes when the going gets tough.

It would be difficult for today's pilots to understand what flying meant to pilots of earlier days. A bare minimum of instruments, no radio, no weather information, no flight plans. We experienced just plain old-fashioned flying in our own private sky that gave us very little concern over mid-air collisions, as there were only 32 airplanes in the whole state of Oregon as late as 1929, and most of these were on the west side of the Cascade Mountains. I was on the east side.

The whole world lay at my feet. Aviation was in its infancy, and I was a part of it and would grow up with it. My crystal ball was a little cloudy, so I could not see exactly what lay ahead, but in my eyes it had to be something good.

Try as I might to get a view of the face of destiny, it eluded me. All my life lay before me, with horizons unlimited. In a few years everyone would own an airplane. They would use their airplanes more than they use their cars, and I would fit into the picture somewhere.

Maybe it is just as well that I was unable to see what really lay ahead. If I had a million guesses at the future, I would have missed on all of them, except one, that is: I said a long time ago that someday someone would build an airplane that would carry 100 people—and now they have done that, and then some.

During this period I would not have accepted a job flying the airmail if someone had offered it to me. I could not have gotten very excited about flying those large planes on routine monotonous daily runs, with some character on the ground telling me what to do over a radio.

There was always a certain amount of glamour associated with the idea of being an airmail pilot. There was a "lot" of glamour associated with the idea of receiving a steady monthly paycheck. Even though the pay was not very high in those days, it was more than we made as barnstorming pilots, and someone else paid for rebuilding crashed airplanes.

It seems that nearly all pilots a generation before me had military training. Jimmy Doolittle, Lindbergh and Rickenbacker are famous names with military backgrounds, and there are many others. They also had other things going for them in order to get the military training—political pull or money, or both. I had nothing going for me. I was swimming upstream all the way. I have been told that half the fun is in the struggle, and you can get the other half anywhere you can find it. Well, I have had half the fun and am ready for the other half now.

We like to think of a fox as being a smart animal. I have no quarrel with this. However, even among foxes, there are some smarter than others. Putting this another way, there are some not as smart as others. Putting it still another way, there are some dumb foxes out there. Well, even dumb foxes can teach their young a lot of important things about how to survive in a hostile world.

I see a parallel here with foxes, pilots, and flight instructors. In the early days of aviation pilots were looked up to. (How do you like that?) What I mean is that they were something special. They were a little above ordinary mortals. (I did it again!)

By the time I came along, the public was beginning to re-assess their earlier judgment of pilots and suspect they were not any smarter than other people. Maybe I had something to do with this frame of mind.

At any period of aviation you choose to focus on, when a flight instructor taught a student to fly, he was teaching him all he knew about how to survive in a potentially hostile sky. This gave the student his "start" in aviation, but that is all it was, just a "start."

This left the student with a great deal more ahead of him to learn than he received from his flight instructor and because of the fact that with pilots, like with foxes, some are smarter than others. Consequently, we eventually had a lot of pilots roaming around up there in the sky who had various degrees of competence.

Speaking of foxes, how about the time I was flying a Gull-Wing Stinson Reliant west of Billings, Montana, back in the early 1940's! Stormy weather, high winds, and very poor visibility. I was following the west leg of a radio beam out over the Crazy Mountains when I became suspicious that I might be following a false beam. I figured the weather was too bad for me to start hunting for the real beam out there over those mountains, so I did a 180 and flew back to Billings, where we spent the night.

My passengers were Mr. Barth, his wife, my wife Margaret, and our two children, Beverly and Curtis.

The next morning we flew over the Crazy Mountains in much better weather and made it back to Seattle okay. This is not an example of using a high degree of flying skill. It is an example of using proper judgment in a potentially dangerous situation. Sometimes there isn't anything that is any more fun than to just be safely on the ground after a ride like that.

Even today, poor judgment causes more airplane crashes than lack of skill. Both flying skill and flying judgment are highly personal things. An example of poor "judgment" is when a pilot continues flying into bad weather and it gets worse and he ends up in impossible conditions where no amount of flying "skill" can save him. An example of poor flying "skill" is stalling out in a turn and spinning in. No two pilots have exactly the same degree of skill or judgment in flying an airplane. I have never found out where I would fit on a scale that was designed to measure flying skill, or judgment. Perhaps we should leave it like that, but somehow I have managed to survive many hours of flying over the years in a sky that is sometimes docile and sometimes extremely unforgiving of human error.

In many lines of activities we figure each day as eight hours in a work day, 24 hours in a whole day, seven days in a week, 30 or 31 days in a month, and 365 days in a year. Even looking at it this way, for too many people, life becomes monotonous drudgery to be tolerated, not really enjoyed. Monotony has not been a big problem in my years of flying. There have mostly been challenge and adventure.

In some cases these flying hours are made up of minutes, and the minutes are made up of seconds. Some of these seconds are made up of small fractions of seconds, and some of these fractions of seconds can hold hidden hazards or hidden joys that are unknown in other professions.

Early in my flight training Tex Rankin explained to me the advantages of looking around the shadow of my airplane for the shadow of other airplanes, especially when flying near an airport or any other place where other airplanes might be encountered. But it was only after 40 years of flying that I discovered that when a night landing is to be made under conditions where no other satisfactory lights are available, any visible shadow of your airplane that is made by the moon can give you a very accurate gauge for leveling off for your landing.

When I discovered this, I was making a night landing on a dry lake that was over 10 miles long. In getting into position for the landing, I could not judge my altitude above the ground within several hundred feet. So when I believed I was several hundred feet above the ground, I held the nose up to a position that would be about halfway between cruising and a three-point position. Then I throttled back enough to let the plane settle slowly.

As I was settling, I just happened to notice the shadow of my plane that the partial moon made on the dry lake. Then as things progressed, I watched the movement of this shadow as it came closer and closer, until it finally touched my wheels just as I landed. This interested me, and I made several take-offs and landings while I studied this situation. I learned that with very little practice there was no wild guesswork involved and that good results are easily obtained and consistent.

Why does it take so long for a pilot to learn things like this? A pilot shouldn't have to fly 40 years to learn this, the way I did. A student should learn this on his first 50 hours of flying. But students today probably are not learning about how the shadow of their plane, made by the moon, can be used to help them on night landings.

Pilots deal with facts, not fantasies, but fantasies can seem almost real as we see a full-circle miniature rainbow with the shadow of our airplane in the center of it, following us through the sky. Then we see a full-sized rainbow that is full circle lying at about a 45-degree angle. Then we see countless wispy shapes with ever-changing patterns, with all shades of color from the brightest white to total black, and sometimes lightning flashes, lacing things together.

Our venturesome spirit tells us to move in, investigate, and see what is going on in there. But we remember we did that once and escaped only by the skin of our teeth. Once was enough, almost too much, and we felt just plain lucky to get out of there alive. So our natural instinct for survival tells us to stay out of there and be content to look at it from a distance.

I can think of no other occupation where we are dealing with "facts" more than in flying. But there are times when facts are hard to come by and fantasies seem real.

The young student looks ahead. Some day, soon now, he will be good enough to solo. Then he starts figuring the steps ahead for his private pilot's license. At the time of his first solo flight, the goal of a private pilot's license is a molehill that looks to him like a mountain taller than Mt. Everest.

After his private license is in his pocket, his commercial pilot license and instrument rating are even tougher hurdles. If and when he gets these, there are still endless mountains to climb—instructor rating, multi-engine rating, seaplane rating, and so on. The obstacles seem endless.

If the ultimate, the airline pilot rating, is ever achieved, that is still not the end of the line. After he gets this, he spends the rest of his flying career going to school just to keep up with new developments and new equipment. By the time he reaches the ripe old age of 60, there are so many new developments and new types of equipment staring him in the face that now he is getting punch-drunk from trying to keep up with all of it.

The younger pilots coming in actually have an advantage over him now. He has had it. Most of the things he has spent his life learning are obsolete now. But if he has survived this far, at the very least he has lived an interesting and rewarding life, and that is what it was all about to start with. Even I have done that.

ONE MORE TOMORROW

Is anybody happier because you
    passed this way?
Does anyone remember that you
    spoke to him today?
Can you say tonight, in parting,
    With the day that's slipping fast,
That you helped a single brother of
    The many that you passed?
Is a single heart rejoicing over
    What you did or said?
Does the man whose hopes were
    fading, now with courage look ahead?
Did you leave a trail of kindness, or
    A scar of discontent?
As you close your eyes in slumber,
    Do you think that God will say,
"You have earned one more tomorrow
    By the work you did today?

APPENDIX A

FLYING TECHNIQUES

When I first started doing commercial flying, I thought I already had all the important answers on how to fly an airplane. When I began to learn there was more to it than that, I did a lot of studying and practicing to get "the rest of the story."

While flying our Eaglerock glider in 1930, 56 years ago, I discovered, just from experience and the feel of the controls and the wind hitting my face (for we had no instruments), that an "extreme" cross control was required in a normal turn when flying very slow, just above a stall. I had no understanding why this was necessary, and this bothered me.

This glider had a wingspread of 36 feet. It did not have a tapered wing; it had a constant cord for the full span. It lifted off the ground at 30 miles per hour behind a tow car, so the slow airspeed turns could have been as low as 25 miles per hour.

One day in the summer of 1931, I was flying my OX5 Waco 10, a beautiful airplane with an attractive paint job and in the best of condition. It had a Hamilton Standard metal propeller. My engine was actually turning up 1,500 RPM on takeoff, which gave the plane exceptional takeoff performance.

I had recently installed an instrument in it that had a ball that showed when I was skidding or slipping in turns. That ball taught me a lot about flying. This instrument also had another feature that registered the position of the nose, up or down.

A friend I had known for several years was admiring my Waco. He had learned to fly two years before I did, and he had done quite a lot of flying. He owned a Waco the same model as mine. His Waco was not in good condition; it needed new fabric and an engine overhaul. I invited him to fly my airplane. He took it up for a flight, and when he came down he said it flew like a dream. But that little ball in that curved glass tube was crazier than a bedbug, because it always rolled to the high side in a turn, and he figured it should roll to the low side. I explained to him that it was supposed to stay in the center in a turn. That was news to him.

Any time the ailerons are moved, it requires a corresponding movement of the rudder in order to keep these two controls properly coordinated. When I learned to fly, my instructors were very strict about properly coordinating rudder and aileron control applications. When these two controls are not properly coordinated in a bank (turn), it is called "crossing your controls," and it is well understood that you are not supposed to "cross your controls" in a bank (turn). When the controls are crossed, it causes the ball to move off center, indicating a skid or a slip.

That ball was teaching me some things about rudder and aileron control coordination I did not know. What the ball was telling me was that I had to have my controls crossed a small amount to keep the ball centered in a bank (turn), and that sometimes they had to be crossed more than at other times. I discovered the lower airspeeds required the most cross control to keep the ball centered, and at higher airspeeds it was hardly noticeable.

Even when I was instructing in the war flight training programs during World War II, these things were not clear in my mind. I felt I had a proper understanding of it, but was not able to explain it to others.

I didn't have any problems explaining this to my students. They didn't have any preconceived ideas on the subject, so they just took my word for it. The books in the training programs said, "Do not cross your controls in a bank." So I was preaching something that conflicted with accepted practice.

It was to require several more years of flying, including corralling wild horses with an airplane, aerial spraying, and hunting coyotes with SuperCubs, before I was able to put the following explanation of rudder and aileron control coordination on paper for all to see.

The diagrams A and B are exaggerated in order to make it easier to understand. A little flying in smooth air, with a ball in front of you and a light touch on the controls, will verify this explanation and could help you smooth out your flying in the low airspeed range, and it could save your life if you really get good at it.

For a specified degree of bank, say 30 degrees, an airplane will make a smaller circle at a low airspeed, say 50 MPH, as in diagram A.

At a higher airspeed, say 100 MPH, as in diagram B, the airplane makes a larger circle. No. 1 in both diagrams represents the distance the outside wingtip travels. No. 2 in both diagrams represents the distance the inside wingtip travels.

This clearly illustrates that the outside wingtip travels farther than

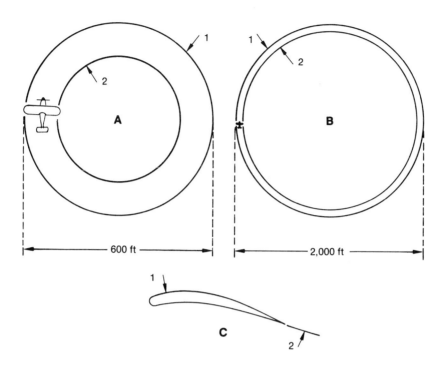

the inside wingtip in the lower airspeed range (diagram A) than in the higher airspeed range (diagram B). Therefore, more top aileron is required to prevent the bank from getting steeper at the lower airspeeds.

The accepted definition for the use of the rudder in a turn, after the bank has been established (assuming correction for torque is properly provided for with an offset vertical stabilizer and proper power setting) is to streamline the rudder with the arc of the circle.

You plainly see the arc of the circle is greater at the lower airspeed. Therefore, more bottom rudder is required in a bank (turn) at the lower airspeed. Condensing all this into fewer words, we find that for proper coordination of rudder and ailerons, a certain amount of cross control is required, more at lower airspeed than at higher airspeed.

STALL-PROOF WING

The first fall I flew the OX5 Waco 9, in 1929, I doped about three dozen pieces of yarn, four inches long, on top of the bottom wings so I could observe the airflow over the top of the wings in stalls, tailspins, and other maneuvers. I already knew the air "burbles" on top of the wing in a stall, but what I learned with this yarn surprised me. I learned there was a direct tailwind on top of the wing in a stall, all the

261

way from the trailing edge of the wing forward to about where the front spar is on the Waco 9, and that in a tailspin the inside wing is stalled throughout the spin.

This gave me an idea for a wing modification that could give us a stall-proof wing that would result in a spin-proof airplane.

Referring to diagram C, No. 1 is a cross section of a wing. No. 2 is a piece of sheet metal I hinged onto the back of my wing.

In a stall the air pressure under the wing raised the back of the sheet metal until the air under the wing came in contact with the air over the top of the wing. This prevented the tailwind on top of the wing, as well as the wing forward of the sheet metal, from stalling.

The sheet metal I installed was 36 inches long by 12 inches wide at the rear edge of my right lower wing. I did a lot of stalls with this sheet metal on the wing and discovered I could not stall the wing forward of this sheet metal. However, on one flight at a high airspeed, the sheet metal developed a violent flutter and tore itself off the wing. That concluded my testing of this idea on the Waco 9.

At a later date, when I was flying the Waco 10, I decided to do further testing on this idea. On the Waco 10, the pilot controls the lower ailerons directly. The upper ailerons are operated by a small streamlined steel tube that connects the lower ailerons to the upper ailerons, so they both work together.

I removed these two steel tubes so I had no control over the upper ailerons. They just floated free in the wind. If they had developed a flutter, I might have been in trouble, but they didn't, even at high speeds.

At low stalling speeds the air pressure under the wings raised these free floating ailerons and prevented the upper wings from stalling forward of these ailerons.

Before disconnecting the upper ailerons, there was nothing I could do to keep the Waco 10 out of a tailspin when I held the stick all the way back.

With the upper ailerons floating free, I climbed to 5,000 feet above the ground, closed the throttle, held the stick all the way back, and dropped, nose high, almost like a parachute, for 4,500 feet, recovering 500 feet above the ground. All the way down I had good lateral and directional control.

This was during the Great Depression of the 1930's. I was scratching with the chickens, trying to stay in business. I thought I was discovering something important. So I wrote to the National Advisory Committee for Aeronautics in Washington, DC, and explained my experiments in detail. In due time I received a letter from them discouraging further research on this idea. I still believe it is worth following up on, but when you are "scratching with the chickens," you do not have the time or resources to do a lot of basic research.

QUICK-STALL-RECOVERY

Throughout my flying career, rudder and aileron control coordination, stalls, and tailspins have been very much on my mind. These are key things that can determine whether you live or die. For many years I had the feeling there was something here we had not tied together yet, and headstones in graveyards confirmed this.

Rather accidentally and ever so slowly, I finally put enough things together to come up with a technique for what I call "quick-stall-recovery." This actually started back in 1933, on our mustang job in the Owyhee Desert area, when I did an accidental stall, very close to the ground, and recovered in time to avoid a crash. At that time I didn't understand what made such a sudden recovery possible.

It wasn't until the 1960's, approximately 30 years later, that I developed an understanding of what I now call a "quick-stall-recovery." I have lost count of how many times I have recovered from accidental stalls in tight maneuvers close to the ground, and it doesn't even bother me anymore, now that I understand this technique for "quick-stall-recovery."

The following is an explanation of how it works: An airplane stalls at a higher airspeed if it weighs more than if it weighs less.

An airplane weighs more in a turn than it does while flying straight and level.

Nearly all accidental stalls are done while turning.

When you stall while turning, or even if you are not turning, a sudden forward movement on the stick, or wheel reduces the weight of the airplane and the load on the wings. You are instantly flying a lighter airplane, so you have instantly recovered from the stall without the necessity of having to dive to regain airspeed, as we used to think it had to be done. You are still banked, but you can shallow your bank easily after you have recovered from the stall. It is as simple as that.

In a stall you have lost the smooth airflow over the top of the wings. As soon as the stick is moved forward, the smooth airflow is restored over the top of the wings.

I have been asked to instruct other pilots on this method of quick-stall-recovery. However, a simple explanation of this, and some solo practice at a safe altitude by the pilot you might be instructing, in my estimation, is better than dual instruction on it because you have to have hold of the controls to feel it.

To give dual instructions on this quick-stall-recovery close to the ground, where its real value exists, reminds me of Dud Rankin's refusal to teach fishtails. Close to the ground there is no room for corrections after an error has been made.

Too many years and too many hard knocks were required, in my life, to come up with answers to these sorts of questions. Things of this nature could and should be properly presented to students today in their first 50 hours of flying. They would not master all of this in 50 hours, but it would give them some worthwhile goals to work toward and eventually make better pilots out of them.

I have an unusual background in the kind of flying that puts the spotlight on these things. I have had around 9,000 hours of mustang flying and several years' flying for coyotes, plus aerial spraying, dropping salt, and flying power-line patrol—all of which results in maneuvering close to the ground, much of it at low airspeeds. I developed the technique for quick-stall-recovery long before I really understood it.

SINKERS

It also took me several years to figure out that many air conditions that cause an airplane to "sink" are not necessarily downdrafts. Air that is moving horizontally (wind) often changes direction or velocity, or both. If an airplane is flying into air that is a headwind of 10 miles per hour, and suddenly the 10 miles per hour headwind stops, then the plane loses 10 miles per hour of lift. The "sinker" that put me into the ground, years ago at Denio, was just such a condition.

Even today, with our modern jetliners, we still have this same problem. It has caused several serious crashes with heavy loss of life. Today they have come up with a more scientific word to describe it. They call it "wind sheer," but it is exactly the same thing we called "sinker" back in the OX5 barnstorming days. Because of our new understanding of wind sheer, crashes caused by wind sheer have now gained a certain respectability and are no longer blamed on pilot error, as they were in earlier days.

One thing that used to puzzle me was that when I flew into an "updraft," my engine speeded up, and when I flew into a "downdraft," the engine slowed down. I was not able to understand why this should happen, and no one I talked to understood it either. Now I understand that when I flew into what I considered an updraft, it was not an updraft. It was a headwind; or to say it another way, it was a change in horizontal wind velocity. A sudden increase in a headwind would relieve pressure on the propeller, which would allow it to turn

264

faster. A sudden decrease in a headwind, or a sudden tailwind, would add pressure to the propeller, causing it to slow down.

COOL AIR–WARM AIR

Another thing that had me confused for some time (but not very long) was that because OX5 Wacos do not climb very fast when flying from the field elevations I was flying from, I would often "hunt" for good air so I could climb faster. I knew cool air was heavier (thicker) than warm air. I figured I could climb faster in cool heavy air than in lighter thinner air. So when I wanted to climb faster, I would fly out over a cool, irrigated alfalfa field where I expected to find heavier thicker air. I would avoid the hot sagebrush flats where the air was warmer and thinner. However, I discovered exactly the opposite is true.

The warm air over the hot sagebrush flats is going up, and I could climb much faster in the warm air. The cool air over the irrigated alfalfa fields is heavy and going down. I could not climb very well in air that was going down.

However, cool air is thicker, and hot air is thinner. I could climb better on a cool morning in thick air than on a hot afternoon in thin air. There was a paradox here for a young pilot of the earlier days whose knowledge and flying experience was limited.

These sorts of things confused me. I like to understand what is going on when I am flying, but it seems the point has never been reached where we understand all of it, or are quite as proficient in handling our airplane as we would like to be.

Most of my flying has been in taildragger airplanes, with a tailskid or a tailwheel, where the landings should be three-point landings. All three points should touch the ground at the same time, in a smooth contact with the ground. And sometimes that is the way I make them, but I have never known a pilot who can do this consistently, every time. After all my years of flying I still cannot always make an airplane do exactly what I want it to do.

AILERON RESISTANCE

On an experimental flight I made in 1930, with the Waco 9 from the HL Meadow in southeastern Oregon, I had the left lower aileron disconnected, so I was flying with control over only the two right ailerons and the upper left aileron.

On this flight I discovered that a raised aileron has more effect at lowering a wing than a lowered aileron has at raising a wing. The lowered aileron causes all the aileron resistance that requires the pilot to apply rudder to counteract, and does only about one third of the work required to raise the lowered wing.

This discovery gave me an idea. If I could develop an aileron control that would raise ailerons and not lower ailerons, all aileron resistance, that requires a corresponding rudder application to overcome, would be eliminated. This would greatly simplify the pilot's job in flying the airplane and would make it much simpler for beginners to learn to fly.

I finally figured out an aileron control system that would do this on over 90 percent of flying; I built a model of this system and sent it to the National Advisory Committee for Aeronautics in Washington, DC, in 1932.

The picture of my model shows how it did this. The first half of the control movement raised ailerons only. This would take care of 100 percent of all normal flying. However, in certain situations or in an emergency if more aileron control was needed, or for such things as taxiing, where lowered ailerons help in directional control, the last half of the control movement lowers ailerons only.

The National Advisory committee's response to this idea was that they didn't like the idea. So, that is where it stands even today, 54 years later. A good idea, not developed and used. However, at a later date, some airplanes did come out with an aileron control system that resulted in raised ailerons going up farther than lowered ailerons came down. This gives some of the benefits my system would have given.

This is a model of my idea for an improved aileron control. I sent this model to the National Advisory Committee for Aeronautics in Washington, DC in 1932. Lindbergh was a member of this committee at that time.

The first half of the aileron application raises ailerons only, thus eliminating the necessity for a corresponding rudder application to overcome aileron resistance, as it is only the lowered aileron that causes aileron resistance; and the raised aileron does about two-thirds of the work. So in almost 100 percent of the flying there would be raised ailerons only, but in emergencies and for taxiing, full aileron control would also lower the opposite ailerons. So nothing would be lost and a lot would be gained.

APPENDIX B _____

GLIDERS

Throughout man's long experience on earth there has been a desire for human flight. Some of the best minds in recorded history had tried to solve the problems that could bring this about, all without tangible results until the Wright Brothers came along.

The steam engine was developed in the early 1800's, and by the early 1870's the internal combustion engine had been developed. Even before this, thinkers and experimenters had everything that would have been required to have built successful gliders, but no one had been able to do it.

Many of the experimenters in those days were trying to build flying machines with flat wings. It was not until the late 1800's that the first successful gliders were built. The gliders built and flown by Otto Lilienthal of Germany were the most successful up to that time.

Before I built my fishing-pole glider in 1925, I had read about Otto Lilienthal, who had made 2,000 flights in gliders he designed and built. One of these flights covered a distance of 1,000 feet. Lilienthal was killed in a crash with his glider in 1896.

Also, I had read about a Scottish engineer by the name of Percy Pilcher who conducted glider experiments in Scotland and later in England. A horse pulled his glider with a rope that went through a series of pulleys, so the glider traveled faster than the horse did. Pilcher, like Lilienthal, controlled his glider by shifting his weight.

Pilcher had visited Lilienthal and had even flown his glider. He used curved wings, in contrast with Professor Langley of the Smithsonian Institute, who used flat wings in his early experiments. But Langley eventually changed his mind and used curved wings. On September 30, 1899, Pilcher's glider had a structural failure and he was killed.

I had also read about other glider activities. Then, of course, since the Wright's first flight with a powered airplane in 1903, we had fought a great war, World War I, where airplanes were widely used, and I was reading anything I could get pertaining to aviation.

When I built my 1925 gliders, I knew I was not pioneering in a new and unknown science, as men like Lilienthal, Pilcher and the Wrights had done. It was just a case that the science was new to "me," and I had very limited experience, knowledge or resources to work with. But I had a compelling desire to build something I could fly with, realizing full well that even though a lot of progress had been made since Lilienthal and the other early pioneers in aviation, we were still dealing with limited knowledge on the subject, and with the same laws of gravity that had killed so many of these earlier pioneers.

When I built my fishing-pole glider, 22 years after the 1903 first flight of the Wright Brothers, I did not have the right answers to all the problems I faced either. At this time I was only 17 years old and had never seen a glider and had never even talked to anyone who had seen a glider, but I had read everything I could find about gliders. I proceeded to design, build, and fly a glider, using 25-cent cane fishing poles for the wing structure and unbleached muslin for wing covering. Everything considered, it was surprisingly successful.

I had built this glider two years before Lindbergh flew to Paris. Two years after he flew to Paris, I was flying an OX5 Waco 9 at Bend, Oregon, teaching flying, barnstorming, charter flights, stunt flying, parachute jumps, etc., and over a period covering 57 years, I have 25,000 hours at the controls of airplanes.

It seems only natural to me that throughout my flying career Lindbergh was my real life hero. He was only six years older than me. Before he flew to Paris, his ambitions were similar to my own, although there was a vast difference between his life and mine, even in the early stages. His father was a United States Senator, so he got around more and came in contact with influential people even as a small boy, and spent considerable time in Washington, DC, and in the White House. My early life was very different.

In looking back through time, to my early glider days, I can see no touch of genius or expertise on my part, just a young man's desire to fly and a venturesome spirit that is difficult to hold down. I can recall no thrill during my flying years greater than the thrill I received as the earth retreated beneath the rising wings of my fishing-pole glider.

Aviation has grown into a great industry since those days, but it is something more than just financial investments, jobs, and transportation. What it does to the lives of those who participate in it is also a very important part of it.

During the period in 1925 when I built and flew my triplane and

biplane gliders, there were no federal or state laws governing building or flying gliders.

Later, in 1929 and 1930, I designed, built, and flew two gliders that
were designed along the same lines as my earlier gliders, but I used
one-inch aluminum tubing instead of fishing poles.

Neither one of these gliders flew quite as well as the biplane fishing-pole glider. The first one was so badly out of balance that on my
first, and only, flight with this glider, behind a tow car with a 70-foot
rope, immediately after liftoff I had to go full forward on the elevator
control. It still climbed steeply until almost directly above the tow
car, the rope pulled off the hook on the front of the glider. The glider
reared straight up into a whipstall, but it did not whip. It fell all the
way to the ground, straight down, backwards, and became an instant
pile of wreckage, with me right in the middle of it. I had a sore tail-
bone for a long time.

This glider had three wings, with the third wing in front. In rebuilding from the wreckage, I eliminated the front wing entirely and installed a conventional tail assembly behind the two wings.

It seems that all large airplanes at this time, such as the Tri-motored
Ford, had a wheel control for controlling the ailerons. I had never
flown an airplane that had a wheel control, so I decided to put a
wheel control on my rebuilt glider.

The Bend iron foundry cast an aluminum wheel for me, and I
mounted it on top of the stick. Moving the stick forward or backward
controlled the elevators, and turning the wheel controlled the ailerons. The bottom of the stick was simply on a hinge that permitted
forward and backward movement. I had redesigned this glider to a
point where I figured I had the center of gravity about in the right
place relative to the center of lift.

On my first flight with this glider, also behind a tow car, I used a
200-foot rope. I told the car driver I didn't want to get very high on
this first flight. After liftoff the glider seemed to be properly balanced, and it responded fine to the elevators and the wingtip rud-
ders.

At about 50 feet above the ground my left wing dropped sharply,
and I instinctively shoved the control stick to the right to get the left
wing up, instead of turning the wheel as I should have done, and the
stick broke off where it was hinged. This left me with no control over
the elevators or the ailerons. However, I was able to raise my left
wings to a level position by using a strong application of right rudder.

Now my life depended on this glider being properly balanced. The
tow car driver knew nothing about my problems, but he slowed down
as he neared the end of the field, and the glider settled down to a
perfectly smooth landing as I nervously pressed the rudder pedals
from side to side, which accomplished nothing. I also leaned as far
back in the seat as I could, to get my weight as far back as possible for

270

the landing. This helped some. This landing also helped me in establishing a little better relationship with God. He had more control over it than I did.

Neither one of these aluminum tube gliders were hang gliders. I used a pine 2x4 for a landing skid and had a seat to sit in, complete with a safety belt. I made quite a few tow flights with this glider after making a more sturdy hinge mounting for the bottom end of the stick, and learning to "turn" the wheel for aileron control instead of pushing it sideways, as I was used to doing when flying the Waco 9.

One interesting thing I did with this glider that I do not recommend was that I tied it to a fence post, using a long rope. Then when the wind was strong enough, it would lift me off the ground. On one such flight I was almost 100 feet high when the wind suddenly slowed down, causing me to lose a lot of lift, and I came down very fast but landed successfully. However, that ended that type of flying for me. I never really had the feeling of the freedom of flight with this glider that I felt with my 1925 fishing-pole glider.

Eventually I dismantled this glider, organized a glider club, and bought a new Eaglerock glider. This glider flew very well, and we did a lot of flying with it. I finally bought the Eaglerock glider from the club and also purchased another Eaglerock glider. I operated these two gliders commercially, one at Bend and the other at Prineville. There were no other commercial glider activities in Oregon at that time, or anywhere else on the West Coast that I knew about; and I did not know of any other gliders in Oregon at that time, either club operated or privately owned.

We used a tow car to get these gliders up on most of the flying but we also used my OX5 Waco on some of the flights. When we moved one of these gliders from Bend to Prineville, one of my students flew the Waco 10 and I flew the glider, a 36-mile flight. I cut loose 4,500 feet above Prineville and had a nice long acrobatic flight to the Prineville airport.

We did a lot of flying with these gliders but were not getting very rich. So we decided to move the Prineville glider to Salem and operate it off the Salem airport. My wife's brother Al agreed enthusiastically to take charge of that end of the business.

We decided to tow the glider over the Cascade Mountains behind the Waco from Bend to Salem. This was 1932. The OX5 Waco was not a super powerhouse for towing a glider from a soft sandy field that was 3,600 feet above sea level.

The only way we could get the glider out of Knott Field behind the airplane was when we had a northwest wind, which happened often. But this gave us a headwind for our flight to Salem, and we had a very low groundspeed even in calm air when the Waco was towing the glider.

On one attempt to tow the glider to Salem, we had just taken off and were about 50 feet above the ground, with Knott Field about half a mile behind us, when one of my spark plugs fouled and reduced me to seven cylinders. I could not remain airborne on seven cylinders with the glider behind me. So I cut Al loose, and he was on his own, 50 feet above the ground, with nothing but sagebrush and rocks under him. He got that glider down in a very tight place without hitting any rocks or sagebrush and did no damage to the glider.

After releasing the glider, I was able to remain airborne and made it back to the airport okay.

On another attempt to tow the glider to Salem, we had taken off into a northwest wind. I was flying the Waco and Al was flying the glider. The small town of Sisters is 20 miles from Bend. By the time we were over Sisters, we had been in the air one hour. At this speed we did not have enough gas to get to Salem, so I turned back to Knott Field.

We finally gave up on the idea of towing the glider to Salem behind the Waco. We hauled it over there on a trailer and had a successful glider operation at the Salem airport for some time. Even at this time I did not know of any other gliders in the state of Oregon.

About this time the Aeronautics Branch of the Department of Commerce started licensing gliders and glider pilots. All of my flying in central Oregon at this time was being done under an Oregon State license. Oregon had no laws regarding gliders, and I never bothered to get a federal glider license, but we taught a lot of people to fly these Eaglerock gliders. We had a few minor accidents but nothing major, and no one was ever hurt in our gliders—anyway not enough to justify going to a doctor.

During this period some glider enthusiasts in Portland, Oregon, and Vancouver, Washington, formed a glider club. They built their own glider, similar to the Eaglerock glider, but their glider was made of wood. The main structure of the Eaglerock glider was steel tubing. According to the information we received, one of their club members stalled their glider about 30 feet above the ground, crashed, and was killed. But they rebuilt their glider and continued to do quite a lot of flying with it on Pearson Field, across the river from Portland in Washington, and most of their members eventually received a federal glider pilot license.

One day one of their club members came to our airport while we were flying the Eaglerock glider. He showed us his federal glider pilot license and asked if he could fly our glider. We had no reason to doubt his flying ability so we said okay. On a tow flight behind the car he cut loose at about 500 feet, pulled his nose up high, started a right turn, and fell off into a right-hand tailspin. He continued to hold the stick back and never recovered from the tailspin. He spun all the way to the ground and crashed the glider. He was not hurt, but the glider was

272

badly damaged and we had to rebuild it. That was the last time we ever permitted a stranger to fly our gliders without first going through our course of training.

One day three representatives from the Eaglerock factory arrived in Bend to talk to us and to observe our glider flying. We were using a long telephone wire for a towline behind our tow car. We would get the glider 1,000 feet in the air before releasing it; then we had nice long flights back to the airport. We used a shorter wire when we towed the glider behind the airplane. We had made provisions for the car driver or the airplane pilot or the glider pilot to be able to release the glider in case of emergency. These men were really impressed. They said we were doing more with the Eaglerock glider than they had ever seen anyone else do with it.

GLIDER HISTORY

In 1911 Orville Wright set a duration record for gliders of 9 minutes 45 seconds. This record was not broken until the summer of 1929 by a glider flight of 15 minutes, made by Ralph Barnaby. On May 1, 1930, Ralph Barnaby received glider pilot license No. 1. We were flying the Eaglerock glider at this time.

Also, in 1930 Ralph Barnaby became famous for having dropped in a glider from a dirigible from 3,000 feet. At that time he had only 25 minutes' experience flying gliders. I had almost that much flying time in my fishing-pole glider in 1925, plus flying my aluminum tube gliders, plus my Eaglerock glider flying. Long before this an early day aviation pioneer in California (Montgomery?) dropped in several glider flights from a hot-air balloon from great heights.

I considered my 1925 glider a great success, even though it had deficiencies because of lack of aileron control. In one very important way the Wrights' two gliders of 1902 were superior to mine. They had provisions for warping their wings, which gave them satisfactory lateral control. The only lateral control I had was to move my weight sideways, and with a wingspread of 27 feet this did not give very good results. The reason weight shifting gave Lilienthal such good results was that he had much less wingspread than I did, so the weight shifting was more effective for him. Further development on my fishing-pole glider would have been a sensible course for me to have followed.

I didn't realize this at that time, but this glider had better lift than either of the two gliders the Wright Brothers built before they built and flew their first airplane in 1903. Of course, I had advantages they did not have. This was 24 years after their glider experience, and I had more information from which to make judgments of design than they had.

When the Wright Brothers built their gliders in 1902, they tried to fly them before they had treated the fabric to make it airtight, and they did not have satisfactory lift until they made the fabric airtight. I had this same problem with my fishing pole gliders. They did not have satisfactory lift until I painted the fabric with calcimine to make it airtight. My friend, Cloyde Artman, also had this same problem with the first glider he built.

There were a lot of things that were not understood by the pioneers until time consuming and sometimes costly trial and error brought forth answers to many of the problems they faced.

The Wrights did not understand the benefits of the canard they had developed. They did not understand the need for a vertical fin. They did not understand the center of pressure travel on wings. All this and more, that is, until they went through agonizing trial and error periods to learn about these things. All of which they had to establish some control over before they could make their first flight.

Cloyde Artman was five years younger than me. We both came along after much of the original pioneering had been done. But we were both doing things that amounted to groping in the dark, beyond the extent of our knowledge on the subjects we were dealing with.

When I was doing commercial flying with OX5-powered Wacos, almost 26 years after the Wright Brothers' first flight, I had a basic understanding of a lot of things about flying. I had the benefit of the experiences that pilots over the past 26 years had had. But I was to learn there were things about flying even yet that were not understood. It required many years of flying before I understood rudder and aileron control coordination and quick-stall-recovery among other things.

The Wright Brothers flew over the sands about 30 miles per hour. Our astronauts travel around 25,000 miles per hour. When I was flying in the late 1920's, I considered 80 miles per hour a satisfactory cruising speed, and I figured I would really be happy if I ever had an airplane that would fly 100 miles per hour. A lot of things have happened since those days. I remember the days when airplanes were not widely accepted. Just plain flying still means something to me that others would find hard to understand.

When I was born, no passenger had ever flown in Europe. The first passenger flight was May 29, 1908. Even the Wright Brothers had never made a publicly announced flight. Their first public flights were August and September, 1908—Wilbur in France and Orville in the United States. Of Wilbur's flying in France—such flying had never been seen before.

July 4, 1908: Curtiss flew the June Bug nearly one mile.

There had never been a successful flight in the British Empire when I was born; the first British flight was February 23, 1909.

274

July 30, 1909: Our government bought its first military airplane from the Wright Brothers.

The world did not know of the Wrights' earlier success until late in 1906. The first official details of their 1905 flights at Huffman Prairie were made public in March, 1906.

January 13, 1908: Farman won the Grand Prix D'Aviation for flying a circuit of nearly one mile. He was airborne for about one and a half minutes. May 29, 1908, he flew the first passenger in Europe. The first man killed in an airplane was Lt. Selfridge, September, 1908.

August, 1909: Hubert Lathem set an altitude record of 508 feet at the Reims Aviation meeting. Glenn Curtiss won the Gordon Bennett Trophy. The fastest airplane was a Bleriot, 60 miles per hour.

After we moved to Bend in 1923, I repaired bicycles, using our garage as my shop. There was no other bicycle repair shop in Bend; so, if you can call it that, I had the first bicycle repair shop in Bend.

That put me right up in the Wright Brothers' league. They also repaired bicycles before they built their first flying machine. No doubt they were better bicycle repairmen than I was. They also made a bigger splash in the aviation pond than I did.

At one point in aviation history, Bill Stout, the developer of the famous Ford Tri-motor, was a young reporter for a newspaper. He was interviewing the Wright Brothers for a story. He asked Wilbur what their plans were for the future, what they were coming out with next, as an improvement on what they had already accomplished. Wilbur's response was, "Our present airplane is the final achievement; it cannot be improved."

Our Eaglerock glider after we built the nacelle to increase the gliding angle and to shield the pilot from the wind.

APPENDIX C

WILD HORSES ON WELFARE
THE SACRED HORSE FIASCO

The people of India have suffered for centuries under a strange religious concept that hold certain cattle as sacred. "Sacred cows" wander the streets and byways, consuming precious forage, and are held absolutely protected while the people starve.

Americans have long been dismayed by that peculiar practice of literally wasting valuable resources...and yet we have permitted the adoption of a governmental program that amounts to exactly the same thing, with complete disregard for the welfare of our people and our growing national debt—the Sacred Wild Horse, that was made "Sacred" and inviolate by the Wild Horse and Burro Act of 1970.

The news that reaches us is that we now have the homeless street people the same as India has. Maybe not as many as India but still far too many, numbering in the thousands. Just one, if the men who wrote, and signed, our constitution, knew about it, would cause them to turn over in their graves.

The countless millions of dollars we are now spending preserving wild horses would be better spent helping our homeless street people.

The horse, and its many kin, is simply a large hooved mammal man has ridden, used as beast of burden, and eaten, since prehistoric times. It is admittedly an appealing animal—not especially intelligent, but endowed with certain characteristics of speed and stamina which man has been prone to irrationally romanticize beyond reason.

Of all man's illogical fancies and follies during his ages-long love affair with horses, few have been quite so exquisitely absurd as the Wild Horse Act.

276

Back in the late 1960's a zealous horse-loving lady out of Reno—the late "Wild Horse Annie" Johnson—spearheaded a campaign to "protect" the wild horses which roam western ranges. The major tactic of the "movement" was to instigate an emotional letter writing campaign by grade school children to congressmen. To say the children's crusade was successful would be an understatement.

Our representatives, taking leave of their senses (that happens a lot on Foggy Bottom) swallowed the tearful nonsense whole. Passage of the Wild Horse Act proved once again that George Washington was absolutely correct when he said, "Government is not reason. It is not eloquence. It is force, like fire, a dangerous servant and a fearful master."

Congress, in its sublime foolishness, not only prohibited the capture and commercial sale of free-roaming, unbranded horses, it also failed to provide a grazing allotment for them.

So, for the years since this act, the sacred wild (feral) horses have been fruitful and multiplied, and multiplied. And multiplied. And consumed vast quantities of range forage at an ever-increasing rate—forage that could have been far better utilized for beef production, and the sustenance for our shrinking deer herds.

The problem—which was perfectly predictable from the beginning—has been recognized, but the solution to the problem has not been arrived at even yet.

Typically, the government has adopted a program to reach a well-defined goal that appears deliberately designed to achieve the least beneficial result, over the longest period of time, at the greatest possible public expense.

Using BLM personnel, hired buckaroos, contracted helicopters, traps on the range, government vehicles and large holding centers, cost of the roundup was $600 per head. Before this, operating under the idea of a "free market system," mustangers were making a profit selling these horses for $30 to $60 per horse.

The Bureau of Land Management is still engaged in a great wild horse roundup, testing whether that program, or any other government program, so conceived and dedicated, can long endure the light of reason.

Using BLM personnel, hired buckaroos, contracted helicopters, traps on the range, government vehicles and large holding centers, cost of the roundup is still several hundred dollars per horse. The overburdened taxpayer is still being stuck for millions of dollars annually, with no end in sight.

What happens to the horses when captured? At the beginning of this program they were adopted by fond, new "foster parents" and shipped all over the United States, but the BLM retained title to the animals.

Something the horse protection people did not and apparently still do not understand is that removing these horses off the range does not necessarily "save" them. The Adopt-a-Horse program works only to a limited degree. Even after long years of promoting the program, it is clear that suitable "foster homes" are found for only a fraction of the horses available for foster homes on these terms. All the rest, after being kept and fed for a period of time at additional taxpayers' expense, were shot and buried. Not even the coyotes or buzzards were allowed to eat them.

This system brought serious objections from the "horse protection people" and the rules were changed again. So now the BLM merely keeps the old and crippled horses, and the others that do not get adopted, in government corrals and feeds and cares for them at taxpayer's expense, until they die of old age, or maybe until some common sense slowly creeps into the lawmaker's heads so these horses could be sold to the highest bidder to recover some of the cost of managing the program.

Don't blame the BLM for the "Sacred Horse" fiasco. Congress, in typical abdication of responsibility, saw fit to create the Bureau of Land Management and vest in it powers none but ancient monarchs ever dreamed of possessing. As supreme sovereign of all that moves, grows, or exists on or below a public land empire in excess of 700,000 square miles (approximately the size of Mexico), BLM can, and rightly, be accused of over-reaching its congressional mandate.

No way, though, can BLM be blamed for the Wild Horse Act. Congress passed that law and ordered BLM to administer it. Congress is the sole culprit in this instance. (There should be no federal law controlling wild horses. Each state should control the horses within that state).

Since Congress has already amended the act to the extent of permitting the use of helicopters in government-run roundups, I suggest a few more amendments—changes that would be not only more reasonable but more beneficial to all concerned—the taxpayers, the consuming public, the BLM, and even the wild horses, themselves.

The horse, without an owner willing to bear the cost of feeding and caring for it, is just another source of scarce protein, leather and glue.

Many horses die from cold and starvation during hard winters. The best efforts of government and romantic programs like Adopt-a-Horse are not going to save thousands of horses from ultimate death.

There are plenty of mustangers around who could and would gather the surplus horses—just as humanely as government is doing it and at no cost to the taxpayer—provided they be permitted to make a buck or two on commercial sale of the animals.

The Wild Horse Act should be amended to allow just that. Keep

BLM in a licensing and supervisory role. Keep Adopt-a-Horse program for whatever slight value it may have. But let private enterprise do the job it has done before and can do again in harvesting surplus wild horses.

There is no good reason why licensed mustangers should not be allowed to capture the surplus horses. They could be supervised by BLM and the horses could be brought into BLM corrals temporarily, much as it is being done at present. The BLM could select appropriate animals to send along to those few people wishing to adopt them. The rest could be returned to the private mustangers who would be permitted to sell them for commercial consumption.

Everyone's interests would be served. Government might even make a few bucks through licensing and taxation of income. Those who wish to adopt a horse could do so.

A dead horse is a dead horse—whether it dies of thirst and starvation in the desert, is killed for pet food and leather, or slaughtered and bulldozed into a trench where not even the buzzards can make use of the carcass when not nearly enough people want to adopt them.

The Wild Horse Act is resulting in the very thing it was supposed to prevent—the needless, wasteful deaths of thousands of horses.

Nobody—certainly not the old-time mustanger, or the rancher or sportsman—suggests total elimination of the wild horse herds. What is suggested is treating them rationally as a renewable natural resource to be harvested like any other.

Let's get off the Sacred Horse kick and get wild horses off federal welfare and stop foolishly wasting valuable forage, protein, leather and glue.

Cal Sunderland & Ted Barber

This editorial was published in the Winnemucca newspaper, *The Humboldt Sun,* over Cal Sunderland's name. This version of it has been lightly edited by Ted Barber.

INDEX

For the benefit of those who cannot find this book in their local bookstore it can be ordered direct from the writer.

Send $12.95 to:

Ted Barber
P.O. BOX 5
Orovada, Nevada 89425

and the book will be sent post paid to any address in the United States. Add $1.00 for addresses outside the United States.